JUDGED TO DEATH

It was time to judge my dessert.

Horatio praised me for thinking of something so clever and with a ten brought our score up to a respectable level.

I held my breath as Bess took one bite of my limoncello cannoli. She was so hard to please, and I hadn't been able to win her over all week. I held my breath as her eyes rolled back in her head, then her face fell forward, and she passed out on her plate.

"Cut!" Ivy marched over to Bess. "Wake her up! She is going to have to be replaced with someone else. I can't have this on camera." Ivy shook Bess's shoulder. She didn't respond.

Horatio was dabbing a wet napkin on his woolen suit jacket where some of Bess's mascarpone had squelched out and hit him. "Of all the unprofessional, drunken—"

"Bess!" Ivy shook the older woman a little harder.

Something didn't feel right. I had a growing pit of dread rolling in my stomach . . .

Books by Libby Klein

CLASS REUNIONS ARE MURDER

MIDNIGHT SNACKS ARE MURDER

RESTAURANT WEEKS ARE MURDER

THEATER WEEKS ARE MURDER

WINE TASTINGS ARE MURDER

BEAUTY EXPOS ARE MURDER

ANTIQUES AUCTIONS ARE MURDER

Published by Kensington Publishing Corp.

Restaurant Weeks Are MURDER

LIBBY KLEIN

KENSINGTON BOOKS
KENSINGTON PUBLISHING CORP.

www.kensingtonbooks.com

KENSINGTON BOOKS are published by

Kensington Publishing Corp.
119 West 40th Street
New York, NY 10018

All Kensington titles, imprints, and distributed lines are available at special quantity discounts for bulk purchases for sales promotion, premiums, fund-raising, educational, or institutional use.

Special book excerpts or customized printings can also be created to fit specific needs. For details, write or phone the office of the Kensington Sales Manager: Attn.: Sales Department. Kensington Publishing Corp., 119 West 40th Street, New York, NY 10018. Phone: 1-800-221-2647.

Kensington and the K logo Reg. U.S. Pat. & TM Off.

First Printing: March 2019
ISBN-13: 978-1-4967-1307-0
ISBN-10: 1-4967-1307-9

ISBN-13: 978-1-4967-1308-7 (eBook)
ISBN-10: 1-4967-1308-7 (eBook)

10 9 8 7 6 5 4 3 2

Printed in the United States of America

*For Aunt Ginny, my inspiration.
You fostered my love of comedy, taught me to cream my face,
and promised to knock me flatter than a flitter if
I misbehaved. I want to be you when I grow up.*

*A special thank you to Chef Ingrid Gustavson
of the Lightfoot Restaurant for generously giving me
a tour of her kitchens and answering my many questions.*

Chapter One

"I don't care how good Dr. Oz says it is, I'm not eating vegan cheese." Aunt Ginny took the last stuffed pheasant off the Fraser fir, wrapped it in tissue paper, and placed it in an old Woolworth's hat box to store until next Christmas.

I put the lid on the box of antique nutcrackers and placed it by the doorway for my handyman, Itty Bitty Smitty, to store in the attic the next time he was here to fiddle with his perpetual chore list. "But Aunt Ginny, you haven't even tried it yet. It's made from cashews."

Aunt Ginny stuck her tongue out. "That might just be the most disgusting thing I've ever heard. I'd rather eat the plastic it's wrapped in."

Figaro made himself his usual nuisance and batted a sparkly red and gold ornament from a low branch across the floor and chased it out into the foyer.

"Come on. You said you'd do this diet with me. You know how much better I've been feeling since I went Paleo four months ago."

"Yeah, I know. Everybody knows. Because you won't stop talking about it. I've never heard anyone go on so much about gluten, inflammation, and free-range vegetables in my whole life. Back in my day you ate what you wanted and got old gracefully. You never complained that you were bloated, or your brain was foggy."

I rolled my eyes to myself. If Aunt Ginny didn't spend the better part of each day grousing about her aches and pains, her jaw would atrophy, and she'd need physical therapy. I picked up the three boxes of Belgian chocolates that she had received for Christmas from her "Secret Santa." I suspected Aunt Ginny's "Secret Santa" was a little redhead in her eighties with a penchant for caramels. "Where would you like these Saint Nick?"

Aunt Ginny snatched the boxes from my hand. "I'll put them in my room with that bottle of Amaretto that mysteriously showed up under the tree."

I threw my hands up. "It's a Christmas miracle!" I followed the trail of glitter down the hall to the kitchen where I found a gold, sparkly Figaro peeking at me with one eye, the other side of his body hiding behind the trash can. I checked the time. Thirty minutes till the event of a lifetime: working side by side with Tim, my ex-fiancé, as his pastry chef in a real, professional kitchen. Just thinking about it made my scalp tingle. "Come on Liberace, let's brush you out before I'm dealing with something gold and sparkly in the litter box."

I plopped down on the floor in the sunroom and ran a brush through Figaro's black smoke fur. He hummed like a Harley, his copper eyes slitty like two winter crescent moons reflecting on the Atlantic.

Aunt Ginny waved a pair of bright orange leather hands at me from the doorway. "What should I do with Georgina's present? These must have cost your mother-in-law a fortune, but who in their right mind needs Italian calfskin car gloves just for driving five minutes to the beauty parlor once a week? And why in the world did she get this gaudy shade of orange?"

My eyes flicked up to the pumpkin-colored swirls atop of Aunt Ginny's head. "I think she got them to . . . match." I smiled.

Aunt Ginny narrowed her eyes. "Well then, you take them. They match your hair, too, smarty pants."

"Hey, don't blame me for Georgina's gaudy taste. At least you didn't get a custom-monogrammed barbecue brand to sear your initials onto your steaks. I can't even regift that."

Aunt Ginny sat in her rocker and wound a ball of twinkle lights into a hive for me to figure out next Christmas. "I'm glad things are going better between the two of you. Especially since it looks like she'll be visiting regularly, now that she and You-Know-Who are an item."

We gave each other a look and shook our heads. The memory of Georgina locked in a passionate embrace with a certain little bald handyman was a disturbing image.

Figaro swatted my hand and tried to bite me, signaling the grooming event was over. I took the ball of lights Aunt Ginny had painstakingly knotted up and put them in another storage bin.

I hiked up my skinny jeans, which were drooping over my hips. I giggled to myself. I hadn't worn anything that could be classified as too big since I played dress-up in Aunt Ginny's petticoats when I was six.

I boxed up the penguin mafia and the Nativity Scene, which somehow always managed to merge into one display, and checked the time on my phone again. Ten more minutes.

Aunt Ginny toddled around the corner heaving a giant light-up gingerbread house onto the stack. "Is it time?"

"Almost." I grinned and took the Sweetie Shoppe from her.

"You've been bouncing around here like a grasshopper on a hot pavement."

"I can't help it. I feel like my fairy godmother finally showed up and said you're going to an all-you-can-eat pie buffet, and everything has negative calories. I've waited my whole life for this day. I thought I had greater odds of fitting into a size seven again."

Aunt Ginny put a papery hand on my arm. "I know how much this means to you, Poppy Blossom. I wish you had just gone to culinary school instead of that fancy college. I want you to slow down and enjoy every minute of it. Even working with Gigi."

I groaned. The thought of Gigi, Tim's cute, little, incessantly perky mentee, was irritating enough to blister a melon. "I will. I'm not going to let Gigi get to me this time. I feel like my life is finally taking a good turn, like I'm going to make something out of myself after all. If I had a beret, I'd throw it in the air."

Aunt Ginny cocked her head. "You've made plenty out of your life. What do you call the Butterfly Wings Bed and Breakfast? You've turned this old Victorian into a beautiful inn."

I taped up a box and glanced at the chipped crown molding and the scuffed baseboards. "We're almost there. We've had a rocky start, but I think in the spring we'll be ready to officially open for guests. If I can ever get Smitty to finish up."

Aunt Ginny crossed her arms. "Thank God for the off-season. Lord Jesus help us come Easter."

I took one last look around. Christmas was packed away for another year. It was time to turn some day-dreams into reality. Today I become a chef, even if it's only for a week. I looked at my phone again.

"It's time." I gave Aunt Ginny another hug. "I'll see you in a few hours after the meet and greet."

A shaking rumble to our left caused me to pause and listen. "Did you hear that?" It happened again.

Aunt Ginny let out a loud sigh and pointed to the box by my feet. It was moving.

I ripped the tape off, and Figaro popped out like a deranged jack-in-the-box covered in tinsel.

"This is why pastry chef Pierre Hermé doesn't have a cat."

Chapter Two

I hopped in my car and cranked up first the radio, then the heat, and took off for Mays Landing and the Cape Community College. The Restaurant Week Competition was being held in the brand new culinary school kitchen arena. Even though it had been twenty-five years since my unfulfilled acceptance to the Culinary Institute of America in New York, I was simmering with excitement like it was yesterday. I had thought my chance to wear the starched whites was deader than banana clips and shoulder pads, but for the next week it was like I was Mr. Roarke's guest on Fantasy Island.

Tonight was the Chef Meet and Greet, a little kick-off social event for Restaurant Week competitors. It was a chance to get to know the other teams and be briefed about the event from the director. I thought it was a nice gesture, kind of a preemptive olive branch of sorts, since these chefs could go from professional courtesy to bitter rivals in less time than it takes to make toast. Tim and Gigi were meeting me there. Gigi's idea, I'm sure, since she had her claws sunk into Tim like a seagull with a soft pretzel. After the social we were going back to Tim's restaurant, Maxine's Bistro, to discuss our team strategy.

The culinary school was at the back of the campus with L'ÉCOLE DES CHEFS lettered across the brown and white bricks. The center backdrop of the grand foyer had the words HALL OF HONORS written in silver. Underneath, there were portraits of various chefs wearing their double-breasted uniforms, in their high hats and medals. Each one had a plaque listing their achievements and where they went after graduation. A row of neon-pink posters that read RESTAURANT WEEK EVENT lined the center corridor and had arrows pointing to the left for the kitchen arena.

I took a peel and stick name tag from the welcome table, wrote POPPY MCALLISTER—MAXINE'S in red marker, and stuck it on my emerald silk blouse over my heart. I fluttered between excitement and nerves just from walking in the door. I had the giddy-terrors.

I was immediately greeted by a brunette in pink glasses. She was a little on the chunky side, wearing a tight black dress. She grabbed my hand and shook it. "Hi, welcome to Restaurant Week, Poppy. I'm Ivy, the director." She consulted her clipboard and made a notation. "It looks like you're the first one here from Maxine's, but Chef Louie is just over by the hors d'oeuvres, and Chef Vidrine . . ." She looked around the room. "Well, she's here somewhere. You'll know her when you hear that Southern drawl."

"This is quite a setup."

"It is, isn't it? They plan to host renowned visiting chefs for intimate demonstrations. At least that's what the course brochure said." She laughed.

"Intimate demonstrations? That looks like seating for a hundred."

She raised her forefinger. "A hundred and six exactly.

I know that because I had tickets printed up for that many audience members for each day. Which reminds me." She pulled the tickets from her clipboard. "Each chef gets two tickets for friends and family."

"Thank you."

"And I'll tell you a little secret, just between us girls." I leaned in. "Okay."

"There are six kitchens at the front of the room laid out like a horseshoe. See? Two-by-two-by-two."

I nodded.

"Chef Phil-eep Julian has requested the one on the far right, to be closest to the judges. *Kiss-up*. And Chef Adrian Baxter has requested the kitchen on the far left, to be closest to the audience. *Show-off*. I recommend taking one of the two kitchens straight ahead under the projection screen. The camera will have the best views there, and the angles will be the most flattering." She cocked her head to the side and lifted her eyebrows.

From one chunky girl to another. "Ivy, you're my hero."

Ivy flashed me a brilliant smile. "Make sure you check out the pantry so you know where everything is come Saturday morning. And help yourself to a cocktail. I've had three." She laughed, spotted someone else coming in behind me, and took off with her hand outstretched. "Hi, welcome to Restaurant Week . . ."

I helped myself to some sparkling water with a lime wedge and headed into the communal pantry. The room was floor-to-ceiling aluminum shelves with rows and rows of storage bins, bottles, and jars containing various ingredients every chef would have on hand, and then some. We would all have to pull supplies from this small space during the competition. With my phone, I took some pictures of the spice rack, the dry goods, and the glass door refrigerator and freezer. I would blow these up later to study, so I could make strategical strikes for my ingredients and not waste time wandering helplessly while on the clock.

I came back into the main kitchen area and looked around. A middle-aged Nick Nolte lookalike in an orange Hawaiian shirt was spearing something with a toothpick and flicking it into his mouth. He saw me watching and gave me a thumbs-up. Across the room from him, a severely dignified gentleman wearing a monogrammed starched chef coat was holding a glass of champagne. He was in conversation with a petite mahogany-skinned girl with a 1,000-kilowatt smile. Her hair was done up in an intricate series of braids swirled around her head. She caught my eye and waved me over. I had just started toward them when a passive-aggressive, high-pitched needle pierced my eardrum.

"Hi-yeee."

Tim and Gigi strode in together, Tim looking a little guilty about something. Gigi was the sock that slid down your foot into your shoe when you walked. She was the underwire that busted out of your bra and poked you in the armpit. Now she was here, holding a shopping bag close to her chest.

Tim pulled me into a hug. He had the very slightest puff of love handles straddling his flat stomach. *That's new.* "I tried to call you, but you'd already left."

"Oh, what for?"

"I know we said we'd drive up separately, but Gigi's car wouldn't start so I had to pick her up."

Gigi grinned and shook her perky little blond bob.

"I'm sorry to hear that. Do you think it will be fixed in time for the first challenge on Saturday?"

Gigi put her shopping bag down to reveal . . . whoa! Either someone got herself a new pair of boobs for Christmas or Victoria's Secret is selling their bras prestuffed.

"I'm not sure when it will be fixed, but probably not until Restaurant Week is over. But you shouldn't feel burdened to be chained to us. You should keep the freedom of driving yourself."

Uh huh. That's about what I expected. "What's in the boobs? . . . I mean bag! What's in the bag?"

I couldn't stop staring at her chest. But then, that was probably what she was going for when she picked out her tight red sweater. I didn't know they sold plunging necklines in the children's section.

Tim was having a similar problem. Judging from his expression, I'd say he was half in love and half trying to figure out if her boobs had always been there, and he just hadn't noticed before.

Gigi pulled two black chef coats out of the bag. They were monogrammed RESTAURANT WEEK 2015. One said CHEF TIM, and the tiny little one said CHEF GIGI. "I had these made special for the competition." She gave Tim a giant smile and handed him his jacket. "Do you like it?"

"Oh yeah, this is great, Geeg. Where is Poppy's?"

Gigi flicked her eyes to me and dropped them from my head down to my feet. "I didn't get her a chef coat because she's not a real chef. She's just helping with prep, but I didn't want her to feel left out either, so I got her this." She reached into her shopping bag and pulled out a bright yellow frilly apron. She held it against my body. It made my skin tone the color of a five-day-old bruise. I looked like Ronald McDonald . . . in an ugly apron.

Tim looked from Gigi's boobs to my face. "That was nice of you Geeg, but I'm not sure about the color."

Gigi waved him off. "All Poppy needs is a good night's sleep, and those dark circles under her eyes will disappear."

I tried to muster up some enthusiasm. "That was very—"

"Thoughtful?" Gigi offered brightly.

"Well, I can definitely tell you put a lot of thought into it."

A stocky man with tight-cropped black hair and plastic holes in his earlobes entered the room and looked around. He crossed his beefy, tattooed arms and shook his head like he'd been lured to an all-you-could-eat seafood buffet only to find one sad pan of fried shrimp amongst several trays of hush puppies.

Tim groaned. "Aww no."

"What is it?" I whispered.

"That's Adrian Baxter. We went to school together. He's a real piece of work."

"Why?"

Tim didn't get a chance to tell me because the tinkling sound of a fork tapping a champagne glass brought the room to attention.

"Oh God, okay, is everybody listening? This is awful." Ivy stood in the middle of the arena, a skinny boy at her side wearing a headset and holding a clipboard. "I have an announcement to make." Ivy's voice cracked, and a worried hush fell over the chefs. "I know this was supposed to be a big event for everyone. Channel Eight was going to have coverage every night of the competition, and the marketing team was going to post real-time stats and updates of your progress on all the social media outlets. But . . . I'm sorry to say . . . that . . . Restaurant Week is . . . cancelled."

There was a collective gasp followed by a murmur of dissension.

Ivy held up her hands to quiet the chefs. "Due to an unforeseen emergency . . . there has been a water main break at the inn where the celebrity judges were booked for the week. My PA here has been on the phone for over an hour trying to get alternative lodging, but all the B&Bs are either closed for the winter or booked solid with holiday specials. The judges are coming in from North Jersey. They can't be expected to commute. Miss New Jersey is coming all the way from Secaucus. The whole competition is ruined."

Tim ran his hand through his hair. "Oh, this is not good. I was counting on the publicity from this to boost business. Now what am I going to do?"

The murmurings in the room were getting angrier. Adrian Baxter lashed out with, "Are you kidding me? I hired additional staff to cover my time for the week's tapings. Are you sayin' I have to pay them for nothing?"

Ivy held her sides and took a deep breath, counting from one to ten and back again. "Look, I know you're all disappointed that you've been inconvenienced. I'll probably lose my job over this. The station manager has been promoting the event for weeks. The only thing we have to fill this time slot is old school board meetings and that video clip of Eunice, the belly dancing otter."

I raised my hand. "I have a bed and breakfast. It's not officially open yet. We've had some . . . kinks to work out, but there are five bedrooms and they're ready if there are no other options available."

"Are you kidding?" She rushed over and grabbed my hands. "Yes, yes! Absolutely, yes. You've saved my job."

The Nick Nolte chef interjected over to my left, "And the competition."

Ivy glanced at him. "Of course, and the competition."

A couple of the chefs cheered and whistled. Tim hugged me again. "Thank you, Mack. It means a lot to me that you would do this. Let me know if you need any help."

I gazed into Tim's eyes and my heart gave a little flip. A lock of blond hair curled over his tanned face and blue eyes, and I reached up to wrap it around my finger. I was pulled away by the director before I made contact.

"Come with me. I'll need you to sign a few waivers promising that you won't use having the judges staying in your bed and breakfast as an unfair advantage, and you won't sue the station for any damages, that sort of thing."

"What kind of damages?"

"You know, the usual celebrity kind. Just legal mumbo jumbo. Don't worry, these are professionals. Nothing will go wrong."

Chapter Three

Ivy took me to the film studio classroom where the TV station had set up their office for the week. I filled out and signed several contracts. I might have promised I would donate a kidney if one of the staff was ever in need. I probably should have read them closer, but I really wanted to get back to the party and hang with the chefs.

When I was finally able to rejoin the group, I saw that they had made themselves comfortable with the cocktail cart. Conversations were a little louder, attitudes were a little bigger. I took a moment to let the gravity of my situation sink in. These were real chefs, with real restaurants. I'm just a widow who makes muffins for a hot Italian barista who likes me.

Nick Nolte came up and took my hand. He had that perpetual tan that came from living by the ocean his whole life, and he carried himself with the easy demeanor of someone more at home on a surfboard than in a boardroom. In a lot of ways, he could pass for Tim's dad. "Nice job, Red. You saved us."

"I'm glad I could help."

"Folks call me Hot Sauce Louie. I got a little hole in

the wall down by the beach called The Dawg Houz. We specialize in gourmet burgers and dogs and deep-fried hand pies."

"Ooh, that sounds delicious."

"You should come by sometime, on the house."

"That's very generous of you. I don't remember The Dawg Houz from when I was growing up here. How long have you been there?"

"'Bout three years. I used to have a food truck called Wheelie Dogs, but the dang thing broke down so often, I spent more time making the repairs than making the food. I finally sold it to a guy in Philly who makes pierogis. I used the money to start up my new joint. Last year we were voted best burgers at the shore. How about you? You got a place around here?"

I felt my cheeks get hot. I knew this was coming, the moment where I had to admit I didn't belong here, that I was a fraud. I'd just hoped it wouldn't come so soon. "No, not me. I'm not a chef. I'm working with Team Maxine's as a favor to Chef Tim. I just make muffins and cookies and things for *La Dolce Vita*, the coffee shop on the mall."

Hot Sauce Louie leaned back and gave me an appraising once-over. "You're the baker behind the gluten-free madness? I cannot get enough of those maple-pecan shortbread bars. I'm addicted!"

I swelled with unexpected pride. "Guilty."

"Wow. I'm gonna have to up my dessert game now."

I giggled like a nerd. It came out more like a horse whinny, and I quickly looked around to see if anyone else had overheard. Tim had been watching me with Louie and was suddenly heading our way.

Hot Sauce Louie nudged my shoulder. "Hey, let me ask you something. There's a little something in those bars that I can't place. What is it?"

"There's a pinch of nutmeg."

"No, that's not it. It tastes a little like booze."

"Oh, that's my vanilla. I make it myself out of vanilla bean pods and white rum."

Hot Sauce Louie slapped his leg. "That's it! It's been driving me crazy. You're gonna have to show me how you do that one of these days."

"I'd be glad to." *Oh my God! Is this really happening?*

Tim put an arm around my shoulder and introduced himself to Louie.

"That's what I love about an event like this." Louie looked around the room. "Getting to work with all these cool chefs and learning from each other. This is what it's all about. I'm feeling the love right here. Hey, girl."

The woman with the braids who had waved me over earlier joined us. She was beautiful, and young. Maybe late twenties.

Hot Sauce Louie pointed from me to the young girl. "Have you two met?"

I smiled and shook my head no.

"Poppy McAllister, this is Vidrine Petit-Jeune."

Vidrine smiled broadly. I reached out my hand but she broke protocol and pulled me into a hug instead. "Thank ya, *chéri*, for offerin' up yaw rooms to save the event. I know my place needs the exposure of an affair like this, what with me being new in town an all."

"I'm happy to do it. This is my team leader, Chef Tim Maxwell."

Tim was also pulled into a hug. He asked Vidrine, "That's a unique accent you got there. Where are you from?"

She laughed. "I was born in Haiti but moved to Mobile, Alabama when I was a young'un, so my accent is very confused."

She was delightful. I liked her instantly. "What kind of restaurant do you have?"

Vidrine pulled a card out of her bag and handed it to me. "Honey, I got a little ol' place just off the mall called Slap Yo Mamma! We specialize in Southern comfort food wit a Caribbean influence."

"Oh, I've heard about that place. My friend Sawyer and I have been trying to get over there and try it out."

"Well you should, *chéri*."

Tim put his arm around me again, "If Sawyer can't go, I'd love to take you."

I smiled. "I'd like that."

Vidrine looked to her left and right before leaning in and speaking in hushed tones. "Did y'all hear who one of the judges is gonna be?"

Louie whispered back, "Who?"

"Horatio Duplessis."

Tim groaned. "Gah! We may as well go home now."

"Why?" I asked. "Who is Horatio Duplessis?"

The tan had slid right from Hot Sauce Louie's face, and he looked like he'd eaten a bad clam. "He's a food critic with a stick up his butt."

Vidrine's hands perched on her hips. "Honey, his reviews can make or break a chef's career. If you don't impress him, no amount of publicity here can save you."

I asked Tim, "Have you been reviewed by him?"

Tim sighed. "He gave Maxine's mediocre reviews a few years ago."

Louie grabbed a cocktail from the cart as it went by. "I don't put much stock in those critic columns. The only reviews I care about are Trip Advisor and Yelp. Real people without an agenda."

"So, I guess you've never been demoralized by Sir Horatio?" Vidrine asked Louie.

"A dude that takes himself that serious would never stoop to the depths of reviewing a joint like The Dawg Houz."

"Then why did you look like you were about to pass out when you heard his name?"

Louie shrugged. "It's freaking hot in here."

Gigi popped up on the other side of Tim and introduced herself to Vidrine and Louie as Tim's sous chef for the competition. "Tim and I are both alumni of CIA in New York. Of course, he was a few years ahead of me."

Hot Sauce Louie had my kind of filter and blurted out, "Ya think!"

I stifled a giggle, but Gigi went on, "Poppy here didn't go to culinary school, she's just on our team to fetch ingredients. Where did the two of you go to school?" Gigi flashed Hot Sauce and Vidrine each a big smile. They both smiled back, unfazed by her prejudice.

Louie shook his head. "Didn't go to school. I'm one hundred percent organically self-taught. My philosophy is either you got the gift, or you don't. Anyone can learn to cook, but only a special few cook by instinct." He gave me a wink. I wanted to hug him right then and there.

Gigi's smile had cracked some, but she was holding on. She looked to Vidrine for redemption.

"Oh honey, I learned everything I know in the school of hard knocks at my momma's knee. Every one of my recipes have been passed down through generations of Petit-Jeune women. But I been working in professional kitchens since I was fifteen years old, and then I had to forge my momma's signature to get a work permit. I've worked my way up from dishwasher to sous chef in some of the most prestigious restaurants up and down the coast. And now I got my own little *tranche du paradis*—slice of heaven."

Gigi's eyes were stiff, and her smile was pasted on. I think I saw a mini-stroke building up behind her retinas, and it was all I could do not to jab her in her double *D*s.

Tim leaned away from the tension radiating from his left side—too close to his left side I might add. I was concerned he would need a Gigi-ectomy. He politely excused our team and said we were going to go mingle a bit.

We left Hot Sauce Louie and Vidrine amiably chatting about their restaurants and backgrounds and wandered toward the other side of the room. Adrian Baxter, Tim's old classmate, started our way, and Tim pivoted us in another direction.

Tim took a deep breath. "He's going to make this week miserable for us, and I really need things to go well if Maxine's is going to survive."

"Why? What's going on with Maxine's?" I asked.

Before Tim could answer, a little Italian in a paisley pink shirt was kissing both my cheeks. "Poppy, I thought that was you. I would know Gia's *bella amore* anywhere."

Tim's back stiffened and the muscles in his jaw were making little veins pop up on his neck.

I recognized the little man from *Mia Famiglia*, the restaurant across the courtyard from the coffee shop where I make the gluten-free baked goods for Gia, the sexy Italian barista who holds a big piece of my heart. "Marco?"

"*Si, sono qui.*"

"Is Gia's mother one of the chefs competing in Restaurant Week?"

"*Si, si, si.* Oliva is competing. But you know she no speaks the English so good, so Marco is here to translate."

"Is she here now?" My eyes darted around the room looking for a little old lady putting the evil eye on me.

Marco dipped his eyebrows and shook his head. "No. She's does not come tonight. She will be here Saturday for first event."

Gigi looked around the room. "I knew there were supposed to be six chefs. She must be the one who's missing."

Marco kissed my cheeks again. "Gia sends his love and says good luck, Bella."

A warmth began to rise from my toes.

Tim tightened his grip on my arm. "Come on, I want to introduce you both to one of the most influential chefs in South Jersey. He's also our toughest competition."

He led us up to the very dignified chef, who reminded me a little of Sam the Eagle from the Muppets, with his bushy eyebrows and tufts of gray hair over a serious expression. He stood ramrod straight off to one side with his teammates, quietly watching the mingle without joining in.

"Chef Philippe, I want you to meet Chef Gigi, of *Le Bon Gigi.*"

Chef Philippe gave a courteous head nod to Gigi. "Mademoiselle."

"And my pastry chef for the competition, Poppy McAllister."

Chef Philippe gave me the same nod. "Madame."

Why'd she get a "mademoiselle"?

Tim went on, "Chef Philippe owns *La Maîtrisse,* a very popular brasserie in Sea Isle."

"Are you also an alumni of CIA?" I asked, before Gigi could pounce on her passive-aggressive soapbox.

Chef Philippe had a deep rich voice with a touch of an accent, like dark chocolate poured over a soufflé. "No, madame. I graduated *Le Cordon Bleu* in Paree, but that was many years ago." He gave me a kind smile.

Ivy's PA came by with the cocktail cart. Tim handed me a refill on my sparkling water and offered champagne to Chef Philippe, who accepted. "I had your *caneton à l'orange* last spring. It was magnificent."

Chef Philippe's eyes crinkled at the corners when he smiled at Tim. "Thank you for your praise."

Tim was about to continue gushing over Chef Philippe's food, but he was forcefully booted out of the way by a brazen attitude with tattoos running from wrist to shoulder of each arm.

"Well, look whooz here. You gonna cheat at this competition too?"

The blood drained from Tim's face, while Gigi and I made matching bookends of horror. Well, one of the bookends may have been a little top heavier than the other.

Tim poked Adrian Baxter on the collarbone. "You've got a lot of nerve coming here and accusing me like this."

Chef Philippe and his team politely excused themselves to go anywhere but here.

Adrian didn't seem to care how offensive or loud he was to the rest of the room. "Why? That's what you do, in'it?" He turned to me and Gigi. "I suppose you're his line chefs. Did he tell you about me?"

I squared my shoulders to poke back at the stocky bear. "That depends. Who exactly would you be?"

He sputtered, "I'm Adrian Baxter. Only the hottest chef at the shore. Everyone's heard of Baxter's By the Bay. We got a raw bar that'll make yooze weep for joy. And this poser and I were in the same graduating class at CIA."

I shrugged. "I don't believe Tim has ever mentioned you." I wanted to ask if it took a lot of training in cooking school to set up a raw bar, but we were already getting some negative publicity with the rest of the room, so I kept my mouth shut for Tim's sake.

Gigi finally managed to get ahold of herself. "Are you sure your restaurant's in South Jersey? I've been a chef in West Cape May for five years, and I've never heard of you."

Adrian sprouted purple down to the dragons on his meaty forearms.

Tim spoke to him in feigned pity. "Ouch. I guess you're not as big a deal as you thought."

Adrian stormed off backwards while pointing at Tim. "I'm gonna wipe the floor with you, Maxwell. Just wait till you see what I got planned for yooze. You may have fooled Isabel, but after this week everyone will know who the better chef is."

Chapter Four

Once Adrian had backed out of the arena, Gigi snorted. "What was that all about?"

"And what did he mean by you may have fooled Isabel?" I asked.

Tim rolled his shoulders back and blew out a deep breath. "Isabel Georges. She's a very accomplished and respected chef in New York City and a CIA alum. I beat Adrian out of a prestigious internship in her Soho restaurant, Lardon, twenty years ago, and I guess he never got over it."

I looked to where Adrian had exited. "Well it sounds like he's got some kind of plan for this week."

Tim looked from me to Gigi to Gigi's boobs. "Come on, let's get out of here before there are any more incidents. Adrian's personality intensifies when he drinks, and the cocktail cart is open for another hour yet."

I told Tim and Gigi I would see them at Tim's restaurant in a bit. Then I went to the main foyer where I'd signed in. Ivy caught me on my way out the door. "Leaving so soon?"

"Yes, I'm afraid so. We're going to strategize before the big event this weekend."

"Good idea. There's some tough competition in the room. The winning chef gets their picture on the cover of *South Jersey Dining Guide* for the summer. That'll bring their restaurant a lot of business, and everybody wants it, so bring your *A* game.

"I'll do my best."

"And hey, I'll be by your place tomorrow around four to welcome the judges when they arrive. I've arranged for town cars to drive each of them to the bed and breakfast. Just send the accommodation invoice to this address here." She gave me a business card for the administrative department of the local television station.

I hoped they'd pay quickly. I would have to go buy supplies for the guests first thing in the morning before baking for Gia. I called Aunt Ginny during my drive back to Cape May and filled her in on our last-minute guests.

Her only comment was, "What are you, some kind of nut?" That was about as on board as I could get her before I arrived at Tim's.

Maxine's Bistro was a converted white clapboard fisherman's cottage down by the harbor. Black, shuttered windows were topped with blue awnings, and weathered, wooden window boxes graced each frame. I parked in the crushed-clamshell parking lot on the side. Tim was waiting for me at the door. "Is this the first time you've been here?"

"Yes, I think it is." *As long as you don't count driving up and down this road at night like a maniac trying to spot you through the windows, it is.*

"Well shame on me. Come on in here and let me show you around."

Tim took my coat and hung it by the door, then he guided me by my elbow through the maze of rooms painted in soft colors of provincial blue and white, each room peppered about with white linen-covered tables and tufted blue chairs. Every table topped with a candle in a jar and the usual linen napkin–rolled cutlery. One set of customers sat at the table in front of the fireplace. Their server was just asking if they needed anything else. She gave Tim a subtle nod when we went by.

"Come on, I'll show you the back of the house."

The kitchen was a small stainless-steel galley loaded with pots, pans, and mixing bowls. Two line chefs in starched whites were standing at the open back door, smoking cigarettes.

"How'd we do?" Tim asked them.

One of the chefs shook his head. "Twenty covers. I sent Gail home early."

Tim sighed. "Alright. Come on, Restaurant Week fame."

I didn't see a pastry station like Gia's momma had at *Mia Famiglia*. "Where do you make your desserts?"

"I don't have time to make desserts, so we use frozen."

"Wait a minute, I think my heart just stopped."

Tim breathed out a laugh and pulled me close. "I've been waiting for the right pastry chef to come along."

"You have?" I teased.

"Mmhmm. Know anyone?"

"That depends. How much does the job pay?" I gave him a coy smile.

His lips twitched, and he looked at my mouth. "I'm broke. I can only pay in kisses."

"Hmm. I already get paid that in my day job."

Tim's mouth dropped, and he pulled me against him when I laughed at his shocked expression.

"I might be able to give you a raise." He leaned down to kiss me.

"What's taking you two so long!"

Seriously, Gigi!

"Come on slowpoke, we don't have all night."

I have all night, but it might be close to your bedtime.

Tim sighed. "Let's go upstairs. Gigi's been waiting for us to go over the game plan."

I followed Tim up a back staircase to his modest studio apartment above the restaurant. The living room was floor-to-ceiling wood paneling. On one wall was a beat-up plaid couch and a glass and chrome coffee table. On the other wall, a dining room table was made from an old door on makeshift legs. It had been refinished to a beautiful stained pecan.

"I didn't realize you lived above the restaurant."

"Yep. It's a lot easier and more cost effective than having a second place. I'm here all the time anyway."

Tim had bailed me out of jail a few months ago, and he said he put up Maxine's for the collateral. He could have lost his home. *He'd risked everything for me.*

"Do you want something to drink?" Tim walked over to a small fridge and looked inside. "Gigi, where is that sparkling water I just bought."

"It should be behind my Brie."

Hold the phone! I tried to make my voice sound as carefree as possible. "Does Gigi live here too?"

Gigi had a smug look on her face, like she had been waiting for this moment to put me in my place.

"No, she's just here a lot."

Define "a lot."

Tim handed me a sparkling water. "We've been going over menu ideas based on what the Restaurant Week mystery ingredients could be."

Gigi leaned back on the couch, and I noticed she was leaning next to a peach and brown crocheted throw. I reached over and tugged it out from behind her shoulder.

"Oh my gosh, I can't believe you still have this."

Tim laughed. "I will treasure that ugly blanket till the day I die."

"This thing is hideous." I shook a corner in the air. "Look at all these mistakes."

"No way, I love it." Tim took the crib-sized throw from me and wrapped it around his shoulders.

Gigi jutted her chin out. "What's so special about a ratty old blanket?"

"Poppy made it for me when we were seventeen."

"They were supposed to be the colors of the Flyers team jersey." I shook my head.

"But after she made it, she washed it with bleach. The look on your face when . . ." Tim couldn't finish the story for laughing so hard.

I was almost in tears from laughing. "It was supposed to fit your bed, but then it took me six months to get it that size. You almost got a pot holder except Aunt Ginny made me keep going."

We were both laughing at the memory only we shared. Gigi looked from one to the other of us, less amused. "Cute. Well, why don't we get started discussing the competition."

I took a seat on the other end of the couch as far away from Gigi as I could get.

Tim cleared his throat and tried to stop smiling. He picked up a legal pad from stacked crates he'd made into an end table. "Okay, so there are five other chefs in the competition. Chef Philippe."

Gigi held up her tablet with a picture of the older, most dignified chef in the competition.

"Right," I said, "Sam the Eagle."

Tim chuckled.

Gigi said, "Who?"

"Nothing."

Tim continued. "Chef Philippe is classically trained. He specializes in French comfort food with an emphasis on plating. Thoughts?"

Gigi looked at the tablet. "I found him to be pretentious."

Tim replied. "He is. But he has the reviews to back him up. What are his possible weaknesses?"

I thought for a minute. "Cooking styles other than French cuisine."

Tim pointed at me. "Exactly. We may not be able to compete head-to-head with his expertise of French sauces, so I say we think multiculturally. And keep an eye on the presentation. Make sure the dishes complement the food. Use contrasting colors. Don't put a yellow sauce on a yellow plate."

Gigi scoffed. "No, of course not. Everyone knows that. Oh, you're saying that because of Poppy. Sorry."

Tim's eyes met mine for a moment, and he seemed amused with my irritation. "Up next, Vidrine Petit-Jeune."

Gigi pulled up a picture of the southern Haitian. "Vidrine didn't go to culinary school. I think that will be to our advantage."

I was about to tell Gigi to put away her soapbox when Tim said something that shocked me.

"Agreed. Not because she isn't qualified and gifted," he said as he saw my dagger eyes. "But because she won't have had the benefit of having been in competition before."

Gigi turned to me. "Yeah, the whole mystery ingredient fad on your TV cooking shows, that didn't start with *Iron Chef*. Culinary schools have been doing that for ages."

Tim nodded. "It's a way to teach a young chef how to think on their feet and improvise with recipes. Now, she may not have been through school, but that doesn't mean she hasn't been through training. She is going to be a strong challenger. Some pretty impressive chefs have mentored her. Plus, she's got a very creative fusion menu as one of her strengths."

Gigi pulled up Slap Yo Mamma! online and read from Vidrine's website. "Caribbean flavor meets Southern charm. She has items on here like coconut-shrimp tacos, passion fruit chicken, pineapple-braised short ribs, and lobster with mango butter."

My stomach growled, and I moved one of the sofa pillows to cover it up.

Tim turned the page on his legal pad. "I think it's safe to say that Chef Vidrine is able to think creatively in creating her recipes, but experience is on our side. Next is Chef Louie."

"Gourmet burgers and dogs," I said.

Gigi gave me a look like a skunk had curled up in my lap.

"What? Everyone loves burgers and dogs. I hear his place is one of South Jersey's top ten places to eat at the shore."

Tim tried to be diplomatic about it. "While he isn't exactly the same caliber of say, Chef Philippe, Louie has a strong following. The Dawg Houz has lines down the block every day. And these aren't your garden variety burgers and dogs. I've had his cherry gorgonzola burger and black truffle fries. Wow. He may look like he just washed up with the tide, but he knows his umami."

Gigi leaned in to speak to me with maximum condescension and give Tim a better view down her sweater. "Umami is the fifth sense in tasting. Sweet, sour, salty, bitter—umami."

I smiled at Gigi. "I know what umami is."

"Oh, I didn't realize they covered that on television."

Tim cleared his throat again. "So, Hot Sauce Louie. Weaknesses?"

"I'd say the same as Vidrine," Gigi said.

I considered throwing a pencil at Gigi's cleavage to see if I could get it lodged in there. "I don't know, I think he has maturity on his side. He might surprise us. Plus, he used to have a food truck, so he's okay with working in a very small kitchen."

Tim jotted down some notes. "Good work, Poppy. I didn't know about the food truck. But then someone who's been around the culinary scene as long as Louie has probably got a few tricks up his sleeve."

Gigi pulled up a picture on her tablet and showed Tim. "Okay, Oliva Larusso. I know very little about her."

I knew this one intimately, so I chimed in. "Traditional Southern Italian. No formal training. She's been cultivating her family recipes for generations. *Mia Famiglia* is one of the most popular restaurants in Cape May. I am surprised, however, that Momma . . . I mean Oliva—"

Gigi smirked.

"Would enter Restaurant Week because she speaks very little English. That's why her sous chef, Marco, will be joining her. You met him tonight."

Gigi said, "Oh yes, the one who kissed you on your face and said your boyfriend says hello."

Tim paled.

"I don't remember it quite that way, but yes. Hand me that pencil."

Gigi passed me one of her pink troll doll pencils.

I held it in between my finger and my thumb to judge how hard I would have to throw it. "That was Marco. Her strengths will be that she makes very, very good Italian food. Weaknesses, I don't know that she makes anything else. Chef Oliva doesn't even think of her food as an ethnic category. To her, pasta is just part of everyday dinner."

Tim's voice was slightly strained, and he had a nervous eye on me with the pencil. "Okay. Same guidelines for Oliva as for Philippe. We mostly stay away from French and Italian, unless that is the most appropriate use of the ingredients."

Gigi nodded.

Tim closed his legal pad.

"Um," I started. "Are we going to talk about that bit with Adrian?"

Tim looked at the exposed beam ceiling. "Adrian Baxter. He's a good chef. He'll be tough competition. Eclectic menu. Nouveau American cuisine."

Gigi and I looked at each other then back to Tim.

"Uh huh. What about that whole scuffle at the mixer?" I asked.

"Yeah, he said you cheated at a competition," Gigi said.

Tim hedged a bit. "Adrian and I have never gotten along. We were in the same graduation class at CIA, and, somehow, we had the same course schedule. My second year I actually tried to switch classes to get away from him, only to find out Adrian had also requested a switch. We both ended up in the same switched class anyway."

I laughed aloud and had to apologize.

"He's overconfident, but very accomplished. Our ranking went back and forth between first and second in our graduation year. The competition where he says I cheated, someone sabotaged his ingredients in a head-to-head cook-off, and I beat him. That put me first in my class at graduation, and he's still bitter about it."

"Then there was that internship at Lardon," I added.

Tim rolled his eyes. "At the end of the day, I think Isabel gave me the internship because Adrian annoyed her."

"Did you cheat?" I asked.

Gigi launched herself at me. "No way did he cheat. How can you even ask him that?"

"He was eighteen years old. You do dumb things when you're eighteen." As soon as the words were out of my mouth, I regretted them.

Gigi sat back and tried to fold her arms across her chest. "Well you would know."

Tim stood up. "Okay, let's not go there."

Gigi put both her hands up. "She started it."

I pretended to twirl my pencil and launched it at her cleavage. It wedged right in the valley, and the troll doll dinged her on the chin. I covered my mouth with my hand. "I'm so sorry. Your new boobs."

Tim's eyes nearly fell out of his head, and he had to excuse himself.

Gigi blushed and extracted the number two from the Bobbsey Twins. "Maybe we should just go over our duties for the event."

Tim came back to the room and sat down. His face was scarlet, and he couldn't look at me or Gigi without his shoulders shaking up and down again. "Okay, there are three courses. Each day we'll have three mystery baskets, one for each course. We have to incorporate the ingredients from the basket into the dish."

"This sounds exactly like the competition shows on the Cooking Channel," I pointed out.

Tim looked at me, tightened his lips, and looked away to keep from laughing again. "I'm sure that's where they got the idea from. Except we have more time to make the dishes, we have three team members working at the same time, and the event coordinator has agreed that there won't be anything disgusting or extremely expensive in the boxes, since whatever we make, we have to serve in our restaurants the same night."

Gigi had finally stopped pouting. "It's pretty hard to get local customers to try goat stomach or monkey brains."

Tim made a face. "Ech. Plus, no one is eliminated from the competition. We just accumulate points and notoriety."

"If no one is eliminated, what's the downside?"

Gigi adjusted her sweater placement. "If we make a bad dish, everyone will know about it. People will want to eat in the restaurant that made the winning dishes. So, Tim and I will work closely together to be sure our dishes complement each other and there are no failures."

Tim consulted his notes. "Now that I know Horatio Duplessis is one of the judges, it's more important than ever for everything to be perfect. Gigi and I will prepare all three courses. We've been practicing here in the kitchen after hours for weeks."

I'll just bet you have.

Gigi flashed Tim a big smile.

I asked Gigi, "Why didn't you enter the competition yourself for *Le Bon Gigi*?"

Gigi blushed. "We're closed for the month of January, plus Tim has been my mentor since I arrived in Cape May. I've been wanting to work closer with him, and this seemed a good way to do that."

"Okay," I said, "what do you want me to do?"

Gigi pulled a beginner's guide to chopping out of her shopping bag and handed it to me. "You will do our prep work."

Tim nodded. "Right. You can save us so much time by being our gofer to the pantry, prepping our meats and veg, getting our plates ready, that sort of thing."

All the air was just sucked out of my sails. "That's all you want me to do?" What about flambéing a cherries jubilee? Or folding together a light-as-air cheese soufflé? We'd had four years of high school culinary classes together and plans to run our own restaurant, and he wants me to chop onions and fetch him plates? There were no words for what I was feeling right now. At least no words I could say without Aunt Ginny taking a switch to my backside.

Tim looked me in the eyes. "It's a very important competition, Mack. I got a lot riding on this one. I need you there to support me."

I could hear the universe making a giant flushing sound as all my hopes and dreams were sucked away in a current of condescension.

I didn't break eye contact, but Gigi leaned into my field of vision. "And trimming the silver skin from meat is tedious. You can be a big help." She smiled broadly. "And don't worry, I'll be in the middle of you and Tim the whole time."

Just like always.

Chapter Five

I loaded the last of the B&B's groceries into the commercial refrigerator. I was still in love with my new peach and copper kitchen. We'd had to make several renovations to turn Aunt Ginny's Queen Anne Victorian into the Butterfly Wings B&B. Of all the work that we'd done, this room was my favorite.

Figaro was pouncing from bag to bag to check for invaders . . . or treats . . . it was hard to say which. Aunt Ginny was rifling through the bag on the counter looking for chocolate of some kind. As if I put chocolate into everything. "It's in the bag with the cassava flour."

"Ha! Chocolate chips! What are you making with these?"

"I thought I would make black forest French toast for the guests."

"That sounds more like a dessert than breakfast."

"I know, but a lot of people look for that sort of thing when they're at a B&B, and I think I can make a Paleo version for you and me, so we can try it." I tipped my chin up to give Aunt Ginny a smile and caught her holding a spoonful of peanut butter rolled in chocolate chips. "What are you doing?"

She gave me an indignant look. "Any caveman that can think of turning coconuts into pancakes can think of this."

That's why I had a second bag of chocolate chips in my purse. Aunt Ginny always fell for the decoy chips. "Did you call Mrs. Galbraith?"

"Yes, and she made a big deal about it being last minute and all, but she will be here starting tomorrow to clean the rooms."

I whipped up a smoothie with some tangerine juice, frozen fruit, spinach, and collagen powder. "I'm heading over to the coffee shop to make some muffins and bars to last throughout the week. This event filming schedule is brutal. Somehow they manage to make an hour of baking take all day to record."

"How is Gia going to get by without you? Is he going to freeze everything and dole it out?"

"I think that's the plan, yes."

"Aren't you going to miss being with him every day?"

I gave Aunt Ginny a sidelong glance. "I'm definitely conflicted about it. When I'm with Gia, I feel like my heart explodes, and my brain goes mush. But when I'm with Tim, I'm home again. He's all I've ever wanted, and the years just melt away. It's only for a week and a couple of days. I'll be back to my regular life at *La Dolce Vita* soon enough."

Aunt Ginny kicked a bag with her toe and sent Figaro galloping across the room. "That's the problem with love. You can love two people at the same time. I don't know who I would have ended up with if I'd met all five of my husbands at that picnic in Seaside Heights. Yet, I loved every one of them."

Love? Did I say I was in love? Am I? I know I feel overwhelmed with both of them, like my whole world stops spinning and each moment could last forever.

My heart speeds up, and my breath catches in my chest. *Is that love?* My love for my late husband, John, kinda skipped that step, what with our doing everything in reverse order and all.

Aunt Ginny interrupted my thoughts. "What are you going to do?"

"About what?"

"Choosing between them."

"I don't know. I don't think I have to do anything yet. It's not like either one has declared his feelings or asked me to be exclusive."

"Well, when the time is right, you'll know what to do."

One thing I did know, the day would come when one of the three of us would have a broken heart. And if I caused either of them pain, that alone would surely kill me. I threw a straw in my cup and held it up to Aunt Ginny. "Do you want some of my spinach smoothie before I go?"

Aunt Ginny froze with the spoon halfway to her chin, and through a mouthful of peanut butter said, "I'm full."

Gia met me at the back door with a hot latte in hand. "There's the next Food Network star."

I choked down a laugh. "Discovered from a one-hour news segment on local cable access, just like Cat Cora." I took the latte and gave Gia a grin. "How did you know I was here?"

"I can hear your car coming all the way from Aunt Ginny's house down the alley. You need to get that muffler fixed."

I looked at my Toyota Corolla. It was pretty old. "Hm, I never noticed."

Gia rolled his eyes. "Just like a woman. I bet you've never had the oil changed."

"The light didn't come on."

Gia went off in Italian, which I understood very little of, but I gathered the gist was that I didn't know how to take care of a car. I'd argue that he was being a chauvinist . . . except . . . I didn't know how to take care of a car. John had always done that stuff for me.

"Give me your keys. I will have my brother Piero take a look this week. In the meantime, you can take my car." He handed me the spare keys to his Alfa Romeo.

My jaw dropped. "I couldn't. What if I get into an accident?"

Gia shrugged. "I have insurance."

We'd swapped keys. It felt sexy and mysterious, like an important line had been crossed. I told myself I was being silly. It's not like he was giving me the keys to his house or the PIN to his bank account. "If you're sure."

Gia winked. "Come and tell me all about the greet and meet."

The back room to the coffee house had a stainless-steel kitchen with a brand new, cobalt-blue Viking range with double oven on the left and a walk-in refrigerator on the right. In the back corner, Gia had an office smaller than my closet with a walnut desk and two chairs.

I put my coffee down on the polished countertop, put Gia's keys in my purse, and put on an apron. Then I started the ovens, washed my hands, and went to the storage room to gather supplies for the day's baking. "It went well for the most part. I have the judges staying at the bed and breakfast for the week now. Their original place was flooded."

Gia leaned against the counter, his arms folded

across his chest. "I'm surprised the other chefs didn't have a problem with that."

"Well, it was either that or the event was going to be canceled. Many of them have been hit hard by the economy and fewer tourists are visiting, so they're banking on the publicity from this event to stay afloat." My mind went to Tim living in that tiny studio apartment over the mostly empty restaurant. I didn't want to let him down.

Gia nodded. "It's been slower here, too, but we have a strong base of locals that keep us going."

I pulled out a recipe I'd been thinking about for a Paleo version of a strawberry Pop-Tart and assembled my ingredients. "Other than that, all the chefs seem pretty nice. Except for this one guy that Tim knows from college, Adrian."

Gia handed me a mixing bowl. "What's wrong with him?"

"I don't know. He was really abrasive and cocky, and he accused Tim of sabotaging him when they were in college and ruining his class ranking."

"Did Tim do that?"

I measured my almond meal and arrowroot starch and added them to the bowl. "I don't think so, but when I asked him outright he didn't exactly say no."

"That was a long time ago. People make mistakes when they're young."

"See, that's what I said."

The bell for the front door jingled. Gia went to wait on his customer while I finished the pastry dough and formed it into a ball. I chopped some frozen strawberries and scraped a vanilla bean, and then dropped them into a saucepan with some honey and gelatin. At the last minute I grabbed some balsamic vinegar and added a tablespoon to the berries to bring up the acidity.

Gia returned when I was rolling out my pastry dough. "Can you fill a special order for four dozen of your espresso brownies for a party tomorrow night?"

I checked my supply of allergy friendly chocolate chips. I only had enough for the double batch of brownies for the pastry case up front. "I can if they don't mind me replacing the chips with chopped dark chocolate."

Gia went back out front, and I stirred the Pop-Tart filling. The bell jingled again, and Gia came back a minute later. "She said that was fine. Where is your recipe? I will get everything together for you and be your sous chef."

I giggled. "You want to be my second in command?"

Gia spun me around. "I want to be your number one." Then he kissed me, and it was like he'd set me on fire.

When he was done, all I could say was, "Wow."

He smacked me on the backside and said, "Don't burn your sauce." Then he began to collect ingredients for the brownies while he whistled a little tune. "Are you excited about the competition?"

"The what? Oh, yeah." I wasn't thinking clearly about anything except what had just happened. "Yeah, that. Um . . . yeah. I'm not doing as much as I originally thought, but I still feel like I'm living out a fantasy, you know? I don't want to do anything to mess it up again."

"You won't mess it up. Maybe the time wasn't right before. Now will be your time."

"I hope you're right. This is definitely the major leagues. I hope I don't make a fool of myself. Bringing out the wrong ingredients or being asked to get something and not knowing where it is—or *what* it is."

Gia chuckled. "Don't worry. You are better at this than you think you are."

"I sure hope so. Chef Philippe and Chef Adrian both went to top-tier culinary schools, and have professional pastry chefs on their teams. Chef Vidrine has been mentored by top chefs for years. Only Hot Sauce Louie is self-taught like me, and his restaurant is ranked in the top ten in Cape May. I don't know what I'm doing in the same room with them."

"You need to believe in yourself like I believe in you."

My heart swelled, and I had to swallow some emotion. "And don't worry about the shop. I have four batches of muffins, the brownies, Pop-Tarts, and a couple cookie bars to make for you to freeze today. That should get you through the week. You won't even notice that I'm gone."

He stopped chopping chocolate for a minute. "Bella, my heart will always notice when you are gone."

Chapter Six

Gia and I worked together for hours making enough muffins, brownies, and lemon bars to feed one of Georgina's charity events. Although I'm not sure what charity would want only Paleo and gluten-free baking. Maybe the Celiac Foundation? Anyway, between the many shots of espresso, dance breaks to Dean Martin, and just trying to control myself around a sexy Italian for six hours, I was wired. I was also covered in melted chocolate and tapioca flour. I needed to rush home, take a shower, and eat something healthy before Ivy arrived with the celebrity judges.

Gia pulled his Spider convertible to the back door for me. He gave me a long kiss good-bye and tucked me into the silver sports car. I very gingerly pulled out of the alley, terrified that I would hit something during the two-and-a-half block drive home.

Three black town cars were parked at the curb in front of my house, and a fourth one was pulling up. Neighbors were coming out to check their mailboxes for mail delivered by fairies, because the mailman had been gone for hours, and they knew it. I checked the clock on the console: two-thirty. The judges were early. Well crapalulah!

Aunt Ginny was standing in the yard wearing the frumpiest-looking flowered dress I'd ever seen. It looked like the cover-up they give you at the gynecologist for your Pap smear. I didn't even believe it was hers. She had to have gone to the thrift store this morning just to punk me. "Today of all days."

I pulled into the driveway and Aunt Ginny stuck her face in the driver's side window. "Whoo, look at this. Did the hot barista give you a car?"

"No," I said, a little grouchier than I'd intended. "And what are you wearing? When I left this morning, you were in a navy and white striped sweater from Ralph Lauren. This looks like something you'd give a first grader to wear as a smock for art class."

Aunt Ginny quirked a smile and raised an eyebrow. "I wanted to give the highfalutin judges an authentic South Jersey welcome."

Three guests were getting out of their town cars and Ivy was on her way over to greet me. "For the love of God, go change," I said. Aunt Ginny stormed off, and I turned to give Ivy a smile. But a last-second thought caused me to call over my shoulder, "No ball gowns!"

Aunt Ginny stopped, dropped her head, then disappeared into the house.

"What was that all about?" Ivy smiled.

"Nothing, but I'm sure I'll come to regret it at some point today. So . . . they're early."

"I know, I'm sorry. One of the judges is Bess Jodice. She used to be the Dean of Culinary Arts at Cape Community College. Now her cookbooks are on the *New York Times* best seller list. You may have read her column in *Food and Wine Digest.*"

I shook my head no.

"Well, she arranged a tour of the kitchen arena for the judges this evening, so everyone was picked up early. Only you know who the studio forgot to tell?"

"Me?"

"Well, yes, but I mean me, the director of the Restaurant Week segment. Do you know how long I had to work to be given my own special interest, week-long mini-series in a non-fiction time slot?"

I shook my head.

"Six years. Jazmin got to do it in two, but Jazmin has a tiny waist and big boobs, so, you know, she earned it faster."

"Aww." I patted Ivy on the shoulder.

Across the yard, the celebrities were getting restless.

There was a dapper gentleman in a white suit and perky, salmon-colored bow tie with matching pocket square. He wore a white trilby hat cocked at a jaunty angle over a gray handlebar mustache. He looked like the Monopoly Man, and he was poking my Butterfly Wings B&B sign with his walking stick.

Next to him was a young Adonis in designer jeans and a pale blue cashmere sweater. He had perfect hair in the shade of dark chocolate, icy blue eyes, and very straight, very white teeth. He was busy taking numerous selfies in front of the B&B. He called out to the older gentleman. "Where is the paparazzi? I thought they'd be swarming this place by now."

The older gentleman looked around. "Clearly the staff has been sworn to secrecy. It's a good indication of a well-run establishment that they have been discreet about our arrival."

I whispered, "Who are they?"

"The older one is Horatio Duplessis, restaurant critic for the *New York Journal Food Digest*. He's a bigwig in the industry. The word is, he came out of retirement just for this event."

"So, he's the one I've been hearing about."

"Oh yeah. We had two chefs drop out of Restaurant Week when they got wind that he was coming."

"I thought there were only six slots?"

"There are. Hot Sauce Louie and Oliva Larusso were last-minute replacements. And over there, the yummy one, is Stormin' Norman Sprinkler, channel eight's eleven o'clock weatherman." She tapped her temple with her pen. "Not a lot going on upstairs, but with those looks, who needs brains?"

"How is a weatherman one of the judges for a cooking competition?"

Ivy pursed her lips and slid her eyes to the side. "This is a low-budget show, okay. We got local celebs. Most of the Chamber's money is being spent right here on wining, dining, and lodging the judges in order to get a big name like Horatio Duplessis. Even the basket items have been donated by local suppliers in exchange for free advertising."

"Yoo-hoo. Is anyone going to take our bags?"

We had to peel our eyeballs off the weatherman because we were being hailed by an older woman with a gray bob wearing a mumsy plaid pantsuit. Ivy said through gritted teeth, "That one's Bess. If you can make her happy, you'll be the first."

We walked over to the group, and Ivy introduced the judges to each other. I offered my hand to Bess. "I'm so sorry about the delay. We didn't expect you just yet. I'm Poppy, the owner of the Butterfly Wings B&B."

Bess stared down at my hand and made a distasteful recoil. I had a smear of strawberry jam on my wrist. I wiped my hand on my hip. "Sorry, I've been in the kitchen all day making Pop-Tarts and . . . stuff." Bess wasn't listening; she was mesmerized by a vision in white coming down the front porch.

Aunt Ginny had chosen to punish me by donning a vintage beekeeper's suit and helmet. I could just make out her smirk through the netting. She was being closely followed by Figaro, who would pass out if he even saw a bee on the other side of the window.

Ivy nodded toward Aunt Ginny, "What's that all about?"

I sighed. "Retribution."

Bess greeted Aunt Ginny like the two were old friends. "Do you keep bees here?"

"Not yet, but I thought I would start. I need some safe hobbies."

"I have my own hives up in Asbury Park." Bess got closer to Figaro who promptly flopped over. Bess looked at him with concern.

Aunt Ginny said, "Don't worry about him, his head is hollow." And the two of them walked arm in arm toward the house, leaving Bess's four large bags at my feet.

"I guess I'll just get those." I hefted two of the bags and looked back at the town cars. "There are only three judges? Who's in the fourth car?"

Ivy shuffled through her clipboard. Her hand flew up to her mouth. "Oh no." She ran to the fourth car and threw the door open.

The most stunning woman I had ever seen got out of the back. Flowing mink-brown hair, eyes the color of emeralds, and flawless skin. "It's about time!" She stamped her long, leather-clad, perfect leg and ground her lipstick-red stilettos into the grass. "My agent specifically said that it was in my contract that I'm to make a big scene at all times."

Ivy consulted her paperwork. "Do you mean a big entrance? That's what I have here."

The woman tossed her hair with a flick of her head. "Yeah. A big entrance. You were supposed to come open the door for me. I was sitting there for like an hour."

Stormin' Norman stuffed his cell phone in his pocket and stumbled over to the town car. "I'll open your door for you . . . Miss?"

"New Jersey."

"What?"

"It's Miss New Jersey. Like as in Miss America. Or Miss Placed. And my door is already open."

Ivy cleared her throat. "Poppy, I'd like to introduce you to Brandy Sparks, this year's reigning Miss New Jersey."

Brandy took a big step to get her stiletto unstuck. "My bags are in the car." She headed toward the house, stopping at Figaro, who was sitting tall and staring at her with big copper eyes. She looked at the giant fluffy cat and said, "Eeww," then kept walking.

Stormin' Norman grabbed her suitcases. "Can I have the room next to hers?" He rushed after Miss New Jersey, past Figaro who again flopped over. Norman didn't seem to notice.

"Well, that just saves the best for last." Horatio gave me a kindly smile. "You don't get to be as old as I am without learning to look after yourself. Hop to, Ivy." Ivy jumped and scooped up the dapper gentleman's luggage. Figaro was still lying on his back when Horatio looked down at him. Figaro blinked.

Horatio said, "Odd," and stepped over the smoky gray cat.

"Is that everybody?" I asked Ivy.

The town cars started pulling away while we took

the first load inside. "We're missing two people, Ashlee Pickel and Tess Rodriguez, the co-hosts of *Wake Up! South Jersey*. It's a millennial morning show out of Egg Harbor that airs from ten to eleven on weekdays. I don't know what's keeping them."

I made my second trip out to the yard for the rest of Bess's luggage. The house was waking up with chitter-chatter as the guests got to know one another. Figaro and Stormin' Norman had Miss New Jersey cornered in the sitting room. I put Bess's luggage down in the foyer and stretched my arms. *Who needs four bags for one week?*

Miss New Jersey was huddled in a chintz wingback chair. She cried out, "Eeww. Can you please make him go away?"

I looked from Figaro to Norman and asked, "Could you be more specific?"

"The cat. I'm allergic."

Oh dear. I shooed Fig from the room. He stood out by the stairway and wrapped his body around the door jamb, so he could still see Miss New Jersey with one eye. He stretched one paw just over the threshold of the sitting room.

While Ivy gave the judges an overview of the week—the times they would be picked up by their cars and when they would get their hair and makeup done before taping—I opened two bottles of wine and set out a cheese tray.

One by one, I showed the guests to their rooms. I put Bess Jodice in the Swallowtail Suite, where first she had to check the mattress for bedbugs. Then she had to check the pressure in the shower, and the windows to see if they opened easily or had a draft. Once those tests were passed, I was given instructions about breakfast. She required tea at exactly 185 degrees, served

only in bone china. She needed no sweetener as she
had brought her own honey from her personal hives.
There were to be no flowers that had smells in her
room, but orchids were fine. She will not eat eggs for
breakfast unless they come from her own laying hens.
No, she did not bring any eggs, or hens, with her, and
I would do a much better job of decorating her room
if I would add a chenille throw and a couple of beaded
pillows for a pop of color.

I wanted to ask her if she had any insider stock tips
she could share with me, but I refrained. My trial bed
and breakfast opening a few weeks ago had been a failure. I couldn't afford to have another.

I was going to put Stormin' Norman in the Monarch
Room, but at the last minute changed my mind and
sent him to the Adonis Suite. Mostly because I knew it
would make Aunt Ginny giggle later when I told her
about it, but also because it was the farthest away from
Miss New Jersey in the Scarlet Peacock. I made sure to
show Brandy how to lock her door and chased Figaro
from her room. Finally, I got the suave Horatio Duplessis settled in the Purple Emperor Suite, our nicest
room with a king-sized bed and a view of Mrs. Pritchard's
rose garden. I was just going over how to work the elec-
tric fireplace when sounds of a fracas in the front yard
got everyone's attention.

Ivy called to me from the bottom of the stairs.
"They're here."

They were making a ruckus over who would wear
the pink minidress on camera. The whole house had
joined to watch, including Figaro, who was standing
next to Miss New Jersey. Miss New Jersey sneezed.

Out on the front lawn, hair was whipping around,
French manicures were being ruined, earrings were

being pulled. It was like watching a honey badger and a wolverine go head-to-head.

Aunt Ginny narrowed her eyes watching the two young ladies and tsk'd. "Squirrels!"

Horatio stepped forward. "Ladies! Pah-lease."

The girls stopped scrapping and noticed they had an audience. They got ahold of themselves, and immediately did the most critical task that came to mind and reapplied their lip gloss.

Ivy nudged me and rolled her eyes. Then she said, "Ashlee Pickel, Tess Rodriguez, this is Poppy McAllister, your innkeeper for the week. She will show you to your room. Then I have a limo that will take us to tour the Restaurant Week set before we go to dinner."

Ashlee and Tess were well matched in temper, but opposites in appearance. Ashlee was a pale and willowy wheat blonde, while Tess was olive skinned, brunette, and curvy. From eyelashes to toenails they were both highly glossed, and while their pink-shimmer lips smiled prettily, their eyes flashed mutual animosity.

"Wait just a minute, *chica*. We have to share a room?"

"Does that producer know who we are?"

"Yeah. We're Ashlee and Tess."

They sang their theme song in harmony, "Babes in the mor-ning."

I tried to apologize. "I'm so sorry ladies, but this is the only other room I have. You do have your own bathroom though. Only the Scarlet Peacock uses the one in the hall."

Stormin' Norman came up the stairs as I was letting the girls into their suite. He made a big show of which room was his. "If you ladies don't have a lot of space in yours, I have a suite." Then he took his sweater off in the hallway and went into his room.

The girls both looked at me in question.

"I guess he was hot."

Tess watched the back of his door. "I'll say."

I opened the girls' room, and Figaro ran out.

"How many cats do you have?" Ashlee asked.

I stared at Figaro, dumbfounded. "Just the one."

Figaro flopped over.

I showed the girls their room and how everything worked. They snapchatted the experience for posterity until Ivy called, "The limo is here!"

Thank God. I ushered the girls back to the foyer where the other judges were getting their coats and wraps to leave. Everyone except for Bess Jodice.

"I'm not going. I've seen the old place. I was Dean of Culinary Arts for twenty years before I transitioned careers to write my award-winning column for *Food and Wine Digest.* I think my portrait still hangs in the main lobby." Her chest puffed out and she rolled her eyes shut and grinned.

Ivy stood holding Bess's coat, unwilling to adapt to the change in plans. "But, what about dinner? I have reservations for all of us at Barberini's."

Bess shook her head. "Oh dear, no. I don't go out to eat often. I just can't stomach restaurant food unless it's five stars. I find it's safer to just eat at home. That way I can control the quality of ingredients."

Aunt Ginny had snuck into the foyer by way of the dining room. "We got a McDonalds in North Cape May across from the strip mall. I like their Quarter Pounder." Then after a glare from me, "I mean, I used to . . . before I was sentenced to the Paleo Diet." Aunt Ginny backed into the shadows of the sitting room.

Ivy shrugged and handed me the coat. "Okay, but if you change your mind, you'll have to call an Uber, since the town cars won't be back until checkout a week from now."

Miss New Jersey took her winter-white pashmina and draped it around her shoulders. "I'm starving, let's go." My heart lurched as she headed for the door, and her entire back was covered in tufts of gray cottony fur as if a very naughty feline had maliciously rolled around in the center of it. Figaro licked his paw and rubbed it on his ear. Miss New Jersey sneezed.

It's gonna be a long week.

Chapter Seven

"I told you this was a bad idea." Aunt Ginny passed me the coffee so I could refill the carafe for the third time in an hour.

"You didn't say any such thing," I hissed back.

Aunt Ginny refilled the basket of assorted muffins for the dining room. "Well you better believe I thought it. We tried this with free guests a few weeks ago, and they left us bad reviews. Now you've brought in celebrities, with high expectations and higher demands. They've about run me off my feet. How do you think this is going to end?"

"I'm not sure the hosts of a local cable access show classify as celebrities."

"Well they've been ordering me around like they think they're Kathy Lee and Hoda."

I put another pitcher of cream and bowls with sugar cubes and packs of stevia on the tray. "I know, I'm sorry. Thankfully, they are just here for nine days."

"Governments have been overthrown in less time." Aunt Ginny picked up her tray and together we headed into the formal dining room, where our six guests were leisurely enjoying their bottomless refills and the late-morning sunshine.

Figaro lay on the floor at Miss New Jersey's feet; he swatted at her fringed boot. The woman's eyes were red and puffy.

"Are you feeling well?"

"It'd my allergies," she snuffled. "I think dat cat wath in my roomb last night."

I placed the coffee service on the buffet. "I'm sorry. He doesn't usually go into the guest rooms." I tried to discreetly nudge Figaro with my foot to move him away from Brandy. He smacked my foot with his paw. "I can't imagine how he got in there."

Aunt Ginny put the muffins in the center of the dining room table. "We'll be sure to keep a close eye on him today."

Horatio held up a little silver dish. "Would you have any more of that delightful fig jam?"

I took the silver bowl from the restaurant critic. "I'm sure that we do. I'm so glad you like it."

Aunt Ginny scooped up Figaro, who protested with a powder-puff swat to Aunt Ginny's hand.

Back in the kitchen Aunt Ginny told Figaro, "You need to leave that girl alone or I'll lock you in my room all day."

He squirmed out of her arms and landed with a soft thud.

Aunt Ginny washed her hands. "Menace."

I refilled the silver bowl with Aunt Ginny's home-made fig jam. "I can't believe they've eaten most of the jar in one breakfast."

"I can't believe they raided the kitchen last night and ate a week's worth of fruit and cheese."

"Remind me to ask Smitty to make us a STAFF ONLY sign for the kitchen door."

"Sure. You'll probably get it by next Halloween, but sure."

The kitchen door swung open and Bess poked her head in. "Poppy, is that pasture-raised bacon on the buffet or the low-budget stuff?"

"It's organic, pasture-raised, antibiotic-free bacon."

"With or without nitrates?"

"Without."

"Oh good. I think I'll have some after all."

She returned to the dining room, and Aunt Ginny stuck her tongue out behind her.

"Eight days to go."

I tied my hideous yellow apron around my waist and looked at my reflection in the locker-room mirror. "It looks horrible."

Vidrine shook her head side to side. "Mmh-mmh-mmh. Well, it's not horrible. Just hard to coordinate with that mess'a red hair."

"You know how long it took me to pick an outfit this morning? I had on black, I looked like a bee. I had on red, I looked like I'd be serving a dollar menu."

"Well, honey, blue was the way to go."

"I look like a Minion."

"Yeah. But not in a bad way. And you're rocking those skinny jeans."

Ivy stuck her head in the locker room. "Ten minutes, ladies."

Vidrine gave me one last smile. "See you out there, *chérie.*"

"Good luck today. Or . . . break a leg . . . I don't know what chefs say."

I joined Tim and Gigi in our kitchen, the one straight in front of the camera that Tim had chosen at my suggestion.

Gigi gave a sly smile, more to herself than to me. "Good, it fits."

"Of course it fits. Each tie is a yard long."

Tim reached around Gigi to squeeze my arm. "You look adorable."

Well that wiped the smirk right off Gigi's face. I looked around the stage. Vidrine gave me a wave from the kitchen next to ours. Then there was Hot Sauce Louie around the bend next to her, followed by Philippe, standing at attention in the spot he requested next to the judges' table. On the other side of us, to our right, was Momma's team, er, Chef Oliva's team, from *Mia Famiglia*. Marco gave me a finger wave. I waved back, and Momma gave me such a deep scowl that her eyebrows had time to braid themselves together. Then, lastly, on the other end of the horseshoe, was Adrian, next to the audience. He was standing spread-eagle with his arms crossed in front of him, flexing his tattoos, and shooting threatening looks straight at Tim.

Tim noticed him too. "God, just look at him there, acting like he has a personal vendetta."

Gigi put one hand on Tim's arm. "Don't worry about him. You got this."

Aunt Ginny waved from the stadium seating, where she was sitting next to Sawyer. The gorgeous, chestnut brunette with the heart-shaped face had been my best friend since elementary school. If anyone in the room could make Miss New Jersey feel insecure about her looks, it'd be Sawyer. I gave her and Aunt Ginny both a big smile and waved back. They were my plus one and plus two. I was glad to have someone in my corner.

Wait. Who was that making their way through the crowd over to them? Ooooh no. This can't end well. Mrs. Dodson was leading a group of pink and white-haired biddies and cronies into the stands. They were all there, Mrs. Davis, Mother Gibson, Mr. and Mrs. Sheinberg. Ivy must have given tickets to the senior center to boost audience attendance. One by one, they all found me.

"Where's Poppy? I don't see her."

"Over there."

"Where? I don't see a redhead anywhere."

"There, in the hideous apron."

"Oh, I thought that was the mascot. Hiya Bubala!"

I gave them a little palm side-to-side wave.

"You look like Raggedy Ann."

I gave a little smile, and a thumbs-up.

The house lights dimmed and brightened, signaling that we were about to begin. A skinny boy wearing thick glasses and a bright yellow headset led the judges to the table on the far right of the last kitchen—over by Chef Philippe. They each found their name cards.

First was Horatio Duplessis, who tipped his hat to the audience. "Thank you for extending the invitation."

Next in line, Bess Jodice give a little unsanctioned speech. "It is so good to return home to my alma mater. I know you all have been missing me as much I miss these hallowed halls." Bess turned and looked around the audience. "I have so many good memories here, molding the minds and hands of tomorrow's chefs. In fact, I see some of my former students in this very room. You can be sure that you've left an impression on me that will never be forgotten. Thank you."

Bess sat down next to Horatio and the audience gave a timid clap.

Stormin' Norman Sprinkler gave a bow, blew kisses into the audience, and took a selfie with some culinary students in the audience. He tapped out a message on his phone, then put his hands in a prayer position and bowed again.

Miss New Jersey hadn't taken her place. She was waiting by the camera, watching Ivy.

Ivy motioned for her to come take her seat, but Miss New Jersey threw her hands up to her hips and stamped her foot.

Ivy rolled her eyes and huffed. Then she consulted her clipboard and picked up the microphone. In a flat tone she read, "Ladies and gentlemen, it is my pleasure to introduce the woman New Jersey has voted the most beautiful woman in the state . . . and one day the world . . . an honor that will be determined at the upcoming Miss America Pageant later this year. Ivy quirked an eyebrow and paused. Please welcome, Brandy Sparks, Miss New Jersey."

Techno club music piped in overhead, and Miss New Jersey made her big entrance. She did a runway walk down in front of the kitchen stage then down in front of the audience seating. She stopped, threw out a hip, waved, did a three-hundred-and-sixty-degree pivot, threw out the other hip, waved again, then finally walked to her seat.

Ivy muttered, "I don't know who all that was for, the camera isn't even rolling yet."

I found Aunt Ginny in the audience, and we shook our heads at each other.

Ivy took her place at center stage to address the room. "Can I have everyone's attention please? I want to welcome you all . . . again . . . to our first Annual

Cape May County Restaurant Week Competition. Wow, that's a mouthful."

Everyone laughed politely, and the audience applauded.

"This event is being sponsored by South Jersey Tourism and the Chamber of Commerce. As you can see, the event is being recorded for WSJL Channel Eight during the six o'clock news, and then an hour-long special will air on the same channel at nine PM. Everything the chefs do, the dishes they create, and their scores each day, will be tweeted, instagrammed, snapchatted, and uploaded to Facebook throughout the event by our social media team, aka Roger."

Ivy's skinny, yellow headset-wearing PA stood and gave the audience and chefs a salute.

Most of the seniors had no idea what she had just said, so they gave a polite wave back.

"Every kitchen has a pot of boiling water, the double ovens are preheated to 350 degrees, and the bowls to your countertop ice-cream makers are in the freezer. You've all had time to familiarize yourselves with the dry goods and cold storage in the shared pantry. Each day's competition will be a special three-course meal consisting of an appetizer, an entrée, and a dessert."

A quiet muttering in Italian was heard from Oliva's team.

"Is there a question?" Ivy asked Oliva.

Marco stepped forward and gave a nervous laugh. "No, she just ask is that special because it so small? In Italy, every dinner is minimum five courses."

The audience and the other chefs broke out into laughter.

Ivy continued with the instructions to the chefs. "Each chef will be given a mystery basket with three ingredients that must be incorporated into their dishes. You have one head chef, one sous chef, and one pastry chef per restaurant team. Each chef on your team has to prepare one of the three meals using their mystery basket."

What? What was that?

Gigi gasped, and her hand flew up to her mouth. Tim ran his hands through his hair and shifted his weight.

Ivy turned to the audience. "And each head chef has agreed to offer their three competition dishes in their restaurants each night of the event, win or lose."

The audience whispered excitedly amongst themselves about that little twist.

"And now for the big announcement." Ivy smiled and waited for a dramatic pause. "In addition to the publicity and bragging rights, *South Jersey Dining Guide* has offered an award of ten thousand dollars to the chef with the highest score at the end of the competition."

A collective whoop went up from the kitchens, and the testosterone level in the arena doubled. Even Tim had a crazed look in his eyes, like he was mentally spending the prize money.

"Now here are your hosts, *Wake Up! South Jersey*'s very own Ashlee and Tess, who will introduce our panel of celebrity judges."

Ashlee and Tess came out to work the crowd and get the judges involved while Ivy went from kitchen to kitchen to answer any questions. When she got to us, Gigi lunged at her.

"Did I understand that each member of the team has to create their own dish?"

"Yes, that's right. The judges thought it would cut

down on production time if all three dishes were prepared at once, so they aren't sitting here all day, plus it will better showcase the talents of each restaurant and how well you work as a team. Bess Jodice says a chef is only as good as the rest of their line."

We're screwed.

"We didn't realize that." Gigi pointed a finger at me. "She's not a real chef. She's just his ex-girlfriend."

Ivy looked from me to Tim and back to Gigi, who was manic at this point.

"We need time to get a real chef from one of our restaurants." Gigi turned to Tim. "I could call Alice and see if she can get a babysitter."

Ivy consulted the clipboard in her hands. "The team captain for Maxine's Bistro is . . . Tim Maxwell."

Tim gave a tight-lipped nod. "That's me."

"There's no time for you to make a substitution now. If you're worried about your standings, all you can do is drop out and apply again next year."

Tim's lips tightened. He looked from Gigi to me.

I was so humiliated, I was trying to disappear into the set, but I had on this stupid apron the color of flashing tow truck lights.

"No, we're staying in. I think Poppy can do it. She may not have formal training, but my girl's got some skills."

Ivy grabbed my hand. "Good. I think she can do it too. Plus, we have nowhere else for the talent to stay if you drop out. Oh my gosh! Ashlee and Tess!"

Ivy ran to the front of the arena to rein in Ashlee and Tess who were trying to teach the audience that consisted of mostly culinary school students and senior citizens, their morning show theme song.

Gigi started to hyperventilate, and I wasn't far behind. Tim gathered us into a tight huddle.

"Everybody just breathe. This isn't a big deal.

Poppy knows how to bake. She's been making fantastic desserts since we were young. We can make this work."

I nodded confidently, but I was totally faking it.

In a small voice, Gigi said, "I never looked in the pantry."

Tim cocked his head to face Gigi. "You didn't?"

She sniffled. "I thought I was going to be next to you the whole time, and Poppy would bring us everything. I never even looked in the pantry."

I was feeling slightly more confident. "Stick with me when we go back there. I have it practically memorized."

Tim smiled. "Okay now, see. We can do this." We put our hands in the middle and very discreetly cheered, "Maxine's."

Ivy was addressing the stage again. "Before we begin, as a clue for today's theme, we'd like to offer our distinguished panel of judges some mimosas."

Miss New Jersey and Stormin' Norman whooped and gave each other a high five. Horatio twisted his mustache and gave a dignified nod. Bess declined the mimosa and gave the same speech about her tea and honey that she'd given at the bed and breakfast. Roger ran off presumably to Google how to make tea.

Miss New Jersey held up her hand. "Cand I getb someb of dat tea too. I'mb all stuffed up from that dab cat."

Ivy punched on her headset. "Bring two cups, Roger."

Once everyone was settled, the tea was poured, the audience was silenced, and the chefs took their places. The cameras began rolling and Ashlee and Tess introduced the competition and opened it with the mystery baskets.

I stood next to Gigi who was next to Tim, and we

each had a mystery basket in front of us. My heart was pounding through my chest. *I'm not ready for this. Whose dumb idea was it to be a chef? I'd rather face a firing squad. It would be more relaxing. I wish I was back home watching* Chopped *on the Cooking Channel. I need to apologize to every chef I ever criticized. If I screw this up, any potential relationship with Tim is going to erupt into a fiery bag of poo on someone's porch. Hopefully Gigi's.*

"Today's theme is Brunch at the Jersey Shore. You have one hour. Chefs, open your baskets."

Chapter Eight

I threw my basket open. Brunch dessert. Brunch dessert. My basket contained sweet corn, blueberries, and a box of Fralinger's salt water taffy. My heart sank. "What the?"

Ashlee squealed to Tess, "Oh my God, this is so exciting!"

Tess squealed back, "I know, right? The appetizer baskets have pork roll, tomatoes, and soft pretzels."

Ashlee leaned into the microphone. "And the entrée baskets contain rib eye chip steaks, asparagus . . . eww, gross. I don't have to eat the asparagus, do I?"

"That's not in my contract," Tess quipped.

"And Italian water ice. What the heck are they going to do with that, Tess?"

"I don't know, Ashlee, but they'd better work some magic. They only have one hour!"

I stared in horror at my basket while the hosts listed the ingredients for the cameras. I should be able to do this. I've been eating dessert for breakfast most of my adult life. Somewhere, I heard Ashlee or Tess yell, "Go!"

Gigi broke me out of my trance by grabbing my arm and hurtling me toward the pantry.

She hissed in my ear, "I need salt, olive oil, rosemary, oregano, garlic, marjoram, eggs, cream, and vodka!"

I gathered the ingredients for her quickly while muttering where the stations were for staples, herbs, spices, dairy, and booze.

She flew back to our kitchen in an invisible tornado. Other chefs ran in and out in a blur. I still didn't know what I was going to make.

Tim grabbed my arm. "I can't find heavy cream or porcini mushrooms."

I grabbed the items and hurled them to him. He ran out behind Gigi.

I was alone in the pantry, and my lip started to quiver. *I have to get it together, I can cry later. What the heck am I gonna do with salt water taffy? It's just sugar and coloring with some artificial flavor. Wait. It's just sugar! I'll melt it down and make a sauce.* Then I knew what I was going to do. I grabbed dry goods and lard to make a pie crust, along with sugar, eggs, and cream to make sweet corn ice cream. I shoved a Meyer lemon in my apron pocket to balance out the blueberries, and ran back to my station.

The room was buzzing with excitement—the head chefs calling out orders down their line, Ashlee and Tess chatting up the judges about the mystery basket ingredients, and Aunt Ginny yelling to me from the stands, "Make a pie!"

I unwrapped all the pale orange taffy pieces, put them in a saucepan with a little cream, and turned the burner on low to melt them down. That would make a peach-cream flavored sauce for the pie. Then I took a cup of flour, and with a nervous hand, accidentally dropped it into my bowl. The cloud of dust that wafted up to my nose smelled strange. I licked my finger and tasted the flour. Baby powder? I opened the sugar and tasted it. Salt. I opened the vanilla and sniffed. Soy sauce. *What is going on?*

My hands started to shake, whether from fear or anger, I didn't know which. *What is this? Is this a test? Is this some twist on the competition to see who notices their ingredients are wrong? Or did some idiot mismark everything?*

I grabbed Tim and Gigi. "The ingredients are wrong!"

Tim was well on his way to making some kind of frittata. "What!"

Gigi had goo all over her hands. "What are you talking about?!"

"Everything is marked wrong. Let me see what you have."

Gigi was putting mint and tea leaves into her pork roll meatballs. Tim was trying to make a syrup out of Meyer lemon water ice and salt.

Tim's face flamed red. "Adrian! I bet he's behind this somehow." He dumped the pot of liquid down the sink and we all started over.

I sniffed a bunch of dry herbs in the pantry till I found one mismarked tarragon that smelled of oregano and gave it to Gigi. I found a jar of honey for Tim to use in his syrup. Then I put together substitutions to make a galette crust. There was definitely no time to make a pie. I had lost fifteen minutes with the ingredient search, now I had to make mini galettes because a big one would never bake in time. I whisked my peach taffy sauce, threw together my corn, milk, and cream mixture. I added some honey because we didn't have sugar, and I had to use some sour cream because I didn't have time to cook a custard with eggs. I prayed the judges wouldn't notice there was no vanilla in the ice cream; I just couldn't find any. I whipped the mixture up and threw it in the ice cream maker. I also threw a sheet pan in the freezer. Thirty minutes left on the clock.

Gigi was making some kind of tomato vodka sauce, and Tim was putting a frittata into one of the ovens. Aromas of deep fried dough, bacon, and artificial banana taffy were filling the room as the smells from various dishes melded. I tossed together my pie crust using what I hoped was whole wheat bread flour, lard, and the salt which had been marked sugar. My dough really should have had time to rest, but I was already way behind. I rolled it out to the thickness I wanted, and grabbed the sheet pan from the freezer. I placed the frozen sheet pan on the rolled-out dough to chill it, fast. I could hear Ashlee talking to the judges.

"What is Maxine's pastry chef doing with that sheet pan, Bess?"

"She is using it improperly. There is a right way to do a thing and that is not it."

Horatio leaned in to the microphone. "It looks like she's trying to chill her dough. It will never be flaky if it's too warm. I'd say that was a smart move."

I dumped my blueberries in a large mixing bowl and added some honey, then I grated my Meyer lemon and zested it into the bowl. I gave it a quick taste. It needed a little something. I ran to the pantry and found whole nutmegs in a jar marked juniper berries. *Those two things don't even look alike.* I added a fresh grating to the berries. I considered dressing up the berry mixture with a fussy liquor, but the theme was South Jersey Brunch, and, who am I kidding, we aren't that fancy here.

Roger came by and asked each of us what we were

making and took a couple of pictures to upload for social media. "What exactly is a galette?" he asked me.

"A galette is a free-form pie where you dump your filling in the middle of your crust, then fold up the sides and bake it on a cookie sheet. It's supposed to look rustic, and it's a life saver if you're too short on time to make a fancy pie crust." *Or if you're in an insane competition with your ex-boyfriend whom you really want to impress, but you're running out of time, and you don't want to be the only chef with nothing on the plate.*

I brushed a quick egg wash on the mini galettes, popped them in the oven and prayed. Then I checked the clock, turned up the temperature to 375 degrees, and prayed again. I tasted my peach cream sauce and saw that it was done, so I removed it from the heat and poured it into a shallow container to let it spread itself thin. Then I popped it in the blast chiller to thicken up. Tim and Gigi both had plates, and they were decorating them, so I went to get mine. I found four little square dessert plates and grabbed a handful of fresh mint from the oregano box, then checked on my ice cream. I gave it a taste. It could use a little salt to enhance the corn. I couldn't add it now or it would melt, so I waited to sprinkle a tiny dusting on top when it was plated.

I had a couple of minutes before I could take the galettes out of the oven, so I took a survey of the room. Every kitchen was in chaos. The chefs were furious. I saw Chef Adrian hurl a pan of something into the garbage. Vidrine was in tears.

Ashlee was interviewing Chef Louie. "What have you made for the judges today, Chef?"

"Dude, I made steak and potato hash, but . . ." He shook his head no. "Something is *no bueno.*"

Ashlee responded to Tess, "Well it seems Chef

Louie's team is also having problems today, Tess. Are the judges worried?"

Tess started asking the judges questions, but my timer went off just before Ivy called the five-minute warning.

I put my galettes in the blast chiller, so they wouldn't turn my ice cream to corn soup, and I grabbed my sauce from the freezer. I drew peach cream sauce in swirls around the edges of my plates. Then I plated up four beautiful rounds of sweet corn ice cream and stuck a mint leaf in each one, followed by a light sprinkle of salt. I got my pies from the blast chiller, and placed one warm flaky galette by each mound of ice cream.

Tess called, "Time's up!" We all stood back from our stations. Tim and Gigi came to see what I had made. Tim smiled at my plates, but Gigi shook her head. "That's it? Pie and ice cream? We'll never win with desserts like that."

"Geeg, cut her a break. She saved our butts with the heads-up about the pantry items. You almost made mint meatballs."

Gigi huffed and stomped away.

Tim wiped a bit of flour off my nose. "Nice catch today, Mack."

"What do you think this was all about anyway?" I whispered. "You think it was part of the challenge?"

Tim looked at Adrian's kitchen. Adrian was complaining about something to Ivy, and he was pointing at us. "I'm not convinced of that. But, if it was deliberate sabotage, it had to be Adrian. He said he had something planned. This had to be it."

"But why would he sabotage everyone? We all have to share the pantry."

Ivy called a timeout. "I need everyone to stay right where you are. No one touch anything." She pulled out her cell phone and walked from the room.

"Oh boy." I looked around the room. "Everyone looks pretty angry. I bet they all put something that was marked wrong in their dishes."

Tim nodded. "Everyone except us."

The realization hit us both at the same time, and we looked at each other with a mounting sense of dread.

I breathed out. "Oh no."

Tim paled. "Everyone except us."

Chapter Nine

Adrian rumbled into our kitchen like a monster truck in a demolition derby. "I can't believe you had the gall to pull this old stunt again."

Tim puffed his chest out and clenched his fists. "You've got a lot of nerve to sabotage the competition, and then accuse me of it."

Adrian peeled out, and stirred up the whole arena. "Who else in here was a victim of Tim Maxwell's sabotage today?"

A tearful Vidrine raised her hand.

The senior citizens in the audience turned into a roomful of Romans at the Colosseum. "Get him! Take the skinny chef downtown!"

Hot Sauce Louie threw a dishtowel to the ground and rolled his sleeves up.

Marco explained to Momma what was going on. Then he had to wrap both arms around her waist to restrain her from flying across the kitchen and going full MMA all over Tim. Even in Italian, we could understand that the string of profanity coming out of Oliva's mouth was strong enough to cook ceviche.

Gigi ducked behind Tim. "Whoa, that little old lady is terrifying."

Tell me about it.

Ivy returned and ordered the audience to calm down, and Adrian to go back to his kitchen. "I've just gotten off the phone with my boss. They aren't pulling the segment. They think the sabotage angle will make great ratings, so there are no do-overs. You don't have to put the same wrong ingredients in your dishes at your restaurants tonight, but they want the mistakes on camera. Roger, make sure you tweet that the ingredients were sabotaged. We're moving forward, and the judges will give fair and honest feedback. Don't pull any punches because someone screwed with the ingredient labels."

That started a cacophony of complaint from the chefs, but Ivy wouldn't hear it. "Tell it to the panel when you present your dishes."

One by one, each head chef addressed the judges with their three dishes. We went in order of kitchens starting from the judging table around the room. *I wonder if Philippe knew he'd be first when he requested that kitchen.*

Chef Philippe presented his dishes to the judges, and to everyone's surprise, he hadn't used any of the wrong ingredients. Bess gave him high praise. She loved the idea of putting rib eye in a quiche Lorraine in place of ham. "I really appreciate that you gave me such an inventive twist." She held up a score card and gave Chef Philippe a ten.

Horatio Duplessis was less enthusiastic. "Congratulations on avoiding all the sabotaged ingredients."

"Thank you, monsieur. I realized zee ingredients

were wrong right from zee start, and we were able to correct in time."

Horatio narrowed his eyes and nodded, thoughtfully. "Hmm. Very lucky for you, wouldn't you say?"

The tips of Chef Philippe's ears blossomed pink. "Yes, very lucky."

Bess's scores tanked for Hot Sauce Louie and Vidrine. "How could you possibly have so many years working as chefs, and still move in blind ignorance? You discredit the art of cooking by not being able to tell the difference between flour and talcum powder. Shame on you. It is obvious that neither of you have had a proper education like that of *L'École des Chefs*."

Vidrine burst into tears.

Louie responded to Bess, "Dude, that's so harsh. I noticed something was wrong when I tasted the food, but it was too late to fix anything. We're working against the clock here."

We watched from our kitchen in silence. I was trying to deal with rising queasiness. I knew Adrian and Oliva had both fallen for the sabotage. Philippe was our only buffer, preventing us from looking totally guilty for tampering with the pantry.

"Chef Tim, please take your mark." Ivy took the judges our plates with Roger's help. "Rolling."

Ashlee and Tess introduced Tim to the judges for the camera's sake, and asked him what he had made.

"Judges, today we have made for you, an appetizer of pork-roll-studded meatballs in fresh Jersey tomato sauce, a Philly cheesesteak frittata with peppers and porcini mushrooms, and a blueberry galette with sweet corn ice cream drizzled with a peach salt water taffy sauce."

The judges tasted our food, and Horatio was the first to comment. "The meatballs are delicious, and this frittata is wonderful. It's so creamy. But I don't taste anything out of place. How did you avoid using mismarked ingredients?"

"One of my chefs noticed her flour smelled of baby powder and began tasting everything. She discovered that many of the ingredients were mismarked and informed the rest of my team."

He called me his chef. My heart did a little leap.

Tess interjected from the side of the judges, "Which chef was that, Chef Tim?"

Tim responded, "Chef Poppy, my pastry chef."

One of the cameras swung to face me. Aunt Ginny and the biddies cheered, but I recognized that this was not necessarily a positive direction for the proceedings to take. It might look too convenient that I was able to recognize the problem foods. For all I knew, Tess and Ashlee were about to suggest I be burned at the stake.

Bess Jodice took a sip of her tea. "Why didn't you notify the producer of the error immediately?"

Hmm. *That's a good question.* Why didn't it occur to me to let someone know?

Adrian yelled from across the room. "Because they did it! He screwed with the pantry. It's his MO."

Ivy silenced Adrian. "We'll cut that out in post-production."

Tim addressed the judges. "In the heat of competition, it didn't occur to me that the ingredients were sabotaged. We thought they were simply mismarked, and that the other chefs would notice just like we did. We were busy making our dishes and fighting against the clock. If we had thought our colleagues might be compromised, we would have said something."

Good answer.

Horatio dipped his spoon into my dessert. "I like the sprinkle of *fleur de sel* on the ice cream, and the sauce was a very clever way to use the salt water taffy. However, the crust is not flaky as a galette should be, probably from a lack of proper ingredient availability, which was not the chef's fault. Overall, well done."

That's when a light shone from heaven, and the angels began to sing. A *New York Journal Food Digest* critic just gave my dish a "well done."

"Of course, the bar has been set very low." Bess Jodice put her spoon down and picked up her tea. "The frittata is lacking in imagination. I would have liked to see something more avant-garde, like a deconstructed benedict. The pork roll made the meatballs way too salty, and the galette is very dense and heavy because you used bread flour in the crust. As I write in my column for *Food and Wine Digest,* food should arouse to flights of fancy. As the competition progresses, I'd like to see more flair put into the dessert round than pie and ice cream. However, since most of your competitors have presented dishes that are inedible, I have no choice but to grant you a six."

Someone sounding very much like Aunt Ginny booed from the audience.

Stormin' Norman Sprinkler leaned back in his seat and crossed his arms. "I've seen every episode of *Chopped* on TV."

Oh no.

"So, I know what I'm talking about when I say that ice cream is way overdone. I'd like the pastry chefs to think outside the box a little more."

Gigi snickered next to me.

"I disagree, Norman." Miss New Jersey was making googly eyes at Tim. "I think this chef has shown great creativity. I like how he sprinkled salt on top of the ice cream, and that peach sauce is really good with the blueberry pie."

"You know he didn't make that, his pastry chef did."

Miss New Jersey blinked.

"The redhead."

Miss New Jersey shrugged. "Well, it's still good."

Tim gave her a show-stopping smile.

Gigi grunted like a bull getting ready to charge. Or maybe that was me.

Our team received nines and tens with Bess's six, and Tim returned to the protective cubicle of our kitchen, away from the slings and arrows of the other chefs' eyes.

Momma did not fare as well with the judges.

"Chef Oliva, in addition to the fact that you used salt instead of sugar in your cake, I don't taste any salt water taffy."

Marco translated for Momma, and she answered in Italian. "Judges, Chef Oliva say she told the pastry chef to leave the taffy out."

Bess blinked a couple of times. "You can't do that. You have to use all the ingredients in the basket. Why would you leave that out?"

Marco translated. Oliva answered him, and he rolled his eyes to the side. "She say she leave out the taffy because it stupid. It no belong in polenta cake."

Bess shrugged and held up a scorecard with a zero on it. Horatio was a little kinder and gave the older chef a three. Norman gave her a zero, and Miss New Jersey followed with a four.

Chef Oliva narrowed her eyes and began a hot rebuttal in Italian. Marco thanked the judges and dragged her back to her kitchen.

Adrian, the final chef to be critiqued, showed us all why it's a bad idea to argue with the judges. Not only do you look like a weenie trying to make excuses and justify why you baked a baby powder cake, but every judge gave him a zero for being a tool.

Horatio Duplessis refused to try Adrian's entrée or dessert. "I can smell the soy sauce in your mousse from here. The fact that you were not able to distinguish soy sauce from vanilla only shows that you wasted thousands of dollars on a fancy culinary school education that did you absolutely no good. If I were the dean of the CIA, I'd sue you for slander just for using our name."

"You listen here you group of wannabe chefs." Even the dragons' nostrils on Adrian's biceps were flaring. "Tim Maxwell has sabotaged this competition, just like he sabotaged that exam twenty years ago! He's a fraud."

Tim flew into a rage and tackled Adrian in front of the judges' table.

Bess grabbed her teacup and moved away from the fight, while Norman and Miss New Jersey leaned over the table to get a better view of the brawl. Ashlee and Tess stepped over the fight and grabbed spoons to try Adrian's bread pudding before it crashed to the floor.

Ivy walked nonchalantly in front of the camera. "Cut! Did you get the tackle? That's a wrap! Take it to post!" She walked over to Tim and Adrian. "Okay, break it up guys. Great energy for the camera. Everyone be back here same time tomorrow morning. Oh, and as of right now, the pantry is off-limits between filming, and anyone caught in there will be disqualified, 'kay?"

The culinary school students came down from the stands to clean the kitchens and talk to the chefs.

Tim and Adrian each attempted a final punch before getting to their feet. With a few parting slurs, they retreated to opposite corners of the arena.

Tim threw a towel across the room, and it landed

in the sink. "I'm leaving. If you're coming with me, let's go."

Gigi grabbed her purse and followed him out the door.

Sawyer and Aunt Ginny came to congratulate me, followed by the biddies and the Sheinbergs.

"I'm so proud of you."

"That was smart thinking with the taffies, Poppy honey."

"Bubula, you did great!"

"Why you wearing that ugly apron? You need me to find you a better one?"

Adrian laid eyes on Sawyer from his end of the kitchen, and had an immediate attitude adjustment. "Well, hello beautiful. Where have they been keeping you?"

Sawyer giggled.

Oh my God. Snap out of it!

It was all too overwhelming. While the seniors chatted with the crew, and Adrian chatted up Sawyer, I slipped out to the locker room. I had to take a couple deep breaths to calm my nerves. Tears sprung to my eyes. I was kicking myself for not telling Ivy about the ingredients right from the start. How could I be so stupid to think it was part of the challenge? Now, thanks to Adrian dragging Tim's name through the mud, everyone thinks we cheated.

The door opened, and Vidrine entered the locker room. She was a lot less Southern charm and a lot more Jersey girl than earlier that morning. "Honey, the next time you know the sugar bin is full of salt, how about letting a girl know about it, okay?"

"Vidrine, I'm sorry. I should have said something right from the start. I didn't think—"

She cut me off. "No, you didn't think. And if I get

sabotaged again, no matter who is behind it, you better believe I'm gone come up swinging, *chérie.*"

She spun around on her pink Birkenstocks and headed out the door.

I tore off the hideous yellow apron and threw it on the floor. I stomped on it a couple times, but that only made me feel marginally better. I cried a few more tears before washing my face. I pulled my cell phone out of my purse and opened the gallery to the pantry pictures I took Thursday night. I scrolled through until I saw the container of juniper berries. I zoomed in. Tiny little blue-black pebbles, definitely not big brown nutmegs. Whoever tossed the pantry did it after the meet and greet and before this morning. That could literally have been anyone, but only one person was threatening that they had something planned for us, something in way of revenge. Maybe that plan was to frame Tim for sabotage, accuse him on camera, and destroy his reputation with all his loyal customers. If it was, I'd say Adrian Baxter had accomplished his mission.

Chapter Ten

"Poppy, do you have any Alka-Seltzer? The food today was jus debloraple. No offense."

"I don't think we have that, Ms. Jodice, but I can make you some peppermint tea if that will help." *Or maybe some strong coffee to sober you up.*

"Tea'll do jus' fine. Don't sweeden it! I have my own."

"Yes ma'am." I left Bess in the library and returned to the kitchen where I'd been trying to hide since I'd slunk home from the competition.

Aunt Ginny sat at the banquette drinking a cup of coffee. "Queen Bess again?"

I put the kettle on to boil. "Yep. And she's brought a bell with her to signal when she wants me for something."

Aunt Ginny shook her head. "You know who I bet she would get along with?"

I gave Aunt Ginny a sly look. "Georgina."

"You read my mind. Just how many mimosas did she have at that catastrophe?"

"I didn't see her have any. Just that pot of tea Roger had to keep refilling."

"Maybe she slipped Roger a twenty to make the tea out of bourbon."

A stout matron of a woman entered the kitchen wearing a serviceable gray dress with a starched white apron and white cross-trainers. She was carrying a basket of clean laundry under one arm and a submissive Figaro under the other. "I found this curled up on the bed in the Scarlet Peacock. I've given him a stern talking to."

I took Figaro from Mrs. Galbraith. "That's Miss New Jersey's room. I don't know how he keeps getting in there." I put Figaro down and he slinked away.

"I am finished with four of the rooms. I haven't been able to get into the Swallowtail Suite these past two days. The DO NOT DISTURB sign has been up."

"Thank you so much Mrs. Galbraith. I really appreciate you coming in this week on such short notice."

Mrs. Galbraith thrust the basket of clean linens into my arms. "I am unaccustomed to not being trusted by the guests. But since yours is a new establishment, I will overlook the slight until you can build a name for yourself as having a safe and ethical establishment. I hope you understand that I expect to be paid for all five rooms, even though I can only clean four."

"Yes, Mrs. Galbraith. Of course."

Aunt Ginny stuck her tongue out behind the chambermaid's back.

Mrs. Galbraith checked the tiny clock that was pinned to her starched white collar. "I'm off for the day. I'll return at eleven tomorrow. Keep that cat downstairs. I found him curled up on the bed in the Scarlet Peacock again, and he's shedding on my clean steps."

"Yes ma'am. I will do my best."

Mrs. Galbraith left the room and Aunt Ginny muttered, "Battle-axe."

I put two peppermint teabags in a warmed china teapot. I tossed Aunt Ginny a look of mild chastisement for her to ignore. "Stop calling Mrs. Galbraith a battle-axe. We have to be nice to her. You know I can't get a replacement this time of year."

Aunt Ginny snickered.

I poured hot water into the teapot for the peppermint to steep. "How does Figaro keep getting into Brandy's room?"

Aunt Ginny looked around. "Speaking of . . . where is the little devil now?"

"Oh great. I'll have to go look for the furry menace after I deal with the tipsy menace." I put the teapot and tea cup on a silver tray and took it to the library where Bess had been joined by Horatio.

"Did you see the look on Chef Adrian's face when I gave him a zero?" Horatio leaned back in his chair and laughed. "Smug son of a . . . oh hello, Poppy. You did very well today."

I put the tray on an antique coffee table for Bess. "Thank you, Mr. Duplessis."

I stopped dead in my tracks when I caught Bess gluing scraps of tissue paper onto a tall vase. I tried not to freak out, but that vase cost more than I was getting for her stay here. "What are you doing?"

"It's called decoupage. I'm trying to sprrruce the room up for you. Conshider it a gift."

"That's Lalique crystal, from France."

"Yesh, so ugly on their own. Now it will be a Besss Jodiccce original."

What would happen if I grabbed that vase and ran

from the room? Would that jeopardize her judging our team in the competition?

From the stairway, I heard Miss New Jersey sneeze. A moment later, she came into the library with a squirming pillowcase, which she handed to me. "Dis is yourbs. It wath in my closet."

The pillowcase said, "Merrroooowwww."

"I am so sorry. I'll go lock him in the back."

I cradled the naughty bundle in my arms and spoke to it. "Why are you so bad? The one person in the house who is allergic, and you've got to be all up in her business." I walked into the kitchen with Figaro in the pillowcase. Aunt Ginny took one look at us and laughed.

"This is going in your room for a while." I let Fig out in Aunt Ginny's large bedroom off the back of the kitchen. He turned and gave me a look that said, "I don't care. I've been trying to get out of that closet all day." Then he sashayed up to Aunt Ginny's king-sized bed, jumped up to her pillow and turned in circles twice, then lay down. Before I closed the door, I saw him open one eye, look at me, and quickly close it again.

I collapsed with Aunt Ginny at the table. My feet were killing me, and my back was on fire. "I think we're going to have to advertise that we have a cat in the B&B, to warn people with allergies." I took a sip of my tepid coffee. "Where was I before I was summoned by her majesty? Oh, the pantry. So now everyone is furious with us, as if we had something to do with the pantry fiasco. Why aren't they mad at Chef Philippe?"

"The fella covered in tattoos threw all the suspicion on Tim when he pitched that fit. He was a little over the top if you ask me. People put on a big show like that to cover up when they're involved in something."

"Even if Tim did cheat twenty years ago, not that I'm saying he did, but he wouldn't be foolish enough to do the same thing today, against the same competitor."

"He would have to be an idiot."

"Exactly."

"Do you think Tattoo Chef did it himself?"

"Yes. And . . . no. I don't know. He's a bully, and he's full of himself, but he also seems too prideful to make bad food on TV for revenge."

A tinkling sound of annoyance floated into the kitchen on the air of superiority and announced that servitude was required. Aunt Ginny leaned back in her seat and picked up her coffee. "I'm on a break."

I heaved myself out of the kitchen and into the library where Bess and Horatio were now joined by Miss New Jersey and Stormin' Norman. I walked in just as Horatio was saying, "I think the producers are behind it, trying to create a scandal to boost ratings."

Bess started wiggling to the edge of her chair. "Well, any chef worth his salt would have noticed from a mile away." She tried to stand and stumbled. "I think they all need to go back to ssschool for shome decent training."

I put out my hand to catch her. "Would you like some coffee?"

She ignored me. "And I'll tell you shomething. I've had my share of bad chhhefs, whoo! Poppy, what brand of tea ish this? It doesn't taste like Harney & Shons. Any good bed and breakfast that is not capable of blending their own tea like I am would know to sherve Harney & Shons."

"I don't believe it is, but I will make a note to consider replacing it."

"Good. Shee that you do. And while you're at it, your shilver tea tray could use a good polish." She threw her arm up over her head and fell back into the wingback chair.

Horatio rested both of his hands out in front of him on his walking stick and shook his head. "Poppy, you were the chef on your team who realized someone had undermined the pantry, weren't you? I know you agree with me that a chef should taste their dish several times as they create it."

"Absolutely." *I've been known to eat half a pan of brownies before getting them into the oven.* "But, I'm not a real chef. I'm only helping Chef Tim for the event."

"Don't sell yourself short, dear, you're a chef down in your bones where it counts. You have a gift. Don't let anyone rob you of your dreams by being overly critical. You wouldn't believe how many times I've seen a student give up because a teacher told them they couldn't do something."

"Thank you, Mr. Duplessis. That's very kind of you to say. Was there anything else you all needed?"

Stormin' Norman barely looked up from his iPhone. "Can you make a good recommendation for dinner tonight? I'm starving after that failure today. If it were up to me, all the chefs would have been chopped."

Miss New Jersey was also on her iPhone. "Oh gawd. Stop with the *Chopped* already, fanboy. Poppy, where is that dreamy chef's restaurant located? Maxine's?"

Here Figaro. Here kitty, kitty, kitty. "Uh . . ."

Horatio sat forward on the couch "No, that won't

do. It would be unethical to eat in a contestant's restaurant."

Miss New Jersey drew her bottom lip out. "We eat here every morning."

Bess gave a slight nod of her head. "Yesh, but Poppy isn't a restaurant chef. She's an innk . . . an innk . . . a bed and breakfasht owner. And it takes no special training to do that."

Horatio scowled at Bess. "I don't know. I've known many a lousy chef who thinks they know more than they do because of the address on a diploma. It takes more than exams to make a proper chef. A good teacher can recognize the spark of excellence in their student, and cultivate it. Sometimes the best chefs come from the most humble of beginnings."

I looked around the wood-paneled library with its floor-to-ceiling bookshelves filled with Aunt Ginny's collection of first editions and leather-bound classics. The fire burning in the stone fireplace cast a warm glow on the blue and cream Oriental rug. I thought it was rather elegant in here.

"Give me a greasy spoon any day. As a highly regarded food critic, there's always a bunch of foolishness whenever I'm noticed. I usually have to wear a disguise when I go to a fancy dining establishment. As soon as the front staff recognizes me, it's all over. Chefs parade out their best dishes, service is impeccable, the plating is pure artistry. One look at what the other diners are getting, and it's easy to realize the staff is putting on the Ritz just for me."

Miss New Jersey blew her nose. "You poor dear, that sounds like hell."

Was that . . . was that a joke?

Horatio straightened his bow tie. "It makes it impossible to leave an unbiased review, and I believe professional chefs should be held to scrupulous standards. In any event, I'm ready to retire. I've had enough jetting around, eating rich food, enduring ridiculous dishes with molecular gastronomy like salmon foam and balsamic pearls." Horatio gave a little shudder. "I'm ready to get in my own kitchen and make my own meals. I long to get back to the basic simplicity of well-made gourmet."

The front door flew open and a tumbleweed of bad attitude rolled into the house in the form of Ashlee Pickel and Tess Rodriguez. They were elbow deep in at least one argument. Possibly two. Ashlee was hollering about being upstaged, and Tess was spouting off complaints in Spanish. Neither seemed to need the other to understand them, so long as the volume was loud.

Horatio waited calmly for an opening then asked, "Would you ladies care to calm yourselves down long enough to join us for dinner?"

"I'm not eating anywhere with her!"

Tess jabbed two fingers toward her eyes. "*Prefiero empujar mis ojos con tenedores*! Norman! You're having dinner with me! *Vamonos*!"

Norman sprung off the couch like Tess held an invisible ejector button. "Where do you want to go?"

"Just shut up and follow me."

Horatio turned to Ashlee. "Just the four of us then?"

Bess struggled to her feet again. "I've had enough bad fooo for one day. I have a migraine commingonumuan. I'll jush go to buh."

She was running her words together so badly that I only understood about half of them. I helped her over to the stairs while suggesting a popular burger place on the mall to the others. "It's walking distance, and I doubt the staff would recognize you."

I led Bess up to her room, and went to let her in. She blocked me from reaching the handle and asked me to send up some saltines to help settle her stomach. When I returned, her lights were off, and I could hear her snoring through the door.

I did not envy the hangover she would have in the morning.

Chapter Eleven

"Aren't the others coming down to breakfast this morning?" I put the Southwestern egg casserole on the buffet, and took the bowl of fresh salsa from Aunt Ginny. I picked up the coffee, and, judging by the weight of the carafe, found it to be nearly empty.

Ashlee passed up the eggs and helped herself to a broiled grapefruit half. "I haven't seen Tess all night, that tramp. She didn't sleep in the room, so God only knows where she is. She could have been taken and sold into human trafficking. Hey, can I get the Wi-Fi code again? I have to post to my Instagram. I'm up to eight hundred followers, and I don't want Tess to get ahead of me."

Your level of concern is staggering.

Horatio brought his plate over to the buffet for some of the spicy casserole with chorizo sausage. "I don't think it's a coincidence that our weatherman hasn't come down for breakfast either."

Aunt Ginny brought in a basket of fresh biscuits and butter. Horatio had one in hand before the basket touched the linen tablecloth.

Miss New Jersey had her head lying on her forearm on the table. A cup of coffee cooled at her side.

"Are you okay, Brandy? Do you need anything?"

Miss New Jersey looked up through bloodshot eyes and a nose Rudolph would be proud of. "I just took someb allergy medicine. Imb okay." She blew her nose into a tissue and dropped it on my floor.

On my way back to the kitchen I passed Figaro slinking his way around the buffet toward his victim. "Nope." I reached down and scooped him up with one hand. I deposited him in the kitchen where he glared at me reproachfully.

"What is your problem with her, Fig? Have mercy, the woman can hardly breathe."

Figaro showed his remorse by swatting an empty pineapple juice jug across the floor.

Aunt Ginny refilled the carafe of coffee and handed it back to me. "Do you think Bess is okay? No one has seen her since before dinner last night."

"I think she's just sleeping it off. Better have some aspirin on hand for when she gets up."

I took the coffee and another pitcher of cream into the dining room and refilled Horatio and Ashlee's cups. Miss New Jersey was more interested in peppering me with ridiculous questions about things that were none of her business.

"How long have you worked for that sexy blond chef on your team?"

I played it very cool. *Don't you even mention Tim's name, you baboon!* Okay, I didn't say that out loud. What I said was, "Oh, Tim. Um . . . I guess I've known him for about thirty years or so."

Her eyes lit up. "Oh, so he's like a brother to you?"

"Ah, no. I wouldn't say a brother, exactly."

"But you probably know a lot about him, right?"

I put the heavy carafe down, so I wouldn't be tempted to whack the beauty queen upside the head with it. "I think so, yes. Why?"

Her green eyes sparkled, and she laid her chin on her fist. "He is so gorgeous. I would love to go out with him. Tell me everything you know."

I knew it wouldn't be fair to Tim to ruin his chances of happiness with a beautiful woman. He and I weren't married or anything, and I still didn't know where my heart was between him and Gia. So, I knew I had to do the adult thing here and be honest with Brandy. If it was meant to be between me and Tim, it would happen.

"He's gay."

I turned on my heel and fast marched out of the room. Okay, that was a fail. As I swung through the kitchen door, Figaro tried to sneak out. I grabbed him just in time, looked him in the bright orange eyes, then gingerly put him back down and opened the door a crack to let him at her. I would buy her a pack of Benadryl later, on the house.

I was dreading the competition today. I had to give myself a little pep talk in the ladies' room to work up the courage to enter the room. The kitchens were silent. The air was thick with suspicion. All around the arena, chefs were scowling at us, full of anger and malice. I caught Adrian glaring at Tim while sharpening his knives, and instinctively wrapped my arms around myself.

There were a lot fewer empty seats, and a lot more white hair in the stands today. Mother Gibson had brought her church group, and they were all wearing matching T-shirts that said TEAM POPPY. Tim chuckled when he saw them, but it did not go over well with Gigi, who humphed and said, "It's Team Maxine's. There is no Team Poppy."

Tim looked at me and whispered, "I'm Team Poppy."

Sawyer was holding a sign that said GO ADRIAN! I pointed at her sign and made a swirly motion with my finger. She looked at the sign, lurched in her chair, and quickly spun it around where the other side said GO TIM!

Tim shook his head. "Subtle."

Aunt Ginny had made herself the authority on all things competition related. She marched back and forth in front of the rows of seniors like the fish feeder at a SeaWorld orca show. "And that one down there with the tattoos, he used to go to cooking school with Tim. He's got his knickers in a knot saying Tim cheated at another competition years ago."

Tim sighed.

"But I think the one to keep your eye on is that fussy old Frenchie by the judges."

Chef Philippe frowned and turned his back to the audience.

"He said he noticed the ingredients were all wrong, but did he tell anyone?"

The crowd of seniors shook their heads. "No, uh-uh."

"Exactly, and no one is threating to tan his hide like they are Poppy's. No one really knows what happened in that pantry yesterday."

Mrs. Dodson gave a dignified nod. "You mark my words, they'll all be tasting every single ingredient today. Oh yes."

Tim leaned down to speak in my ear. "They do know they aren't helping our cause with this, don't they?"

I shrugged. "They march to the beat of their own drum . . . one played by a drunk, deaf monkey."

The judges finally arrived: Horatio looking dapper in a three-piece plum suit with canary-yellow bow tie; Bess, obscured by a giant pair of dark sunglasses and aided by Horatio's walking stick: Norman in a cashmere sweater the color of a gathering storm. He winked at Tess, and she rolled her eyes in return. The judges took their places as before. The makeup girl came over to give Miss New Jersey a touch-up, then settled on a full overhaul to cover the effects of Figaro.

"Okay everyone!" Ivy entered the arena with Roger in tow. "Let's get started. Take your places, please. Audience, quiet on the set. Now before we begin, after yesterday's fiasco with the ingredients, the culinary school students have painstakingly gone through the pantry and replaced and relabeled everything. I posted a guard in the pantry overnight, and there were no incidents."

Roger yawned and gave a thumbs-up.

"The good news is, we created a lot of buzz on Facebook and Twitter. Last night's show had the highest ratings of anything we've ever broadcast. We even got a mention on the network news at eleven. I'm just thrilled! Well done. Break a leg today, everyone! Ashlee and Tess, you want to take your places and introduce today's baskets?"

Ashlee growled at Tess and they grappled over the roving microphone until Ashlee wrenched it free with a few expletives.

Tess rubbed her teeth with her finger to clear any smeared lipstick, flashed the camera a sweet smile, and welcomed the viewers to night two of the Cape May County Restaurant Week Competition. "Before we get cooking, Ashlee, should we offer the judges a little something from the wine cellar?"

"I know I always want a glass of red with my dinner,

Tess." Ashlee also flashed a brilliant smile for the camera.

"I know you do, girl." The girls both giggled for the camera.

"And as a little clue to tonight's main course, we have a lovely rosé from the *Côtes de Provence*."

"Oh, I love it when you speak French, Ash."

"*Merci beaucoup, mon ami*," Ashlee read from the teleprompter.

Ashlee poured the glasses of wine, but Bess waved her off. "No. Not for me. I'll shtick with my tea."

Ashlee turned questioning eyes to Ivy, unsure of what to do.

"Cut!" Ivy strode over to the judges' table. "Bess, we're kinda doing a thing here every night with the drinks. Are you sure I can't have Ashlee get you a glass of rosé? For the camera?"

"I never touch the shtuff."

Aunt Ginny could be heard in the stands. "And roosters lay chocolate eggs."

"I jus' want my tea. Every leaf is hand rolled from the finest quality jasmine I grow in my greenhouse tea garden."

Ivy cocked her head to the side as if considering her response. Then she snapped her fingers, and Roger flew out of the room to, once again, make a pot of tea while Ashlee handed out the remaining glasses of wine.

Norman reached for her before she could walk away. "Leave the bottle, baby."

"Fine." She tromped back to the staging area. "It's not like we don't have more." She poured herself a large glass and knocked it back.

Roger returned with the steaming china pot, and everyone took their places. Ivy and Roger wheeled out the mystery baskets and placed them before each chef.

I was getting jittery and my breakfast casserole was rescrambling in my stomach. I tried to peek through the wicker weave to see what was waiting inside. I couldn't make out anything definitive, but I could smell flowers. Lavender? There's lavender in my basket. What can I do with that?

Back on camera, Tess and Ashlee introduced the basket ingredients. "Okay chefs, today's theme is Afternoon in Provence."

Miss New Jersey blew her nose. "What does Rhode Island have to do with pink wine?"

Norman turned to her. "Provence, not Providence, you dumb bimbo." Then he took a quick selfie with his glass of rosé.

"Open your baskets."

Inside the brown wicker hamper was a bunch of fresh lavender, along with crème fraîche and several bags of Pop Rocks. *Since when are Pop Rocks French? I need to make something more sophisticated than yesterday. These other teams have actual pastry chefs who work in sugar art every day. They're gonna make my sad little desserts look like they were made with an Easy Bake Oven.*

"You have one hour. Go!"

We all rushed the pantry together, creating a bottleneck. Hot Sauce Louie shoved Adrian. Chef Oliva barreled into the fray like a human cannonball. I worked my way into the room where chefs had lids off and jars open to make sure the flour was flour and sugar was sugar. Chef Philippe gave me a hostile look from head to toe, then shoved his nose into a jar of marmalade and inhaled.

Gigi bounced in front of me while I was getting powdered sugar and flour. "I love working with frogs' legs! I need butter, vinegar, and ginger to make a sauce from the Speculoos Cookie Butter, no substitutions."

"I thought I showed you where everything was yesterday."

"Yeah, I wasn't listening."

I grabbed her ingredients and got myself some butter and eggs while I was at it.

Vidrine gave me a hip check into the side of the freezer on her way out, and I crushed one of my eggs. The diaphanous goo oozed down the front of my apron. She glanced over her shoulder and called out, "Behind."

I gathered everything I would need to make lemon-lavender crème brûlée with grape-lavender shortbread. At the last minute I grabbed some pistachios for color and crunch and ran back to my station.

I put some ramekins on a sheet pan and placed them in the oven to preheat. Then I whisked together egg yolks, cream, and sugar in a mixing bowl. All around the room, chefs were dipping fingers in the spices and eating pinches of salt and spoonsful of oil and nodding. I would have laughed if my head weren't already on the executioner's block with most of them. It looked like whatever prank, error, or sabotage that had happened yesterday wasn't being repeated today. Everyone seemed to have what they expected to have. I zested and juiced a couple of Meyer lemons and added them to my filling along with a half a teaspoon of lavender extract.

Tim edged over to my workspace. "Hey, baby, can I buy a lemon?"

I snickered and handed him two. "What are you making?"

"It's Meyer lemon-glazed duck season."

"Wabbit season."

"Duck season."

Gigi pushed her way between us. "Will you two stop fooling around. We're on the clock, and that gnocchi isn't going to make itself, Maxwell."

Tim wiggled his eyebrows. "I gotta go."

I grinned back and tasted my lemon-lavender filling. Then I took it to the bottom oven and poured it into the hot ramekins. I checked the time and pulled out the food processor.

Next to us, Vidrine was calling a time-out. Ivy yelled that there were no time-outs.

"But honey, my blender won't blend. It's an emergency!"

Bess hollered over from the judges' table. "For God's sakes, ush shomething elsh."

Vidrine started to cry in frustration, until Louie handed her his blender and peace was restored.

I measured flour, sugar, and butter for my shortbread. I would have to be very careful with the lavender. Lavender sneaks up on you. Too little, and the judges won't know it's in there. Too much, and your dish will taste like hand soap. I thought my cookie dough was well balanced with a nice floral back note.

There was a loud whir, followed by Vidrine screaming. "*Sa ki mal!*"

The kitchen arena came to a momentary standstill when a pink sauce exploded from Vidrine's blender and doused her in a sticky mess. She cried to Ivy and the judges like Tonya Harding to the Olympic Committee. "A blender isn't supposed to spin that fast. Someone must have tampered with it." Her sous chef handed her a dish towel to wipe her face.

Gigi muttered, "Drama queen."

I glanced at the clock and put the lid on my food processor. I pushed the buttons, but nothing happened. I checked to see that it was plugged in, and then swapped outlets. It still wouldn't come on. I jiggled it around, starting to panic, when there was a loud ruckus on the other side of the kitchen.

Adrian threw a sauté pan across the room. I felt my blood run cold. Oh Lord, I hope he doesn't cry sabotage again. I jammed the food processor lid on over and over, but the dang thing wouldn't fire up. In a huff, I grabbed a wooden spoon and mixed my dough by hand.

Chef Louie called out, "Does anyone have a stand mixer my pastry chef can use? Ours only works on high."

At first, no one moved. Then Chef Philippe's pastry chef offered up hers. She said she was making meringues, so they could swap.

Ashlee leaned against the judging table. "What do you think about what's going on in the kitchens today, judges?"

Miss New Jersey said, "I don't think all their stuff works."

Horatio hung his head, then said, "We can all see that, Brandy. Do you have a thought about how they're handling it?"

Tess approached the other end of the judges' table and patted Miss New Jersey's hair. "That's all right *chica*, you're very pretty."

Bess was struggling to keep her head up. "I think it's a real shame and a discredit to the art. Chefs have to know how to work without all the fancy appliances today. Back when I started teaching, we didn't have immersion blenders and food processors in every kitchen. A chef had to learn to cook with his bare hands."

Aunt Ginny was overheard muttering to Mrs. Dodson, "Who was she teaching? Cleopatra?"

The audience laughed, and Aunt Ginny asked Mrs. Sheinberg, "What are they laughing at?"

Mrs. Sheinberg answered, "Just some crazy yenta."

Adrian was royally freaking out now. "How do you expect me to make a sauce when none of my burners will light?"

I patted my dough flat on the worktop and looked over my shoulder at our stove. All the burners were lit, and several pots were frying, sautéing, and boiling. A brilliant flash followed by a loud whoosh came from Oliva's kitchen, and Marco screamed in pain. His arm was on fire.

I abandoned my dough and ran to Marco, as did Adrian and Tim. Adrian pulled his chef coat off and used it to put the fire out. Marco was burned badly on one arm up to his elbow. Hot Sauce Louie ran through our kitchen with a bucket of ice water, accidentally bumping Gigi who dropped her platter of frogs' legs into Tim's Meyer lemon sauce. We plunged Marco's arm deep inside the bucket to stop the burn. Ivy yelled for Roger to call campus paramedics. Oliva had the grease fire under control, but she was angrily trying to tell Ivy something while pointing at the deep fryer.

Ivy looked at the deep fryer and back to Oliva while shaking her head. "I'm sorry, I don't understand."

I picked up *troppo caldo* and *temperatura*. "She's saying something about the temperature of the fryer being too hot."

Louie looked at the gauges on the deep fryer. "There is no way that oil is three hundred and fifty degrees. Look at how it's smoking." He bent down to adjust the dial and it came off in his hands.

Across the room, Chef Philippe calmly worked on his dishes.

An uneasiness began to niggle at the back of my brain. These were too many coincidences. What started out as a minor inconvenience had turned into something more nefarious. And this time someone was badly hurt.

The campus medics arrived and took Marco to the hospital. Ivy shouted that there were only twenty minutes left on the clock, but she would give everyone an extra five and hide it in the video. Vidrine, her braids dripping with pink sauce, threw her arm out toward Chef Philippe. "Does he also get extra time? He didn't even stop to check on Marco!"

Ivy cracked her neck side to side. "Come on! Work with me people. Just finish up! Chef Adrian, use the empty station in Chef Oliva's kitchen to make your sauce. Roger! Put an update about Marco on Snapchat!"

I rushed back to my kitchen where Gigi was in tears that her dish was ruined. She apologized to Tim because his sauce was now all froggy. He put his arm around her and told her it would be okay. And I angrily pounded my shortbread dough and rolled it out between two sheets of parchment. I quickly cut some scalloped circles with a biscuit cutter and put them on the sheet pan. I opened the bottom oven and shook my crème brûlées. They had the slightest jiggle, which meant they were done. So, I took them out and put the shortbread in their place. I tucked the custards into the blast chiller, and whisked together a lavender-grape glaze on the stove top, with cream, powdered sugar, and Pop Rocks.

Ashlee stuck a microphone under Tim's nose. "Chef Tim, Miss New Jersey wants to know what you're making."

Tim sent a wave to Miss New Jersey, and I thought Gigi would drop a lemony frog leg.

"I'm making a Meyer lemon-glazed duck breast with sweet potato gnocchi." He punctuated it with a wink.

Miss New Jersey answered back. "That's so hot."

Adrian called out from his new station in Oliva's kitchen. "Yeah, well I'm making a duck confit salad with candied Meyer lemons over arugula, and it's gonna be the best thing yooze ever tasted, gorgeous."

Miss New Jersey yawned. "Whatever."

I sprinkled my lavender-lemon crème brûlées with some raw sugar and crossed my fingers that the blow torch would work. After a couple of clicks, the blue-white flame fired up. Thank God! I caramelized the tops so they would harden and crack. Crème brûlée top crust is the bubble wrap of the pastry world. There was something very satisfying about breaking that shell.

Tess hollered from the judges' table, "Five minutes!"

Then Aunt Ginny yelled from the audience, "Five minutes, Poppy!"

I pulled my shortbread out of the oven and dipped each one in the grape-lavender glaze, and then I sprinkled chopped pistachio nuts on top. I watched the clock count down until I had thirty seconds left. I wanted to give the shortbread glaze as long as possible to set. Then, I placed two cookies on the plate next to the ramekins and dusted the plates with a few lavender blossoms.

"Time's up! Step away from your counters."

We all backed away from our tables. Gigi leapt into Tim's arms and gave him a hug, which he returned— in force—as I stood to the side and watched in horror.

Aunt Ginny pointed in our direction. "That's going to be a problem." Two rows of white and pink hair shook their heads in mutual displeasure.

Ashlee stepped to the camera and made a grand gesture with her arm. "Chefs, it is time to present your dishes to the judges."

Tess stepped in front of her cohost and struck a seductive pose. "Why don't we go in reverse order today and start with Chef Adrian Baxter."

Ashlee twisted her torso around to get her face next to Tess. "Chef Adrian, what have you made for the judges?"

Ivy yelled cut so she and Roger could set the judges' table with the first round of dishes. Frozen items were stored so they didn't melt before their respective chef's turn at judging.

Horatio righted Bess who was leaning heavily onto him. She sagged over to Stormin' Norman who tried shifting her back. The judges had the chance to stand and stretch, and Ashlee and Tess took the opportunity to have a cat fight.

In the stands, Aunt Ginny was facing the other seniors, and everyone was taking notes. She had Sawyer going seat to seat with what looked like a clipboard. The biddies were all a flurry of discussion, pointing at the chefs.

What are they up to?

Tim unwound Gigi from his side. "I think we did good today. We have three good dishes."

Gigi gave my crème brûlées a side eye.

Tim nudged her. "Don't you think Poppy's desserts look great?"

Gigi shrugged. At least, I think she shrugged. Her chef's coat hung on her like a bell due to her newly enhanced top shelf, so very little movement registered. "They don't look half bad. I just hope they don't taste like perfume. Lavender is very tricky."

I'd had about all I could take of Gigi, the small and

annoying. "Well at least they won't taste like lemon frogs' legs."

Gigi frowned and looked down at her appetizer that had been dabbed with paper towels and served with cookie-butter sauce.

Adrian came from out of nowhere and pounced on Tim. "Did you sabotage my cooktop?"

Tim's eyebrows dipped. "I wouldn't even know how to do that. I'm not an electrician."

"Well somebody cut the gas line on the range in my kitchen and none of my burners work. If I find out it was you, I'll take you down so fast you'll never even see me coming."

The uneasy feeling crept back on me, and something started to click in my head. "You weren't the only one with an equipment malfunction, Adrian."

"What?"

Gigi tossed her blond curls. "Yeah. Weren't you paying attention? Marco's deep fryer practically exploded."

"Vidrine's blender was tampered with, Louie's stand mixer, our food processor."

Tim and Gigi both swiveled my way. "What was wrong with your food processor?"

"The motor's dead. The lights come on, but the wheel won't spin."

Gigi cocked her head to the side. "Is that why you made your dough by hand? I just thought you didn't know how to operate it."

"It's a food processor Gigi, not a spaceship. It has two buttons."

Gigi huffed and turned away.

Adrian poked a finger in Tim's chest. "That just proves my point that you will do anything to win."

Tim turned back to Adrian, anger rising. "I didn't tamper with anything."

"Oh yeah!" Louie and Vidrine had come to join the argument. "Then who did, dude? 'Cause we lost precious time today trying to get our equipment straight. We had a double oven that only got up to two hundred degrees. My pastry chef had to bake her tarts in Vidrine's kitchen."

"And honey, my kitchen is messier'n a possum's nest after that blender nonsense."

I pointed to Oliva's kitchen. "No one was affected more than Marco. What kind of deranged lunatic would cause a grease fire to win a local cooking competition?"

Adrian leaned in. "You're just proving my point, Red."

Philippe had made his way over to join us. "*Mon dieu!* We are all just chefs. Only one person here would have the know-how for mechanics. Hot Sauce Louie, what ever happened to your food truck that you said you had to repair all the time?"

Vidrine sucked in some air and slapped Louie with her dish towel. "Are you behind this!"

Tim and Adrian each took an offensive step toward Louie.

Aunt Ginny yelled from the stands, "What's going on? Poppy! Should I get this on my iPhone for the YouTubes?"

Louie put his hands up. "Not me, dudes. My kitchen was sabotaged too." He turned on Philippe. "I don't remember you complaining about broken appliances today, Philippe."

Adrian rolled his sleeves up. "Yeah. In fact, yooze didn't even come help when Marco was on fire, did ya?"

"Zat's what you think. We tried to make zee duck sausage, but the grinder would not grind. And I worked on my food because I am a highly trained professional."

I glanced over at Marco's blackened station and caught Momma calmly eating a plate of pasta.

I lowered my voice. "Please, everyone. Just stop fighting. We can't turn on each other now. I think that's what they want us to do."

Louie tossed his head. "Like, what who wants us to do, babe?"

I lowered my voice. "The television crew. Haven't you noticed? Even though Ivy yelled cut ten minutes ago, the red light on the camera is still on."

Chapter Twelve

"What are you all doing? Get back to your kitchens!" Ivy returned to the arena. "We're rolling in two minutes. Where is Bess Jodice? Why isn't she at the judges' table?"

"Maybe she's out . . . you know." Norman put his thumb to his mouth and knocked his head back.

Ivy clicked on her headset and shouted, "Roger! Find Bess Jodice ASAP." She lowered her voice and shielded the microphone with her hand. "Yes, the drunk one."

The chefs retook their places. Ashlee and Tess had stopped their cat fight long enough to drink a couple glasses of rosé. They were hovering over the judges' table, giggling, when Roger finally brought Bess back to her seat. "I found her lying on the couch in the lobby."

"I'm so sorry. I know thish will come as a shurprise to everyone, but I'm jush not feeling too well. I'll be glad when thish day is over. I guess I'm not as young as I ushed to be."

Ivy, once again in control, started the judging process. One by one the chefs presented their dishes. Nothing could please Bess except for Philippe's *duck au citron* with lavender rice.

Horatio was not nearly as impressed with Philippe. "It was a crime against the culinary gods to put that much lavender in the rice. It was like eating a bottle of cheap perfume. What were you thinking?"

"Monsieur, I was thinking that I am a chef. A chef trained by the master Pierre Escargot himself. And you are simply one who thinks he knows food because his picture is in a newspaper."

Mother Gibson slapped her knee. "Ooooh. You tell him, Frenchie."

Tim knocked my elbow with his. "I told you his duck a l'orange is amazing."

"It's definitely a classic French dish."

Horatio was not impressed with Tim's now frog leg-studded *duck au citron* either. "The only dish on Team Maxine's that has any flair is this lovely lemon-lavender crème brûlée and shortbread. What a delightful use of the Pop Rocks candy by putting them in a glaze. Well done."

Well, I don't know what everyone's problem with Horatio is. I think he's charming.

Miss New Jersey had a different sort of review for Tim. "I love this duck breast and these little orange thingies?"

"Thank you. Those are called sweet potato gnocchi. I'm glad you like them."

"Oh, I do, and speaking of calling, here's my number."

Adrian ran his hands across his buzzed hair. "Are you kidding me! He's influencing one of the judges!"

Ivy had to reprimand Miss New Jersey. "Brandy, you

can't say stuff like that on camera. We'll cut that out in post. Roger! Don't tweet that!"

Everyone else received scathing, albeit barely coherent, reviews from the former culinary school dean. Bess's harsh remarks left Vidrine in tears over her grilled duck breast, but Hot Sauce Louie received his criticism with calm dignity, muttering to Tim as he walked by, "Dude, why is that old lady so mean? She needs a vay-cay."

It was only for Horatio's kind words of, "I really like how you turned the duck into a burger, Chef Louie. It was very unexpected," and "The lemon-scented rice was lovely, Chef Vidrine. Just lovely," that either of them held their heads high at the end.

Judging Oliva was a challenge because she had lost her translator and sous chef. "You do understand that the theme was Afternoon in Provence? But you made duck scaloppini. That's an Italian dish. You didn't keep to the theme. Do you understand why we are giving you a low score?"

Oliva smiled and nodded politely.

Roger recorded the judges' feedback to play through Google Translator. When Chef Oliva heard the translation and saw the low scores, she gave some Italian feedback of her own—feedback that would not make it past the network censors and would have to be edited out of the final segment.

We wrapped for the day and the audience dispersed to their duties and gossip. Tim gave me a quick kiss good-bye, and he and Gigi were off to Maxine's Bistro to prep for dinner. Aunt Ginny and Sawyer made a beeline for the kitchens.

"You did good today, Poppy Blossom. I want to taste that creamy bruleay you made."

"Come to my station. I made two extras in case one of them was a flop."

On the way to our station, Sawyer linked her arm in mine. "What was up with Tim and the blonde?"

"That would be Gigi. She's recently been augmented."

"Oh, good Lord. Well, she was stuck so far up Tim's butt, if he farted she'd be in the pantry."

"Hey. Where is my sixth ramekin? One is missing."

Aunt Ginny grabbed a spoon and the remaining custard and gave the caramelized sugar a whack. "That's all right, we can share this one."

I handed Sawyer another spoon. "What were you all doing in the stands during the judging?"

Aunt Ginny and Sawyer paused with the spoons in their mouths, looking very guilty.

Sawyer started to say something, but Aunt Ginny kicked her under the counter and she changed it. "Nothing. We were watching you."

Aunt Ginny tried to distract me with flattery. "Oh, my goodness, but this is delicious. Why you aren't working in a high-class restaurant I'll never know."

"Uh huh. Don't do anything to get me in trouble."

"You don't need me for that. You're doing a fine job of getting into trouble all by yourself."

Adrian inserted himself into our circle to get close to Sawyer. "Heya, slim. Did you like what you saw me do today?" He took her spoon, dipped it in the crème brûlée, and took a bite. "Mmm." He turned to me. "This is delicious. I see why Tim has you on his team."

The molten ball of hatred in my belly for Adrian just gave a little fizzle like it had been hosed with ice water. "You think so?"

"Oh yeah. Tim is a master strategizer. He's always working a scheme to get what he wants."

My Tim? The Tim who ate three chili dogs and a plate of nachos before getting on Lightening Loops at Great Adventure, then threw up on the loop and it landed in his lap on the way down? That Tim?

Sawyer patted Adrian's bicep. "You did pretty good today yourself."

Adrian shrugged. "Two good scores and two bad ones. I'm hanging in the middle." He handed Sawyer back her spoon. "How 'bout having coffee with me sometime?"

Aunt Ginny slowly pulled the dessert across the counter.

Sawyer giggled, and I pinched her on the arm behind Adrian's back.

"Um. I don't know. Aren't you too busy for that? What with Restaurant Week and all."

"Naw, I got backup at Baxter's By the Bay. We're too popular a place for me to leave the kitchen unattended, so I called in some favors and got a couple temp cooks."

Sawyer looked around Adrian to me. I gave her a warning scowl, which she ignored. "I would love to. I know just the place. It's over by my bookstore."

Adrian grinned. "Good. How's about tomorrow night?"

Sawyer nodded. "It's a date."

After Adrian was out of earshot, I asked, "What are you doing?"

"What? It's just coffee."

"With the one chef who's trying to destroy Tim's reputation."

"No, he's not. If Tim would just admit he sabotaged Adrian years ago, he would let it go."

"But Tim didn't do that."

"How do you know?"

"Because I know Tim."

"Do you, Poppy? Because you haven't seen Tim for almost thirty years. Maybe he's changed. Hey! What happened to all the crème brûlée?"

Aunt Ginny licked her spoon. "I thought you were finished."

"Well, I am now."

Aunt Ginny rubbed her belly. "Are you two ready to go? I'm starving. Why don't we go to an early dinner? My treat?"

I took off my apron. "It will have to be a fast one. One of us needs to be at the B&B to wrangle Figaro and set out the evening cheese plate."

Aunt Ginny nodded. "I think it's your turn, so . . . you have fun with that."

"Yes, well, thanks for your support." What was I gonna say? Aunt Ginny was in her eighties. She didn't have to help me at all if she didn't want to. But I sure wasn't going to admit that to her. The more time she spent working with me, the less time for her to sneak off and get into trouble. "Let me get my things, and I'll meet you both in the parking lot."

I went to the locker room to retrieve my purse. When I closed my locker, Vidrine was there waiting for me, her eyes blazing. "What did I tell you would happen if I was sabotaged again, *chérie*?"

"Vidrine, listen to me."

She leaned in until her nose piercing was just inches away from me. I had to force myself not to stare at it.

"You have to know that I had nothing to do with the equipment malfunction today."

"And why would I know that?"

"For one thing, I was sabotaged too."

"Yeah, you had to make cookie dough by hand. Boo hoo. I had sauce blow up in my face."

"I got lucky. And if you ask Marco, so did you. Think about it. Whoever sabotaged the equipment had to have done it between the event yesterday and this morning. Every minute of my time can be accounted for at the bed and breakfast. Can you say the same? Where were you last night?"

"Working in my restaurant, making the same dishes I made yesterday morning. Just like everyone else."

"How do you know that's what everyone else was doing?"

"For one thing, it's in the rules." Vidrine considered me for a moment. "Honey, someone is out to get us. It may not be you, but you have fared remarkably well so far."

"You haven't done so badly yourself. Horatio really liked your duck in passion fruit sauce."

"I'm glad someone did. Stormin' Norman thinks he's learned to be a master chef from watching the Cooking Channel."

"Yeah? Well, Norman told Tim my shortbread needed more baking powder."

Vidrine leaned away and softened her shoulders. A little smile played at her lips. "I'll bet he's never baked anything in his life. At least he's just pompous. Bess is downright mean. She hasn't liked anything my team has made for two days." Vidrine scrunched her nose up and mimicked a stuffy old lady. "Chef Vidrine, your food isn't fit for school lunches. I suggest you get yourself to a good culinary program and learn the basics."

I grinned. "Wow, that was really good."

"Honey, I've been a professional chef for almost ten years now. I've seen a lot of stuff in restaurant kitchens. Some of it, I can't talk about. But one thing I know for sure, a fancy education is no match for good instincts, experience, and *pasyon*. I wish I could make that old bat eat her words."

"I wouldn't let Bess discourage you. The only one she likes so far is Chef Philippe."

"Yes, well. Horatio is a *New York Journal* food critic, and he can't stand Philippe's cooking. Maybe his food seems more inspired if you're loaded."

"We all need to stick together. We don't know who is sabotaging the event. It could be someone from the TV studio. It could be students of the college. It could even be one of the judges."

"Well, *chér*, that may be. But my gut says it's a chef. This competition comes with a highly coveted award. Don't underestimate any of these guys. They aren't all who they pretend to be."

"What do you mean by that?"

We heard footsteps coming our way, and Vidrine shook her head that she couldn't say more.

Philippe's pastry chef entered the locker room, her face flushed and tear-stained.

Vidrine grabbed her tote bag. "I'll see y'all tomorrow."

When she left, I asked the pastry chef if she was okay. She nodded, then started to cry. She ran out the door and down the hall before I could ask her what was wrong.

Chapter Thirteen

Figaro met me in the foyer, swishing his tail like an old lady tapping her foot.

"What are you doing?"

A pair of bright orange eyes blinked. Fig lifted a paw to his mouth and paused. His ears swiveled back and forth like a satellite dish searching for a signal.

I bent down to snuggle him up. "Were you waiting for me to come home?"

Figaro gave me a powder puff swat on the hand.

"Hey! You don't have to be rude about it."

Miss New Jersey opened the door and he jumped in front of her and arched his back. She threw her hands up and yelled "Achk!" Then she sneezed twice.

I scooped Fig up and held him close. "I'm sorry. I don't know what's gotten into him lately. He's not bothering anyone else."

"Thadt cadt is evil."

"I mean, I wouldn't say evil." *Terminally naughty maybe.*

"I'm going up to my roomb now. Keep him downb here."

"Okay," I tried to sound bright and cheerful. "Let me know if you need anything."

She disappeared up the stairs. I held Fig out away from my body, his furry legs and poufy tail dangling in midair. "Why?"

Figaro sneezed. Then he grabbed my hand with his front paws and nibbled my finger.

I took him into the kitchen where Aunt Ginny and Sawyer were waiting with coffee and cookies.

Aunt Ginny was pouring cream into her cup. "Did he scare her again?"

I rolled my eyes and nodded.

Sawyer asked, "Who?"

"Miss New Jersey," I said. "They are having a feud." I put Fig in Aunt Ginny's room and shut the door before I joined them at the table.

Sawyer held out her cell phone. "Look at this Twitter feed. If you search hashtag CMrestaurantweek, most of the buzz is about the sabotage. Almost nothing about the scores for today."

"Poor Tim. He doesn't need bad publicity. Business hasn't been very good at Maxine's."

Sawyer took a bite of chocolate chip cookie. "Adrian says his place is booming. It was hard for him to get off this week to compete."

I took half of a cookie. My pants were feeling a little tighter than they were a few days ago. I chalked it up to stress. "What do you mean he's off? I thought he had to make his competition dishes for dinner each night of the event."

"Technically, his restaurant has to make the dishes. He gives them the recipes, and they re-create his three courses for the menu."

"So, he hasn't gone in at all?" I exchanged looks with Aunt Ginny. "What has he been doing with his time each night?"

Sawyer saw our exchange, and nervously put her

cookie down. "I don't know. I didn't ask him. I just know he said he's free to take me for coffee. Why? What are you thinking?"

"Whoever is behind the sabotage would have to have had access to the arena after hours, and the time to tamper with the appliances."

Aunt Ginny stirred her coffee and tapped the spoon on the side of her cup. "Not to mention a motive to want to win the competition at any cost."

I nodded. "Adrian seems very motivated to me. And as far as I know, all the other chefs are busy in their own kitchens after the competition. Tim works until two in the morning. Then we're back at the college at eleven the next day for taping."

Sawyer sat back and picked at her fingernails. "Well that doesn't mean anything. Whoever tampered with the equipment would have to have the mechanical ability to know what they're doing. They didn't just break the appliances, they rigged some of them to keep working and create disasters."

Aunt Ginny said, "That's a good point. But who would have that kind of know-how?"

I took a long drink of my coffee while trying to decide how to answer. "Well, there is one chef who we know has mechanical ability. Hot Sauce Louie used to have a food truck."

"I remember," Aunt Ginny said. "He had the best foot-longs. Whatever happened to that?"

"It broke down a lot, and he got tired of fixing it."

Sawyer's face and shoulders relaxed. "Well see, there's your culprit. He'd know how to jack up an appliance."

"Just because he knows how to work on a drive shaft doesn't mean he knows how to rewire a gas range. And it definitely doesn't mean he'd be willing to put someone's life in danger just to win a contest."

A chime went off in the kitchen, signaling that the front door had just been opened. "Poppy! Are you here?"

"That sounds like Ivy." I went to meet the director in the foyer. "Hey. What's up?"

"We're having a little judges' meeting. Do you think I could get some coffee for everyone?"

Bess and Horatio were sitting in the library while Norman tried to light a fire. Bess croaked out "tea," which we'd all expected.

"Yes, of course. I can bring in some fresh-baked cookies, too, if you'd like."

Horatio took off his hat. "That would be fabulous."

Bess waved her hand in my direction. "Do they contain nuts?"

"No."

"Did you do a better job with them than you did that shortbread this morning?"

I bit back what I really wanted to say. "I made them special for the B&B."

"Okay, then."

I tried to release the stress that went hand in hand with dealing with Bess, and counted down the days till Restaurant Week was over. I returned to the kitchen to make the refreshments with Sawyer's help. A few minutes later we headed into the library with the trays. Miss New Jersey had come down for the meeting wearing her bathrobe and the green goo of an avocado masque on her face. I had to blink twice to be sure of what I was seeing. I glanced at Ivy to capture her expression.

She shrugged. "I told everyone not to worry about how they look, but to come as they are."

I set out the cups and saucers. Sawyer poured while Ivy discussed the judges' concerns.

Norman picked up a cookie. "Are these made with white sugar?"

"Coconut sugar."

"Do you know how many carbs are in each one?"

"About twenty."

He put the cookie back on the plate.

Miss New Jersey sipped at her coffee, careful not to smudge her masque. "I'mb not eating anything gwoss. If they get bugs or fish eyes or something like that in their basket, you can count me out."

"There is nothing like that in the schedule. Oh shoot." Ivy searched her tote bag. "I forgot my daily planner. I must have left it over in the staging area at the arena. Poppy, do you know anyone who can run out to the college for me? I really need that schedule, and none of the chefs or judges are allowed on the premises before eleven AM tomorrow. I would get Roger, but he's working in the cutting room, getting the video ready for airing tonight. I can offer two passes to see the Mariah Carey concert in Atlantic City as a thank you."

Sawyer practically dropped her carafe on the end table. "I can go for you."

Ivy's eyes lit up. "You can? That would be such a life saver." Ivy described what she was looking for and where Sawyer should look.

Sawyer grabbed her keys and flew out the front door, and I took over filling the coffee cups and making Bess's tea.

Ashlee whined, "I don't see why Tess gets to do the kiss and cry with the judges, and I have to roam around the kitchens like a nomad looking for interviews. I'm trying to pull out the 411, but no one wants to give. They're all too busy 'crafting their dishes' and 'working on their plating.' Whatever."

Ivy nodded along.

Tess rolled her eyes, her head, and her shoulders. "Ahck! You're so basic. Just do your job, *chica*."

Ashlee turned the whining up a notch. "Hey, the struggle is real, okay."

Tess grabbed a cup of coffee, and dumped six stevia in it. "I can't even."

Ashlee started to pout. "Don't be salty with me. I've seen you without makeup."

Ivy took out a pair of perfectly round pink glasses and put them on. "It's okay to feel your feels. That's cool. But I need everyone to just take a chill."

Horatio twisted his handlebar mustache. "I don't understand what any of you are saying right now."

Bess's chin had drooped to her chest, and she snored lightly.

Norman took a cup of coffee and placed it on his lap. "The way things are going in those kitchens, I want you to make sure the ingredients are fresh too. I don't want food poisoning because someone thought it would be a great idea to sabotage the refrigerators. Ted would never let that happen on *Chopped*."

Horatio took a napkin and two cookies and placed them on his lap. "I've had worse in professional restaurants. I've even called the health department before finishing a meal a couple of times."

My mind went to Figaro, and I really hoped there was no errant cat hair on the cookies.

Bess snorted herself awake and stirred her private stock honey into her personal tea. "Well, I had low expectashions from the start. I know a lot of these chefs and their hishtories. Many of them aren't properly trained, they haven't had quality of educashion, and they aren't properly trained."

Ivy typed something on her phone. "Okay, noted."

Horatio muttered, "Stewed again."

Bess tried to hold her head high. "If you are referring to me sir, you are incorrect. I am as shober as the day ish long. I'm jush not feeling well."

Ivy leaned forward in her chair. "I really need you to be at your best health tomorrow, Bess. You and Mr. Duplessis are our professional authorities on the chef's abilities, and we really need your reviews to be on point."

Norman looked up from his phone. "Hey. What about me?"

"My reviewsh are alwaysh on point. I can tell you right now who has true shkills and who is pretending." She looked around the room and over to me. "Eve-ry-one."

I swallowed hard. I left them to their meeting and retreated to the safety of my kitchen, where the only judgment I had to sit under came from Figaro and Aunt Ginny.

Chapter Fourteen

I awoke in a panic and shot upright in bed. "I should have made donuts."

I looked around. I was still in the bedroom. Thank God, it had been a dream. No way would I make deep fried jellyfish for the judges. My heartbeat softened, and my breathing slowed to normal.

Figaro thought we were under siege and chose to save himself. He missiled off the bed and out of the little kitty door I'd installed when I moved into the attic.

"What about protecting your master?"

I could hear him galloping down the hall without a concern in the world for my welfare. I could also hear the sound of someone in the throes of distress in the bathroom below my attic apartment. Who is directly below me? Bess. Oh dear. Better have the aspirin ready again this morning. I checked the time. Five-forty AM. There was no use going back to sleep for twenty minutes.

I sped through my yoga routine. I was almost able to do a warrior three pose without falling over. Almost. I picked myself up off the floor, rolled away my mat, and went to get cleaned up. Forty minutes later I was showered, dressed, lashes layered in mascara, and ready for day three of the Restaurant Week challenge. But first, I had to serve the talent their breakfast.

I made a small inspection of the guest stairs this morning instead of my usual route through the hidden pantry. Down on the second landing, I almost tripped over Figaro, who was making a beeline for Miss New Jersey's open bedroom door. *Seriously. No wonder he keeps getting in there.* Miss New Jersey came out of her adjoining bathroom next door, buck naked with her hair wrapped in a towel.

I averted my eyes. "Oh! Um. Good morning. You know, anyone could come out of their rooms at any time into the hall."

"I don't mind."

"I see. I think I just saw Figaro go into your bedroom."

"Ah! Not again." She placed her hands on her hips without a bit of shyness.

"Um. I think maybe if you'd close your door when you leave the room, that might help to keep him out."

"I could try that."

"Yep. Yep. That'd be good. Okay then."

I tried to make a quick getaway, but she stopped me. "Oh Poppy. I just want gluten-free toast this morning. Bess throwing up all night has totally, like, turned me off."

"Of course. Did you tell me you had food allergies? Do you have celiac?"

"What's shellac?"

"Celiac. You know, because you want gluten-free toast."

"I'm just going low carb this morning."

"Um . . ." I started to tell her that gluten-free bread still had carbs, just not gluten, and that the two were not synonymous. But it seemed unlikely to make any kind of difference, so I just said, "Okay, sure."

I continued toward the kitchen. When I got to the bottom landing I heard a thud. "Stay out, dumb cat." A door slammed. And Figaro bounded down the stairs ahead of me.

Aunt Ginny was in the kitchen making coffee. "The baked oatmeal is almost ready, and I've got the melon balls in mint sauce in the pink crystal."

"Thank you. I think we are going to need to add toast this morning. Miss New Jersey has requested it, and Bess either has a wicked hangover or a stomach virus."

"How in the world is she going to judge a cooking show if she's throwing up?"

"I don't know. Maybe Ivy has a backup plan."

"She'd better."

"I'm going to send a note to Mrs. Galbraith to let her know to disinfect Bess's room today."

"She hasn't been able to get in there yet."

"At all?"

"I think Bess is afraid of being robbed by the staff, so she keeps the DO NOT DISTURB sign up all the time."

I took a mason jar of gingerbread syrup and a bowl of fresh cream out to the dining room table. Horatio and Ashlee were already waiting, even though breakfast had just begun. Aunt Ginny brought in two carafes of fresh coffee and placed them on the buffet. By the time I came back in with the melon salad and juice, Norman and Tess had joined the group. When Miss New Jersey rolled in last, wearing a pair of thigh-high boots and a burgundy sweater as a dress, she had to shoo Figaro out of her seat to sit down.

I cringed when I saw the pile of gray fur on the tufted seat. I should have checked that before bringing in the food. I left them to their meal while hiding in the kitchen and eating with Aunt Ginny. We ate quietly while listening for snippets of gossip.

"Which chef do you think is the most likely to be behind it?"

"I think Chef Tim. Like, seriously. He's gotten off too easy."

"D'no way. Chef Tim is hot. I think id Louie."

"He doesn't even belong in an event like *Chopped*. He just makes burgers."

"My money is on Philippe. Did you see the way he just stood there with his duck while the other chef was on fire? I can't even."

"I think it's the production team. They are the only ones who can get in there after hours."

Aunt Ginny and I shook our heads at their wild assumptions. We never did see Bess for breakfast, which wasn't a surprise. I just hoped Ivy had a replacement worked out in case Bess was too sick to get out of bed. We quickly cleaned up and called the judges their Ubers to take them to the college. Aunt Ginny and I would follow in Gia's silver sports car.

Aunt Ginny had one hand on the driver's side door handle. "How's about I drive?"

I laughed. "You're hilarious."

"What? I want a chance to take this hot rod on the road."

"I'd rather be the suspect in another murder investigation."

"Famous last words."

Chapter Fifteen

Aunt Ginny took her place in the stands, and I stowed my purse in the locker room. Upon entering the kitchen, I heard, "Whoop-whoop-whoop."

A little bald hobbit danced his way over and my handyman stood before me. "Heya, Boss."

"Smitty, what are you doing here?"

"The college called me in to make some repairs before the event today."

We're doomed. "Did you figure out what made the deep fryer flare up like that?"

"Someone tampered with the thermostat. They also fed the condensation hose back into the bottom of the fryer. Once things got hot enough, the bottom of the oil basin filled with water. You all were lucky this whole place didn't catch on fire."

"So, it definitely wasn't an accident?"

Smitty thought so hard, his forehead gave birth to a giant, furry unibrow. "Not a chance in a million. Hoses don't cut and move themselves. Someone sawed through the electrical wiring of that first range over there too. The igniter won't spark without electricity."

"Were you able to fix everything?"

"Everything that I found."

We're all gonna die.

"Itty Bitty Smitty!" Ivy walked into the arena with Roger by her side.

Smitty turned and gave a backhanded salute. "Reporting for duty, ma'am."

"Did you finish?"

"Yes ma'am. Everything is rewired and repaired. Except for that one mixer. I can't find anything wrong with it."

"Which one?"

"The one in the far-right kitchen by the judges' table."

Hmm. That's the mixer Philippe's pastry chef was kind enough to swap with Louie's team.

So, it wasn't really broken.

"Good work, Smitty. Can you hang around today just in case something else breaks?"

"Nyah-nyah." Smitty made wobbly moves with his left hand, then shrugged. "I guess so."

"Great. Why don't you go make yourself comfortable in the audience, if there are any seats left. On day one, I couldn't give tickets away. Now they're being scalped on Facebook for fifty dollars each."

Smitty saluted again and took a seat over by Aunt Ginny and Sawyer. As soon as he sat down, Aunt Ginny was on him. She shoved a flyer in his face. He peered over his glasses to read it then took out his wallet.

What is she up to now?

Everyone was in the right place, except for Bess, who hadn't arrived.

Ivy stood in the center of the arena and tapped on her microphone. "Can I have everyone's attention please? I'm sad to report that Marco Ubruzzi is out of the competition due to second degree burns up to the elbow from yesterday's accident. The good news is, he is expected to make a full recovery. Since Chef Oliva is down a man, she has been allowed to replace him with a new sous chef. For the remainder of Restaurant Week, we will be joined by Chef Oliva's son, Giampaolo Larusso."

Tim's breath caught in his throat, and he coughed.

My heart gave a flip. *What? My Gia? Does he even know how to cook?* I craned my neck to see who was making an entrance over by the cameraman. Then, a tall, dark Italian with icy, blue eyes and hair that curled at the base of his neck strode into the arena in a starched, white chef coat.

Ashlee dropped her microphone, and the feedback reverberated throughout the room.

Tess threw catcalls like a construction worker.

Miss New Jersey loudly blew her nose in a tissue. Not the most effective come-on—but I guess when you're a pageant winner you're not as impressed with other people's looks.

Norman sat up straighter and complained to Ivy. "No fair. You promised I would be the most handsome man in the room. It's in my contract."

"I said you'd be the most handsome weatherman in the room," Ivy shot back.

Gia took his place next to Momma, I mean Chef Oliva, and threw me a wink.

I giggled, caught Tim watching me, and tried to cover it by clearing my throat. I was unsuccessful.

Gigi took notice, and, seizing the opportunity, linked arms with Tim.

Ivy called the room to attention again. "It looks like we are short a judge, so . . ."

"I'm here." Bess staggered over to the judges' table.

Horatio twisted the handlebar of his mustache. "Really? She is in no condition for this. She needs to be replaced."

"I agree. With another older woman," Norman said, still apparently stinging from Gia's entrance.

Miss New Jersey pulled out her cell phone. "Maybe I can get Donald Trump to fill in. I've worked with him on the pageant circle in Atlantic City. He loves to be in charge."

Ivy blinked a couple of times. "I'm pretty sure he's all tied up, Brandy."

Miss New Jersey shrugged, and dropped her phone back into her Kate Spade designer bag. "Whatever."

Bess fell into her chair and slurred her words together. "You will do no sssuch thing. You were only allowed to film thiss little debacle here becaushe of my pull with ssthe board. If I go, the dealsssssh off."

"Are you sure I can't get you some strong coffee, Bess?"

Bess looked down her nose at Ivy.

Ivy drummed her fingers against her clipboard. Then she snapped, and Roger ran off with the teapot.

After a slight delay of game—one where I kept stealing glances at Gia only to find him grinning at me, then sneaking looks at Tim to find him looking straight ahead with his jaw clenched so tight his cheeks were white—the cameras were ready to roll, and Tess took her mark.

"Okay chefs, yesterday we spent the afternoon in Provence. Today we celebrate an evening in Italy. Ashlee, bring on the Chianti. Ashlee?"

Ashlee was staring doe-eyed at Gia. "You're way hot."

Tess looked into the camera. "Amigos, chica has gone loco. If you are a loyal viewer of *Wake Up! South Jersey* on Channel 9 weekdays from ten to noon, you know my girlfriend here is cray-cray for the tall, dark, and hottie."

Ashlee let out a long, awkward giggle.

"So, while we get the judges some wine, and Ashlee finds her voice, let's open those baskets, chefs."

We threw open our baskets and took out our items while Tess told the viewing audience what our mystery ingredients were for the day. I had Amarena cherries, which were dark cherries in syrup, lemon liquor, and wonton wrappers.

Tess turned away from the camera. "Are you sure the wonton wrappers are in the right basket? Jes? The producer say jes. Okay, chefs, start the clock!"

We all ran for the pantry, smashing into each other to be first. I reached for a jar of candied orange peel, but Vidrine beat me to it. I took the ricotta, but Philippe grabbed it out of my hand. Are they doing this on purpose? I saw Tim in a rumpus with Adrian over a basket of mushrooms. It seemed the other chefs had decided to retaliate for their unfounded suspicions. I grabbed whatever I thought I could use to make limoncello cannoli and headed out of the pantry. On my way, I collided with a sexy Italian, and I don't mean Momma.

Gia plucked at his chef coat to show me his title. "*Apprendista*," he said, proudly.

I giggled. "Did Momma get you that?"

"She insisted." He wagged his eyebrows.

I gave a small curtsy. "Well I'm wearing the yellow apron of punishment for not attending culinary school."

He shook his head and chuckled. "You are still cute."

"What are you going to make?"

"I have *primi piatti*, or antipasti. There will be a lot of salads."

We both giggled.

Tim came up behind me and spoke stiffly, "We're on the clock, Mack."

"Sorry." I gave an apologetic look to Gia and rushed to my station to begin my cannoli. I had to make some substitutions due to either bad luck or the vindictiveness of my competitors, but I was sure I could make it work.

Ashlee was immediately in front of Gia with the microphone. "Chef Giampaolo, what are you making today?"

Oliva rattled off instructions in Italian, and Gia responded to Ashlee, "I am making pancetta ravioli with fresh herb and mozzarella in espresso basil pesto."

"Ooh, that sounds dreamy. How do you make it?"

Gia flashed her a sexy smile. "I have no idea."

Ashlee giggled and leaned on the counter, the microphone forgotten.

Gia crudely chopped his pancetta while Oliva worked on her entrée and told him what to do. It was an impressive display of multitasking.

"Ashlee," Ivy sang out from beside the cameraman.

"Hmmm?" Ashlee turned around, seemingly surprised to see anyone else there.

"Could you please go around the room and talk to some other chefs now?"

Ashlee dragged herself away from Gia with a tinkling finger wave, and peppered Adrian with halfhearted questions about his veal.

"What are you making?"

"I am creating a beautiful veal par-ma-ja-no with fresh herbs and . . ."

"Mmhm. That's nice."

Tim and Gigi were extra chatty today. For some reason Gigi had turned up the perky to a new level. "What you got there, chef?"

"Veal piccata, a la minute. Whatchu doin'?"

"Settin' my meez."

"All day long, son."

What the heck are they talking about? I hadn't felt left out like this since lining up to choose teams for field hockey in high school. I wrapped my last wonton around a metal cannoli form and got them ready for the deep fryer.

Gigi's smirk at my ignorance let me know she was putting me in my place again. "Oh, sorry. This is chef language. You would understand if you'd gone to culinary school, Poppy."

I didn't have time for Gigi's petty aggression. I focused on my cherries and chocolate chips. "Whatever you say."

The clock was counting down. I zested some orange into my mascarpone and added the limoncello. I looked over at Gia. He was shaking the dough off his hand. He was struggling to make ravioli, but he had a huge smile on his face. It made me grin to myself.

I heard Tess doing the shtick with the judges. "It's eerily quiet in the kitchen arena today. Many of the chefs appear to be tiptoeing around each other in nervous caution. Except for, of course, Chef Oliva's team. But it doesn't appear that there is any sabotage. What do you think about what you're seeing, Channel Eight's sexiest weatherman, Norman Sprinkler?"

"I really like the technique Chef Adrian is using on his herbs. I believe that's called chiffonade, isn't it, Chef Adrian?"

"No, it's called chopping."

Norman blushed.

"Well there you have it. Chef Adrian is chopping."

Tess moved on to Miss New Jersey. "What do you think, Brandy?"

"Everything looks so pretty and fresh. Especially what Chef Tim is working on. Just gorgeous."

"Do you hear that, Chef Tim? What are you making that is so beautiful?"

I looked over at the pile of fuzzy brown clods of dirty mushrooms Tim was peeling on his cutting board and crinkled up my nose.

Tim flashed a grin for Miss New Jersey. "I'm making a porcini and white bean risotto with sautéed monk's beard."

"Monk's beard is a basket ingredient today. Chef Tim, can you tell us exactly what it is?" Ashlee shoved the microphone back under Tim's chin.

Tim held up the thin, spiky, green vegetable. "It's a Tuscan green that tastes a little like spinach, or chard."

Ashlee recoiled. "Eww. It looks like a bunch of pine needles and grass had a baby. Is that in all the baskets?"

Tim trimmed the fine leaves. "I'm going to lightly sauté them and toss them in olive oil. They'll be delicious."

I looked around my workstation for my spice jar and realized I'd forgotten it with the petty drama in the pantry. I went to look for cinnamon in the spice rack, but there was none left on the shelf. I returned to my station and asked Tim and Gigi, "Do either of you have the cinnamon? I can't find it."

Tim shook his head no.

Gigi said, "Eighty-six the cinnamon."

"I'll take that as another no."

Gia appeared by my side waving a jar of cinnamon. "You can take ours. We are finished with it."

I thanked him and couldn't keep my face from

breaking out in a huge smile. "You need to go pay attention to your ravioli," I teased.

He returned to his kitchen where Momma swatted him angrily with a dish towel and complained vehemently in Italian.

Tim sidled up to me, still holding the green stems. "Hey."

"Hey."

"Thanks for being such a good sport this week. I know it's turned out to be a lot more than we bargained for."

I gave him a grin. "It's been an adventure."

"Why don't we go for an early dinner tonight? Something easy."

"Don't you have to cover Maxine's?"

"If we go early enough, Carlos can handle the prep. I'll be there in time for the reservations."

"Okay, that'll be nice." *And very conspicuously timed.* I slid my eyes to Gia, who was whacking at the garlic cloves rolling around on his cutting board.

I placed my cannoli shells in the deep fryer and started on my mascarpone filling. You could slice the tension in the arena with a hacksaw. The chefs were silent, and the audience was scanning the kitchens like the health department inspecting for roaches.

I overheard Aunt Ginny say. "Twenty-to-one odds that someone gets sick eating that clump of grass."

A couple of the biddies held up dollar bills. Thelma Davis held up a stack of coupons for the Acme. *Oh Lord. She's running numbers on the competition. No wonder she's been so flush with cash.*

Mother Gibson waved a stack of her bingo money. "I wanna put fifteen on Poppy ending up with that sexy new chef before the day is over."

I felt a sudden warmth rise to my face.

Tim was bionic, chopping his monk's beard.

Gigi put her hand on his back. "You're not gonna be able to cook that if it's dust, you know."

I added the cinnamon to my mascarpone and tasted my filling. Perfect. Orange, cinnamon, lemony, creamy, that soft bite of chocolate chips and succulent dark cherries. It was going to be delicious.

I took my wonton cannoli shells out of the deep fryer as Tess was interviewing Horatio and Bess.

"Most of these chefs need to go back to basics," Horatio lectured. "Food should evoke strong emotion, not just be slop on a plate."

Bess raised her teacup. "Here here. And you shhhould know more than anyyyone, Horace . . ." Bess's chin dropped to her chest before she finished her sentence.

That'll look good on camera.

Ivy called the five-minute warning.

Horatio pulled at the neck of his bow tie to loosen it. "Chefs have lost the artistry of cooking, focusing instead on new and absurd menu items and molecular gastronomy. I'd like to see more quality over flair in their dishes. Cook from the heart, not from the trends."

Bess was resting her head in her hands. Ivy told the camera to pull in tight on Horatio, so she wouldn't be noticed.

I filled each cannoli shell with the sweet mascarpone and plated two on every plate like logs in a bonfire. Then I dusted them with powdered sugar.

"Time's up!"

An audible hiss of relief fell over the kitchen like plunging a boiling custard into a water bath. No one was sabotaged. Everything was working. It looked like Restaurant Week had taken a turn to the positive.

I stepped away from my station and looked at my cannoli. Two beautiful cream-filled shells dipped in chocolate chips rested on each plate with a twist of lemon. I was proud of what I'd made. Gia came over to congratulate me.

"Beautiful! You do such nice work, Bella."

Gigi muttered, "For an amateur."

Gia winked, and returned to his kitchen.

"Gah! Oh God, no." Tim was staring at his plates in horror.

I scanned his station. "What's the matter?"

He ran his hands through his hair, tugging the pained expression on his face skyward.

"I was distracted because of . . ." Tim jerked angry eyes toward Gia.

I looked down at his plates. He'd forgotten to plate the monk's beard. They were still in the sauté pan. That was a basket ingredient, and it was a required element. This would not go well for Team Maxine.

Adrian was paying close attention to our kitchen instead of his own. "Maxwell forgot his veg! I'm just pointing that out now, in case he tries to slip it on the plate when no one is looking."

Gigi was not practiced in comforting the male ego. "Oh great. They are going to nail us for this mistake."

"Thanks Gigi. Take five." I put one hand on Tim's arm. "It will be okay. I'm sure your veal piccata is so good, it will make up for it."

It was time for the chefs to offer their dishes to the judges. Oliva was expected to sweep all three dishes, and I had it on good authority that she'd made one of her specialties, veal and pork Bolognese with fresh pasta.

We were going in order of score, so Philippe was first to present.

"What have you made for us today, Chef Philippe?" Tess asked.

"Blanquette . . . err . . . I mean Tuscan veal stew with onions and mushrooms."

Bess mumbled something unintelligible, but held up an *L*, which we realized was an upside down seven.

Norman and Miss New Jersey also gave high scores to Philippe.

Horatio chewed thoughtfully. "*Je préférerais manger un chat.*"

Philippe simply nodded. "Thank you."

"Ouch. He's taking that really well."

Tim whispered in my ear. "What'd he say?"

"Horatio said he'd rather eat a cat. See, there's hope for us, even without the monk's beard."

Adrian could do nothing to please Horatio or Bess, but Miss New Jersey and Norman were impressed with his dishes.

Gigi's petit lasagna fared well, but Tim's entrée received twos because he forgot a basket ingredient.

Stormin' Norman poked his fork at his plate. "Do my eyes deceive me, or am I missing monk's beard on my plate?"

Tim's lips tightened into a line. "I apologize, judges. I forgot to plate the monk's beard."

"That's a rookie mistake," Norman gloated. "Chefs rarely win on *Chopped* when they leave off a basket item."

Horatio dabbed the corner of his mouth with a napkin. "What happened today, Chef Tim?"

"I was distracted. I won't let it happen again."

Miss New Jersey looked down the table at the rest of the judges. "Wait. Something is missing?"

Norman rolled his eyes.

Horatio looked at Brandy. "Do you see a vegetable on your plate?"

Brandy looked at her plate. "The pine needles? We were supposed to eat that?"

Bess shook her head. At least, I think she shook it. It could have been shaking on its own.

Norman gave Miss New Jersey a look. "Yes, we were all supposed to have it on our plates."

"Oh, well I like it better without." She fluttered her eyelashes at Tim.

"Chef Tim, jussh whaat were you dishtracted by, may I ashk?" Bess's eyes rolled around, and she had trouble focusing on the chef before her.

Tim looked at the ceiling and shifted his weight. "A small personal distress that is growing larger by this interrogation. I left the ingredient off. It was a mistake. I will be more careful about the rest of the week."

Ivy called, "Okay, let's move on."

It was time to judge my dessert.

Horatio praised me for thinking of something so clever and with a ten brought our score up to a respectable level.

I held my breath as Bess took one bite of my limoncello cannoli. She was so hard to please, and I hadn't been able to win her over all week. I held my breath as her eyes rolled back in her head, then her face fell forward, and she passed out on her plate.

"Cut!" Ivy marched over to Bess. "Wake her up! She is going to have to be replaced with someone else. I can't have this on camera." Ivy shook Bess's shoulder. She didn't respond.

Horatio was dabbing a wet napkin on his woolen suit jacket where some of Bess's mascarpone had squelched out and hit him. "Of all the unprofessional, drunken—"

"Bess!" Ivy shook the older woman a little harder.

Something didn't feel right. I had a growing pit of dread rolling in my stomach.

Norman shook Bess and her head flopped awkwardly to the side.

Ivy put two fingers on her neck. She pulled her hand back like it was on fire. "Oh no! Oh no no no! This can't be happening. Not on my show."

One of the biddies yelled from the audience. "What's happening?!"

Ivy looked at the chefs lined up in their kitchens. "Bess is dead."

Chapter Sixteen

Itty Bitty Smitty was the first to speak. "What are the odds of that?"

Aunt Ginny replied, "I gave it two hundred-to-one. I guess I underestimated."

Ashlee spoke into the microphone like she was still on camera. "Did she drink herself to death?"

Norman shook his head. "Ted would never let this happen on *Chopped*."

With a shaky voice and unsteady hands, Ivy said, "Everyone stay where you are. I'm going to call an ambulance." She found her tote bag and pulled out a cell phone. After a minute of silence in the room, Ivy spoke. "I have an emergency. Someone is dead." She walked out of the arena for privacy.

Everyone stood stock-still for about ten seconds, and then the arena erupted into chaos. Everyone was talking at once. The other judges got as far away from Bess as fast as they could. A hundred cell phones were activated. Roger held both hands up, pleading with everyone not to touch anything, but his appeals were flatly ignored.

Ashlee and Tess stood in front of the body and

snapchatted the gruesome details for their followers. "OMG, someone literally just died. I mean, can you even?"

Gia was immediately by my side and pulled me into a hug. "It will be okay."

Tim was deep in conversation with Hot Sauce Louie and Vidrine, commiserating over what this meant for their restaurants. He spotted me with Gia and frowned.

Aunt Ginny, Sawyer, and Smitty came down from their seats to stand in solidarity with me in the kitchen.

Smitty gave me a soft punch to the shoulder. "You okay, kid?"

"I think so."

Aunt Ginny sniffed one of my cannoli. "Good Lord, Poppy. How much booze did you put in these that you killed the drunk lady?"

I grabbed Aunt Ginny's arm. "Shh! Don't say stuff like that. I didn't kill her."

Sawyer pulled me into a hug. "Oh honey. I'm so sorry about your dessert."

Mother Gibson led a group of seniors down to my station. "Ooh child, don't you worry about a thing. We saw everything you put in those desserts. We know you didn't kill her on purpose."

Thelma Davis held her smartphone up to show me her screen. "I recorded the whole thing, so you have evidence, dear."

I looked at the screen, and it showed a ten-minute video of Mrs. Davis unwrapping a caramel and betting fifty-cent-off coupons for toilet paper that Adrian would fly into a rage if he got a low score. "Thank you, Mrs. Davis. I'll let you know."

The Sheinbergs were next to arrive.

Mrs. Sheinberg held and patted my hand. "Don't worry, Bubula, we'll think of something. There are laws against double jeopardy, preventing you from being accused of the same crime twice."

"That's only if she killed the same person twice," Mr. Sheinberg added. "This isn't the same gal you were supposed to have killed before, is it? Eh?"

Mrs. Sheinberg smacked her husband on the shoulder. "No this isn't the same girl, ya schmegegge. This one's older than dirt. The other one was a young thing like Poppy here."

Mr. Sheinberg threw his hands in the air. "Oy, whaddya think I know, eh?"

"I didn't kill her. I didn't kill either of them. We don't really know what happened yet."

Mrs. Dodson had taken the long way around the arena, passing the judges' table to get a good look at the body before making her way to comfort me. "Poppy, you poor thing. You must have the worst luck in the world." She looked at my extra plates of dessert and shook her head. "What a terrible thing to happen to cannoli."

"Really, everyone. It wasn't my cannoli. They're fine. Here, I'll show you." I picked up one of my mascarpone-and-cherry-filled wonton shells and lifted it to my mouth.

They all lunged forward and yelled, "No!" like I was about to jump off the roof or get a bad perm.

Aunt Ginny smacked my wrist with her hand. "We believe you. Just drop the cannoli before you get hurt."

A loud piercing whistle punctured the air. "What are you all doing? I said for everyone to stay where they were."

We all turned to see Ivy, who had now been joined by a petite blonde cop whose hobbies included arresting McAllisters.

"Good afternoon everyone. I'm Officer Amber Fenton."

Aunt Ginny had lost her internal filter long ago. She gave Amber a curious once-over. "Just how small is that police department?"

Amber took off her police-issue sunglasses. "I should have known. I'm going to have to ask everyone to stand back and not touch anything. This is an active crime scene."

I may as well just drive myself down to the station and put on the orange jumpsuit right now.

The kitchen was locked down while Amber's team collected evidence and questioned everyone. Did they notice anything? What did the victim have to eat and drink? Did the victim have anything to eat or drink that could be isolated to just her? Did anyone have a grudge against the victim?

Ivy sat in the corner hugging herself and rocking. "My career is over. I'm going to have to go back to dog grooming. I'm not ready to get bitten by the Anderson chihuahua again."

Amber spent the most time with Roger. "And you made her this special tea every day?"

"Yes, ma'am. Several pots of it."

"And no one else drank any but her?"

Aunt Ginny and I exchanged looks. While Amber cross-examined Roger, Aunt Ginny slowly crept over to the judges' table.

"As far as I know. No, wait a minute. I think Miss New Jersey had some on day one. Because she was sick. I remember bringing in two cups."

Aunt Ginny's wrinkled little hands plucked a tissue from her purse and grabbed Bess's teapot. She lifted the lid and bent down and gave it a good sniff.

Amber caught the movement out of the corner

of her eye. "Put that down and back away from the evidence."

Aunt Ginny gave Amber her most innocent little old lady look, which Amber knew was far from reality, and sidestepped away from the table.

"Well?" I hissed.

Aunt Ginny shrugged. "It's just tea. Not booze at all."

"Then how is she getting drunk?"

It was finally my turn to be questioned by Amber.

"What was your relationship to the deceased?"

"I didn't really know her. She was staying in my bed and breakfast."

"How did she get along with the others?"

"Fine, I guess. She didn't go out with them after the competition or anything, but she would hang out and chat with everyone around the house."

"What has her behavior been like for the past forty-eight hours?"

"Fussy. Pretentious. To tell the truth, she seems to be a very heavy drinker. She's either been some level of drunk or nursing a wicked hangover the entire time she's been here."

"What have you witnessed her drinking?"

"Well, nothing, really. But someone has been draining my sherry and brandy decanters every night."

I filled Amber in about all of Bess's likes, dislikes, and habits that I was aware of, then I was free to go. I was sick with fear that I would be arrested at any minute. It was my cannoli that Bess was eating when she died.

A couple hours later, everyone had given their statements, and the ambulance had arrived and removed Bess in a body bag. I felt my body give an involuntary shudder when the coroner zipped the bag shut. It was so loud it was as if Ivy still had a microphone on her.

All the stress from the past several days broke through and mocked the strength I was trying to show. One tear broke through my little dam of resolve and rolled down my cheek. Tim took my hand and pulled me into his side. Gigi threw herself into his other side.

A young girl in a black vest with CSI printed on the back came to my kitchen, dumped my extra cannoli into a baggie, zipped it up, and dropped it into a duffel bag that said EVIDENCE.

My heart sunk. I was gonna eat that.

"For now, you are all free to go. I'll be back after I receive the toxicology report, but the initial evidence suggests that the victim was poisoned. The crime scene techs have done a thorough sweep of the kitchen and pantry, and all suspicious items have been bagged. I have agreed, under duress, to let your director continue with the filming while we wait for the autopsy. If anything shows up, I'll be back."

The kitchen arena emptied faster than the National Zoo with a gorilla on the loose. Aunt Ginny and Sawyer had attached themselves to me as if they could somehow shield me from Amber. They probably should have removed my glow-in-the-dark apron, because she still spotted us on the way out.

"Finding you at my crime scenes is getting old. Should I move you to the top of the suspect list now and save us all some time?"

Aunt Ginny gave Amber a steely glare. "Only if you want to keep your track record of being wrong."

Chapter Seventeen

"I can't believe we're caught up in the middle of another murder investigation." Aunt Ginny squirted mounds of coconut whipped cream onto three almond-milk mochas. "This town is going to hell in a handbag."

Sawyer sprinkled the tops of each mug with powdered chocolate. "Are we sure Amber is saying the poisoning was murder? Maybe Bess died of self-inflicted alcohol poisoning?"

We took our mochas and went to the library to sit in front of the fire. The rest of the guests were still at the college in some kind of production powwow with the director, so we had the house to ourselves for the time being.

"She used the word victim, so I'm pretty sure she meant murder." I poked the logs to stir up the flames before joining Sawyer on the couch. "But who would want to kill her? She's only been in town for three days. She doesn't even know anybody."

"I don't want to speak ill of the dead," Aunt Ginny said, "but she didn't do herself any favors by turning her nose up at everything all the time. She was a royal pain in the patoot. I'll be soaking that Lalique vase for hours to get the glue off."

"If she was poisoned"—I pointed out what I thought was obvious, but it made me feel better to say it—"it would have to have happened at the college. The only other place she's been is here, and I know I didn't poison her."

Sawyer and I slid our eyes to Aunt Ginny. Figaro had jumped up onto her lap under the guise of wanting to be petted when we all knew it was a ruse to get to her whipped cream.

Aunt Ginny paused in stroking Fig's cottony fur. "What?"

"You don't know anyone who may have poisoned Bess, do you?"

Aunt Ginny narrowed her eyes. "If I was going to poison the guests, I wouldn't have stopped with that one. Those two girls that fight like a couple of wet hens would be on the top of my list. We need to figure out who would have a good motive for doing the old broad in."

"What about the competition?" Sawyer asked. "Isn't ten thousand dollars riding on the outcome of this week? That seems like a good motive. Would any of the chefs be mad enough with their harsh reviews to want to get Bess out of the way?"

"She did give scathing reviews to everyone except Philippe—you would think he paid her off for good scores. Let's see. . . . In less than three days, Oliva put the evil eye on her for saying she underseasoned her entrée. Louie had to go meditate when she said he would be more successful if he marketed his hot sauce as an alternative to paint thinner. Adrian broke a blood vessel in his eye when she told him his duck was worse than a fried bat she ate on a trip to South America.

He was furious, and we've already seen his temper in action. Maybe he should be the prime suspect."

Sawyer's face reddened and she shot back, "Well, she also said Tim's risotto was so dry he should send letters of apology to all his customers and give them their money back. I didn't see him laughing it off."

I couldn't believe Sawyer's gall to attack someone who had been a friend to her for most of her life, in defense of a guy she'd just met a few days ago. "Tim isn't violent. Adrian threw a heavy pan across the room."

Sawyer was leaning over the edge of her seat. "Not violent?! What about that tackle two nights ago when Adrian was trying to protect the rest of the chefs from the sabotage?"

"Are you out of your mind?! He accused Tim of cheating in front of God and everyone. They aired it on the eleven o'clock news."

"That's because Tim ruined his class ranking and his chances at a good internship. He has a pattern."

"Tim said that never happened. It's Adrian's word against his, and I believe Tim."

Aunt Ginny held her hands up. "Girls! Either get ahold of yourselves or go get the boxing gloves before one of you wears a hole in the chintz. You're defending two men that neither of you know as well as you think you do."

Figaro pinned his ears to his head and threw us a reproachful look for disturbing his whipped-cream scheme.

I bristled at Aunt Ginny's unfair commentary but said nothing. Sawyer and I gave each other a look that said I'm still irritated with you, but I love you enough to end this now and bring it up again later, right where we left off.

"Besides," Aunt Ginny said, flattening Figaro's ruff back down. "Nothing is worse than what she said to that poor little Southern girl yesterday when she made her cry."

"That's true." I sat back against the chenille throw. "She told Vidrine her cooking was worse than a first semester, community college student's, and she should do herself a favor and just go back to Haiti now."

Sawyer shook her head. "Why was she so mean?"

Aunt Ginny shrugged. "Sometimes people are mean because they're unhappy. Life didn't turn out the way they wanted it to, and they take it out on everybody else."

"Well, at least Vidrine was over it yesterday by the time I ran into her at the arena." Sawyer took a sip of her coffee while Aunt Ginny and I stared at her open-mouthed. "What? What'd I say?"

"What do you mean you ran into her?" I gave Sawyer a pointed look.

"Remember when Ivy asked me to go get her schedule?"

I nodded.

"When she promised me the Mariah Carey tickets?"

"Yes."

"Well I met Vidrine coming out of the kitchen on my way in."

"But the competition had been over for hours by then."

Sawyer shrugged. "I think she had been practicing or something. She was covered in flour or baking soda or something powdery."

"That's against the rules. No one is allowed in the arena between events because of the sabotage. She could be disqualified."

Aunt Ginny tipped her chin. "Maybe sabotage is what she was doin'. How did she react when you ran into her?"

Sawyer chewed her bottom lip. "Nervous. Surprised to see me. Maybe a little guilty."

"Why didn't you tell Ivy when you brought her notes back?" I asked.

Sawyer was looking more uncomfortable by the minute. "I don't know. I didn't think about it. I was so focused on those Mariah tickets. I didn't really put two and two together that she was somewhere she shouldn't be."

"Well, no one seemed to be sabotaged at today's event," Aunt Ginny said. "Other than Bess, of course. But then the afternoon was kind of overshadowed, what with her dropping dead and all, so we could have missed something."

"Still, I think we need to find out what she was doing there." I sipped my mocha. "It could have been nothing."

"Or," Aunt Ginny pointed out. "She could have been making Bess a special entrée with a side of cyanide."

"Well, if she did, I sure don't know how she pulled it off. She was on camera the entire time. And everything Bess ate during the competition was shared by at least three other judges. Not to mention the fact that Ashlee, Tess, and Ivy sample most of the dishes off camera. No one else was poisoned."

Sawyer drew her feet up under her. "Couldn't she just poison one plate of food and not the others?"

I thought about it for a minute. "I guess you could sprinkle something on the food at the last minute. Like arsenic in a salt shaker, or strychnine in the cinnamon." I thought about the cinnamon I'd gotten from Gia and swallowed hard. "But Ivy and Roger take the plates to the judges. The chefs have no control over which judge gets which plate."

Figaro swiped a paw full of whipped cream from Aunt Ginny's coffee.

Aunt Ginny nudged his paw and smashed the cream into his face. He shook his whiskers and gave her a glare. "Maybe one of those two put something on Bess's plate before giving it to her."

"I guess that would be possible, but what motive could they have for killing Bess? I don't think Ivy would do anything to jeopardize the broadcast. She acts like her entire career hinges on its success."

Sawyer pulled out her phone and scrolled through the feed. "Yeah, but the exact opposite is happening. Everything that goes wrong on the show only increases the buzz on social media."

"Increases it how?" I asked.

"Look here." Sawyer showed me the Twitter feed on her screen. "Everyone is talking about it. 'Cape May Cut-throat Cuisine.' 'Artisanal Death.' 'Local chefs are killing it at Restaurant Week.'"

Aunt Ginny took out her cell phone. "Whoo-wee, look at all the scuttlebutt about the contest on Google. Ashlee Pickel has six video links about the mess-ups on page one alone."

"Okay, so I was wrong. Even bad publicity is apparently good for ratings. But would that really be a strong enough motive for murder? I mean, this is a small-town, local show, watched by tens of people."

"Don't underestimate how little there is to do here in the winter." Sawyer put her phone back in her purse and picked up her mug. "A lot of the chefs involved in this thing have big followings. Besides, have you considered that she may have been poisoned here at the house, and it just kicked in at the college?"

I shuddered. "Oh God, don't say that. That's all I need right now."

Aunt Ginny tipped back her mug of coffee and left a whipped cream mustache in place. "Didn't that weird psychic lady say death and dead bodies would follow you wherever you go?"

I shifted uncomfortably in my seat. "I don't think those were her exact words, no."

Sawyer nodded. "But it was something like that, wasn't it?"

"It might have been, I don't know. There was a lot going on right then, and I couldn't focus entirely on her."

"Well maybe you need an exorcism or something." Aunt Ginny put her mug down and gave me a weird once-over.

"I do not need an exorcism. This is silly. That lady was a whack job. I don't know why you're even thinking about her right now. That's it. I'm not going to get involved this time. As far as I'm concerned, Bess's murder—or whatever it was—has nothing to do with me. I'm staying out of it."

I was so busy beating my dead horse that I jumped when there was a knock on the door. Most likely a guest with a forgotten key.

Aunt Ginny got up to let them in. "Whatever you need to tell yourself."

"I think you're right." Sawyer patted me on the knee. "We don't need any more drama. Let's just focus on our own stuff for a change."

"I'm going to mind my own business, and fly under the radar for this one." I nodded to myself, comfortable in the finality of my decision. "Let's just get to the end of Restaurant Week and quietly go on with our lives."

Aunt Ginny peered through the peephole. "Well, that will have to start tomorrow, Cagney and Lacey, because right now, the cops are here."

Chapter Eighteen

Sawyer and I tried to hurl ourselves off the couch. The combined motion of us both flailing around at the same time only threw us back with our feet in the air like turtles spinning on their shells. I finally heaved myself up and made it to the foyer. I flung the front door open, and Amber shoved a court order in my face. "I have a warrant, McAllister."

I yanked my shirt down over my hips, stepped to the side, and swept my arm in an arc. "Gentlemen, I believe you already know where everything is." Three uniformed officers filed into the foyer and went off in different directions.

I handed Aunt Ginny the warrant. "Here, put this with the others."

"Sure." Aunt Ginny crumpled it into a ball and tossed it over her shoulder.

Amber huffed. "You do know that is a legal document. I could make your life very difficult for doing that."

Aunt Ginny held up two clenched fists. "This one's

six months in the hospital, and this one's sudden death. Which one do you want today?"

"Heh heh heh." I put out my arm and slid Aunt Ginny behind me. "She's only joking. Not threatening an officer at all."

Figaro prowled over and flopped at Amber's feet. His whiskers and nose still covered in white foam.

Amber jumped a foot in the air and reached for her sidearm. "Oh, dear God, that cat has rabies!"

"No! No, he doesn't." I picked Fig up and wiped his mouth off with my sleeve. "It's whipped cream. We were drinking mochas."

Amber holstered her weapon. "Your whole family is getting to be a menace."

"Why don't you just tell me what you're looking for. Maybe I can help you. I assume you want to see the room where Bess Jodice was staying?"

Amber peered at me through slanted eyes and tilted her head to the right, then the left. "Okay. If you could show me which room the victim was in, that would be helpful. But don't try anything."

"What am I gonna try?" I handed Figaro to Sawyer and retrieved my master set of keys from the kitchen. Then I led Amber up the stairs. "Bess was in the Swallowtail Suite. No one has been in her room since she arrived. Not even Mrs. Galbraith, my chambermaid. She's had the DO NOT DISTURB sign up the whole time." I turned to make sure Amber was still with me and got caught in a four-man pileup with Amber who was being tailgated by Aunt Ginny followed by Sawyer still holding Figaro, who was in her arms washing the remnants of whipped cream off his face. "Why are you all coming?"

Aunt Ginny gave me a pointed look. "Because I want to see what's going on."

I looked from her to Sawyer. "I don't want to stay downstairs by myself."

Amber huffed again. "Can we just get this over with?"

"Fine." I reached the top of the stairs and turned left on the landing. I unlocked Bess's suite and eased the door open.

"Holy cow!" Sawyer cried. "Would you look at this mess!"

I was stunned speechless. Ms. No-restaurant-is-high-enough-quality-for-me had left a disaster of carnage. Bags of Oreos, boxes of Little Debbies, a giant empty container of Cheetos, and two cases of Diet Dr. Pepper. The motif was Sunday afternoon in the sorority house.

Aunt Ginny stood silently at my side, her chin hanging down to her chest.

Amber pushed her way past us, pulling on a pair of blue latex gloves. "Please don't touch anything. There may be evidence in here."

"Evidence that she was a slob." Aunt Ginny finally found her voice.

"And a phony," I added. "She turned her nose up at my linzer cookies, saying she would only eat jam if it were made from raspberries out of her own garden. I know those Pop Tarts didn't come from her garden!"

Amber was systematically going through Bess's luggage. "So, I guess this suitcase full of Cheez Whiz and Ritz Crackers would seem odd to you as well?"

"Unbelievable. We couldn't make anything that made her happy, could we?"

Aunt Ginny shook her head no, trying to take in the explosion of convenience store shelves before us.

"And the competition! The way she treated the other chefs. She said their food was barely edible."

Sawyer nudged a bag of Starburst with her toe. "To think, the whole time she was secretly up here eating like this."

Amber used her pen and held up a baggie of lumpy brown goo. "Any idea what this is?"

I cringed. "Oh, dear God! I don't want to know."

Aunt Ginny reached out and grabbed the baggy and opened it. She sniffed. Then she stuck a finger in and tasted it.

"I really don't think you should . . ." Amber trailed off.

Sawyer made a sound like she was about to hurl.

"Why would you do that!?" I hollered. "You could get Ebola or rickets or something."

Aunt Ginny looked in the bag with a quizzical expression and smacked her lips. "Fig jam."

"What?"

"It's my homemade fig preserves." Aunt Ginny handed the bag back to Amber. "I know because I can taste the port. It's my secret ingredient."

"Why would she have a bag of your fig preserves?"

Aunt Ginny pointed to a notebook on the desk. "I think she was trying to figure out my recipe. She'd been making notes about it." Aunt Ginny scanned the writing. "She almost had it."

Amber flipped through the notebook. "Her handwriting was fine three days ago, then it starts to get erratic sometime after she arrived."

"Well, it was nothing we did." Aunt Ginny squared her shoulders.

Amber looked around the room. "What's that?" She pointed to a mason jar with a fancy lilac bow.

I took a step into the room followed by Sawyer, who

was glued to my hip. "That's her special honey, made from her own bees. She goes through about a cup of it a day."

Aunt Ginny gave me a lopsided smirk. "It's probably that stuff that comes in the plastic bear."

Amber bagged the honey and the gallon-sized zipper bag of tea leaves that was next to it.

One of her crime scene officers joined her with a small tin of loose tea from the kitchen. "This is all I could find."

Aunt Ginny reached out to grab it. "Hey, that one's mine. The crazy lady never touched it."

"That's true." I said. "I made her a pot of peppermint yesterday because she was sick to her stomach. But other than that, she would only drink her own special blend."

Amber took the tin from the officer and dropped it in an evidence bag. "We have to test everything. It's protocol."

Aunt Ginny balled a fist at her side. "I have my own protocol when someone takes my things."

I grabbed Aunt Ginny by the shoulder and led her from the room. "We'll wait in the library until you're done."

The three of us made our way back down the stairs. Figaro jumped out of Sawyer's arms now that the excitement was over. We sat in the library in silence trying to process what we'd seen.

After a couple of minutes, I said, "That explains why she brought so many suitcases."

Aunt Ginny and Sawyer nodded.

A couple minutes later Sawyer added, "I bet she was going to steal your jam recipe and put it in her next cookbook."

Aunt Ginny and I nodded.

Another minute of silence passed before Aunt Ginny finally said, "Just what was in that tea?"

And we all stared at each other knowing we were on to something.

Chapter Nineteen

Amber came down the stairs holding several baggies of confiscated evidence. "I've sealed off the victim's room. I don't want anyone in there while the investigation is open."

"You mean to tell me you put yellow crime scene tape across one of my suites while I have guests in the house?! Is that really necessary? No one can get in there but me."

Amber pulled off her latex gloves and stuffed them in her pocket. "That's why I put up the tape. You and your aunt have a way of tampering with my crime scenes."

"But what if one of the guests posts a picture of that on social media?"

"Not my problem."

"Why are you treating us like we're criminals? We didn't kill her. The victim didn't even die here."

"It's procedure, McAllister."

I could feel my blood pressure rising. Amber was always so dramatic and unreasonable. It made me want to grab her blond ponytail and swing her around the room. "Could you at least clear me as a suspect. It's completely ridiculous to think that I might be on that list, but then you *have* falsely accused me in the past."

Amber leveled her gaze on me. "I wouldn't rule anything out just yet. I'll be in touch." She sashayed out the front door followed by her three uniformed officers like Rizzo and the Pink Ladies, the last one slamming it shut behind them.

"Well, that didn't go well at all," Sawyer stated the obvious.

My cell phone played the duuuun-duh-dun-duh theme from *Dragnet.*

Sawyer looked around the room. "What was that?"

"I set a Google alert for every time someone posts about the bed and breakfast online." I checked my screen. "Oh, come on! How is that even possible?! Someone tweeted a picture of the crime scene tape covering the Swallowtail Suite."

Sawyer looked on my phone. "Who is Scarlet Dragon?"

Aunt Ginny came around the corner, chuckling.

I held up my cell phone. "What did you do?"

She sobered up quickly. "What? People will be lining up around the block to stay in the crime scene suite."

"I don't want those kind of people. I want harmless little old ladies who sit around doing crafts and drinking tea."

Aunt Ginny crossed her thin, papery arms across her chest. "Like the psycho who just died?"

Sawyer, the ever-helpful, switched loyalties. "Oooh, she's got you there."

"Thank you, Sawyer. That will be all." I rolled my head around my shoulders.

Sawyer blew me off. "And what is the deal with that tea? Do you think that's how the killer poisoned her?"

"If her bag of tea was poisoned, Miss New Jersey would be dead right now. She had some on Saturday."

"Miss New Jersey is younger and in better shape," Aunt Ginny said. "Maybe the poison needs more time to work on her."

"We'll have to warn her to go get that checked." I looked at the time on my phone. "I have to go meet Tim for dinner."

"It's time for me to meet Adrian for coffee too. Where are you going for dinner?"

"Brother's Pizza."

Aunt Ginny prodded me. "How are you going to be able to stick to your Paleo Diet around pizza?"

"They have salads."

"Uh huh." Aunt Ginny gave me a look that said "you're not kidding anybody."

"I have an idea." Sawyer grabbed her coat. "If you're willing."

"What kind of idea?"

"Well, it's a little sneaky," she said.

Aunt Ginny chuckled. "Then it's right up her alley."

Brother's Pizza in West Cape May was just a couple of miles from the house. A small joint in a strip mall, you could smell the garlic and oregano from Sunset Boulevard. Tim was waiting for me at one of the beige Formica tables at the front of the red dining room. An ancient juke box sat in the corner, and there was a metal stand with a stack of *Shoppe* periodicals.

Tim gave me a quick kiss and helped me out of my coat. "I ordered us a *panzerotti*. I know how much you love them."

"They have gluten-free *panzerotti* now?"

Tim blew out a low breath. "Aww, Mack. I'm so

sorry. I forgot about the gluten thing. Do you want me to get you something else?"

"Uhhh, no. No. I'm sure it will be fine." Oh, it was so not going to be fine. But I knew what was in store in just a few minutes, and I didn't want the evening to begin with a disaster. Even if it was destined to end with one. "Amber came by and searched the house."

"She can't possibly think you had anything to do with that lady's death."

"Well, it's Amber, so, you know. Rule number one: blame a McAllister."

"Gah! Did she find anything?"

"Only if the smoking gun was a bag of Tootsie Rolls."

"A what?" Tim laughed.

One of the brothers came over with our hot and gooey *panzerotti*. I could feel my resolve fly away like the steam from the bubbly cheese. I was just going to have one bite, you know, so as not to be rude and all. I mean, if a man asks you out on a date, it's very poor manners not to join him in his *panzerotti*. Especially if you knew he was about to have a very bad night.

"Oh hey, look who it is." Sawyer had just entered the front door of the dining room and was unbuttoning her coat. She had Adrian in tow. In regular jeans and a short sleeve bowling shirt, he wasn't half bad looking. The other half was still terrifying. "It's Poppy and Tim. Hi Poppy and Tim."

Adrian froze. Scowled. "Nope. Can't do it." Spun around and headed back for the door.

Sawyer caught his arm. "Come on. We're all adults. How bad could it be?" She flashed Adrian her brightest million-dollar smile and he melted.

He looked back at Tim and me and hung his head, resigned to just get it over with.

Now I had to work on my side of the peace treaty, who currently had a death grip on my *panzerotti*. "It'll be fine. Just breathe."

Tim gave a tight smile to Adrian and gestured for him to join us.

Adrian pulled out the chair for Sawyer, turned his chair around backwards, and fell into it with a glower.

Sawyer rubbed her hands together to warm them. "What are yooze eating? You got a *panzerotti*? I love those."

Sawyer's Jersey Girl was coming out more than usual. She must have been really nervous.

I tried to pull a piece out of Tim's claw. "Inside out pizza, what's not to love?"

Adrian asked Sawyer, "You want a *panzerotti*? I'll get you a *panzerotti*. Wit the works. But I'm not paying for them." He gestured to Tim and me. "This ain't no double date." Adrian went up to the counter to order, and Tim looked from one of us to the other.

"What's going on here? What are you up to?"

"Nothing." Sawyer smiled. "We were just in the neighborhood and thought we'd get some pizza."

Adrian returned to the table with two root beers and settled next to Sawyer.

Then we sat in uncomfortable silence.

Sawyer gave me an imploring nod to say something.

"So, Adrian. How well did you know Bess?"

"Never met her. But then I didn't go to community college. I went to CIA in Hyde Park. We didn't exactly swim in her little pond."

"Is she well known in the industry?" I asked.

Adrian shrugged. "How would I know? I never heard of her."

"How about you, Tim?" Sawyer tried to extend the olive branch.

Tim shrugged and gave his head a shake.

Well this was just a delight. We would have to do it again, never.

"I got a second restaurant I'm opening in the spring," Adrian announced. "We're just too busy at Baxter's By the Bay. Standing room only every night. I can barely get out of there for a night off. We're up for review to get a Michelin Star, so this is probably my calm before the storm."

Tim looked up from the ball of dough he had squashed with his rage. "I probably need to get to Maxine's soon. My dinner rush is about to start, and things will fall apart if I'm not there." Tim took out his wallet and threw a couple twenties on the table just as Adrian and Sawyer's *panzerotti* arrived.

Visions of Tim's near-empty dining room sprang to my mind. My heart sank. He just wanted to leave. Sawyer's scheme to get the boys together to air out their differences and make up was as bad as a left-bank peace treaty. I wasn't sure Tim would be able to trust me again after tonight.

Adrian leaned forward and tilted his chair toward the table. "A good manager can teach his line how to get by in his absence."

Tim considered Adrian's challenge and met it with a shot of his own. "My staff is top notch, but if I take a night off, the whole kitchen stays in the weeds. I just don't have the same kind of leisure time that you obviously have."

Sawyer, uncomfortable with the rising tension, tried to calm the conversation by throwing gasoline on the fire. "Were there any classes that you two took together in college?"

I threw my foot out and kicked her under the table.

"Ow." She turned to me and hissed, "What? No good?"

Adrian's face broke into a wicked grin. "We took all our classes together. Even the ones we tried to get out of. That's how I know this guy better than any chef at the shore. He used to be my best friend."

Tim threw his hands up in the air. "Dude! Let it go! How long are you going to hold this over my head?!"

Adrian pointed a tattooed sausage finger in Tim's face. "Until you admit what you did."

"You just had bad luck."

"Howz come I was the only one whose ingredients were changed? Huh! Tell me that!"

"Man, I don't know. I wasn't the only one in the class."

"I got a D from Chef Santos. That knocked my ranking down from first to second."

Thank God it was January, and Brother's wasn't full of tourists. Two grown men scrapping like bucks while their ladies sit by and calmly eat a *panzerotti* was just another day in Jersey for the locals.

Tim jumped to his feet. "You know what your problem is?"

"What!"

"You've always had a chip on your shoulder because you fold under a little competition."

Adrian leaned his chair back. "And you can't win without cheating. Just like you're doing this time, trying to get an advantage by flirting with Miss New Jersey." He turned to me. "How do you put up wit dat?"

Tim punched his arm through the sleeve of his coat. "You're impossible. You know, you probably did kill Bess because she said your veal was like eating a shoe. You never could handle criticism. It's why you were put on academic discipline."

Adrian's chair crashed to the floor. "I was never disciplined."

"What do you call those special hospitality management classes you were required to take?" Tim looked at Sawyer and pointed to Adrian. "Oh yeah. And did he tell you about the two-week suspension that he told everyone was a 'study abroad' trip after he attacked Chef Santos when he gave him that D? Did he tell you about that?"

Sawyer looked like a rabbit caught in a net as she turned wide eyes from Tim to Adrian to me.

Adrian flew out of his seat and flipped the table. *Panzerotti* and root beer went flying. The family sitting nearby picked up their plates and moved two tables over before continuing their conversation about the potato transistor Jimmy was wiring for the upcoming science fair.

Adrian jabbed at Tim. "You wanna talk about some rage, just wait." Adrian rolled in a boil out the door and into his red Porsche with the license plate that said #1CHEF. He peeled out of the parking lot and into the night.

Tim muttered, "Sorry Mack. I can't do this right now." He kissed me on the forehead. "I'll see you in the morning." And he followed in Adrian's wake.

Sawyer and I sat together and quietly finished the *panzerotti* we'd been holding before the rest was flung around the room.

I asked Sawyer. "So how do you think that went?"

She shook her head. "Still not the worse date I've ever been on."

One of the brothers came over and picked up the

table. I paid for the *panzerotti* with Tim's money, and put a hefty tip—out of embarrassment—in the apology jar.

I peeled a glob of cheese off of Sawyer's coat. "Come on, I'll drive you home."

We walked out into the brisk night. There was a white halo around the moon. Sawyer sniffed. "It smells like snow."

I sniffed. "Snow and cupcakes."

We looked in the window of the bakery next door.

"Isn't that the weatherman?" Sawyer shielded her eyes from the glare of the streetlight.

"Why, yes, it is. And that would be Ashlee Pickel that he has wrapped around him."

"Huh. I thought he was hooking up with the Latina."

"So did I."

"I wonder if Ashlee and Tess know he's seeing both of them."

I watched the very public display of loose morals. "Yeah. It looks like they're all on the same page with their bad decisions."

Chapter Twenty

After a sleepless night and a silent breakfast service, I pulled Gia's car into a parking space at the culinary wing of the community college. I'd tried to give the keys back to him yesterday, but he insisted we wait until the end of the competition, so I could keep bringing Aunt Ginny with me. There was no arguing with an Italian who had his mind made up.

There appeared to be a relaxed gathering of students enjoying the chilly morning sunshine on the lawn.

Aunt Ginny undid her seatbelt and clutched her purse tight against her. "What's all that ruckus about, do you think?"

"I don't know. Maybe they're decorating for a dance or something."

"All I see is a bunch of posters on sticks."

"Maybe posters on sticks is what's cool today."

"I don't like it."

When we approached the sidewalk, the relaxed gathering picked up their posters and charged us. We couldn't understand them because they were all speaking at once.

"How could you?"

"You should be ashamed of yourselves."

"There's blood on your hands."

These were no students. It was an angry mob of housewives.

"What the—! Get off me!" Aunt Ginny threw her shoulder into one of the women and knocked her back.

I put my arm around Aunt Ginny's shoulder, and we pushed for the doors. A security guard who had been called in for the day tested us like the troll under the bridge with a riddle. "TV people or protesters?"

I tried to form an answer out of the gibberish, but I was stuck on the word protesters. *Protesting what?*

Aunt Ginny was much quicker thinking. "Do we look like we got nothing better to do than stand in the cold with a bunch of poorly drawn posters? She's a chef. Team Maxine's."

He nodded, and let us pass.

"Who are those people? What are they doing out there?"

Aunt Ginny held my elbow and pulled me along. "Just focus on your basket today. One thing at a time."

"But who are they mad at?"

"Focus, Poppy. This too shall pass."

I wasn't the only one who was stunned. The kitchen arena was a grim sight. There was no excited chatter today. Only a general malaise. While Sawyer and I were ducking flying mozzarella at Brother's Pizza, a crusade was being launched. An aggressive backlash had been unleashed against the Restaurant Week chefs overnight.

The South Jersey world of social media had been chewing on each tasty tidbit of scandal revolving around the competition all week, as if Taylor Swift and the Kardashians were involved. Facebook pages were dedicated to the exchange of analysis over whether or not a clever raccoon had tampered with the pantry, or a disgruntled college student had sabotaged the appliances in revenge for failing grades. A new Twitter hashtag, #SJChefFail, was so hot it was being tweeted by one of the Real Housewives.

But when news hit the airwaves that one of the judges had been poisoned during the event, every soccer mom in the tristate area became an activist with a crusade to boycott Restaurant Week and all the chefs. They had zero evidence, but they'd passed around enough rumors to fuel their ire and had frenzied into an angry mob.

Hot Sauce Louie walked over and gave me a hug. "How you holding up, hon?"

"I'm a little shaken. I just don't understand why everyone is so angry without having any facts. We don't even know the cause of death yet."

"Dude, I passed three restaurants on my way here this morning that got signs in the windows, 'POISON FREE FOOD.'"

Philippe was tying an apron around the waist of his starched chef coat, his eyes full of worry. "*La Maîtrisse* had sixteen reservations cancel since yesterday afternoon. Last night was the slowest dinner service we've had in years."

Hot Sauce Louie put one hand on Philippe's shoulder. "Something's gotta be done. I told the little girl with the pink glasses I want out."

"You mean Ivy?" I asked.

"Yeah, that's her. I told her the Dawg Houz can't ride out this wave of negativity. I gotta bail."

Philippe adjusted his chef hat. "And she said yes to this? My team would be very interested in leaving zee competition if that is an option. *La Maîtrisse* has been a landmark in Sea Isle. I will not let her be tainted by this debacle."

"I'm sorry, chefs, but it's just not possible." Ivy strode purposely across the room, waving a sheaf of papers. "I went to bat for you, I really did, Louie. But you all signed contracts that you would compete to the end, no matter what."

"Couldn't there be an exception?" I asked. "Surely these are extreme circumstances."

Ivy shook her head no. "I asked. The executive producer has refused to let you out of your contracts. I'm so sorry. He says there is too much money invested in the event. The shareholders want their return."

"That's soo harsh, man." Hot Sauce Louie pounded his fist in his palm. "You know how many burgers I have to sell to pay my rent? I can't do that if nobody's getting in line."

I felt a hand on my shoulder and a kiss on the top of my head. I instinctively knew who it was without looking.

"Good morning, Bella." Gia smiled at me before he turned to Ivy. "Chef Oliva wants to know what it will take to get out of her contract."

Louie looked at Ivy but pointed at Gia. "See that. Face it, man, this shindig's a dud."

Ivy handed each of us a copy of the competition waiver. Mine was signed on the bottom by Tim Maxwell, in big letters.

I read through the fine print, something I'd had to do for many years working as a receptionist in my late husband's law firm, until I found the clause. "Five thousand dollars? If the chef defaults on his or her commitment they will be fined five thousand dollars? Isn't that a bit steep? The award is only ten thousand."

Ivy shrugged. "They signed. There is a lot more at stake than just the cash."

I thought about Tim and knew there was no way he

could afford to pay the penalty for dropping out. We would have to just bear our way to the end of the week. Lord willing, we would all have businesses to go back to when it was over.

"Hey! You!" Chef Adrian hollered at Ivy from across the arena. "I need to talk to yooze about a little smear campaign against Baxter's on Yelp. I got twenty-seven bad reviews in the last twelve hours. Reviews from people ain't never been to Baxter's. I never had a bad review before this disaster of a show, and I wanna know what you gonna do about it."

Ivy sighed, and rifled through the pages of waivers until she found Adrian's and placed it on the top. "Places, everyone. We start in ten." Ivy clicked on her headset and asked Roger to bring in the cue cards for the hosts, and then she went over to Adrian to deliver the bad news and try to calm him down.

Tim and Gigi entered the arena together, silent, and timid. I tried to give Tim a smile, but it flopped over halfway to his eyes. "What's wrong?"

Tim returned a weak smile. "Someone spray painted 'killer' all over Maxine's last night."

"What!" My heart sank for him. I knew all too well just what that kind of attack felt like, vulnerable and violated. "Did you happen to see who did it?"

He shook his head. "It was the middle of the night."

"*Le Bon Gigi* was hit too." Gigi sniffled. Her eyes were red, and her face was splotchy. "We're ruined."

"I think it's too soon for that." I tried to comfort them. "This whole thing could resolve itself before the week is over. We have to hold on to hope." My eyes flicked up to the stands to Aunt Ginny. This sounded a lot like the same speech she had once given to me.

Aunt Ginny grinned and gave me two thumbs-up.

Tim put on his chef coat and started to button it.

"I don't see how, Mack. My dining room is as empty as my bank account. No one wants to eat in a restaurant where the chef might be a killer. I think the only thing that will help is for the cops to make an arrest. That'll get everyone else off the hook, and the yoga-pants cartel picketing in front of Maxine's can go back to playing Wizardville on their iPhones."

I can't get involved. Not this time. "Is there any way to get a loan to get you over the hump while this works itself out?" I asked.

"Naw. Maxine's is upside down. I'm mortgaged to the hilt from rebuilding after Hurricane Sandy. If things get any worse, I'll be living from handout to handout."

Oh God.

"Poppy, is there anything you can do? You've been through this twice already yourself. Both times you were able to find out more than the cops could."

"I don't know what I can do. I'm not a detective. I've got no business poking around where I don't belong."

Tim's face fell.

Gigi wrapped her arms around his waist. "Maybe we could merge our restaurants together in a formal partnership. *Le Bon Maxine.*"

His eyes popped wide for a second like he was surprised, but then he hugged her back. "That is so sweet, Geeg. But my failure isn't your problem. I just need this whole mess to be over and to have our names cleared from the suspect list before we lose everything."

Gigi was offering a lot of support. Support that I suspected she wanted to come along with some gold bands and "I dos."

I saw the worry lines etched on Tim's face and took a deep breath. *I just can't do nothing and let this happen.*

Tim was there for me when I needed him most. He's walked into danger with me in the past. Well, danger of getting stripper glitter in his eyes, but still—it counts. "Look, I can't promise I'll get anywhere. I think the first two times were a fluke, but I'll do some digging and see if I can find anything out that could help clear us."

Tim smiled up to his eyes and pulled me close to him. "Thank you. That's all I needed to hear. And Mack, I'm so sorry about last night."

"I know. It's okay." I hugged him back and just happened to catch Gigi's expression. Giiiirl, if the eyes are the mirror to the soul, I think I saw Satan's reflection in Gigi's baby blues.

Chapter Twenty-One

A figure fast walked into the kitchen arena draped head to ankle in a dripping Hefty bag. I knew right away who it was because of the pink Birkenstocks peeking out from under the plastic.

"Vidrine, are you okay?"

"Am I inside yet?"

I helped her pull the plastic bag off. "You're in the arena. Is it raining?"

Vidrine patted her braids. "No. That group of angry women is throwing water balloons. At least I hope it's water. I was lucky to have a box of trash bags in the car. Is all that because of Bess?"

"It would seem so."

"Oooh, child. She must have been really popular around here."

Somehow, I doubt it. "Are you planning to ask Ivy to let you out of the competition?"

"No, why?"

"Oh, I just assumed."

"No way, girl. I'm in it to win it." She shook out the

plastic bag and folded it up. "Why? Everybody else want out?"

"I wouldn't say everyone." I guess technically Tim didn't say he wanted out. "Hey, while I've got you, Sawyer said she ran into you the other afternoon."

Vidrine's eyes darted left to right like she was looking for a quick getaway.

I put my hand on her shoulder to try to calm her. I saw Michael Landon do that to a horse on *Little House on the Prairie* once. It didn't work as well on Vidrine.

She called over her shoulder. "What?!" Then looked back at me. "I'm sorry. They want me to take my place now."

"No one said anything."

Vidrine dashed past me. On her way to her station, she stopped to whisper something to Hot Sauce Louie.

He looked my way and gave me a chin up and a big smile.

Hmm. *What is that all about?*

Ivy tapped on a microphone to bring the room to attention. "Okay everyone. The Chamber of Commerce is breathing down my neck to clean this mess up. No one wants to put the nasty business with what happened yesterday behind us as much as I do. But, the show must go on. Now we're missing a judge. The police don't want us to mention anything about the murder to the one or two people in this town who haven't heard about it yet, so we're not going to address it. We're just going to replace Bess with Ashlee and go on as if nothing happened."

A low hum began to crawl around the arena, discussing the poor taste in not giving at least a small tribute to the woman who sat in this room with us for three days of the event.

Even Gigi muttered, "That seems kind of harsh." And you can be sure Gigi was no fan of Bess's.

Ashlee took the now-vacant seat in between Horatio and Norman. Her opening remarks from her new position were, "Aww, how come I have to sit here and taste the poisoned food? Why can't Tess do it?"

Tess was being set up with the wireless microphone. "Sorry, chica. You know I'll come show you some love at the judges' chat."

"No, you won't. You'll ignore me and steal all the air time."

Tess's smile was devious. "Yeah, I will."

I made eye contact with Sawyer in the stands. She jabbed her finger toward Vidrine, who I saw was watching me, and who immediately looked away when our eyes met. Sawyer was doing some kind of crazy sign language that I understood to mean "corner Vidrine and ask her about the other day." I returned a look to Sawyer that said, "I'm kinda busy right now."

"Welcome to day four of the Cape May Restaurant Week Challenge," Tess opened for the camera. "Today's theme is Mysteries of Asia. Ooooohh. I can't wait to see what the secret ingredient is. Chefs, open your baskets."

I flipped the sides down and . . . well . . . *I don't know what the heck I'm looking at. It looks like a hard yellow squid, fish food, and pancake syrup. I do not have a good feeling about this.*

"And the dessert baskets have Buddha's hand, agar-agar, and coconut syrup."

Ashlee cried out from the judges' table, "Eewww."

Miss New Jersey was equally disgusted. "I'm not eating a hand. I don't care whose it was."

"It's a fruit." Norman huffed. "It was on *Chopped Tournament of Stars.* Don't you people like to expand your minds?"

"You have one hour, Chefs. Go!"

Everyone else ran for the pantry, but I was stuck at my station. How was I supposed to know what to make? I didn't even know what my ingredients were. I snapped a yellow tentacle off the Buddha's hand and sniffed. It was kind of lemony. I took a bite. *Oh no. No.* I spit it back out. Maybe I could use the peel in place of lemon rind. The coconut syrup was very sweet. That could easily be used in place of corn syrup. I held up the bag of clear fish flakes and examined them. I was in trouble with this one.

Aunt Ginny turned to Mother Gibson and spoke very loudly while holding her cell phone at arm's length. "I sure wish I had some agar-agar flakes at my house to make a common vegetarian substitute for gelatin."

Ivy grabbed the roving microphone. "Would the audience please refrain from helping the contestants."

I ran to the pantry while Aunt Ginny was overheard to say, "Oh my goodness, do you think anyone heard me speaking to my good friend Lila here. I certainly hope I wasn't too loud, was I?"

Mother Gibson snickered. "I barely heard you."

Gelatin, gelatin, gelatin, Oh! Vidrine, Vidrine, Vidrine. "Hey Vidrine. How's it going?"

Vidrine squealed and dodged around me.

With my catlike reflexes I was able to do . . . absolutely nothing. In fact, I almost tripped myself. Vidrine got away before my brain could process that she was gone. *I will talk to you before this day is over if I have to have Aunt Ginny hold you down to do it.*

I switched gears, temporarily, to my dessert. The only Asian desserts I knew about were fortune cookies and mochi, and I had no idea what mochi was. But I knew what I could do with gelatin. *Thanks, Aunt Ginny.* So I grabbed some milk and cream, and a couple of orchids from the flower case. I put six cute little oval plates in the refrigerator to chill and went about prepping my Buddha's hand. Zest for the *panna cotta* and peel in the coconut syrup to candy for the topping. In a second saucepan, I started heating all my other ingredients. This might be the easiest dessert I'd ever made.

Tess was making her way around the arena checking in on the chefs. "What are you making, Chef Philippe?"

"Today we make *Coquilles St. Confucius.*"

Horatio made a comment from the judges' table that wasn't caught on camera. "I'm seeing a pattern in your dishes, Philippe."

Philippe looked at Tess and waved the comment off.

"And Chef Louie, what is that you're working on?"

"Hey dude, this here's a ginger-scallop burger with tamarind mayonnaise."

"Talk about a pattern," Ashlee muttered.

"Team Oliva?"

Gia and his mother conversed in Italian. "Chef Oliva is making seared sea scallops." He held up the tamarind. "And this weird-bean risotto."

Vidrine called out across the arena, "Honey, that weird bean is a fruit, and it's called tamarind."

Gia translated to Momma.

Ashlee called from the judges' table. "What are you making, Chef Giampaolo?"

Gia grinned. "I am making shrimp cocktail, on a shaved bed of this thing." He held up a radish.

Momma said something to Gia.

"Radish. On a bed of this radish, with some of these little black specs."

Momma spoke to Gia again.

"Nigella seeds." Gia turned and smiled at me.

I laughed to myself, then went and grabbed six ramekins to ready for the *panna cotta*. I spied Vidrine heading into the pantry and ran in there after her. I caught her looking through the spices. "Why are you avoiding me?"

Vidrine started bouncing in her Birkenstocks. "I don't know what you're talkin' 'bout, *chérie*."

"You know exactly what I'm talking about. Sawyer said she saw you Sunday night after the event."

Vidrine wouldn't look me in the eye. "No, she didn't."

"Yes, she did. Ivy sent her up here to pick something up, and you were coming out of the kitchen. What were you doing? You can either tell me, or we can both go tell Ivy."

Vidrine rolled her eyes up to the right. "Um, oh, Sunday, right." Vidrine drummed her fingers on the spice jars. "You know, I almost forgot about it." She snapped her left hand. "I came back to pick up my knives."

"Your knives?"

"You bet your granny's fanny I did. I forgot to get them after the competition, you know? What with my bad reviews and all, I was traumatized, and I needed the knives for my dinner service at Slap Yo Mamma! Any true chef knows they are only as good as their knives." Vidrine's voice dripped with sweetness. "I just had to get them. You understand, don't you? Please don't tell Ivy. Us chefs have to stick together, but I don't have to tell you that, honey. You're one of us. Ooh, I gotta go fix us this messa scallops right quick, *chér.*"

She grabbed four spices and took off for her station.

I looked at the missing spice slots. I had this room pretty well memorized, and there was no way Vidrine was making something with cinnamon, fennel, paprika, and tarragon. Vidrine was up to something. One minute she was as nervous as a hound at the vet, and then, on a dime, she turned to sugar. *What is she hiding?*

"Poppy!"

Oh no, my cream! I ran back to my station and found my *panna cotta* mixture boiling over.

Gigi was scowling. "Pay attention to your recipe, Poppy. We have too much riding on this to be fooling around."

I grabbed the pot and quickly took it off the heat. It was ruined. So much for my easy dessert. Now I would have to start over and with only thirty minutes left in the competition.

I gathered all the ingredients as fast as I could and dumped them into a new saucepan. I put it back on the heat and whisked. I would not leave this one for a minute. I shook the other saucepan with the peel and syrup. It was looking nice and bubbly, so I dumped it out over a wire cooling rack on top of parchment. Vidrine was watching me again. With fifteen minutes left on the clock, I poured my Buddha's hand-scented cream into the waiting ramekins and popped them in the blast chiller. I twisted my candied peel into little corkscrew shapes while I waited. And waited. And waited.

It was strange that everyone had been asking to be released from the competition. Well, everyone except Vidrine. Vidrine was working calmly in her kitchen with her chefs without a care in the world. I bet it would be really convenient for her if everyone else dropped out. She'd win by default.

Aunt Ginny hollered from the stands. "Shouldn't you be doing something?"

I shrugged and looked around. I went to get my waiting plates. Aaah! Who took my plates? I ran to the shelves where the dishes were stored. I looked in all the cabinets. There was nothing good. I looked behind soup tureens and inside casseroles to see if someone had hidden my dishes, but they were gone. All that was left were giant plates you could display an entire lobster on. *This is gonna be a disaster.* I rushed the plates back to my station and scraped the candied syrup from the parchment into a pastry bag.

"I don't know what that goo is," Ashlee said, "but I don't want it."

I piped what I hoped would look like elaborate scrollwork on my giant plates. I retrieved and dipped each ramekin in warm water and gently unmolded a citrusy *panna cotta* just off center of each plate.

The audience began counting down. "Ten, nine, eight . . ."

What!? My heart was racing.

Gigi hovered over me. "Come on, Poppy, hurry up."

I topped each *panna cotta* with the candied Buddha's hand corkscrews.

"Three, two . . ."

Using both hands, I put orchids next to each *panna cotta*, two and two.

"Time's up!"

My hands flew in the air, and I sucked air into my lungs. Leave it to me to somehow take an entire hour to make a twelve-minute dessert.

"I seriously can't believe you pulled that off," Tim said behind me. He ran his hand across my back. "You always do such nice work, Mack. You really have a gift."

Gigi studied my plates. "You didn't get the garnish on numbers five and six in time."

"Those are extras." Why was I defending myself to her? She would only look for something else to criticize.

"Chefs, present your dishes to the judges. Chef Tim, why don't you go first."

Ivy and Roger set the plates on the judging table. The judges shifted uncomfortably in their seats.

"Judges, today we've made for you, shrimp summer rolls with shredded daikon cabbage, dotted with nigella seeds. Tamarind scallops with coconut milk and Thai chilies over rice noodles. And lemony *panna cotta* with candied Buddha's hand. Enjoy."

The judges looked at each other, waiting for someone to go first. Norman shoved his summer roll into his mouth and took a large bite.

Ashlee gasped. "I can't believe you're eating that after, you know."

"What?" Norman asked through a mouthful.

Horatio took a very long time pretending to chew, even though he hadn't actually put anything in his mouth.

Ashlee took out her phone and did a photo shoot of her plates.

Ivy yelled. "Ashlee, what are you doing?"

"I'm posting my food on Instagram."

"Ashlee," Ivy sang. "We're recording now. I need you to taste Chef Tim's food and give him a score. You too, Brandy. We all saw you drop your shrimp in your lap."

"It looks great," Miss New Jersey said, "but, like, I don't want to die over it."

"Why can't we have something good?" Ashlee whined. "Like avocado toast? Or rainbow toast. Can we do a mermaid theme next? That would look so good on Instagram."

"Please focus so we can get through this." Ivy clicked on her headset. "Roger, bring Miss New Jersey a napkin. Let's go, people."

Norman was happily chewing, his confidence almost as odd as everyone else's fears. "I love the summer roll. So fresh. And candying the Buddha's hand on the *panna cotta* was definitely the way to go. Nice job, Team Maxine's."

"Ummm," Miss New Jersey started, "I like the use of cilantro in the little burrito."

"Summer roll," Gigi said, quietly. "And there is no cilantro."

"Sooo, yeah," Miss New Jersey concluded.

Ivy pointed to Ashlee to go next.

Tess stood at the judges' table and taunted Ashlee. "Take a bite, chica! Take a bite!"

Ashlee poked at the dessert. "This pudding tastes kinda gross. And what are these? Fruit roll ups?"

Tim smiled at Ashlee. "Those are candied citrus peels. And your *panna cotta* is still perfectly round."

Ashlee narrowed her eyes at Tim. "I can tell by the smell. And I don't like the goo all over the plate. I feel like this is what poison looks like."

Ivy blew her breath out. "We'll cut that in post." She

clicked on her headset again. "Roger? I need you to get in here."

Horatio had successfully moved everything around and cut his items into little pieces. "A beautiful presentation. Well done."

Tim stood in place not sure how to respond and shook his head. Before he could comment, Officer Amber walked in, and Ivy called a time-out.

"Good afternoon, everyone. If you could all just give me a moment of your time, please."

Tim came back to our station and stood between me and Gigi. "If I'm arrested, please call my brother in Utica and ask him if he can repay me that loan I gave him in 1997."

Gigi and I both said, "Okay."

The room settled to a hush.

"I wanted to give you an update on the investigation. I received the toxicology report this morning. The victim's blood alcohol level was zero."

The room began to buzz, and Amber held up a hand.

My eyes immediately found Aunt Ginny and Sawyer in the stands, and we exchanged looks of shock and horror. We were convinced that Bess was the lush emptying my decanters. I'd accused her to Amber as such.

Horatio took out his pocket square and mopped his brow.

Amber waited for things to calm down again. "The victim had been given a lethal dose of botulism. The symptoms of botulism poisoning are very similar to that of being under the influence of alcohol. None of the foods the CSI team took into evidence were affected. Her special blend of tea was also free from contaminants. The forensics team found traces of botulism on the victim's teacup and in her honey, however, the highest levels of the toxin were found on her spoon."

Amber slowly made her way over to the judges' table. "Now, I've been reviewing the tapes from the past three days in the media booth with the editing crew. And the recordings clearly show that the spoon the victim used every day was taken from the setting to her right."

Horatio let out a high-pitched squeal like a baby pig, and covered his heart with his hand. "That's my setting! My spoon was poisoned? Does that mean I was the target? Oh my. Oh my God, the room is spinning. Someone is trying to kill me. I knew this would happen one day. I just didn't think it would be here." Horatio's face became twisted and pink. He mopped his forehead with his pocket square again.

Tim's hand slid over and covered mine. He gave me a squeeze.

"We don't know for sure that you were the intended victim, but I'd like you to come down to the station with me to answer some questions."

Horatio was so overcome; his words came out strangled and unintelligible.

Ivy dropped her clipboard. "What? Now?! I'm in the middle of a taping. I can't lose another judge."

Amber was not swayed. "You'll think of something. My team has already taken Roger in for questioning. I'm asking for anyone with information on the murder of Bess Jodice to come forward."

No one moved.

"Look, I'm sure that someone here saw something this week. I'll leave a stack of business cards on the table. Please call the station with any leads, even if you don't think it's anything important, it might be." She took Horatio by the elbow and led him out of the arena, quivering and wringing his pocket square.

My cell phone went off in my back pocket. It was a message from Sawyer. "This changes everything."

My eyes met hers. *Don't I know it.*

Chapter Twenty-Two

"This is just awful." Ivy paced back and forth talking to herself. "What am I going to do? First Bess, now Horatio. They were my anchors. They were the only judges who knew what they were talking about."

Norman's head shot up from his cell phone screen. "Hey!"

"Now they're gone, and we haven't done the judging yet. I have to fill that seat. I can't do the show with just these three idiots."

Miss New Jersey had been examining her manicure. "Who are you calling an idiot?"

"I need a new judge. Maybe someone from the audience. The viewers will never notice if I swap out one old lady for another." Ivy looked into the stands where a hundred and six sets of eyes were held in rapt attention, taking in her nervous breakdown. "What lucky audience member wants to volunteer to fill in for Horatio?"

No one answered.

"Come on, it'll be fun. You get to taste all these wonderful dishes before any of your friends."

Itty Bitty Smitty called out, "You'll get to be buried before your friends too."

"No one is going to die," Ivy implored.

"Are ya shuwar?" Mrs. Sheinberg asked.

Ivy's eyes rolled up to the right. "Yeeeesss. I'm mostly sure."

Well that is very convincing.

Nothing.

Aunt Ginny raised her hand. "I'll do it. I've already lived forever anyway."

I felt a small flurry of panic jump in my chest. I wanted to call out "You better sit down, old woman!" But Adrian beat me to the complaint.

"No way! She's working for Team Maxine! Unfair advantage."

Ivy wouldn't hear it. She was desperate. "You'll be great, Mrs . . . Poppy's aunt. Please come join the others."

Aunt Ginny took Horatio's seat. "Call me Ginny. Can I get clean silverware? Preferably without traces of botulism."

Ivy jumped. "Oh my gosh, of course." She clicked on her headset. "Roger, oh." She clicked it off with a sigh and turned to the cameraman. "Frank, could you please go get four sets of silverware from the dish pantry?"

Frank came back a few minutes later with clean silverware and glasses.

Ivy filled the judges' glasses with fresh wine, and the judging began again.

One by one, the chefs presented their dishes, and Norman took the first bites. When he gave the thumbs-up, everyone else nibbled at the food.

The chefs should have worried less about Aunt Ginny's partiality, and more about her lack of a filter.

"What'd you do to this shrimp? It's tough as an old rooster. This bisque tastes like a dishrag. You ruined these scallops with that smelly sauce. I don't care what was in the basket, no one wants to eat something called Buddha's hand pie."

The chefs waited in their kitchens, whispering amongst themselves about Bess and Horatio, how Norman was sure his food wasn't poisoned, and the career-destroying competition they'd gotten roped into. After an hour of critiquing, the filming was finally a wrap for the day.

Aunt Ginny made a beeline for my kitchen. "So, I've been thinking. If Bess was the intended murder victim, it was probably because she gave such harsh reviews, right?"

I nodded my head. "I guess so."

"So, everyone would be a suspect except Philippe."

"Ahhh, okay. It's true that Philippe received mostly praise from Bess."

Aunt Ginny went on. "But if Horatio was the intended victim . . . that changes the suspect list entirely."

The wheel in my brain fired off a spark and the thoughts started to line up. "I see where you're going with this. Horatio was especially critical in his reviews of Philippe. If Horatio was supposed to be the victim, Philippe goes from being in the clear, to the prime suspect."

Aunt Ginny snapped her fingers. "Exactly! Horatio was as brutal to Philippe as Bess was to everyone else. We need to find out how Philippe felt about the judges."

Sawyer and Smitty made their way through the throng of culinary students who were gathering the dishes, and joined us. Sawyer picked up a spoon and dipped it in my last remaining *panna cotta*. "You're missing one again."

I looked at my counter where there were supposed to be two desserts. "Darn it! Who keeps taking my extras?"

One of the culinary students rolled a cart over to pick up the dishes. There were my four perfect little plates with piles of yellow zest swimming in puddles of melted ice cream. I pointed to the drippy mess. "Who made those?"

Sawyer looked from her *panna cotta* to the dish tray. "Louie's team made the ice cream."

"Those were my plates his pastry chef stole from the walk-in."

Smitty took the spoon from Sawyer and scored himself the last bite of my dessert. "I liked the goo design you put on your plates. I thought it was fancy." He tasted the *panna cotta* before Sawyer could grab the spoon away from him. "Hmm. So that's what those ugly yellow fingers taste like."

Aunt Ginny grabbed my arm. "I have an idea. Come with me."

She wound her way around the kitchens of Vidrine and Louie, and dragged me into the kitchen of Philippe who was locking his box of knives. "Chef Philippe, I really enjoyed your *Coquilles St. . . .* whatever you called them."

Philippe's eyes crinkled when he smiled. "*Merci*, madame. I am so pleased." He waved a finger. "But you were not so happy with my sous chef's appetizer, were you?"

Aunt Ginny stumbled for words. "Um . . . I believe that was the limp shrimp on a cracker, wasn't it?"

"It was a shrimp canape."

"Well, it was a nice try, anyway." Aunt Ginny hurried

along. "Chef, I was wondering, have you ever considered putting out a cookbook of your recipes?"

Philippe stammered. "Oh, I don't think . . . m-maybe someday."

"Oh, you should, shouldn't he, Poppy?"

I nodded my head yes. Aunt Ginny was digging her fingernails into my palm, so I was afraid if I opened my mouth, I would cry out in pain.

"I think it would be a best seller. Bess had a lot of successful cookbooks, didn't she?"

Philippe picked up his knife case. "It is something to dream about." He tried to get away from us, but Aunt Ginny threw her hip into him. She jabbed me in the side.

"Oh! Um . . . did . . . did you know Bess very well?"

Philippe stopped and considered us for a moment. "No. I never met her before zee event. But then, I spent many years in Paree before I open *La Maîtrisse*."

"Really?" Aunt Ginny tried to sound nonthreatening. "She certainly loved your cooking. I think you may be the only chef that she appreciated."

Philippe cleared his throat and looked behind us for an exit.

"That's true," I said, "I was sure you were going to win the whole competition because of it."

"That would be quite a boon for you," Aunt Ginny added. "Do you have plans for the prize money? You know, if you do win?"

Philippe rocked back on his heels. "I want to expand my kitchen and have a walk-up coffee shop window open to the beach."

Wow. That's a really good idea.

Philippe took a big step to the side, so Aunt Ginny blocked him again. "Wasn't that just terrible about

Horatio this afternoon? You must be so glad to see him off the judges' table. He was brutal with your reviews."

Philippe narrowed his eyes. "I think the reviews by the judges are purely for television ratings and zee Facebook."

"You don't think we've been given honest reviews?" I asked.

"I do not. My recipes are tried and tested to be zee very best. It is why I have zee Michelin Star. The judges are imbeciles if they do not recognize that."

Aunt Ginny goaded him further. "I don't know. The pageant girl and the weatherman, maybe. But Horatio Duplessis is a well-known food critic. His column is in the *New York Journal Food Digest* for a reason." Aunt Ginny nodded to me.

"I've heard his reviews can ruin a restaurant overnight. Have you ever been reviewed by Horatio? You know, for his column?"

Philippe's lips tightened. He waved his hand in dismissal. "I do not believe so. I do not put much stock in restaurant editorials. The only people who read them are trying to impress someone. *La Maîtrisse* is very well regarded in South Jersey. We are listed as one of zee ten best restaurants at the shore, and we are booked several weeks out. It doesn't matter what Horatio or any magazine says. It is all a bunch of nonsense written by people who were not good enough to become chefs themselves. Now if you ladies will excuse me, I must get to *La Maîtrisse* and prepare for dinner. Zat is, if I have a restaurant left after this disaster of a week." He tucked his knife case under his arm and pushed past us.

Aunt Ginny gave me a look. "What do you think?"

"I'm not sure. He said he didn't know Bess, and he seemed unfazed about his reviews from Horatio. And ten thousand dollars is a lot more money to someone who's struggling to pay the bills than to someone who's successful. Not much motive to poison either judge there."

"If he's telling the truth."

"True."

"You're going to have to check out Horatio's column on that doohickey in your office."

"My laptop?"

"That's it. We need to see who in this room has been reviewed by the high and mighty food critic."

"And what about Bess?"

"Run a search on your doodad, and we'll see what comes up."

Note to self, search on my doodad.

I looked around the arena for Tim to say good-bye; he and Gigi were nowhere to be found. But there was my Italian, leaning against the counter in Momma's kitchen, watching me with a mischievous grin in his eyes.

"Are you leaving, Bella?"

"Yes, I need to get Aunt Ginny home. I wish you'd let me give you your keys back. I feel silly driving your car when you're coming up here every day yourself."

He reached out and took my hand. "Momma doesn't drive, and the Spider is only for two." He pulled me closer and gave me a hug. "You did good today."

"I almost didn't finish on time. I ruined the first batch."

"I never had any doubt. Do you feel better now that someone else was taken in for questioning?"

"I don't feel like I'm in danger of being arrested tonight, but we'll see what tomorrow holds."

Momma came in from the locker room, her purse

in her hands, her coat over her arm. She threw me a scowl and rolled her eyes up to Gia. "*Andiamo.*"

"Gia, before you go, has *Mia Famiglia* ever been reviewed in Horatio's column?"

Gia turned to his mother and asked her my question.

She shook her head no and said something that I interpreted as she didn't think so.

"She said she never heard of Horatio or his column before this week."

"Come on Poppy, get the lead out!" Aunt Ginny was waiting on the other side of me, her purse in her hands, her coat over her arm. She and Momma made a pair of matching old lady bookends. I had a fleeting vision that this could be my future. I shook the thought loose before it could get comfortable.

"I'll see you tomorrow." Gia kissed my forehead.

I helped Aunt Ginny put her coat on, and, with a final nod to each other, we readied ourselves for the dash through the angry mob of Facebook activists.

Chapter Twenty-Three

Aunt Ginny, Sawyer, and I were assembled in the kitchen over a pot of decaf. I'd taken some of Aunt Ginny's black walnut Christmas cake out of the freezer and gently warmed it, wishing the gluten-free cake could act as an antidote to all the gluten I'd eaten this week working for Tim. My face itched, I had heartburn, and I was so bloated I was back in my yoga pants.

I had set up my laptop and was researching *New York Journal Food Digest* articles. "Horatio's column goes back almost thirty years. That's longer than some of these chefs have been alive." I typed *La Maîtrisse* in the search bar.

Sawyer dropped the stack of *Food Digest* back issues she'd picked up at the library onto the kitchen table.

Aunt Ginny took one from the stack. "You girls mess around with your hickeys. I'm going the old-fashioned route."

Sawyer and I made funny faces at each other at Aunt Ginny's mention of hickeys, one of her random words when she couldn't remember what something was called. We giggled silently before falling down our Internet rabbit holes.

"I remember when everything on the Internet was free. Now everyone wants you to pay for subscription access to see it," I groused.

Aunt Ginny flipped through her magazine looking for Horatio's column. "Oh, if only those two girls you got staying here could have heard that. They'd think you're as old as I am."

"I think they already do. . . . Oh! I found something. Six months ago, Horatio reviewed Philippe's restaurant." I scanned the review. "He said the food was bland and derivative and lacking imagination."

"No!" Sawyer swung her head around to read over my shoulder.

"Chef Philippe's choice of wine does nothing to elevate the *boeuf* bourguignon which comes out of the kitchen both tough and overly salted. The vichyssoise was not chilled, but served room temperature. It's a careless chef who does not properly clean the sand out of the leeks, resulting in an unpleasant gritty experience and showing a lack of proper training."

Sawyer puckered her lips. "Ooh, ouch."

"There's a rebuttal printed. A couple weeks later Philippe wrote the paper saying, "Mr. Duplessis's review of *La Maîtrisse* is so far off the mark that I can't help but wonder if he was in the right restaurant. Perhaps his palate is not as refined as he thinks. He should stick to what he knows, fast food and failure."

Aunt Ginny sucked air in through her teeth. "That old frog bold-face lied to us. He said he didn't think he'd been reviewed by Horatio." She got to the end of her magazine, closed it, and picked up the next one.

Sawyer went back to her tablet. "I'm going to look for reviews on The Dawg Houz."

"Okay, I'll look for Adrian."

Sawyer stopped typing. "Why are you looking for Adrian?"

"Because we have to look at everyone."

"Fine. Then I'm going to look up Tim."

"You can't be serious."

"We have to look at everyone."

"Fine."

We both started typing furiously. I prayed that Sawyer wouldn't find anything bad about Tim, but she hit pay dirt first.

"Ha! Maxine's Bistro. Tim was reviewed two years ago."

I held my breath while Sawyer read the review, Aunt Ginny peering just over the top of her magazine.

"Actually, it looks like Horatio gave Tim a semi-decent review. He says his crab cakes were dry and tasteless, like they'd been made out of sawdust, but his lobster bisque gave meaning to the crustacean's premature death. And his chicken piccata is tangy and tender, everything you'd want it to be."

"That's not so bad. I wonder why his reviews have been so critical during Restaurant Week."

"Because now Tim is competing against top chefs."

"What is that supposed to mean?"

"Just that it's easy to get good reviews when there isn't any competition."

Aunt Ginny put her magazine down.

I picked up my coffee. "There's plenty of competition in Restaurant Week, and I think Tim is doing well."

"Well sure," Sawyer shot back. "So, would Adrian if he were cozying up to Miss New Jersey." Sawyer started typing again, and I knew she was looking up Adrian.

"I've already got him."

Her tapping silenced.

Aunt Ginny's eyes shifted from me, to Sawyer, back to me.

"Baxter's By the Bay has received multiple reviews in Horatio's column."

Sawyer took a deep breath.

"Six years ago, Horatio said that Baxter's By the Bay has all the charm of a shopping mall food court, but half the class."

Aunt Ginny said, "Oof."

"Three years ago, Horatio said that Baxter's Raw Bar was the perfect cure for constipation. Just one of Chef Adrian's bad clams will cause an immediate evacuation of everything you've eaten for days. That nickel you swallowed when you were seven, get ready for change."

Sawyer deflated.

"And four months ago, Horatio said, 'Adrian Baxter's cooking is showy and without substance. I was hesitant to review Baxter's again, but I'm a firm believer in second chances, so I finally acquiesced to Mr. Baxter's many pleas. Regret, thy name is Crab Imperial. The title of chef should be earned and not just handed out willy-nilly by teachers selling expensive diplomas. Until Chef Baxter can learn how to properly season a bouillabaisse, this restaurant critic will not be returning.'"

"Good heavens." Aunt Ginny looked from me to Sawyer.

"Wow," I said. "This kind of moves Adrian up to suspect number one on the Horatio-as-the-victim page."

Sawyer crossed her arms on the table and leaned

forward. "Whoever killed Bess is probably the same person who's been sabotaging the other chefs, right? Well I happen to know for a fact that there was no way Adrian could have sabotaged the equipment, because he was out with me after the first round."

"Did you spend the whole night together?"

Sawyer blushed. "No."

"Then there was plenty of time where he could have snuck into the kitchen in the middle of the night."

"Just how was he going to sneak into the community college after hours? They have a security guard."

"I don't know, but someone did."

The kitchen door flew open and Miss New Jersey burst over the threshold. She held her arms straight out, a fuzzy gray ball squirming at the end of them. She sneezed. "Dis wab in my roomb again."

"I'm sorry." I took the ball of fur from her and offered her a dose of Benadryl. She looked terrible.

"Ip I can tade ady ob da pood tomorrow, I will make dure you ged a bad rebiew, no matter wad desserd you mate." She sneezed two more times, then did a runway pivot and took her leopard print stiletto boots back out of the kitchen.

"I've told her not to leave her door open when she leaves the room." I held Figaro out in front of me and glared at him. "Can cats smile? I think he just smiled." I gave him a cuddle and a pet that he didn't deserve, and put him down next to his water bowl. He stretched and gave himself a congratulatory bath.

Aunt Ginny picked up another magazine. "Maybe the person who sabotaged the kitchen isn't the same person who killed Bess. Maybe the killer thought the sabotage would provide good cover for a murder."

We searched the Internet in silence for a while longer. The words were starting to run together on my screen. "I can't find anything for The Dawg Houz or Slap Yo Mamma! in Horatio's reviews, good or bad. Of course, Slap Yo Mamma! is brand new. Vidrine has only been open a couple of months."

Sawyer put her tablet down. "I guess that does open up the suspect list. Louie has the most mechanical ability to be able to sabotage all those appliances, and Vidrine was sneaking around the arena after the competition. Something just feels off with both of them."

"That's true," I agreed, "but don't forget that Adrian has the biggest window of opportunity since he's the only chef who has every night off."

Aunt Ginny took another magazine from the stack.

Sawyer took a bite of her cake and tried to shift the suspicion off of Adrian again. "Well, I don't believe that flimsy excuse that Vidrine gave you about retrieving her chef knives. She was up to something."

"I get the feeling it involves Louie."

Sawyer nodded. "Only Louie and Vidrine don't have any connection to Horatio that we've found."

"None of Horatio's bad reviews mean anything if Bess was the intended victim."

"Yes," Sawyer went on, "but they could be the key to finding out who the killer is if Horatio was the target after all."

"Ah ha!" Aunt Ginny tapped her open magazine.

"What did you find?" I asked her.

Aunt Ginny spun her magazine around, so Sawyer and I could read it. The article was from five years ago and it was titled MIA FAMIGLIA, A ONE TRICK PONY. "The only thing that makes this restaurant so successful is the lack of other good Italian eateries at the shore."

"Oh no. I have to show this to Gia. Either Momma lied, or this is going to be the first time she's heard about this."

Aunt Ginny cut herself a piece of cake. "If Horatio wasn't the intended victim before, he will be now."

Chapter Twenty-Four

I heard Horatio come in sometime late last night. I guess the cops were considering him a victim and not a suspect. Of course, I'd been a suspect before, and I was released on bail. Bail that Tim had paid for by putting up Maxine's as collateral.

On my way down the stairs I heard Miss New Jersey scream, "Oh no you didn't! That is my best pair of leggings!"

I knocked on the door. It opened enough for two hands to thrust a squirmy gray cat at me.

I took Fig down the stairs to the kitchen and opened a can of gourmet mutilated fish guts. "Your breakfast, my lord." Figaro smashed his face in the bowl and went to town. Then I made the coffee. Aunt Ginny and I shared a philosophy. Coffee first. Coffee second. Then we get on with the day. After my second cup of coffee, I made a gorgeous blackberry crumble and a batch of fluffy pancakes for the morning meal.

The guest breakfast was a quiet affair, each one taking their plate to a different room of the house to eat. Miss New Jersey went out on the sun porch. The door opened a minute later, and Figaro was booted into the kitchen. Tess and Norman took their plates to the library, and Ashlee sat alone at the dining room table. I'd made her the avocado on toast that she'd requested, so she was happily taking pictures of it.

Horatio retreated to his room. No one saw him again until we all arrived at the community college, where he was standing out front holding a press conference.

"I'm sorry to say, the dire reports of my person being in jeopardy have not been exaggerated. An attempt was made on my life that was unintentionally thwarted by my dear friend and colleague, Bess Jodice. She was a champion of quality in the world of epicurean education, as well as an inspiration and a mentor in the field of culinary journalism. Her effusive words of assessment will never be forgotten by the eager students who were fortunate enough to learn from her. This week I've seen ingredient tampering, equipment vandalism, and now a heinous murder. A most wretched person is going to great lengths to sabotage this restaurant week competition. And for what? All to win an award for making dinner. Something most mothers do seven nights a week without ever receiving a bit of praise. When did the art of cooking become elevated to celebrity status? Instead of saving lives, protecting the innocent, or teaching the next generation, chefs are being lauded like superheroes for frying chicken. Somewhere in that room is a chef who should be ashamed of themself. I don't have any information about the investigation, but I certainly hope the police are able to bring to justice"—Horatio teared up and had to take out his white pocket square and dab his eyes until he composed himself—"to whoever is responsible for this hateful atrocity."

Too overcome with emotion to answer questions fired off by the yoga-pants cartel, Horatio excused himself and ducked into the college.

Aunt Ginny and I pushed our way through the crowd and followed his footsteps to the kitchen arena. A muscular, red-haired officer stood guard at the entrance. I recognized him as one of the officers that had stood watch at my house a few weeks back. "Hi. I see you're back from your time off."

"Yep, Doc says I'm ready for the field again." He turned to see Aunt Ginny and flinched.

She gave him a toothy smile. "Remember me?"

He reached up to his collarbone and clicked on his radio. "Officer Birkwell requesting the situation at the college to be upgraded from Code Yellow to Code Orange, with a possible 10-96."

Aunt Ginny narrowed her eyes. "That better not be about me."

He gave a crisp nod in my direction. "What can I do for you ladies?"

"I'm competing in the event. I'll be here all week. Are you on duty?"

"The department has agreed to allow the event to proceed, as long as an officer is present at all times."

Aunt Ginny poked him in the arm. "Very smart. Keep all the perps in one place so you can keep an eye on them."

I sucked in a lungful of air. "Aunt Ginny! I'm sure that's not what they're doing." I looked at Officer Birkwell. "Is it?"

His neck blushed in patches. "Actually, yeah."

Aunt Ginny gave me a smug look. "See. You can learn a lot from watching *CSI*."

Office Birkwell cleared his throat. "The captain thought it would be a good way to observe and report while we collect evidence and complete our investigation. All the suspects are in this room, so one of us will be nearby at all times."

Aunt Ginny grabbed my elbow. "Come on, you gotta get that ugly yellow apron on, and I've got to get my lead sheets"—she rolled her eyes up to Officer Birkwell—"I mean crossword puzzles, ready for the day."

She started to pull me away from Officer Birkwell, but I managed to turn back and whisper, "What's a 10-96?"

He answered under his breath. "Psych patient."

Yeah, I get that. I let Aunt Ginny make her way into the arena, but I veered off to the locker room. I stored my purse and grabbed my hideous yellow apron. Horatio's words had rung deep in my heart. Perhaps we do put too much praise on certain careers. Athletes, movie stars, musicians, and, I guess, chefs. At the end of the day, how much do they improve the quality of the lives around them by being able to smoke a rack of ribs? Or make a fudgy brownie. Or a vanilla-scented strawberry shortcake. *Where am I going with this?* I guess each one of us has something near and dear to our hearts. I know that if the world were ending, I would ransack the Hostess factory long before I would try to save my DVD collection. Priorities.

Entering the arena, I considered the other chefs and wondered which one could be Bess's killer. The problem was, there were two possible victims with two very different suspect lists. Throw in the sabotage, and we might be dealing with two different perpetrators entirely.

We'd passed the midway point of Restaurant Week. We were all so hopeful and excited in the beginning, now desperate for it to be over. The current standings were posted, and Team Maxine's was in third place just behind Adrian, with Philippe in the lead. Leaving out the basket ingredient really hurt us on day three. But at least we weren't in last place. That spot was reserved for Momma, who had received zeros on two of the four days for ignoring the theme and making what she wanted.

I walked past Sawyer, who was being regaled by Adrian with stories of his success.

"We were so busy last night, I was turning people away at the door. Everyone wants to try my award-winning coconut scallops after yesterday's high score."

"Thank goodness you're opening a second restaurant right away." Sawyer reached out and touched the dragon on Adrian's arm. "That way no one will have to be disappointed."

I felt my eyes roll of their own volition and kept walking.

Louie was talking to Philippe. "I haven't had a single customer all week, dude. Not even Fat Betty for her daily deep-fried macaroni and cheese burger, man. And she loves those. If business doesn't pick up soon I might have to sell The Dawg Houz and buy my food truck back."

"*La Maîtrisse* is slower zan we have ever been." Philippe covered his heart with his hand. "Where are all my loyal customers? What will happen to Philippe?"

Gia's greeting warmed me from the inside out. "Hey, beautiful."

I gave him a bright smile and held in guffawing like a hillbilly. *Hey, Sexy.* Okay, I didn't really say that, but I thought it. "Hi. I have to show you something."

"What is it?"

I handed Gia the magazine with Horatio's review of Momma's restaurant. He scanned it quickly, his expression clouding over. "I have to tell her." He gave me a tight smile and tapped me on the arm with the magazine, then went off to deliver the bad news.

Things were dire for everyone's restaurant. Well, everyone's except Adrian's. Curious.

I found Tim and Gigi in the corner discussing possible basket themes based on what we'd seen all week. "What about a Japanese theme? I could do sushi. Or Russian. Do you know how to make borscht?"

"Tim, can I ask you something?"

Gigi turned on me. "Poppy, if you would spend more time preparing for the event and less time running your mouth, we might actually be in the lead."

"I beg your pardon, I don't remember anyone accusing my *panna cotta* of being flabby and without excitement."

Gigi huffed. "My summer rolls were delicious! They are just holding the real chefs to a higher standard, and they know you're an amateur."

"Well this girl's amateur desserts helped cover for your coffee-dusted hot pockets."

Gigi's face burned crimson. "They were empanadas."

"Yeah, well Horatio called them 'empa-nadagoods.'"

Gigi spun around and stormed off.

Tim watched her go and chuckled. He leaned down and kissed me on the forehead. "Don't worry about Gigi. You've been a real trooper this week, and I appreciate all your help with the competition. If anyone can sniff out the saboteur and save Maxine's, it's you."

My stomach did a little flip and my breath caught. I reached up and curled that lock of blond hair at the base of Tim's neck around my finger. Our eyes met, and seventeen-year-old Poppy's emotions came flooding back.

The moment was interrupted when across the room we heard "Gyaaahhh!"

Momma broke into a fit and was head down rushing at Horatio. Her pastry chef caught her by the spandex of her girdle through her flowered dress and spun her around toward Gia who wrapped his arms around her voluminous waist to restrain her.

Tim had worked in professional kitchens for a lot of years and wasn't as fazed by the sight of a chef losing their cool. "What'd you want to ask me?"

"How important are reviews for a restaurant?"

"It depends. Some people never read reviews, so they won't know how you're ranked. They'll come to your restaurant to try it out, and if they like the food, they'll come back, period. Others will check out Yelp and Trip Advisor, and only go to restaurants that have the highest ranking. No matter who those reviews come from or how many reviews that person has left. You could have twenty glowing reviews by real customers who loved your food, and the guy next door has fifty reviews all written by himself under different accounts. Some people will only try the restaurant next door because of a ranking that was built on lies and ambition."

"What about restaurant critics' reviews, like Horatio's column?"

Tim shrugged. "Not everyone follows restaurant critics. Some people would rather follow a favorite blog or Instagrammer. But, bad critic reviews can dissuade influential clients like foodies, celebrities, and wealthy customers looking to celebrate a special occasion. They can even influence rankings with the *Michelin Guide* or *Forbes Travel*."

Hmm, now who told me they were up for a Michelin Star? Philippe maybe?

"Places, everyone!" Ivy called out from the front of the arena.

Tim grabbed his apron and tied it around his waist. "Some critics have built their fan base from writing scathing reviews. The worse the review, the better the fame. People love to read about chefs getting ripped apart."

"Have you seen your review by Horatio?"

Tim shrugged the question off. "Yeah, getting a bad review by Horatio Duplessis is like a rite of passage. But you can't let it bother you."

"So, you don't remember what he said?"

"It wasn't important, but I think it was something about my crab cakes being dry and tasteless like they'd been made out of sawdust."

For someone who doesn't remember, that was word for word.

Tim looked around and gave me a quick kiss. "Good luck today, Mack."

We took our places, and the baskets were brought out. While Ivy hooked Tess up to the microphone, I pulled out my phone and looked up Baxter's By the Bay on Yelp. Adrian had twenty-eight five-star reviews left since last night. All from new accounts with no other reviews. All written in the same style with the same bad grammar. The night before he'd had twenty-seven one-star reviews left from various accounts around South Jersey. A couple of the faces I recognized from the protest line out front.

Tim said bad reviews were a rite of passage, but these guys cared more than they let on.

Chapter Twenty-Five

"Before we get started with today's competition, I have good news. I'm so excited to announce that Roger is back. Please everyone, a round of huzzah for Roger!"

Roger bounced into the arena and gave a big wave and a couple of bows. The audience cheered for the hometown boy who had gone up against the police department and, so far, had won.

If both Roger and Horatio have been released, who do the police still have their eyes on as their prime suspect?

Ivy gave the countdown to begin taping and Tess announced the mystery ingredients for the day. Whoever designed these baskets must have been working their way around the world. France, Italy, Asia, and tonight's challenge—the British Country Dinner. My basket had Earl Grey tea, black walnuts, and treacle. I had watched enough episodes of *Nigella* to know that treacle could be used just like honey or corn syrup, so no problem there, but the only thing I knew how to make with black walnuts was Aunt Ginny's Christmas cake, and one hour was sure not enough time to make a Bundt.

I could try cupcakes. No, that would be far too pedestrian for Horatio, not to mention the fit Norman would have with it. We needed some "wow" dishes to bring our score up. *I could do madeleines.* Madeleines look fancy, but at the end of the day they're really easy. They're first cousins to the muffin, and they bake really fast. But no way would that be enough to win the day over Philippe's pastry chef. I needed something lovely to dip them into. *I don't know what to make. Man, I need some chocolate. Ooh, chocolate. Earl Grey chocolate? That could be interesting.*

I searched in the pantry to find all the ingredients needed to make chocolate pots of cream. I backed into Philippe, who had his arms full of bacon, garlic, thyme, button mushrooms, and pearl onions. I knew the entrée basket contained squab because Tim was complaining about deboning it, so I had a suspicion about Philippe's dish. "If you had a bottle of red wine I'd think you were making *Coq au Vin.*" I gave him a friendly smile. I'd seen it made on *The French Chef* a hundred times and had the recipe memorized.

Philippe frowned like I'd caught him doing something naughty. Then he took the bottle of Merlot off the shelf and shoved it under his arm. He cut his eyes to me one more time before darting back to his kitchen. *Did I just plant that idea or was that his plan all along?*

I steeped my Earl Grey teabags in heavy cream for five minutes while I set out all my ingredients for the two dishes.

With Horatio back on the judges' panel, Aunt Ginny was up in the Thunderdome shaking down the seniors to place their bets. The biddies were pointing to the judges and waving dollar bills and coupons in the air, and Sawyer was jotting down notes in a steno book. I wanted to be frustrated with them, but instead I found myself wondering what odds my dessert had today.

Over at the judges' table, Miss New Jersey was staring blankly into space. Stormin' Norman and Ashlee were both making faces into their phones. They could save a lot of time if they'd just take pictures of each other. Only Horatio was paying attention, and he was avidly grilling the chefs in the kitchens. Probably looking for signs of poison or sabotage that could head his way. I felt sorry for him. Not only had he lost a friend, but he was also dealing with news that he might have been the original target for murder. Since the killer was still free, his life was in danger just by being in the room.

I made my Earl Grey chocolate pots of cream first, since they would need thirty or so minutes in the oven. While they baked, I mixed together my black walnut madeleines.

The room was filling with smells of roasting chicken and butter. Tess was working her way around the room, interviewing the chefs about their dishes. Roger was following along, taking pictures and tweeting updates.

"What are you making, Chef Tim?"

"I'm making breast of squab topped with honey aioli and cocoa nibs, with a side of fiddlehead fern and parsnip mash."

"Oh, nice. You're the first chef who isn't making sautéed fiddlehead ferns. Good for you. You hear that Brandy?" Tess called across the arena.

"Can I have a sample, Chef Tim?"

Tim flashed Miss New Jersey a huge smile and held up a spoon. She left her place at the judges' table and slinked her way over to the kitchen. Then, without breaking eye contact with Tim, she leaned deeply over the counter and put her mouth around the spoon.

Both Gigi and I had been frozen in place, watching the shameless display. We all waited for Ivy to yell cut, but she never did. Mrs. Dodson, however, called out, "Hussy is as hussy does."

Mother Gibson and her church group were shaking their heads. "Oh no, she didn't. Child, that girl is trouble."

The other biddies shook their heads in agreement. "Mmmhmm."

Miss New Jersey purred, "I'm going to give that a ten." She pulled Tim's hand to her lips and wiped her mouth with his finger. Then she spun around and sashayed back to alight upon her perch.

Gigi and I looked at each other, and an understanding passed between us. "The enemy of my enemy is my friend." From that moment on, we were all about blocking Miss New Jersey from making moves on our chef.

I put my madeleines in the oven and retrieved my plates. Roger was on his way to Vidrine's kitchen to post pictures of her food. I intercepted him before he got away. "Hey, it's good to see you back with us."

"Thank you. That was the scariest thing that's ever happened to me."

"I can imagine." *Believe you me.* "I wanted to ask you something. Bess was staying at my bed and breakfast, so the police have been questioning me, and I was wondering, from one innocent person to another, what did they ask you about?"

Roger looked around. "I'm not really supposed to talk about it, but they were asking a lot of questions about Ms. Jodice's tea and her honey."

"What did they ask about her tea? Have they tested it yet? Did they find something funky in it?"

"No, they didn't know anything as far as I could tell. They were more interested in what I did with it, and like—where did I get it? How did I make it? Did anyone else touch it? And of course, who set the tables?"

Who sets the tables? Why didn't I think of that? "Who did set the tables?"

Roger looked like he might cry. "I did. But I used the flatware from the pantry. It was all clean. I'm a film student. I don't know anything about table setting. I didn't know it was backwards."

"No, of course not." I patted Roger's bony shoulder. "I believe you. And the culinary students, they broke it down every day and cleared the dishes?"

"Yeah. They're getting credits for attending the competition and helping with cleanup since they can't use these kitchens for their own studies this week."

I nodded. "Uh huh, uh huh. And have you heard any of them talking about Ms. Jodice? Anyone claim to know her or dislike her?"

Roger's voice squeaked. "She was an old lady. Her name is all over this building, so they knew she was a big deal, but everyone here was in elementary school when she retired. No one had ever met her."

"How about Horatio Duplessis? You hear anyone talking about him?"

"Oh yeah. Every kitchen I go to. These chefs all hate Horatio. Apparently, he's ruined some of their lives."

"Mmm hmm. Who specifically said that?"

Ivy hollered from across the room. "Roger! Keep it moving."

"I'm sorry, I gotta tweet. But it's all the chefs. I've even heard . . ." Roger nudged his head and rolled his eyes toward Tim and Gigi. "You know . . . they aren't his biggest fans either."

I couldn't believe it. I hadn't heard them say anything. I guess I don't know everything that's going on between Tim and his mentee. "Well, let's both hang in there. And if you hear anything about that tea you'll let me know, okay?"

Roger gave me a timid smile.

When I returned to my station, I heard Vidrine being interviewed by Tess for the camera. "Honey, I don't use recipes. I got all my momma's knowledge stored in my heart. When I cook, I cook by love."

The audience was eating it up. Rows of pink and white hair were nodding their approval.

Mrs. Dodson hollered down to Aunt Ginny, "I bet she's sleeping with Nick Nolte over there."

Mrs. Davis took out her wallet. "I'll take that bet."

"Your restaurant is a new one to Cape May," Tess was saying. "When can locals try your island cuisine for themselves?"

"We're open seven days a week right now. Monday through Saturday for dinner, and Sunday mornin' for brunch. Y'all should come down and see us at Slap Yo Momma! You won't be disappointed."

My head shot up so fast from embellishing my plates that for a minute I saw stars. I found Sawyer in the audience. Her eyes were as big as two cippolini onions. She'd heard that same thing I had. Vidrine only served brunch on Sunday. She'd lied about needing her knives for Sunday dinner. I was so mad I could just shake her. *Why you gotta go and lie to me like that?*

You can believe I planned on bringing that up, too, just as soon as I was finished with today's challenge. I plated two madeleines next to a warm, gooey pot of baked chocolate custard and watched Vidrine. Her entire team was finished and standing confidently behind their counter. I looked around. Team Louie was also relaxed behind three sets of finished dishes.

"Five minutes!" Tess gave the warning, and the other kitchens continued to hustle. Everyone rushed to plate their dish and garnish it just right. Everyone except Teams Vidrine and Louie.

I gave a final tap of powdered sugar through a sifter over my plates. I had six desserts. Four for the judges, and two extras just in case one was dropped, or . . . I wanted to eat it.

I was finished two minutes ahead of time. I looked at Tim's plates. His roasted breast of squab was beautiful, and the buttery turnip and fiddlehead mash made a nice bed for the golden-brown meat.

Gigi had made gorgeous Cornish pasties. "Is the marmalade inside?"

She blinked. "What?"

"The marmalade. Is it inside the hand pies? It's a basket ingredient you're required to use."

The blood rushed from Gigi's face. "Oh no."

"Quick, put a dollop on each plate like a dipping sauce." I grabbed a handful of rosemary and plucked four tiny tufts. "Here, put this on the marmalade. It will cut the sweetness."

Gigi did as I said and didn't question. She was rattled after that brazen display by Miss New Jersey.

"Time's up!"

We stood back and waited for our turn to face the judges. Making a TV show took a lot longer than real life. Everything was spread out with breaks, so the camera could get just the right shot, or the host could deliver their line perfectly. Sometimes we had an hour between finishing our dishes and the food actually being tasted. Other than the hour we spent cooking, there was a lot of hurry up and wait. Today was no exception.

All in all, we did very well at our turn before the judging squad. I was especially proud of Horatio's comment to Tim about the dipping sauce for the Cornish pasty. "I really like the way the sous chef cut the sweetness of the marmalade with the addition of the herbs. Well done."

I tried not to gloat too hard, but come on—it was Gigi. Queen of the kitchen, ruler over every move I made. Criticizer of all things great and small. I had to gloat a little. Gigi wouldn't look me in the eye. It was hard enough for her to say thanks through gritted teeth.

Tim whispered, "Good job, chefs. Hopefully that pushes us ahead of Adrian."

Gigi clapped her hands together. "Louie was done early today. I hope that isn't a bad sign for us."

It's a bad sign of something.

Adrian was up next, and he was telling the judges all about his bold use of Worcestershire, when Ashlee grabbed her throat and screamed.

"Ack! There's peanut butter in this! I'm allergic to peanuts! Someone poisoned me!"

Horatio shot up from his chair. "Oh, good God!"

Officer Birkwell called for an ambulance on his police radio.

At first, we thought it was a stunt, but Ashlee was swelling up before our eyes.

Tess just stood there holding the microphone. "Where is your EpiPen, you stupid cow?"

Adrian started jumping around like a cricket in a

frying pan. "I didn't use any peanuts. Really, there are no peanut products in my food, I promise."

Ashlee pointed under the table. "I have an EpiPen in my purse."

Ivy ran back and forth screeching. "Roger! Roger! Call an ambulance!"

Tess was still very calm. She rested a hand on her hip. "Someone get her her purse."

Norman grabbed Ashlee's purse and rifled through it. He pulled out a long gold tube and handed it to Ashlee.

Her whole face was swollen and blotchy and she was starting to gasp for breath. "That's mascara, idiot."

There was nothing we could do. No amount of first aid was going to help. A peanut allergy only had one remedy.

Adrian was on his knees, his head in his hands, pleading. "I . . . I didn't use any peanuts. I don't know where they came from."

Miss New Jersey grabbed Ashlee's purse and dumped it out on the judges' table. "There, find your EpiPen. I don't know what that looks like."

Ashlee was holding her hands over her throat. Her face was bugging out like a toad. She pawed through the contents on the table, panic in her eyes. "It's not here."

Tess walked calmly to the table. "What do you mean it's not here? You aren't supposed to go anywhere without it."

"I . . . can't . . . breathe."

We all felt helpless and terrified.

Mother Gibson waddled out of the stadium seating and fast shuffled over to Ashlee. Then, with her fist way up in the air, she called out, "Lord Jesus, take the wheel!" And her hand came down and punched Ashlee's thigh.

The panic began to subside in Ashlee's eyes, and her breathing slowed to a less terrifying gasp.

Mother Gibson slapped a used EpiPen on the table. "My grandson Oliver is allergic to peanuts. I never leave home without one."

Chapter Twenty-Six

The kitchen arena was a swarm of activity. Campus paramedics arrived first, followed by the rescue squad, and, bringing up the rear, the Cape May County Police.

Office Amber arrived and took over like she does. "This room is under lockdown. Nobody leaves unless I say so."

Ashlee was wrapped in a blanket to prevent shock, something Adrian was also in great need of. He was off to the side of his kitchen sitting on an upturned crate smoking a cigarette with shaky hands. Roger tried to tell him that he couldn't smoke on campus grounds, but Adrian had a crazed look in his eyes, so Roger wisely chose not to press the issue. The rest of us pulled up chairs, crates, and countertops wherever we could, to watch the drama unfold.

"Someone tried to kill me." Ashlee croaked out through swollen, alien-looking lips. "Probably Tess. She's been trying to steal the spotlight for months."

Tess tossed her hair and exhaled. "How exactly would I poison you, chica? I've been busy interviewing the chefs this entire time."

"You could have poisoned my food from any kitchen. You've been in all of them."

Amber took out her flip book and a pen. "Your name, please."

"Teresa Maria Consuela Rodriguez."

"Did you know the victim was allergic to peanuts?"

Tess examined her manicure. "Jes, I knew."

Ashlee flapped her blanket like wings. "I told you she did it."

"Did you slip a peanut product into the victim's food?"

"No."

"Did you at any time come into contact with the food in this arena?"

"No."

"Did you see anyone working with or around peanuts or peanut products?"

"No."

Ashlee whined. "She's lying."

Tess stretched like a cat. "Watch the footage from today's taping. You'll see on camera that I haven't touched any of the dishes."

Amber turned to Ivy. "I'm going to need access to all your tapes from today."

"Of course. Anything you need."

Amber let the paramedics take Ashlee to the hospital to be checked out. Then she asked all the chef teams to gather close together in the center of the arena. One of the officers took out a cell phone and held it up like he was filming us.

Amber asked the chefs collective questions. "Were any nuts used in today's dishes?"

The chefs were stunned into silence, so I answered for all of us. "The dessert baskets contained black walnuts, but they aren't in the same family as peanuts."

Amber sighed. She pointed to her other officer. "Go collect all the remnants of the walnuts." Then over to Ivy. "Anything else?"

Ivy shook her head no. "Not in the baskets."

"Whose food was the victim eating when she came into contact with the allergen?"

Everyone in the room pointed to Adrian.

Amber's eyebrows shot up. "Okay. Name please."

"Adrian Baxter."

"Mr. Baxter, did you use any peanuts or peanut products in your cooking today?"

"No ma'am."

"Perhaps in a sauce or a seasoning packet? Sometimes allergens are hiding in other foods."

"No, everything was cooked fresh from whole ingredients. Nothing came into contact with peanuts while in my hands. I can't vouch for the purity of the ingredients in the pantry after the situation last Saturday."

Amber took notes. "Right, the ingredient sabotage. Did anyone notice any sabotaged ingredients in their foods today?"

Everyone murmured no.

"Did the victim mention that she had a peanut allergy?"

We all answered more emphatically this time. "No!"

"It isn't a crime to cook with peanuts. The burden is on the one with the allergies to protect themselves. I just need to know where the peanuts came from so I can rule out malicious intent."

No one moved.

"Really? Nothing? All right, people. This is officially a crime scene."

The uniformed officers rolled yellow crime scene tape over every exit. Amber called for a CSI team to come do the second sweep of the kitchen this week, while she systematically began questioning everyone in the arena. And things had been looking so positive an hour ago.

Mother Gibson was beaming with her newfound hero status. She was basking in the glow of her many congratulatory praises. I joined the group of seniors in the stands to offer my own tribute. "Thank God you were here today. You saved her life."

"I always carry one of Oliver's EpiPens in my bag. I accidentally gave him a sugar cookie that had touched peanut butter cookies once, and he stopped breathing. It scared the life out of me. Thank God, my daughter was with us when it happened. I wonder why that little blonde girl didn't have her own EpiPen. Peanut allergies are so dangerous."

"You're right. Things could have gone very badly for her."

Mrs. Dodson slanted her eyes and nodded gravely. "It really makes you wonder. Who would want to ruin Restaurant Week, plus kill the old judge and the young girl?"

Mrs. Davis twirled a finger in her woolly pink hair. "How is it all connected? You wouldn't think anyone who had a motive to kill that judge would even know Ashlee Pickel. And there's no way Tess would do anything to hurt Ashlee. They're friends. You should see them on camera together."

I smiled at Mrs. Davis. "You watch *Wake Up! South Jersey*? The millennial morning show?"

"I don't watch the whole thing. I start it at eleven when the *Today* show goes off. I can't stand that other show that comes on with the vulgar women."

Aunt Ginny took the notebook from Sawyer and

scanned it. "Twenty-to-one odds that Horatio Duplessis is the next to be poisoned. Fifty-to-one odds that it's Miss New Jersey." Aunt Ginny looked to me. "Unless you have some inside information about the pageant winner that would change those odds?"

I recoiled. "I don't know anything."

Aunt Ginny cocked her head. "Alright."

"You know who I like?" Mrs. Davis asked. "Willard Scott. I hope one day he wishes me happy birthday from the Smuckers people."

Mrs. Dodson looked up to the ceiling and shook her head. "How in the world would that ever happen, Thelma? Willard Scott is as old as you are. You think he'll still be working on the *Today* show when he's a hundred?"

Mother Gibson laughed. "Oh, sweet Jesus."

Mrs. Davis tilted her head to look up at Mrs. Dodson. "Well I have no idea. Maybe he can prerecord a bunch of them. Besides, not everyone retires just because they get old."

The CSI team arrived and began rifling through the pantry and all our dishes. They bagged and tagged samples of Adrian's food, and all the dishes that Ashlee had eaten from. Chef Oliva and Vidrine were off the hook since they hadn't presented yet.

Sawyer grabbed my elbow. "Come on, I want to taste your dessert before they pack it all in that duffel bag."

We jetted down to the kitchen to find one of my desserts was already missing. "Come on!"

I warmed the last ramekin in the microwave. We each grabbed a madeleine and dunked it into the warm gooey Earl Grey chocolate. My madeleine was heading for my mouth when someone swooped in and snatched it out of my hand.

Aunt Ginny plopped the tiny cake in her mouth. "You can't have gluten. I'm just saving you from yourself."

Like I'm going to draw that line now, after the rest of this week? I wanted to protest, but Roger ran into the room calling for Ivy. "Channel Eight news is outside. They want an interview."

Norman jumped up. "I'll do it. They probably want to talk to me anyway. That's my network."

"I don't think they know you're here," Roger said. "They're asking for Tess."

Amber held a hand up. "No way! This is an active investigation. No one leaves this room, and no one talks to the press. I don't want information getting out until I know what I'm dealing with."

Sawyer showed me her cell phone. "Then she won't believe this."

"Twitter already knows that Ashlee was sent to the hospital?" I jabbed a spoon into the chocolate pot and grimaced at Aunt Ginny. "This is gluten free."

"Not only do they know about it, Ashlee is the one who tweeted it. And she recorded a video message to all her viewers from the ambulance."

"Oh man. Wait till Amber finds out."

Sawyer's gaze roved through the arena. She tried to be nonchalant, but I knew who she was looking for.

"He's sitting in his kitchen, brooding."

Sawyer's eyes flicked to mine and then away. "I'm going to go try to cheer him up."

"Good luck with that."

She went in search of Adrian, and I looked around for a miserable blond chef. Gia was interpreting a conversation between Momma and Philippe. I didn't see Momma making any of the rude gestures that were usually aimed at me, so it must have been going well. So where was Tim? For that matter, where was Gigi? And why were they both missing at the same time?

I searched every inch of the kitchen arena until I found Tim sitting in the pantry on a plastic bin of flour. Gigi was crammed in next to him tucked on a low shelf.

"What are you doing in here?"

Tim gave me a weak smile. "Feeling sorry for myself. Wondering how much I can get for my Vulcan range on Craigslist."

I crouched down and put my hand on his knee. "Aw, come on. It's not that bad. At least not yet."

"Who's going to eat in my restaurant once rumor spreads that a chef poisoned not one, but two judges, during Restaurant Week? Who's going to eat in any of our restaurants after this?"

Gigi put her hand on Tim's bicep. "I'm here for you."

Tim jumped up, knocking Gigi's hand off his arm. "Have you found anything out, Mack? Tell me you have an idea about who could be behind this."

"I don't know yet."

"Please keep trying. You have a knack for this kind of thing, and I really need you right now."

Gigi stood and looped her hand around Tim's arm. "We all have our gifts. Mine is cooking. Poppy's may as well be being nosy."

What about my gift of whooping your . . .

"Heeeyyy. There you are."

We all snapped our heads to the pantry door. The opening was filled with perfect mink-brown hair, flawless skin, and legs that started at Gigi's rib cage. Miss New Jersey's curves were swathed in a tight, leopard-print wrap dress, and she knew how to use them for maximum effect.

Tim gave her a sultry smile. "What can I do for you, ma'am?"

Gigi and I shared a moment of silent indignation. *Ma'am?* What happened to depressed and hopeless?

"I thought that since we were on lockdown, we could take this chance to get to know each other better."

Gigi stepped between Tim and Miss New Jersey, much the way a chihuahua would guard her master. "We need to plan our dishes for tomorrow. Now isn't a good time."

Miss New Jersey smiled at Tim, swatting Gigi away like an invisible mosquito. "You don't know what's in the baskets yet."

Gigi answered, "That's why we need so much time to plan. The possibilities are endless."

I could tell Miss New Jersey was trying to wrap her brain around what Gigi was saying. The strain of it was making a wrinkle in her perfect forehead. I had to intervene before she passed out from the stress.

"Actually Brandy, I wanted to talk to you about something. In private."

Gigi threw me a grateful look. "We'll leave the two of you to your girl talk then." She dragged Tim by the wrist back into the kitchen.

Miss New Jersey frowned as she watched Tim leave. "What is it?"

"That was quick thinking earlier, dumping out Ashlee's purse."

"She was turning blue."

"I know. That was very—"

"Freaky."

"I was going to say dangerous, but it was freaky too."

"Cha." Miss New Jersey flipped her hair in agreement.

"Have you had a chance to hang out with either Ashlee or Tess this week?"

"No. I like to do my own thing."

"Sure. I get that. But, not even at the B&B? You guys are there all night."

"Tess is busy with Norman, if you know what I mean."

"I do. What about Ashlee?"

"She's always on her cell phone."

"Do you know what she's doing?"

"The usual. Tweeting, Facebooking, Snapchatting, YouTubing . . .

"LinkedIn."

"What's linked in?"

"Nothing, never mind. Have you ever heard Tess threaten Ashlee?"

"Only that she was going to post an unflattering picture of her."

"Nothing more . . . dire?"

"No."

"Okay, thanks Brandy."

"Sure. Where did Chef Tim go?"

"Mmm, I don't know. You'll have to look for him."

"Okay. How's my makeup?"

"Perfect."

"Phew. I want to make a good impression."

"Don't worry." She could pretty much have worn a bag over her head and she'd still be fine.

Miss New Jersey went in search of Tim—she was Gigi's problem now—and I went in search of Ivy. I had morning-show questions and I hoped she would have network answers.

I found Ivy behind the staging area, trapped as it

were, by Norman. They did not look like they were on the verge of being finished any time soon, so instead of waiting, I moved to plan B.

Tess was sitting alone in her host chair behind the eye of the camera. She was playing a game on her phone.

"Hey Tess, do you have a minute?"

"It's not like I can go anywhere."

"How are you holding up with Ashlee's near-death experience?"

Tess exhaled. "She's such a spotlight hog. She'll probably double her following after this."

"Oh. Okay. Well, keep your chin up."

What the heck is wrong with these two?

"I was wondering, do you have a cooking segment on *Wake Up! South Jersey*?"

"Jes, but it is mostly to show how Ashlee and I don't know how to cook. It doesn't really showcase the chef's talents."

"I understand. I think most chef segments are kind of like that. But I was wondering, more specifically, if any of the chefs in this room had ever been on your show?"

Tess thought for a second. "No."

"Oh, well. It was just an idea I had."

I stood to go.

"Except for Philippe. He was on the show when we first started about three years ago."

"Chef Philippe did a segment with you?"

"Not with me, with Ashlee. It did not go well."

"What happened?"

"Ashlee thought it would be funny to pretend not to like his food. So, when it was time to taste the finished dish, Ashlee spit her bite out into her hand and said it was disgusting. She called JK—that means she was just kidding—but we had already cut to commercial, and then we were out of time. It was just one of those things." Tess shrugged like it wasn't a big deal.

"So, she was never able to tell the viewers that it was a joke?"

"We had to cut to the next segment with the DJ of a silent nightclub on the roof of the Holiday Inn."

"How did Philippe feel about the joke? Was he cool with it?"

"No-oooo-ooo. He was so. Not. Cool. He threatened to sue us, but then he found out our show didn't have any money. So, he swore we would regret it one day."

Well, today might have been the day.

Chapter Twenty-Seven

I had to find Philippe and ask him about that morning show fiasco, and I needed to do it fast. He was our only known link between Horatio and Ashlee. If Horatio had been the intended target instead of Bess, and I think he was, then his harsh reviews of Philippe—both during Restaurant Week and in his column years ago— might have been enough to send the old chef over the edge. Plus, Philippe was the only chef in the arena who had ever been on the morning show, and it hadn't been a love match. I searched the arena and looked for him in his kitchen. Philippe was having a heated argument with Vidrine.

"Poppy. Pssssst! Come over here." Aunt Ginny crooked her finger for me to join her and the biddies in the stands.

I kept one eye on Philippe and went to see what they wanted. "What's up?"

"Which chef did you say used to own a food truck?"

"Hot Sauce Louie, why?"

Aunt Ginny jabbed Mrs. Davis in the side. "See."

"Where is he now?" Mother Gibson asked.

I pointed to Louie down in his kitchen relaying his testimony to Amber. "He's the one who looks like Nick Nolte."

Mrs. Davis giggled. "I remember when he had that little restaurant at the point. He had the best crab cakes this side of the Delaware Bay. Albert and I used to go down there at least once a month."

"I'm sorry, when he had what?"

Mrs. Dodson rolled her head back. "Oh, that's right. What was the name of that little place?"

Aunt Ginny drummed her fingers. "The Seaview?"

"No," Mother Gibson supplied. "The Seaside Café. My Jeremiah loved his Clams Casino."

"That's right." Mrs. Davis held up a finger. "Only he didn't go by Hot Sauce Louie back then, did he?"

"No sir." Mrs. Dodson tapped her cane. "Silly gimmick of a name." She shook her head. "Louis. Chef Louis something."

"Pacione." Mother Gibson tapped the side of her temple. "Chef Louis Pacione. I remember because it sounded a little like passion." She tilted her head to the side and gave a knowing look. "Lord, but he had good oysters. And that's all I'm going to say about that."

My head was swimming. Where was all this information five days and two incidents ago, ladies? "So, you're telling me Hot Sauce Louie had a restaurant before his food truck?"

The biddies all nodded.

I Googled Seaside Café. All I could find was a local news article in the *Star*. "Seaside Café, a popular fish fry, closes its doors after the Health Department receives reports of possible food poisoning. Chef Louis Pacione, a newcomer to the shore, vehemently denies

serving bad clams to *New York Journal* Food Critic
Horatio Duplessis. Mr. Duplessis was not available to
comment."

I felt like the floor beneath my feet just gave a little
shake.

"And where exactly was this restaurant, ladies?"

Mrs. Davis said, "It was a little place down at the
point."

"That sounds right," Mother Gibson said. "Right by
the Seaglass Motel that used to be there."

Aunt Ginny joined in, "Oh, of course. Next to the
dime store and that really good donut shop we used to
have, Angelinni's."

"Now those were good donuts," Mrs. Dodson said.
"We used to get a bag of the powdered sugars and sit
on the bench in front of the sunken ship."

Mrs. Davis had a faraway look in her eye. "It's all
gone now. Only the sunken ship remains. What's left
of it."

I pulled out my phone and went to Google Maps,
since every one of their referenced landmarks had
been gone twenty years. I plugged in Cape May Point
and held the map up to the ladies. "Okay, where was
Louie's restaurant?"

Mrs. Davis looked at my phone and shrugged.
"Where is the sunken ship on that thing?"

I zoomed in to the spot.

Aunt Ginny pointed to the end of Sunset Boulevard. "It would have to have been right there. Remember that lifeguard stand, girls?"

Mrs. Davis blushed. "Remember that lifeguard?"

"Yowzah!" Aunt Ginny giggled.

Mother Gibson held one hand up in the air and shook her head. "Lord, have mercy."

I laughed to myself. No matter what age you are, your personality stays the same. I zoomed in to the spot Aunt Ginny indicated. It was now the very successful Sunset Grill. That property must be worth a fortune right on the beach where scores of people congregate to watch the orange ball drop over the bay. Imagine how successful Louie would be if he still owned it. As soon as Amber finished up with Louie, I was going to ask him about the Seaside Café. But first I needed to corner Philippe to check up on that morning show fiasco. And Philippe had disappeared.

Darn it! I searched the arena and didn't see the stuffy French chef anywhere. Amber had to call in reinforcements, so she could widen the lockdown area to include two classrooms plus the hallway down to the bathrooms, after a potty emergency arose with one of the seniors who had come in the church van with Mother Gibson.

Since I didn't see Philippe anywhere in the kitchen arena, I checked out the classrooms. No Philippe. I walked down the beige hall of kitchen classrooms trying to stalk him while trying to not look like a stalker. When I got near the locker room, I heard a man's voice. It was muffled, but by the caustic tone I could make out that he was angry. I walked quietly to see if I could pick up anything specific. When I got closer, I realized the voice was Adrian's.

"I told you I would pay you back when this is over. . . . No, I'm doing my best here. You know I'm good for it. It should have been in the bag, but there have been complications. . . . How could I know someone would be killed?! . . . Don't be that way. I can turn this around. . . . Don't you dare repossess my Porsche! How will I get to Baxter's? . . . You'll be sorry, Mother!"

I heard a loud metallic punch. I had to get out of here. I was a sitting duck in the middle of this hallway with nowhere to hide. A red-faced Adrian turned the corner. We stood in silence staring each other down. Adrian was breathing heavy. I could feel the anger shooting from his fists.

"What are you doing down here?"

"Um . . . I was . . . looking for you. Sawyer needs you—well, not needs. Wants you. I mean she wants to find you. I think she wants to check on you, to see if you're okay because . . . you know."

Adrian crossed his arms in front of his chest. "Is she really looking for me?"

"She was, yes. She was concerned about you after Ashlee blew up from that allergic reaction after eating your food."

"I didn't use any peanuts!" Adrian answered defensively. "It had to be someone else. I don't even know that girl."

I held my hands up to protect my face. "Okay, okay. I'm not the enemy." *I mean, I kind of am with Tim and all. I'm more enemy adjacent.*

He let his breath out long and low.

"Who were you talking to just now?"

Adrian threw me a glare. "You betta just forget about that." He blew past me and stormed down the hall.

Hmm. No way was that his mother he was talking to. I bet Mother is code for loan shark. It doesn't sound like Adrian is as successful as he wants everyone to believe.

I went back to my search for Philippe. Maybe he was in the men's room. I squeezed my voice high and called into the restroom. "Housekeeping." *Housekeeping,*

Poppy? Are you insane? "I mean, cleaning lady. Is the room empty?" Nothing. Maybe I'd missed him, and he was back in the kitchen. I returned, hiking down the long, quiet hall.

Gia was sitting in the director's chair, relaxed and calm. "Ahh, there you are. I've been looking for you."

I couldn't help but smile. "You were?"

He gave me a mischievous smile. "How are you?"

"Peachy."

"I know that look. What are you up to?"

I flopped down in the chair next to him. "Looking for Philippe."

"I think he's been released to go home."

"Aww, man."

"The officer is starting to let people go after they've given their statements. She sent Aunt Ginny and her friends home thirty minutes ago when they started chanting 'Commie pigs! Commie pigs!'"

"How Aunt Ginny isn't arrested once a month is beyond me."

"I think she could give Momma a run for her money." Gia tipped his chin to where two officers were guarding Momma. One of them had a Taser at the ready.

The room was thinning. "Have you seen Hot Sauce Louie? I just found out he used to have a restaurant at the point years ago that was shut down because of Horatio's reviews."

"He's in the pantry making out with Vidrine."

"What!"

"Yeah, I caught them when I was putting away the tartuffo honey."

"So, Louie and Vidrine are an item?"

"I get the feeling they don't want anyone to know

about it, because they were real cagey when they realized I'd spotted them."

"Oh my God, I almost forgot all about Vidrine. She lied to me about why she was sneaking around up here the other night. Whatever she's up to, I know they're in it together."

"They're definitely up to more than just competing." Gia tipped his head down and gave me a look.

Amber blew a long blast on her police whistle. "Okay, people. You can go for now. The food will be tested, but the CSI team didn't find any traces of peanuts except in the basement vending machines. And no one from the kitchen has been down there today according to security cameras. You are all free to go for now, but don't leave town. This is an active investigation."

I stood and stretched. I was glad to be leaving. I'd have to try and jump—I mean—have a polite talk with, Philippe, Louie, and Vidrine tomorrow.

"And one more thing before you take off. The autopsy report came back this morning. The levels of toxicity in Bess Jodice's blood, along with her reported behavior, would suggest that she was poisoned three days before she died."

If Bess was poisoned at the beginning of Restaurant Week, before she'd given any reviews, where was the motive to kill her? Horatio had to have been the original target. I wondered how he would react when he found out.

Gia put a warm hand on my back. "Why don't you come to the coffee shop? I miss you."

"Won't I be a distraction while you work?"

"I'm closed for the week, but I'll open for us to spend time together."

I felt a flutter of nerves at the back of my neck. Gia wanted to spend time with me, but after this week, I felt like I'd be cheating on Tim. Working as Tim's pastry chef had brought up memories and emotions from when we were engaged. Except for, you know, Gigi being here and bodies dropping left and right. That was putting me right off the mood. I looked in Gia's eyes. Everything was so much easier with Gia. But hearing Tim call me his pastry chef sent chills down my spine.

I'd dreamed of this day for twenty years. This was the life I was meant to have before it all went wrong. Before I let myself be bullied into the business track at William and Mary instead of pursuing my dreams of culinary school. Of course, I had only myself and peach schnapps to blame for the one-night stand that had knocked me up. One frat party was all it took to break off my engagement to Tim and set up my shotgun wedding to John.

John. If only he could see me now. He'd given me a good life with a lot of love, but he knew what my immaturity had cost me. I wonder what he would think about my second chance with Tim now?

I scanned the room for Tim. He was talking to Miss New Jersey, and she was seductively rubbing his shoulder. Gigi was glued to his other side. Gigi caught my eye and quickly linked arms with Tim. He patted her on the hand.

But then, I'm not one for drama. "I'd love to come over. What time?"

Gia grinned. "Time? Let's go now. Momma's pastry chef can take her home."

"Are you driving?" I tried to hide the nerves in my voice. The last time Gia drove me somewhere, my life flashed before my eyes. It was going almost a hundred miles an hour, so it was a quick flash.

"Si, I'll take us in the Spider."

Deep breaths, Poppy. "Okay, let me check with Amber, and I'll get my things." *And maybe ask around for a Xanax.*

"I'll be waiting."

Chapter Twenty-Eight

I was heading to the lockers when a flash of pink disappearing into the ladies' room caught my eye. Vidrine! No one was around so I jumped in after her.

She had veered off to where the lockers were lined up, and was gathering her belongings to presumably go home for the day.

"Hey, Vidrine." I leaned against the locker next to hers.

She jumped a mile and knocked the door back with a slam. "Aah! Poppy! Ah. . . . Hey, girl . . . whachu up to?"

"Don't 'hey girl' me. You lied to me!"

"Whaaa?"

"You said you were only here after hours to get your knives for Sunday dinner. I heard your interview with Tess. You aren't even opened for Sunday dinner. You only do brunch."

Vidrine's eye darted left then right. Her face flushed, and she jabbed at my chest. "You know what, *chér*, you better just mind your own business."

I took a step backwards and put my hand over my heart. "I'm sorry. You're right. I've been putting my nose in your business about this for too long, and I'm gonna stop right now."

Vidrine's face softened, but she was still leery.

"What I'm gonna do instead, is call my good friend Amber in here." *Good friend—Jesus please don't strike me dead for that whopper.* "And I'll let her know just what's going on. She's that blond cop in the other room. This is her business." I started walking for the door.

"Wait. Why is this the cop's business?"

"I think she would want to know that in the midst of a murder investigation, and an attack investigation, that someone found you sneaking around the very pantry, doing God knows what, to the very ingredients that are under said investigation." I waved my hand like it wasn't a big deal or anything. "What am I saying? I'll just let her explain it to you, and I'll go home and put my feet up. Stay here." I had my hand on the door handle and started to yank.

"Alright, stop."

"I'm sorry? Did you say something?"

Vidrine's face fell, and she lowered herself onto the locker room bench. "Look, I didn't do anything that hurt Bess or Ashlee."

"Then why were you really here last Sunday skulking around in the pantry? Were you messing with the ingredients?"

"No! Look, it's not what you think. I didn't sabotage anyone. I didn't hurt anyone."

"Then what?"

"I was scared witless about the competition. Bess fried me like an egg on the first two days. Said I had a lack of proper trainin'. What'd she expect? I was sabotaged! Well, goin' into day three, I was in last place, and that was behind Adrian, even after he told the judges that they had less taste than Miley Cyrus and got himself a couple of zeros. So, I hid in the locker room until everyone was good'n gone. Then I searched the kitchen and pantry to find out the next mystery ingredients, so I could be ready."

"So, you cheated?"

Vidrine picked at her chef coat. "For a good cause, honey. Chefs like you and me and Louie, even that angry Italian woman, we aren't getting a fair shake here. It's your sous chef who keeps pointing out that we all don't have the same trainin' or experience the others have. Bess only respected the chefs who she thought had fancy educations. How is that fair to us who are self-taught? I worked hard to get where I am. Should I be punished for my lack of eighty grand to attend the Culinary Institute of America?"

"I understand where you're coming from. Believe me, I do. I have Gigi whispering in my ear every day that I'm not good enough because I didn't graduate with her or Tim. But what you did isn't fair to the other chefs either. You and Louie clearly got a heads-up about what was in those baskets, because you were done today way before everyone else."

Vidrine took a step toward me, pleading in her chocolate eyes. "Please don't rat me out. I only found out two of the days, and Bess died on one and Ashlee was poisoned on the other. My food wasn't even tasted. Not that it would have mattered a lick. Bess hated everything I made. I was never so glad to see her swapped out." Her hand flew up to cover her face. "Not that I killed her or anythin'. I was just glad to get her off my back, you know?"

On the other side of the divider, a toilet flushed. Vidrine and I froze in horror.

A Japanese student came out of the stall, looked from me to Vidrine, awkwardly washed—and slowly dried—her hands. Threw away her paper towel. Then looked from Vidrine back to me and left the room.

Vidrine grabbed my wrist and begged me. "Please don't tell your friend."

"Tell who?"

"The cop."

"Oh right! Right. Amber. Well, if you want my silence you have to tell me something else. What is up with you and Hot Sauce Louie? My friend saw you two in the pantry."

Vidrine's face glowed a rosy mahogany and her eyes nearly popped out and rolled around the locker room floor. "No, he didn't, he didn't see anything." She grabbed her bag and flew out the door.

I never said it was a he.

As she ran away, the sound of her pink Birkenstocks speed squeaked down the hall like a toddler with a new whistle.

I would have expected that reaction over the whole unethical cheating revelation more than the making out with Louie question. Hm.

I grabbed my things and made my way back to the kitchen arena to meet up with Gia and head out to the car.

"I thought you got lost."

"No, but I finally got a confession. I'll tell you about it on the way home. It'll distract me."

"Distract you from what?"

From the impending Grand Prix ride. "Oh look, the angry mob has tomatoes."

Gia took my hand and led me through the protesters into the early evening, as the sun was getting low in the sky and the temperature was dropping for the night. A chill wind was starting to blow, and I wrapped my coat tighter around me. The activists did not have time to pelt us with tomatoes because they had to rush off to pick up their kids from soccer practice. Gia's Spider had not been so lucky.

"*Oh, mio Dio! Mia macchina!*" Gia threw his hands up in the air and started waving them around. "*Chiama la polizia!*"

The soccer moms started packing faster.

Gia dropped down to his knees on the tarmac and mourned his ruined paint job.

I was speechless. His car was in my possession for five days, and now it would need a two-thousand-dollar trip to Maaco.

Chapter Twenty-Nine

We drove home mostly in silence. I say mostly, because I was silent. Gia muttered angrily in Italian the entire length of the Parkway, his hands flying around like he was having a conversation. That was after we went through the automatic carwash, twice. One of Amber's officers had come out and taken the police report for him to submit to the insurance company. The three protesters who hadn't moved fast enough denied throwing the tomatoes—apparently, the tomatoes had flung themselves out of their bags and into the parking lot—and now the group had lost their permit to assemble. I saw this as a silver lining. But then I wasn't the one with acid burns on their prized Italian sports car.

Gia parked in the alley behind *La Dolce Vita*.

Oh man. He's even making me walk home. He must be furious. I'd had the long drive to think of a dozen different ways he could possibly tell me it was over. Our business relationship, his interest in me, our friendship. I promised myself I would wait until I was alone to cry.

I got out of the car and shut the door. "You know I'll pay . . ."

He cut me off by pulling me into his arms and holding me so tight, that for a minute I wasn't sure what was happening.

"Bella, can you please forgive me?"

"Forgive you for what?"

"For being so angry that I didn't talk to you all the way home."

I was definitely taken aback. "I'm just so sorry that this happened. I should have parked farther away from them."

His eyebrows dropped together for a moment. "Oh, Bella, if I made you think for one second that I held you responsible." He shook his head. "I am so sorry. It was not your fault. It was those horrible protesters."

"I still feel responsible. At least let me pay the deductible."

"You will not! I don't care about the car. I care only about hurting you. Please, you will break my heart if you are still upset." Gia clutched his chest for effect.

I chuckled. *Talk about dramatic.* "I forgive you."

His face broke into a smile and he pulled me into a kiss. "Thank you, Bella." Then he kissed me again. He kissed me all the way up against the door and kept kissing me while he unlocked it and threw it open. Kissing me inside, he threw his foot against the door and slammed it shut, threw his keys on the counter, and spun me over to the other side of the kitchen against the walk-in refrigerator, all the while never breaking contact. My heart was pounding so hard I could hear it outside my head. *Thump-thump-thump. Thump-thump-thump.* Gia unbuttoned my coat and threw it over a chair. *Thump-thump-thump.* He rubbed his hands over my back and pulled me even closer to him.

BANG-BANG-BANG.

We froze. "Is that my heart?" I gasped out through ragged breath.

Gia shook his head and went back to what he was doing.

BANG-BANG-BANG.

"There it is again."

"We know you're in there. Come let us in, it's cold out here."

"Oh my God, is that Aunt Ginny?"

Gia looked into my eyes, his disappointment evident.

"Poppy! Let us in."

Gia shook his head. "And she is not alone."

He slowly walked to the front of the café, turning on lights as he did. He unlocked the door and let in not one, but six senior citizens.

Aunt Ginny had brought the whole gang. "Did you know your front door is locked?"

"Si, because I am closed."

Aunt Ginny took off her coat. "Oh good, then no one will bother us."

Mr. Sheinberg followed her in and shook hands with Gia. "We followed you home down the Parkway, Mario Andretti. Somebody's got a lead foot."

Mrs. Sheinberg smacked her husband on the arm. "Well you kept pace with him the whole way, didn't ya."

"I had to." Mr. Sheinberg took off his coat and cap. "Ginny said to follow that car."

Aunt Ginny marched around like she owned the place. "What took you so long? We've been out front for ten minutes. We were freezing our assets off." Then she looked at me. "Why is your mouth so red?"

Mrs. Dodson's eyes got really big, and she jabbed Aunt Ginny in the side. "I think we're interrupting something, Ginny."

Understanding dawned in Aunt Ginny's eyes. "Oh, you want us to go?"

Gia put on the bravest face he could. "No, of course not. Please, everyone come in and make yourselves at home."

Oh no. "You'll regret that," I whispered.

Gia chuckled. "In Italy we say, '*Se mi ami, tu amo la mia famiglia.*'"

"What does that mean?"

"Love me, love my family." He gave me a quick kiss and headed to the espresso bar to make coffee.

Love?

I entered the dining room dazed, like I was walking up in the clouds or under water. What just happened? It wasn't a declaration, just a saying. Like teach a man to fish, or don't look a gift horse in the mouth.

"Poppy honey, are you listening to me?" Mrs. Dodson was staring at me, tapping her cane on my foot to get my attention.

"I'm sorry, what?"

"I said, did you hear the news?"

"No, what news?"

Mrs. Davis fluttered her hands. "It was all over Channel Eight. The morning show is in trouble. Now that Ashlee is gone, Tess is pushing for a replacement."

I was horrified. Gone? "Ashlee died?"

Mrs. Davis looked at me like I was crazy. "Died? No! She's just staying in the hospital overnight."

"Okay, now I'm confused. Tess is pushing for a Restaurant Week replacement while Ashlee is in the hospital overnight?"

"No." Mrs. Dodson shook her head at my denseness. "She is pushing for a permanent replacement because Ashlee is in the hospital overnight."

"Isn't that a bit extreme?"

Aunt Ginny shrugged. "Millennials."

There was a *tap-tap-tap* on the front window. Sawyer was waving wildly to me.

I opened the door and let her in. She was giddy and out of breath. "Wait till you see what I found." She took off her coat and draped it over a chair.

"What is it?"

Gia came in with a tray of cappuccinos. I ran to help him. He nodded to the cup on the end with a latte foam heart and a dusting of chocolate powder. "That one is yours." Our eyes met, and he winked.

I took the cup, and he put the tray down. The seniors dove into the coffees.

Mr. Sheinberg asked, "Are there free refills?"

Mrs. Sheinberg rolled her eyes and smacked him on the arm.

"Whah? McDonalds has free refills. I just want to know what I'm in for here."

Gia's lips twitched. "Everything is on the house tonight."

"Oy, in that case." Mr. Sheinberg clinked his cup against his wife's. "Keep 'em coming, Mario."

"Poppy, sit." Sawyer patted the bench next to her. "You have to see this." She started a clip on her phone. She had to start it three times because there was much grousing over who could and who couldn't see the picture.

Finally, Gia brought in his iPad, and Sawyer pulled it up to play on the bigger screen.

It was the video of Philippe on the morning show. Philippe was demonstrating how to make a French onion tart.

"Mmm, that would have been a good recipe too. I made one once from *Mastering the Art of French Cooking*. It was delicious."

Mrs. Dodson shushed me. "I can't hear him."

Ashlee wasn't interested in learning how to make the tart or letting Philippe talk about his restaurant. She was too busy trying to juggle the onions and talk about learning to juggle in camp when she was thirteen. A very exasperated Philippe asked why she had him on the show if she didn't want to see him cook. Ashlee said, "Think fast," and threw an onion at Philippe's head. The onion knocked Philippe's hat off, and he got so flustered that he stuttered through the rest of the recipe. Then his sleeve caught fire and Ashlee laughed while a stagehand had to run out and swat Philippe down with a towel to put him out. When it was finally time to taste the recipe, Philippe's sous chef brought out a finished tart that had been made ahead of time.

I jumped to my feet so fast that I knocked the coffee table with my leg and sloshed everyone's cappuccino.

Aunt Ginny yelped, "Poppy? What's wrong."

I was pointing at the iPad. "Oh my God, back it up! Back it up!"

Gia rolled the video back a few seconds.

"Stop!"

The video paused on the sous chef in dark braids smiling down at the finished tart.

"That's Vidrine!"

The room erupted into a volley of questions and theories.

"Is Vidrine secretly working with Philippe?"

"Do you think she's getting bad reviews on purpose to increase Philippe's chances of winning?"

"Maybe she's competing against him to get revenge for putting her on that fakakta television spot."

I assured everyone that I did not have any secret backstage insider information, but I would be sure to fill them in if I got "the skinny."

Neither Gia nor I mentioned anything about Louie and Vidrine making out in the pantry. I wanted to get those details straight from Vidrine herself. Then I would be sure to pass them along to Sawyer and Aunt Ginny later.

After several refills, a few pastries, and a handful of conspiracy theories, we finally said good-bye to Sawyer and packed the seniors up to send them on their way home. Aunt Ginny was the last one out the door. She gave me a pointed look as Gia was helping her put her coat on. "I know how long it's supposed to take to go from here to our house."

"Message received."

Aunt Ginny narrowed her eyes through the last crack of the door before it clicked shut.

We were alone. I turned to Gia to apologize for the invasion. He had me in his arms before I could get the words out. "Don't make it so hard for me to leave."

Gia smiled. "I want to make sure you'll miss me until tomorrow."

"That's a promise."

We gathered up the cups and saucers and plates and took them to the kitchen. Gia helped me into my coat and handed the keys to the now tomato-pocked Spider.

"Are you sure?"

"Bella, please."

I took the keys, glad that Gia still trusted me with his car, but also glad that I didn't have to walk at this time of night. "How will you get home?"

"I'll walk. I only live a few blocks from here."

"Do you want me to drive you?"

He raised one eyebrow. "Definitely not. Besides, I have some paperwork to do here before I go home."

"Okay, I'll see you in the morning."

He kissed me one last time. "I can't wait."

I don't know why the thought of him working late made my heart skip a beat, but it did. What was wrong with me? Turned on by paperwork? For a brief moment, I thought of Tim with Miss New Jersey and Gigi, and the jealousy wrapped around my neck like a noose. I was a big fat hypocrite, and I didn't like it. Not one bit.

Chapter Thirty

I found Horatio sitting in the library reading a biography and drinking a glass of port by the fire.

"Hi, how long have you been back?"

Horatio consulted his watch. "A couple of hours. Officer Fenton wanted to assign me a security detail, but I don't think that's necessary. Everything that happens seems to be at the college. I feel safe here."

"I'm glad. How are you holding up?"

"The stress is worse than having a deadline with nothing to write about."

"I don't know what that's like, but it sounds awful. I'm looking into things on my end to try to find whoever is responsible for these terrible attacks. Hopefully, I'll know something that'll help soon."

Horatio twisted his mustache. "Oh, please don't do anything. I appreciate it very much, but I would hate to see you put yourself in the sights of a killer. Then they'll come after you. I would so much rather you stay safely out of it."

That was very sweet of him. He reminded me a little of my Uncle Teddy with his white hair and dapper demeanor. I tried to reassure him. "Don't worry about me, I'll be fine. I have a lot of friends looking out for me. "

Horatio nodded, thoughtfully. "That's good."

"I've been reading some of your restaurant reviews."

A wary caution crossed Horatio's eyes. "Oh?"

"You've been a restaurant critic for a long time. Is there anyone who would want to hurt you, maybe because of an unfavorable review?"

"You make a lot of enemies in my line of work. It goes with the territory. I get at least one death threat a year. But this is the first time anyone has gone beyond empty words."

"Are there any chefs in the competition who could be serious enough to try to follow through on a threat?"

Horatio looked at his hands in his lap for a moment. "There is one chef—he thinks I've been blocking him from getting a Michelin Star. I've reviewed his restaurant several times, and he just doesn't have what it takes."

I suspected Horatio was talking about Adrian. Out of all the chefs competing, Adrian was the only one who'd had multiple reviews. "What do you mean by 'what it takes?'"

"Anyone can learn to cook. Cooking is a little science, a little art, and a lot of passion. But for some, it's just a job. Then there are those who have the gift. They were born to be chefs. They feel it in their bones. They know by instinct what tastes will complement each other, and how to best bring out undiscovered flavors. They're only alive when their hands are creating. Unless something happens to squash that gift, those are the ones who go on to greatness."

"And you don't think this chef who wants the Michelin Star has this gift?"

"He's ambitious, but his menu is full of overpriced,

deep-fried seafood. He offers nothing you can't get from the freezer section of the grocery store. Yet he has a degree from one of the most prestigious culinary schools in the country. That's just plain lazy."

"Could he be the one sending you threats?"

"I don't know. Threats are not usually signed. People like to hide behind screen names and anonymity. It's rare for someone to own up to their words."

Thinking of Adrian and his erratic behavior this week, I asked, "I know people can be crazy, but do you really think this chef would kill you because of a bad review?"

Horatio chose his words carefully. "If the ego is bruised deep enough, it can cause a regret that can't be shaken as the years go by. Then, I think any one of us is capable of justifying murder."

That was such a grim thought, but it happened every day. There was so much senseless killing and pain in the world—and for what? The reasons ran far and wide, but it usually came down to the killer was hurting, so they wanted to hurt other people. I would never understand how someone could get twisted up enough to justify the horrific things that happened in the world today.

Horatio was also deep in thought, probably about the same thing.

"I'll leave you to your book. Rest well tonight."

He gave me a weak smile. "I'll try. Thank you."

I headed up the guest stairs to check on Bess's door, to make sure the crime scene tape was still in place. I found Figaro scratching at Ashlee's door. "Are you lost, sir?"

Merrrow.

"I believe your usual victim is in the other room over

there." I bent to pick up the furry smoosh-face. "Or have you decided to terrorize everyone equally now?"

Figaro swatted my hand and wriggled out of my arms. He went back to sniffing at Ashlee's door and scratching to get in.

I don't know how we are ever going to get the Butterfly Wings B&B successful with this pest in residence. I need to find some kind of distraction to keep Fig away from the guest rooms.

Norman's door on the Adonis Suite opened, and Tess poked her head out. She stopped short when she saw me. "Oh. Hi."

"Hi there. I hope Figaro hasn't been bothering you." Tess shook her head no.

"Well that's good. I heard tonight that *Wake Up! South Jersey* was having some trouble."

Tess came out into the hall and quickly shut the door behind her. "Jou can't believe everything you hear on TV, and I would know."

"Do you think the show will get a replacement for Ashlee?"

Tess wobbled her head when she talked. "I don't need a replacement. I can do the show on my own."

The door flew open, and Norman, a towel wrapped around his waist, glared at Tess.

Tess shrugged. "What are you looking at?"

Norman slammed the door shut, leaving Tess in the hall with me and Figaro, who was now moaning at Ashlee's door for someone to let him in.

Tess sighed and let out a string of profanity. She jiggled the knob on Norman's door. Norman had locked her out.

I scooped up my squirmy cat again. "Well, I'm going to turn in. Sleep well."

I carried Fig up the stairs to our attic apartment and scolded him for being so naughty. Then I nuzzled him for being so cute. He patted me on the mouth.

Downstairs, Tess had gotten back into the room, and I could overhear pieces of a hissy fit.

Norman was obviously angry about something. "You promised!"

"You're loco! I never promised you anything!"

"What did you tell them?"

"I said you'd be interested."

"That isn't what we agreed!"

"I don't care what we agreed."

"I did everything you wanted!"

"Shhh, keep your voice down. Someone will hear."

The voices got too muffled after that. Then Fig and I heard a door slam, followed a few minutes later by the bell in my room signaling the front door being opened and shut.

"What do you think that was about?"

Fig blinked his bright orange eyes.

"You're right. It can't be good. I wonder what she asked him to do."

Figaro jumped out of my arms onto the bed.

"Fig, I think you're right again."

Chapter Thirty-One

I got to the college early looking for a chance to corner Vidrine. Aunt Ginny was driving up with Mrs. Dodson and Mrs. Davis, so I was alone. The same uniformed officer stood guard at the front door, and I wondered if the increased security was because of events that happened inside, or outside. The protesters were gone, so I felt safe enough to park near the front. Hopefully that wouldn't be an epic mistake.

I said hello to Officer Birkwell and went straight to the locker room to stow my purse and coat. Then I waited. Twenty minutes later, Vidrine finally arrived.

"Mornin'."

She flinched hard. "Wha! What are you doing?"

"What do you mean what am I doing? I'm waiting for you."

Vidrine quickly looked around me in every direction. "Why?"

"I need to talk to you. Relax. No one else is in here this time."

Vidrine covered her heart with her hand and took a couple of breaths.

I held up my cell phone. "I want to show you something." I hit play on the video I'd queued up.

Vidrine's eyes swelled as soon as Philippe said "French onion tart." "Where did you find that?"

"A friend."

Vidrine rolled her eyes and sighed. "So, I used to apprentice for the great Philippe Julian. So what?"

"Don't you think it's strange that you didn't mention this before? It makes you look guilty."

Vidrine threw her head back. "Uhck! I'm not allowed to talk about it, okay?"

"What in the world does that mean?"

"Have you ever heard of a non-compete?"

"Yeah."

"Well, before Philippe took me on as his apprentice, I had to sign a contract that stated if I ever told certain . . ." She gave me an exasperated look. "Certain trade secrets about Philippe or *La Maîtrisse*, that I could be sued for a huge amount of money."

"I've never heard of such a thing."

"Yeah, well, me neither. But I wanted to apprentice under Philippe in the worst possible way, so I signed it."

"How did it go?"

"In the worst possible way."

"Oh."

Vidrine moved in close to me so no one else could hear if they happened to be lurking inside a locker. "Look, do I have your word that this will go no farther than your ears?"

I held up two fingers. "Scout's honor."

Vidrine considered me for a minute. "I tried to tell you this the other day, but Philippe's pastry chef ran in here cryin' like a baby, bless her heart, and I couldn't spill it."

"Okay, well tell me now."

"Working with Philippe started out good. Real good. It was a dream come true to work in the most popular restaurant at the shore. But after a couple of months, it all started to fall apart."

I nodded for her to keep going.

"For one thing, he's miserable in the kitchen. He's on his best behavior here because he knows the cameras are on, but he has a wicked temper. It wouldn't surprise me if that's why he picked the station on the end instead of right in front of the cameras."

"I thought he wanted to be closest to the judges' table."

"Doubtful. He's probably using cheat sheets in the kitchen and he'll want to hide those."

"Cheat sheets?"

Vidrine took a deep breath and slowly let it out. "The great and mighty Chef Philippe doesn't know how to cook anything from scratch. He doesn't have any of his own recipes. Haven't you noticed? Everything he makes is from Julia Child's cookbooks."

"Holy macaroni! How did I not put that together?"

Vidrine counted off on her fingers. "Day one, Julia's quiche Lorraine using chip steak instead of ham. Day two, he made Julia's *duck à l'orange* using lemon. Day three, *blanquette du veau*—he didn't even alter the recipe. He just made the other basket ingredients on the side."

"You know, I figured out that he was making *coq au vin* with the squab yesterday. When I teased him about it he got real cagey, like he was trying to hide it."

"Philippe wants to protect his image at all cost. He doesn't want this secret getting out."

"I bet that's what Horatio meant when he said he

was seeing a pattern in Philippe's dishes. Horatio really knows his stuff. He probably recognized the recipes."

"Philippe hates Horatio. With a passion. If he applied that much passion to his food, he'd be a completely different chef."

"He hates Horatio that much because of one bad review?"

"When he saw that review he went nuts. He wrote this rebuttal to the paper about how his recipes were perfect and time honored."

"Well, I mean, technically they are."

"Yeah, but they aren't his. And Horatio called him out for it. The hostess at *La Maîtrisse* was told that if she ever saw him at the door, she was to call the cops immediately. Philippe vowed to get even one day."

"Even how?"

"I don't know. But you can bet your grits I've been thinking about that all week, *chér*."

"How does someone graduate *Le Cordon Bleu* in Paris, and still not know how to cook?"

Vidrine tipped her chin back and raised both her eyebrows. She laughed. "Honey, there is no way on God's green earth that that man went to *Le Cordon Bleu*. I doubt he's been to the Paris Casino in Vegas. For one thing, Chef Philippe doesn't speak French."

My mouth dropped open. I tried to snap it shut. Then I remembered when Horatio told Philippe he'd rather eat a cat over his food. Philippe had said thank you. My mouth popped open again. "That does explain some things."

Vidrine leaned back against the lockers, crossed her arms in front of her chest and nodded. "One night, we had a guest from Quebec who tried to order in

French. The waiter came and got Philippe. He had no idea what she was saying. He said he was too busy and the waiter would have to work it out. I had to translate for him, and my Haitian French is rusty."

"Is that why you left *La Maîtrisse*? You couldn't stand the hypocrisy?"

"Not exactly. Philippe wants to publish a cookbook, but you need recipes to do that. I left when I caught him taking credit for some of my original recipes in his file. That's when I knew I had to get out of there. And if you ask me, he's doing the same thing to his new pastry chef."

Ivy popped her head in the locker room. "Oh hey, there you two are. We're about to get started. Five minutes."

Vidrine and I snapped to attention like we'd been caught with contraband.

"We'll be right out," Vidrine called. Then after Ivy left she said to me, "Now remember your promise to me, *chér*."

"I will. You have my word."

I headed to my station to begin the Restaurant Week challenge for day six. Only one more day of the competition remained. I was glad to see the back of it. But if I didn't hurry up and clear Tim's name, he might not ever recover from the damage that was done this week.

What I'd learned in the past twenty-four hours was that Philippe was a fraud who swore he'd get revenge on Horatio. Adrian had made death threats to Horatio because of bad reviews blocking his ambitious plans. And Louie had a restaurant shut down because of Horatio's accusations of food poisoning.

I loved Vidrine to pieces, but she'd already lied to me a few times. Maybe everything she just told me about Philippe was a lie. How did I know I could trust her? Not to mention that little scandal about Louie and Vidrine cheating with the baskets. They had something going on, and it was more than just cooking.

It seemed everyone had something they wanted to keep hidden. Maybe something they were willing to kill to protect.

Chapter Thirty-Two

Ivy stomped around the stage having a fit. "What is going on, people?! We have a show to do!" Neither Tess nor Norman had shown up yet. Ashlee was still in the hospital. Bess was still . . . dead. We had a packed audience and six teams of chefs at the ready. But no one to host, and we were short two judges. "Poppy, where is your aunt? I called her last night and asked her to fill in today. She said she'd be here."

I looked in the stands. Sawyer and Itty Bitty Smitty had an empty seat in between them. I had a moment of panic. Not that anything had happened to Aunt Ginny, but that Aunt Ginny was about to happen. She didn't want to ride in with me this morning. What didn't she want me to see?

The lights dimmed, and overhead, music started to play—the theme song from *Chariots of Fire*. The stage spotlight danced in circles, and everyone looked around waiting to see what was going on. But I knew. I knew what was going on. And there was nothing I could do to stop it.

Aunt Ginny entered the arena dressed like Norma Desmond, in a gold lamé kimono over a black pantsuit with a matching gold lamé turban. She held her arms up to her adoring fans. The seniors cheered and roared along with the display while Aunt Ginny took a slow lap around the stage and the judges' table—pausing and spinning in front of the camera.

She walked past my kitchen, and I threw out the question, "How much did this cost you?"

She tossed me a grin over her shoulder. "Twenty bucks to the kid in the control booth."

Ivy stood slack with her clipboard and headset forgotten at her side; her round, rose-colored glasses sat crooked on her nose.

Not a word was spoken until Aunt Ginny finally took her seat next to Horatio, the music stopped, and the house lights came up. She turned to Miss New Jersey, who was mesmerized, and said, "That's how you make an entrance, honey."

Ivy looked at me.

What could I do? I don't control Aunt Ginny.

Tim was holding his sides, laughing. I threw him some shade, and he laughed even harder. "I hope you're going to be just like her when you're that age."

Ivy clicked on her headset. "Roger, could you come here please?" Then she took off the headset, put her clipboard down, and attached the wireless microphone to her black sweater. "Testing one, two. Testing. Okay. I will fill in for Ashlee and Tess today. Roger, you'll be me. Who wants to be Norman?" Ivy looked around the audience. "I need a man."

Mrs. Davis put her hand down, disappointed. "Don't we all."

Mrs. Sheinberg nudged her husband in the side and he jumped. "What?"

Ivy headed over to the stands where they were sitting. "Fantastic. Thank you so much Mister—?"

"What? What's happening?"

Ivy took Mr. Sheinberg by the elbow. "Great. Come with me." She led him down to the judges' table and sat him in Norman's seat. "You'll be our fourth judge today."

Mr. Sheinberg bowed his head and started praying the twenty-third Psalm. "Yea, though I walk through the valley of the shadow of death, I will fear no evil . . ."

Mrs. Sheinberg assured the concerned seniors, "His life insurance is paid up."

Ivy stood in front of the camera and opened the segment. "Welcome to today's event, everyone. We have some special guests on our esteemed panel of judges." Then as an aside she said, "We'll do the introductions while the chefs are preparing today's dishes."

Frank, the cameraman, gave her a thumbs-up.

"Chefs, open your baskets. Today's theme is Latin Love. Too bad Tess isn't here. This basket was picked for her. Our mystery ingredients in the appetizer basket are Iberico ham, jicama, and salt and vinegar chips."

Aunt Ginny must have forgotten that she was on camera for the entire day. "I threw up after eating a bag of salt and vinegar chips when I rode the Wild Mouse rollercoaster on the boardwalk years ago. The vinegar burnt all my nose hair when it came back up."

Miss New Jersey crinkled up her nose. "Eww. I don't want the chips on mine."

Ivy paused, and took a deep breath. "The entrée basket contains skirt steak, plantains, and poblano peppers."

Mr. Sheinberg raised his hand. "I can't eat the peppers. They give me the toots."

Mrs. Sheinberg hollered from the audience. "If you eat those peppers, you're sleeping in the basement."

"Oy, whaddayathink I told 'em for already, eh?"

Ivy closed her eyes and drummed her fingers on her thigh. Blowing out her breath long and low she said, "And finally, the dessert baskets contain passion fruits, *dulce de leche*, and lemon drop chilies." She paused and looked at the judges' table, as though waiting for commentary.

Four sets of eyes blinked back at her.

She turned back to the camera, and Mr. Sheinberg said, "Why is she looking at us? Are we supposed to say something?"

"Chefs, you have one hour. Just go."

I ran to the pantry looking to corner either Louie or Philippe. Philippe darted around me like I had the plague. He grabbed some shallots and herbs, tried to hide them from me, and dashed back out to his kitchen.

Vidrine caught my eye and gave me an "I told you so" look. She grabbed her ingredients and followed Philippe out.

Louie was standing in the walk-in, scratching his head. I sidled up next to him. "Whacha lookin' for?"

"Dude, I can't find the sour cream anywhere."

I reached up to the shelf on the right, next to the eggs, and handed him the red container. "Some of my friends were talking about one of their favorite places the other day, a little place on the point called The Seaside Café."

"I can't believe anyone remembers that old place. We had some good times there."

"They said you had the best crab cakes."

Louie grinned and rocked back on his heels. "The crab was fresh, and the secret was Ritz Crackers instead of bread crumbs." He winked.

"So, what happened? How'd you go from prime real estate at the point to a food truck?"

A shadow cast over his expression. "It was the bum's rush, man. The Health Department shut me down because of a rumor started by the great Horatio Duplessis. One phone call that I was serving bad clams, and they slapped me with a mondo fine. They never even sent an inspector."

"They just shut you down based on his word?"

"Horatio Duplessis was a god around these parts. He was one of the first restaurant critics at The Shore, and mean as a snake. I've never seen a more uptight and bitter chef wannabe in my whole life. Once word went out in the paper, warning against the 'food poisoning danger' at The Seaside Café, my clientele dried up, man. In the middle of the summer! Once we were allowed to reopen, we couldn't get customers no matter what special we ran. We missed the whole season. I couldn't make enough money to cover the dumpster fees, so I had to shut 'er down. I sold the place for less than it was worth just to get out from under it, and bought my food truck. By the next summer, the place was busier than a one-legged man dancing a jig. And guess who the new owner was close personal friends with?"

I was afraid to say it. "Horatio?"

"You got it, dude!"

Louie's sous chef poked his head in the pantry. "Your grill's ready, Chef."

"Thanks man, I'll be right there."

I grabbed some cream cheese and eggs while I was standing there. "You must be furious with him."

Louie shrugged. "Whatever. Life's too short to dwell on the past. Now I got my little hole in the wall, and we're doing great. No one even follows restaurant columns anymore. They only care about Yelp and Google."

"Do you miss having a big restaurant?"

Louie leaned his forehead down to mine. "Don't worry, I have a plan." He wiggled his eyebrows. "I'll be expanding my operation by next summer." Louie put a finger over his lips and backed out of the walk-in.

I wondered if that plan involved Vidrine. She admitted she'd been cheating. Could they be in it together to win the prize money for their joint venture? Would they go so far as to kill one of the judges?

"What are you doing?" Gigi hissed from the pantry threshold. "You've been in there for five minutes! You'd never make it in a real, professional kitchen."

"I'm coming." *What do you think I do at the coffee shop every day?* She probably thinks I'm sitting around eating chocolates and watching soap operas.

I grabbed a lime and a pack of lady fingers and went back to my station. I was making miniature passion fruit-chile cheesecakes. The cream cheese would dull the heat from the peppers and let the citrus flavor come through. *Thank you, Nadia G.* The surface area-to-mass ratio would enable them to bake very quickly. *Thank you, Alton Brown.* I was able to crush the lady fingers with my hands because I was full of unhindered rage. *Thank you, Gigi.*

I tossed the crumbs with a little melted butter and pressed them in the bottom of six mini springform pans. Even though I'd tasted everything along the way, I'd yet to taste my finished desserts—the extras kept disappearing on me.

I capped the bottom of each springform pan in foil and set them aside in a roasting pan. I whipped the cream cheese until light and fluffy and added the *dulce de leche* and egg yolks. Then I added the zest and juice of a lime. I finely chopped my bright lemon chile peppers and folded them into the creamy mixture then dolloped it into my mini cheesecake forms. I gently filled the roasting pan with an inch of water, and very slowly and carefully, took it over to the oven.

BOOM!

There was a blinding flash, and I was thrown backwards. The high-pitched ringing in my ears had me disoriented. I was in a room made of intense white light. The noise was deafening and silent at the same time. *What happened*? *Am I dead*? I slowly became aware of pain. My head was throbbing. I felt like there were needles poking me behind my eyes. I tried to shut out the light, but it wouldn't be extinguished. It was coming from inside me. I was woozy like my head was detached and bobbing in the ocean. A shadow hovered over me. The white light slowly started to fade, and the shape took on form. It was Aunt Ginny, and she was yelling something I couldn't understand. She sounded like she was in a tunnel a mile away.

Then there was nothing.

Chapter Thirty-Three

My head is killing me. Did somebody punch me in the face? I tried to move my hand up to my forehead, but it was attached to wires and tubes. A machine next to my shoulder beeped.

"Shh! I think she's waking up! Aunt Ginny, she's moving."

I could hear Sawyer's voice, but I couldn't see anything. *Oh my God! I'm blind!*

"Here, Bella. Let me help you." Gia's warm hands touched my face and lifted the covering off my eyes. Light started pouring into my head.

"Ow."

Aunt Ginny's face dropped down nose to nose with me. "Yeah, that's gonna hurt for a while. You got a concussion."

"From what?" The shadows started forming shapes that I recognized. Aunt Ginny was on my left, holding my hand. Sawyer was jammed up next to her. Gia was on my right holding my other hand. *Where is Tim?*

"Don't you remember?" Sawyer asked, concern in

her voice. "Your oven exploded. It threw you clear over to Vidrine's kitchen."

"My oven exploded! Are you freakin' . . . somebody . . . who tried to kill me?!"

Aunt Ginny patted my hand. "Okay, settle down. Don't get yourself all worked up."

I tried to sit up, but the pain in my head sent a shock of blinding light. "Was anyone else hurt? Why are my ears ringing?"

Gia adjusted the pillow behind my back. "Just you. And that can happen with an explosion. It's only temporary."

Sawyer handed me the bed control button to raise my head. "The doctors said you were very lucky. That heavy roasting pan full of water took the brunt of the blast."

"Oh no! My cheesecakes!"

Gia chuckled. "That's the least of your worries right now."

"Knock, knock. You decent, boss?"

Sawyer pulled the curtain aside to let Itty Bitty Smitty in. "She's just come to a few minutes ago."

"Whoa, you been out for an hour?"

"What happened after we left, Smitty? Did they find out how this happened?"

Smitty took off his ball cap and stuffed it in his back pocket. "What do you want first, the good news or the bad news?"

"The bad news, always the bad news," Aunt Ginny said.

"Someone cut the gas line from your stove, and used it to rig your oven to explode when you opened it."

"Jiminy Christmas." Aunt Ginny whistled.

"Police found a hacksaw in the back of Louie's truck.

He denied knowing anything about it, but was taken in for questioning."

"Chef Louie tried to blow me up?"

Smitty nodded. "It looks that way."

"What's the good news?"

"That ugly apron you were wearing caught fire from the blast. The material melted into an impenetrable shield. Once they put you out, it was ruined beyond repair."

I weighed that against the reality that I could have been in the morgue instead of the emergency room. "That does make me feel a little better."

Smitty grinned. "I knew it would."

Aunt Ginny sat on the edge of the bed. "Was anything else tampered with? Who else was sabotaged?"

Smitty turned sad cow eyes back to me. "It was just Poppy's kitchen."

"So, Louie was really trying to hurt *me*."

Aunt Ginny made a face. "Do you think he'd be dumb enough to just toss the evidence in the bed of his pickup and come on inside to make his burger of the day?"

"You think someone else planted it there to frame him?" I asked.

"Louie's a little burned out," Aunt Ginny said, "but he's not a fool."

"Everyone suspected him of tampering with the equipment a few days ago." Sawyer patted my hand. "He'd be a good scapegoat."

"Or," Gia added, "he's clever and he knew hiding it in plain sight would make a good alibi for being framed."

"Either way," Aunt Ginny said, "someone doesn't like you asking questions."

The emergency room doctor pulled back the curtain

to the medical bay. "Hey, there you are. I'm glad to see you're awake. You have a mild concussion, but I still want to admit you overnight for observation."

"No, I don't want to stay overnight. I feel fine."

Aunt Ginny pushed me back on the bed. "You aren't going anywhere, missy. You will stay here the night as the doctor says."

"But I have things to do. We have the guests, and I have to make breakfast tomorrow."

Sawyer raised a hand. "I'll do it."

Aunt Ginny muttered. "Oh, God help us."

"You're going to cook breakfast tomorrow? Is this going to be a Charlie Brown Thanksgiving-style breakfast of toast, popcorn, and jelly beans?"

"Hey! I know how to make a couple of things. . . . Aunt Ginny will still be there, right?"

Smitty pulled his hat out of his pocket and pulled it down over his bald head. "I could get doughnuts."

Aunt Ginny stood and stretched. "Don't worry. We'll do an overnight oatmeal. They'll be happy to have something hearty and simple after a week of heavy meals."

"But . . ." I started to protest.

Aunt Ginny narrowed her eyes and jabbed her finger at me. "You're staying!"

"Okay," I said, "but just for one night."

Aunt Ginny blew me off. "We'll see." She kissed me good-bye.

Sawyer leaned down for a hug, and I whispered, "Where is Tim?"

Sawyer turned up one side of her mouth and shook her head. "He stayed at the competition. He said he'd check on you later." She squeezed my shoulder in support. "I'll check on you later. Get some rest."

Then it was just me and Gia. He gave me a big smile, but he couldn't hide the concern from his eyes.

"You left in the middle of cooking?"

"Some things are more important." He pulled my hand up to his mouth and kissed it.

"So, I'm not saying this is a relationship competition or anything . . ." I trailed off.

"But I'd be winning?" Gia cocked his head and gave me a teasing look.

I laughed in spite of myself. "Won't Momma be upset that you left?"

"Momma doesn't even understand what Restaurant Week is. We told her she was competing for a year's supply of Rice-a-Roni."

"Why would she go in for that?"

"Honestly?"

I nodded.

"I asked her to enter the competition to keep an eye on things."

"You did what!" I tried to sit up too fast, and the room wobbled side to side. "Why would you do that?"

"A whole week working with your ex? I wanted to know what I was up against. It was a secret mission."

"So, Momma's your spy?"

"Si. She's been making me call her Mata Hari all week."

"I don't like the idea of you spying on me."

He covered his heart with his hand. "I wasn't spying on you. I was spying on Tim. I wanted to know if my heart was going to be broken sooner rather than later."

I gave him a look and shook my head. I wanted to tell him that he had nothing to worry about, but I didn't know how true that was. Although, he was the only one here, and that counted for a lot.

A nurse came in and said she was there to take me to my room.

Gia leaned down to kiss me and whispered, "I want you to promise me you'll rest. I don't know what I would do if something happened to you." He kissed me, and the heart monitor alarm sounded. He pulled back quickly. "I know I'm a good kisser, but I don't want to kill you."

The nurse chuckled. "That was me. I had to unplug it for transport. Although if my boyfriend kissed me like that, I'm sure I'd set off alarms too."

I sat in my hospital bed feeling sorry for myself. My head hurt, my back hurt, my eyes hurt. Even my hair hurt. My roommate sounded like she might have typhoid. I hated this dreary room. It was the color of misery and broken dreams. And to top it all off, I was seething. Someone had tried to kill me. Or at least they'd tried to scare me enough to stop me from asking questions.

Was it Louie? I was just talking to him in the walk-in. He didn't act like someone who was looking into the eyes of his next victim. Maybe he had an accomplice do it.

Which would most likely be Vidrine. It was hard to know where her lies ended, and the truth began. If it began at all. She clearly wanted to win the Restaurant Week competition enough to sneak in and cheat—and possibly sabotage the other chefs.

Of course, no one wanted to win worse than Adrian. He knew I'd overheard his conversation with Mother. And just who was he calling Mother? His bookie? A loan shark? A hitman in the mob? What kind of trouble had he gotten himself into? He'd sounded like he needed to win, or there would be dire consequences. He's probably the one who sabotaged everyone. After he'd lied about Tim sabotaging him in college. That could all have been misdirect, like Aunt Ginny said.

If I find out Gigi did this to me, to get me out of the way, I'm gonna snatch her bald. See how she likes those fake boobs in a women's prison. If this is how she repays me after I helped her block Miss New Jersey from flirting with Tim . . .

Tim. To say I was hurt that he wasn't here was an understatement. I was attacked. I could have died. Didn't he care? I couldn't believe he stayed in the competition just to try and beat Philippe.

Philippe, that phony Frenchie. Doesn't even speak the language. Vidrine said he would go to any length to protect his secrets. He knew I was on to him. Not to mention that he's the only chef who has a connection to Ashlee and the morning show.

Ashlee! I threw the thin covers off my legs. I wonder if she's still here in the hospital. I picked up the phone in my room and called the information desk.

"Cape Regional Hospital."

"Hi, I'm looking for a friend of mine. I want to send her some flowers. Her name is Ashlee Pickel. Room 212B? Thank you so much." I returned the phone to the receiver. Ashlee's room was somewhere in this wing, and I was going to find it.

I swung my feet over the edge of my bed, waited for the room to come to a stop, and dropped to the floor. The breeze that blew through the back of my hospital gown reminded me that one size does not fit all. I tried the ties but could only find them on one side. So, I rifled through the drawer in the closet and found a backup gown. Putting it on as a robe, I got tangled in the tubes of my IV. Why do I even have an IV? I hit my head—I'm not having surgery. I untangled myself, adjusted the shoulder snaps, and drug my IV pole with me in search of Ashlee Pickel.

Ashlee was in a room down the hall, and she was apparently on the Celebrity Plan. Her room was pink, and private, and bigger than mine, and I had a half-dead geriatric patient who could code blue before I returned.

"Poppy, hi! Are you here to visit me? Did you bring me anything?"

"Bring you anything? Where would I put it if I had?" Ashlee's room was packed with more flowers than the National Arboretum. Her TV was playing a home re-decorating show on HGTV, and she was lounging in pink silk pajamas, painting her nails, and eating a take-out hoagie. An open box of Godiva chocolates sat on her swivel table in the middle of a dozen get well cards.

"Do you want a Nespresso? They just brought me more pods with lunch."

"You've only been here twenty-four hours. How did you get all this?"

Ashlee shrugged. "Fans."

"I don't think I really have to ask, but how are you doing?"

"Great. My ratings are higher than ever. You should see my Facebook page. This hospital scare will put me over the top better than anything else could have."

"Over the top of what?"

"Tess. She's had more followers than me ever since she posted those pictures of herself in a bikini in Cancun two summers ago. I've finally passed her."

I moved a giant panda out of the visitor's chair and sat. "You seem to have recovered well. Do you know when you'll get out of here?"

"I could have gone this morning, but I told them I was feeling depressed that someone had poisoned me. Now I get to stay and do a depression analysis."

Is that the same as a psych eval? Probably not a bad idea. "I was thinking about what happened to you at the community college. Do you know of anyone who would want to hurt you?"

Ashlee shrugged the question off. "Tess would love to do the morning show by herself, but it's in our contract that we have to have a cohost." Ashlee picked up a shopping bag. "Would you just look at all this fan mail! One guy even proposed marriage if I pulled through."

"But only if you pull through?"

Ashlee nodded very serious. "Oh yeah. If I mysteriously die, the offer is void."

"Who knew you were allergic to peanuts?"

"Tess knew."

"Right, but anyone else?"

Ashlee shrugged. "Ivy knows. My agent made it clear that I couldn't be asked to eat anything containing peanuts on or off camera before she signed me and Tess on the show."

"Really? Ivy? And we're assuming probably Roger?"

Ashlee blew her wet nails to dry the pink polish. "I dunno."

"Uh huh. What about Philippe? I saw the clip from his segment on the morning show."

Ashlee stared blankly. "He was on the show?"

"You hit him in the head with an onion."

"That was Chef Philippe?"

"Yeah. And he was pretty angry after you spit out his food. Has he said anything to you this week at the college? Threatened you in any way?"

"No, nothing. I didn't even recognize him. Look, the television station sent over a new iPad in case I get bored."

"Wow. I have a crossword puzzle book from three years ago, and my TV is stuck on Telemundo."

Ashlee looked confused. "Are you in the hospital too?"

I looked at my IV pole and down to my regulation-issue gown of carefree modesty and back into Ashlee's unblinking eyes. "I am, in fact."

"Oh wow. Twinsies. You aren't tweeting about it, are you?"

"No."

"Oh good. I just plugged my phone up to charge."

"I just wanted to stop by and see how you were. It was a good thing Mother Gibson had an EpiPen. You could have died."

"I know. I don't know what happened to my EpiPen. I had just two minutes before I would have passed out."

"That's . . . oddly specific."

"Oh no, I've timed it before. I know what my threshold is, and I had two minutes and eighteen seconds left."

"You've . . . timed it?"

Ashlee took a bite of hoagie and spoke with her mouth full. "This was the best decision I've ever made."

"Decision about what? Decision to be poisoned?"

Ashlee paused with the hoagie by her mouth. "No . . . decision to . . . come to this hospital. To do this Restaurant Week, of course. This event is good exposure for my career." She put the hoagie down on its paper sheet.

"I'm sure it was."

"You know, I'm suddenly feeling very tired." Her arms shot up and she yawned. "I think I need to be alone to get some rest now."

I stood to go. "I understand." I happened to notice that one of the bouquets of roses had a card attached that said GET BETTER SOON, CHICA. "That's nice, Tess sent you flowers."

Ashlee slid her eyes to the roses. "That's from another Tess. You don't know her."

I said goodnight and dragged my IV pole back down to the purgatory wing. My visit with Ashlee had left me with more questions than answers. Back in my room, my cellmate was silent. I was tempted to take her pulse. She resumed a hacking fit when I crossed in front of her bed, letting me know she was still alive. For now.

I rounded the corner, through my privacy mesh, and there was a single red rose propped up against my pillow with a note. It was from Tim.

Dear Poppy, I'm so sorry I couldn't be there with you. I've been so worried. You are the most important person in the world to me. Ivy said if we left, we would forfeit, and Gigi was sure you would want us to go on without you, to win the competition in your honor. I knew you were well cared for with the paramedics, plus you had Aunt Ginny and Sawyer. But I regret staying. I should have gone with you. Can you ever forgive me? Get better and come back to me soon. Even though I'm an idiot. All my love, Tim

It sounded like a reasonable explanation, but why he would believe anything Gigi said about me in the first place? Is he that blind to how she feels about him? If this had happened when we were still dating, would he have dropped everything and come to the hospital to be with me? Maybe I'm expecting too much from someone who I have no commitment with. There's no ring on my finger. Still, Gia was here.

Chapter Thirty-Four

I stared at the second hand ticking its way up the dial to the twelve. Just one more lap. I told myself I'd wait until nine AM before I made my escape. It had been a long fitful night of nurse rotations, vitals checks, and patient zero in the next bed.

I hadn't woken in the middle of the night to find a chef standing over me with a butcher knife, so that was good. Of course, I would have to have slept first for that to happen. Instead, I lay awake most of the night, going over each day of Restaurant Week. The sabotage, the chefs' reactions, the scores, the sneaking around, and the murder of Bess Jodice. I texted Sawyer a few times in the middle of the night and ran my ideas by her. She would have a lot to catch up on in the morning when she awoke. I did manage to cajole the doctor on call into taking out my IV around five AM, so that gave me hope.

The clock struck nine, and I threw the covers off and swung my feet over the edge of the bed. I dressed in my clothes from yesterday. They were still a little damp from my washing them in the sink to remove the passion fruit cheesecake fallout from my T-shirt and jeans. I was sure to have pneumonia by the time my hospital stay was over. I left a note on the bed saying that I'd left. If I'd had to wait for the doctor on call to come around, I'd never get home, and I needed a shower desperately.

Itty Bitty Smitty was waiting at the front door with his pickup running. "Ginny will kill me if she finds out I drove the getaway car."

"Are you gonna tell her?"

Smitty grunted. "Are you sure you should be doing this? What if there's something wrong with you that they haven't found yet?"

"I'm not giving them the chance to look. Just drive."

Smitty pulled away from the curb and headed for the Cape May Bridge. "What's so important you got to go back into that den of chaos where they're trying to kill ya?"

"I don't think they're all trying to kill me."

Smitty furrowed his bushy eyebrows. "One is enough."

"I can't disagree with that logic."

"Which one do you think it is?"

"I don't know. Adrian has the desperation. Philippe has the lies. Louie has the accomplice."

"What about the judges?"

"They could have just killed me at the house and been done with it."

"Oh, I see what you mean. What about the TV station people?" A pest control van tried to cut us off. Smitty rolled down his window and yelled, "Hey! Wise guy! Stay in your lane, ya Wacker! Nyahhh."

"Whoever attacked me is trying to shut me up because I've been asking too many questions. What motive would the TV people have to kill their judge and a host?"

Smitty grunted. "How do you know one person was trying to kill both victims? Horatio Duplessis has a lot of enemies who could have planned his attack, but maybe Ashlee's assailant just seized the moment. Any nut job in that room could kill any other nut job this week and the cops would try to connect the crimes to the old lady. But maybe they aren't related at all. Who in the room knew Ashlee was allergic to peanuts?"

"I asked her. She said Tess and Ivy knew. She never really gave me a straight answer about Philippe, but I'd assume he would have been told not to make anything with peanuts for the morning segment. In a weird way, Ashlee wasn't worried about the attack at all. She was more interested in growing her fan base."

Smitty pursed his lips together and gave me a look. "See. Nut jobs."

We pulled up in front of the house, and Smitty looked warily out the passenger window for signs of Aunt Ginny.

"Don't worry. If she catches you, I'll tell her I threatened to make you dig us a swimming pool."

Smitty grunted and shook his head.

On my way past the front parlor, I could hear the breakfast service in the dining room. Horatio was praising Aunt Ginny's meal for the day. "Normally you get raisins in oatmeal, but yours is chock-full of different fruits and spices. And do I taste rum? What's your secret ingredient?"

I paused on the fourth step when I heard Aunt Ginny say, "Fruitcake. I must get a dozen of them every Christmas. Ethel and I been passing the same one back and forth for six years now."

Aunt Ginny crumbled a fruitcake into a pot of oatmeal. There was no coming back from that. I fired off a text to Ivy that I'd been thinking about Bess's murder and Ashlee's attack, and could she meet me at the college in an hour. Then I hopped into the shower.

I stayed under the hot water until I was pruney. Never had clean felt so good. I pulled on my jeggings—well, I tried to anyway. They wouldn't go up over my derriere. I knew they fit two weeks ago when I bought them. I couldn't wait for Restaurant Week to be over. Today was the final day, hallelujah. I had to pull out another pair of black yoga pants. Whoever heard of losing weight over Christmas, only to gain it all back, and then some, from one week of baking fancy desserts.

I fixed my hair and makeup, using a generous amount of concealer to hide my bad-eating breakout. I was ready to meet the day. Ish. On my way down the stairs, I paused on the first landing. Figaro was scratching at Ashlee's door again. I picked him up and turned his orange eyes to mine. "What has gotten in to you?"

Merrrooowwwww.

I looked at Ashlee's door. What was he trying to get in there?

Norman's door opened, and Tess popped her head out. She was wearing a little bathrobe the size of a toddler's hooded bath towel. She froze when she saw me.

"It's none of my business," I started, "but how long have you been staying in Norman's room?"

"Lady, please. I had to get away from Ashlee the moment the rooms were assigned. She would have made me crazy."

I pointed to the door of the Monarch Room assigned to both girls. "So, you haven't been in here at all?"

"I don't even have a key. Ashlee, that crazy bimbo,

took both keys and said I had to be nice to her before she would give me mine." She nodded to the Adonis Suite. "This was easier. Perks of being a celebrity."

Figaro wiggled out of my arms and dropped to the floor. He went back to sniffing under Ashlee's door.

I gestured to Norman's room. "So, is it serious?"

"Only as far as he thinks." She put a finger to her lips and grinned.

"What happened to the two of you yesterday?"

Tess shrugged. "Overslept. Oops. We made it there, but you had already been blown up and taken to the hospital."

"Yeah, I saw the flowers you sent Ashlee. That was nice."

Tess rolled her eyes. "Believe me, sometimes it's easier to just give her what she wants. Attention. Well, I need to get ready for today." She gave me a finger wave and shut the door behind her.

Figaro was scratching Ashlee's door again. He was desperately trying to get at something.

"Alright inspector, let's see what has you so worked up." I used my master key and opened the door just enough to look around.

Figaro bonked his head against the corner and pushed his way into the room. He dove under the bed, disappearing under the Battenberg lace skirt.

"Fig, no!" I rushed after him and dove to my knees. I reached around until I found a squirmy ball of fluff. I pulled him out along the floor—he offered no assistance. He was intent on something under the bed.

When I wrestled him free, his head was stuck in an open jar of peanut butter. I used my cell phone flashlight to look under the bed. There was a sleeve of crackers, a few sandwich baggies, and a pair of rubber gloves.

If Tess didn't have a key, Ashlee would be the only one able to get in here other than staff. So, who hid the peanut butter under the bed?

Fig turned his big orange eyes on me, and, licking the peanut butter from his whiskers, he gave me a smug look that said I told you so.

Chapter Thirty-Five

I snuck down the stairs to get out of the house before Aunt Ginny could harangue me for leaving the hospital.

"Who broke you out? Kim? I knew that girl would get you in trouble one day."

I was so startled, I missed a step and had to grab the banister to keep from falling. Aunt Ginny was lurking in the shadows of the front parlor, lying in wait to catch me. *Do I remember nothing from high school?*

"How did you know I was home?"

"The hospital called thirty minutes ago when they found you missing. I oughta tan your hide for doing something so foolish."

"Or . . ." I held a finger up. "We could call it even for that getup ya got on right there."

Aunt Ginny was dressed in marine-blue harem pants and a matching gauzy long-sleeved top bejeweled with aqua sequins and tiny gold bells. There were gold bedroom slippers on her feet.

"Who are you supposed to be?" I asked. "The Little Mermaid?"

Aunt Ginny huffed. "That's ridiculous."

"Cher?"

Aunt Ginny rolled her eyes. "It's called a bedla. It's a belly dance costume."

"You planning on wearing that to judge in today?"

Aunt Ginny threw her hands on her chiffon hips. "I have it on good authority that today's theme is . . . well, I'm sworn to secrecy. But I'm dressed appropriately for it."

"Just out of curiosity, who told you today's theme? It wasn't Mr. Ricardo, your frisky salsa teacher, was it?"

"No." Aunt Ginny cocked an eyebrow. "But that does remind me that I have to check the event schedule at the senior center. I'll see you up there. I'm driving with Edith and Thelma."

Aunt Ginny went in search of some trouble, seeing as it had been a few hours since she'd found some. I jetted out the door to make the drive to *L'École des Chefs.* My long night in the hospital had given me some theories to test, and, by God, I was gonna test them.

Ivy met me in the foyer at the Hall of Honors and took me to the film lab. "I don't know what you're looking for, but if you can get my career out of the dumpster, I'm willing to show you anything."

"I want to see the footage from day one, before any editing."

She took me to a tiny little booth of a room. It was dark and smelled like Red Bull and Cheetos. There were four monitors lined up side by side on a long black table. A skinny black device covered in toggle switches and equalizers sat at the front of the table.

Two black mesh chairs rolled up to a couple of wireless mice and keyboards ready for us.

Ivy opened the first file in the list. "The police have already reviewed this, and they found no evidence on camera that anyone connected with the event tampered with the place settings."

The video began playing with Ashlee and Tess introducing the judges for the camera. "This isn't what I'm looking for."

"This is the beginning of the competition."

"Yeah, but I want what you recorded before the competition."

Ivy sounded confused. "What do you mean?"

"You know what I mean. You've had the camera rolling before and after the competition, capturing our fights and arguments. Watching our reactions to the sabotage and the judging."

"Whaaat?"

"I've seen the lights on the camera, and Frank never leaves his post. Now do you want my help or not?"

Ivy looked away. "It's not what you think. Unless you think the network wanted to catch any hint of scandal to expose and boost ratings. Then it's exactly what you think."

"I also think you're the one who sabotaged the ingredients on the first day."

Ivy looked behind us quickly to be sure we were alone. She swallowed hard. "Look, this is my first big show. I may have moved around a few labels in an effort to create some drama and chaos, and it paid off. Our ratings have skyrocketed. We've broken records for Channel Eight. Viewership has never been this high before. There's been talk of picking up our little show on the network. That will be great exposure for Team Maxine's."

"Not if that exposure makes it look like Tim was the one who cheated, and murdered Bess Jodice."

Ivy threw her hands up. "That wasn't me. I had nothing to do with poisoning Bess. And I wasn't involved with the equipment sabotage or Marco being hurt, or Ashlee being peanut buttered. The worst thing that could have happened with mixing up the pantry items was someone would've eaten a couple bites of talcum powder—and that won't hurt you—I checked. I'm just as shocked as everyone else about how this week has tanked, but the producer has insisted on moving on with the show."

"Exactly who is this producer you keep mentioning? Is it someone you work with at the station?"

Ivy shook her head. "Not exactly. Charlie is the segment producer—he's my boss. But the exec is silent. Like a venture capitalist. Executive producers put up the capital and make the arrangements, call the shots. Their money—their rules."

"So, you've never met the exec?"

"No."

"Do you have a name?"

"R. Snaarg."

"Arsnarg? What the heck kind of name is Arsnarg?"

"R is his first initial. Snaarg is the last name."

"Okay, well I was hoping it would be something obvious like Philippe Julian or Adrian Baxter, so we could pinpoint one of the chefs. So, where is the footage you took before the event? The footage you didn't want us to know about."

Ivy pulled up a separate folder on the hard drive and typed in a password. The files were dated, and time stamped with notes about who flew off the handle and what fights broke out.

"That one." I pointed to the first time stamp an hour before filming officially started.

Ivy clicked it and the media player opened the video. The chefs were slowly coming into the arena and milling about their stations. The judges' table was set with name cards and place settings. Horatio approached the table and examined the cards. He switched two of them, moving Norman farther down the table and moving Bess next to him. Horatio had made it clear that he didn't like Norman when they'd first arrived at the bed and breakfast. No one touched Bess's flatware. No one rearranged the table. Horatio took his seat, fished around for his pocket handkerchief, mopped his brow, tucked it back in his pocket, and waited patiently for the taping. After a while, the other three judges came in and milled about. Three different chefs came over to shake hands with the judges. Adrian, Philippe, and Tim. Then, a few minutes before the competition began, Roger took the judges from the room to await their cue to enter for the camera.

When Ashlee and Tess made the introductions, the camera angle changed and we couldn't directly see the judges. Anyone could have tampered with the place settings while the camera was focused on the girls, although I was in the room at the time, and I never saw anyone walking around. Once we were in our places, we stayed there.

When the camera panned back to the judges, we saw Bess pour herself a cup of tea, examine the silverware in front of her, and clearly pick up Horatio's spoon. Horatio had his eyes on the kitchens and didn't notice. Bess stirred her honey into her tea with the poisoned spoon. I shuddered involuntarily. We were watching the murder take place right before our eyes.

We scanned a few more files, keeping our eyes on the activity around the place settings. I had really hoped the file would show someone pick up a spoon and replace it with a poisoned one. I closed the last file with the footage from the judges' table on day one. "There has to be something I'm missing. Can we watch the first clip again?"

Ivy pulled it up and we watched the judges sitting at the table waiting for the day to begin. Everyone's hands were visible the entire time. The chefs came over to shake hands.

"Wait. Stop there."

Ivy paused the video. "What is it?"

"I thought I saw something."

"Like what?"

"I dunno. Like a flash or a flicker."

Ivy backed the video up a minute and we watched it again, keeping our eyes on Bess's place setting. "I don't see anything," Ivy said. "Are you sure it was there?"

"Maybe my eyes are imagining things." Then it flickered again. "There. Can you play it in slow motion?"

We watched the playback for the third time, this time at half speed. There was a slight flicker while the chefs were at the judges' table. "What was that?"

Ivy shrugged. She examined the video closer. "I'm not sure. It looked like the recording jumped. Like it was a bad cut. But the time stamp hasn't changed."

I examined the judges' table. Nothing looked any different. What was missing? One of the three chefs swapping out a spoon? A fourth chef? "Who would know how to edit the file to remove a few seconds of recording, but doctor the time stamp to show no time had passed?"

"The whole postproduction team would."

"We need to talk to them as soon as they come in.

Someone edited out a section of video, and I'd be willing to bet it shows whoever replaced Horatio's spoon with the one that poisoned Bess."

"I'll call you as soon as they come in."

"Good." I closed the file, so no one would know what we'd been looking at until we could question the editing team. Another file name caught my eye. TIM AND GIGI SECRET ROMANCE DAY 4. "What's this?" I opened it.

"I'm not sure you should see that," Ivy cautioned.

The video was a close-up of Gigi teasing Tim. She was circling his name on his chef coat with her finger, and he was smiling down at her with a look like the one Gia gave to me.

"I'm sorry. I thought you and your boss had a thing going."

"It's fine." I tried to shrug it off. I couldn't close the file because my hand was shaking. I walked from the film booth in a haze. I guess that's that, then. It didn't look like I'd be making any painful decisions in my future. From the look on Tim's face I'd say he'd already made it.

Chapter Thirty-Six

I tried to calm my shaky nerves. Tim and Gigi hadn't arrived yet. I had no right to be upset, but that logic didn't stop waves of heartbreak from pummeling me.

Aunt Ginny breezed in with a gift bag and held it out. "What's the matter with you? You look like you're about to cry."

"I'm just realizing that I've been a fool."

"Honey, we're all fools. Anyone who looks like they've got their life together is just a good actor. Here, I got you something."

I took the bag and pulled out an attractive black apron with the title CHEF in silver filigree writing, front and center. I felt my face break into a sly grin. I slid my eyes in appreciation to Aunt Ginny. She gave me a conspiratorial nod in return then took her place at the judges' table.

I put the apron on and waited for Gigi to arrive.

Gia entered with Momma and headed straight for me. "Bella, I went to the hospital to check on you this morning. They said you'd left without being discharged. Why didn't you call me?" He wrapped his arms around me. "Are you feeling okay?"

I looked into his face. He was so beautiful, from the inside out. Why was I so determined to keep my emotions in check with him? "I'm fine. Just a slight headache. I wanted to finish the competition."

He took my hand. "Are you sure you should be on your feet today? Maybe you should be resting."

"Really, I'm fine."

Louie approached me, his head down, caution in his eyes. "Poppy, you gotta believe me. I never would have rigged your oven to blow like that. I don't know where that hacksaw came from, but it wasn't mine."

"I see they released you."

"They checked that thing for my fingerprints, but it had been wiped clean. I asked the police why they thought I was smart enough to wipe my fingerprints off, then dumb enough to toss it into the open bed of my pickup. Twenty minutes later they let me go."

Several chefs came over to welcome me back, tell me they were glad I wasn't hurt, and threw me compliments about my new and improved apron. It made me feel a part, like I was one of them. An equal sibling in the Chef family. I hated what I had to do today to knock a couple of them down.

Tim and Gigi finally arrived with matching Starbucks cups. Two, not three. I could tell the moment Gigi saw my apron, because she stopped in her tracks and spewed a mouthful of coffee on her chef coat.

Oh, that was worth it.

Tim's eyes lit up. "Hey Mack, you're here. I was so worried about you."

"Uh huh."

He gave me a hug which I did not return. "Thank God you're okay."

"Places, everyone." Ivy came through the room with Tess close behind. "We begin rolling in five. In honor

of today being the last day of Restaurant Week, I've set
up the room across the hall as a sort of green room for
you. There will be snacks and drinks set out all day.
Feel free to use the area as a lounge whenever we have
a break."

Tim and Gigi stowed their things and hid their
coffee cups. Tim was watching me. His eyebrows dipped,
and he cocked his head to the side. He switched places
with Gigi and whispered, "Are you mad at me?"

I knew I couldn't get into it now. If I started unload-
ing my feelings from the past week I might not be able
to rein it in. I couldn't even look at him. "We'll talk
later."

Sawyer hustled over to my station and handed me
an envelope. "Here's what you asked for. Let him
have it."

I popped it open and read the contents. "Well, let's
see where this goes."

Ivy held up her hand and counted down on her fingers from five. Sawyer ducked into the stands next to
Smitty and Mrs. Dodson.

Tess spoke into the camera. "Welcome to day seven
of the Cape May County Restaurant Week Competition. Today's theme is Lively Morocco. Chefs, open
your mystery baskets."

Tess went over the mystery ingredients, but my
mind was on Adrian and the information that Sawyer
was able to dig up for me. As soon as Tess shouted,
"Go!" I was off to make an interception.

I followed Adrian to where he was taking spices and
raisins off the shelf. I handed him the envelope. "We
know everything."

His eyes narrowed, and he looked in the envelope.
When realization dawned on him as to the gravity of
what we'd discovered, he dropped his raisins.

I went back to my station empty-handed because I had no idea what was in my basket. Almond paste, sesame seeds, and dates. I looked over to Philippe's kitchen. He was in deep discussion with his chefs. Probably because Julia Child's recipes didn't translate easily into Moroccan cuisine.

Adrian walked through my kitchen and hissed, "You don't understand."

I went to the pantry and grabbed some phyllo dough, honey, and walnuts and went back to my kitchen. I would make baklava.

Adrian came through again. "It's not what it looks like."

Tim and Gigi gave me questioning looks. I answered with a shrug.

I laid out my phyllo dough and realized I would need butter.

Adrian made another pass. "Image is everything in this business." He knocked Tim on his way by. Tim's hand slipped, and he chopped a big chunk off a carrot.

I went to the pantry for a block of butter to melt.

Vidrine was in there. "What is going on with you two?"

"Adrian's got his knickers in a twist over something I showed him."

"*Chér*, be careful with that one. He can fly into a rage lickety split."

I took a stick of butter back to my workstation and started to unwrap it.

Adrian came by again, his nostrils flaring. "Mother is a shark. She will eat you alive if yooze try to burn me with this." He knocked my butter off the counter and went to the pantry.

I was no fool. I knew what he wanted. He thought I would follow him in there, so he could corner me, but it wasn't going to work. I could wait all day.

He came out a couple minutes later with two potatoes. "I need to talk to you, now!"

"Cut!" Ivy called a time-out. "Chef Adrian, why do you keep entering Chef Tim's kitchen? If you need something from the pantry you could go around."

Adrian pointed a potato at Tim and shouted. "Chef Tim is blackmailing me!"

"What?! I am not!"

"Ah . . . yeah, he is. He's using his pastry chef to intimidate me."

The audience snickered.

That made Adrian heat from a simmer to a boil. "Tim Maxwell has been out to get me since I stepped foot in this arena a week ago. He sabotaged my ingredients causing me to get a low score, he cut the line on my range, so my food was substandard, he probably poisoned Ashlee Pickel so my dishes couldn't be judged, and now he's ruining my concentration with this blackmail." Adrian waved the envelope in the air. "I'm the best chef in this room, and he's threatened by my skills."

Tim put his knife down and leaned on the counter for support. "I haven't done anything to you. Everything that's happened this week, you've brought on yourself."

Adrian rushed Tim and roared. "You've been out to destroy me ever since our culinary school final!"

The camera spun toward Tim. I knew everything that was happening would be in the editing room computer in a file labeled TIM AND ADRIAN SHOWDOWN by this evening. I wanted to warn them, but there was no stopping this crazy train.

Tim's face was purple with rage. He pulled his chef coat off and balled his fists in front of him. "Yeah! I did it! I mixed up your ingredients! Alright!"

Gigi took a step backwards. The audience gasped.

Money started changing hands between the seniors. Mrs. Davis waved her fingers. "Pay up."

Gigi lost the ability to stand and dropped to her knees.

Adrian threw his arm out and pointed at Tim. "Aha! Finally, you admit it!"

"Yeah, I admit it. I was twenty years old. I was young and stupid. It was a horrible mistake that I've been ashamed of for years. But you still graduated second in your class with honors. I didn't ruin your life, you've done that all on your own. You're so full of yourself that you can't handle the slightest criticism. If your scores suck, it's because you argue with the judges and insist you know better."

"I do not!" Adrian started to protest, but the judges were all nodding in agreement.

Tim stomped his foot forward, and Adrian shrunk down. "And I had nothing to do with the pantry or any other sabotage this week. I'm just trying to make the best food I can to represent Maxine's and get my picture on the cover of *South Jersey Dining Guide*. I don't even know what you're talking about with this blackmail stunt."

Adrian held the letter up prepared to complain some more.

"The envelope is from me."

The audience gasped, and the camera swung in my direction. I sighed. *Here we go.*

Ivy picked up the handheld microphone. "Are you blackmailing Chef Adrian?"

"Of course not."

"What's in the envelope?"

Adrian opened his mouth, snapped it shut, and then shoved the envelope into his chef coat. "Nothing. It's not important."

Tim crossed his arms and flexed his biceps. "A minute ago, you were trying to ruin my reputation over that envelope. Now, what's in it?"

The arena hushed. The room was quiet enough to hear the feedback from Mr. Sheinberg's hearing aid.

Ivy applied some pressure. "Come on Adrian, what's in the envelope?"

Sawyer yelled from the stands. "It's a security camera photo and receipt from Handyman Haven that shows Adrian bought a hacksaw last Saturday night."

The audience gasped again, and seniors started passing money down to Itty Bitty Smitty.

Aunt Ginny hollered back from the judges' table. "I called that one! I get half!"

Adrian was ready to bolt. "I can explain. It's not what you think."

Louie blew a gasket. "You tried to frame me for rigging Poppy's oven!"

Roger's thumbs moved like lightning, tapping out the updates for social media.

Gia was on Adrian like thunder. He grabbed him by his chef coat and pulled Adrian to his toes. "Did you fix Poppy's oven to explode? Did you? I will make you regret the day you were born."

Momma was at Gia's back swatting him with her apron and chattering reproof.

The blood drained from Adrian's face. "No! No no no no no. I didn't. I didn't touch Poppy's oven or try to frame anyone for it! I only cut the line on my own range. That was all!"

Oliva spouted a line of obscenities in Italian. Gia translated, and cleaned it up. "Did you tamper with the thermostat on the deep fryer?"

"No, I swear. Look, I came in late Saturday night after we'd all been sabotaged and cut the line on my stove. I knew some of you thought I had sabotaged the pantry, and I wanted to throw suspicion off of myself—because I didn't do it. But I didn't touch anything else. Not Saturday, and not since. Really. Look, I stashed the hacksaw in the walk-in behind a box of turnips. Go see for yourself."

Ivy took off running for the pantry with Frank wheeling the camera behind her. The chefs all crammed in the small doorway to watch Ivy check the huge refrigerator. She bent over boxes of carrots and lettuce and fished around behind the turnips. She turned and looked into the camera, then pulled up a small hacksaw.

Adrian breathed a sigh of relief. "See. The police found the hacksaw that was used on Poppy's oven in Louie's truck yesterday. It was taken into evidence."

Vidrine added, "Plus it was a lot manlier."

Philippe laughed. "What is zat, a toy hacksaw?"

The color rushed back into Adrian's cheeks. "No, it's a regular manly hacksaw. It's just—travel size."

"I think that's the one the Girl Scouts use," Louie snickered.

Everyone followed Ivy back into the arena where she held the tiny hacksaw up for the audience.

When they'd stopped laughing, Mrs. Dodson called out, "Is he the one who poisoned Bess with Horatio's spoon?"

The audience chatter kicked up again.

Adrian held up his hands, pleading. "I didn't. Food is my life. I would never resort to manipulating it to harm anyone. No matter how much of a low-life-slug-critic Horatio Duplessis is. And I didn't even know the lady who died. I'm innocent. I'll take a lie detector test. You can watch my every move on camera. See for yourself."

"Why should anyone believe you, Adrian?" Tim asked. "You've been lying about the sabotage all week."

Adrian rounded on Tim. "Are you going to call me out for lying after you've held on to your lie for twenty years?"

Tim backed down.

I made a face at Ivy. "Maybe the person responsible for sabotaging the ingredients should come forward so everyone can stop accusing everyone else."

Ivy shook her head no.

I nodded mine yes.

She rolled her eyes. "Fine. I switched the labels in the pantry."

Mrs. Dodson whooped and tapped her cane. Seniors started passing money down to her.

Adrian was so shocked you could have knocked him over with a gentle breeze. "But—"

Ivy implored the chefs. "I wanted to drum up some drama for ratings. I didn't know you would all get in such a twist and start sabotaging everything else."

Louie called out, "Who sabotaged the appliances?"

Vidrine added, "And who killed Bess?"

No one was willing to fess up to either, and the room grew rambunctious.

Ivy held her hands up. "Okay, settle down everyone. We don't have all the answers yet. All we know is that Adrian sabotaged himself." Ivy crooked her finger at Frank to follow her with the camera and took the microphone over to interview Adrian. "Tell us why you did it. Why would you sabotage your own oven to try to win the competition?"

Adrian wouldn't answer, so I answered for him. "Because he's bankrupt."

The audience jabbered amongst themselves and checked their dailies. One of the seniors from Mother

Gibson's church jumped to her feet and did a little hallelujah dance. "It's me! It's me! I said he was really broke." She collected her money and waved it around.

Horatio twisted his mustache. "That isn't news. It's common knowledge that he's broke. He's in debt up to his eyeballs. For golly sake he still lives at home. Everything he owns is in his mother's name, and Helen Baxter rules with an iron fist."

Adrian pleaded with Ivy. "You don't know my mother. All she cares about is the bottom line. She's the Baxter in Baxter's By the Bay. She has no eye for artistry. All she cares about is profit. If I don't bring Baxter's bottom line up, Mother is shutting us down. My whole future rides on winning this competition."

Mother is really his mother.

Adrian looked much smaller with the turbo knocked out of his engine. "This contest was my last chance to drum up a success. But the sabotage, then the poisoning, then the other poisoning. They've ruined my business."

Horatio blurted out, "Your business can't be more ruined by this event than by what you've done to it yourself."

Adrian closed the distance between himself and Horatio in seconds. He slammed his hand down on the judges' table. "You ruined me with your horrible reviews of Baxter's. What do yooze have against chefs? Why yooze got to be so critical?"

Horatio raised his palms in the air. "I'm a critic. It's my job."

Adrian shoved his hands in his pockets and stepped away from the table. "Why do you have to be so mean about it?"

"Huh," I breathed out loud to myself.

"Huh, what?" Tim asked me.

"If Adrian was trying to murder Horatio, he would have attacked him just now. He didn't even touch him."

"Maybe that's because of the camera recording his every move."

"Maybe. Or maybe Adrian isn't a cold-blooded killer. Maybe he's all talk."

Chapter Thirty-Seven

Ivy moved to the center of the arena and put her hands in a time-out position. "Okay everyone, let's take ten then come back and regroup."

Philippe was incredulous. "Take ten? Why are we not getting zat cop in here? He is clearly your killer."

"We don't know that," Ivy answered. "And I'm not going to get the police involved based on circumstantial evidence."

Philippe threw his apron off and stormed out of the arena.

I ducked after him. It was time to fry this fake Frenchie.

I followed him down the hall toward the main foyer and the Hall of Honors. He strode to the back of the foyer and turned a corner. There was a door with an Emergency Exit sign lit overhead. Philippe pushed his way through the crash bar, went around the hall, and entered a room full of vending machines. He smacked the side of a vending machine, kicked the bottom corner with his foot, and a Twinkie popped out.

"How did you know it would do that?"

Philippe jumped. "What do you want with me, madame?"

"How about the truth?"

"Zee truth about what?"

"For a start, I saw the morning show footage."

Philippe looked away. He unwrapped the Twinkie and shoved it in his mouth. When he was done chewing he said, "They made me look like a fool."

"I know," I soothed. "It wasn't right."

"They did not care about what I was making, or how to caramelize onions. They only want to look cute in zee apron on camera. Then they humiliate me by spitting my food out like it was bad. I will never do another TV spot again."

"No one could blame you for that."

"Is zat why you corner me down here? To ask me about this ancient history?"

"Did you slip Ashlee some peanut butter to get even?"

"My God, woman! Who do you think I am?"

"You tell me."

"I am Philippe Julian, Chef de cuisine. I study under zee master, Pierre Escargot at *Le Cordon Bleu*. I do not kill people."

"Mm hmm. *Préférez-vous les recettes traditionnelles?*"

Philippe screwed his face to a pained expression.

"I asked if you prefer the traditional recipes."

Philippe shrugged. "I know."

"I ask because every one of your recipes is a Julia Child masterpiece. I would know because I've seen every episode of *The French Chef*, and I've read both volumes of *Mastering the Art of French Cooking* cover to cover."

Philippe's Adam's apple bobbed in his throat.

"Everything you've made this week has had very minor substitutions, but I'd recognize the recipes anywhere. I'm willing to bet that you were making a *boeuf bourguignon* with Moroccan spices and raisins before we were called to a time-out."

Philippe blushed crimson.

"*Tu ne parles pas français.*"

Philippe just stared at me.

"*C'est oui, ou no?*"

"Sure, whatever."

"I said, you don't speak French, do you?"

Philippe remained silent.

"The thing is, *Le Cordon Bleu* only started translating classes to English in the late eighties. That was after you would have attended."

Philippe's ears started to glow hot. He lost the accent. "What is your problem with me?"

"And Pierre Escargot is a character from a '90s variety show on Nickelodeon. You've never even been to Paris, have you?"

"Why do you care so much about what I do, lady? I haven't been giving you a hard time. Why can't you mind your own business?" He punched the vending machine on the side. It released a Kit Kat this time.

"I think it's fascinating that you know just the right spot to do that." I looked around the room. "And that you knew where this room was. Especially since the lobby upstairs marked this hall as an emergency exit only. Didn't Bess say she recognized someone in the competition? Yet all the other chefs went to top-tier culinary schools or were self-taught. You're the only one who lied about it."

Philippe kicked the trash can. "Fine! Enough! I went here."

"Why isn't your name on any class list? I searched a decade of yearbooks for you online last night."

Philippe dropped his face in his hands. "Isn't it enough that I had to be mocked by that witch every day? I won't put up with your mocking too."

"I'm not mocking you. I just want you to come clean."

"I failed, okay? I flunked out of community college. So, what!" Philippe started pacing the tiny room. "Some of the most successful chefs never went to school at all, like Vidrine and Louie, as you already pointed out. Being classically trained doesn't make or break you. Just look at Adrian Baxter, Culinary Institute of America, second in his class, and he lives with his mother, flat broke." He tapped his chest. "I reinvented myself. I'm successful now. I have nothing to be ashamed of."

"Unless you killed Bess Jodice for recognizing you."

Philippe turned on me. "I wish I had. Because whoever killed her, did me a huge favor. It was only a matter of time before she figured out who I was, and tried to ruin me. She was a bitter woman who loved to taunt the weak and sensitive. She made my life a living hell. She constantly humiliated me on her Wall of Shame, and then she failed me. Oh, but she loved my dishes in the contest. If she had remained a judge, I would have won for sure. That was going to be my sweet revenge. No, I didn't kill her. I wanted to rub her face in my success."

"Wall of Shame? What is that?"

"Her Wall of Shame is where she posted failing grades on her special bulletin board. Took pictures of your flops and hung them up to embarrass you. Picked apart your recipes until you were terrified of ever holding a whisk again. She was vicious. You would think she invented cooking the way she judged who was worthy to practice the art and who wasn't. She didn't just mark you down. She destroyed you. You don't know what I had to do to get over her torture and move on with my life. It was always my dream to be a chef. To create delicious masterpieces. People would line up for hours waiting to dine in my restaurant. So, I memorized the cookbook of the greatest chef of all time."

"Why don't you just make up your own recipes?"

Philippe flew at me, spittle flying out of his mouth. "Because I can't! I don't have that gift. I can follow a recipe, but I just can't make my own."

"Of course, you can. You've been doing it all week."

Philippe straightened. "What?"

"Making up a recipe is the same as playing with new ingredients and putting that twist on something familiar. It's being creative with flavors to turn the usual upside down. Like swapping out chip steak for ham in a quiche Lorraine. Or using coconut oil in place of shortening. Swapping like for like. Adding a pinch of this, a dash of that."

Philippe's eyes narrowed as he considered my words. "You just lack the confidence."

"Having the Devil as a professor will do that to you."

"She sounds perfectly horrible."

"She was, but what she did to me was only a fraction of what she was capable of."

"How do you know that?"

"There is one student who will live in infamy for giving his class food poisoning. She tortured him worst of all. He didn't fail, he just disappeared one day, never to be heard from again."

"You don't remember his name, do you?"

"Remember it? It was on our exams. His portrait hangs on the Wall of Shame to this day."

"What! It's still here? Why didn't you say that sooner?"

"It's an unwritten rule, you don't speak that name here."

"Where is this Wall of Shame? I want to go see it for myself."

"I'll tell you where it is, but I'm not going down there. Never again."

Philippe wrote directions on the back of the Kit Kat wrapper and told me I was on my own.

I followed his scrawl to the letter. Down the hall, to the left, descend the dark stairwell. Around the corner. Then, through the double doors that say boiler room. There, I found the Wall of Shame.

It wasn't the Polaroid snaps of fallen soufflés, burnt pies, or lopsided cakes that caught my eye. It wasn't the failing exam sheets covered in red pen, the newspaper articles about school competitions that had not been won, or the vicious cartoons mocking students for their mistakes. It was the portrait of a young Horatio that hung in the center of the wall over the name Horace R. Snaarg that took my breath away.

Chapter Thirty-Eight

"I knew you'd eventually find your way down here. I tried to warn you to stay out of it. Now you've forced my hand."

I didn't have to turn around, I knew that voice. Why did it have to be him? He'd been praising my cooking and encouraging me to follow my dreams all week. He'd given me hope that I had what it took to be a professional chef. Was any of it real, or was he just playing me? My heart trembled with disappointment. "You're R. Snaarg, the executive producer behind Restaurant Week? It makes sense now. Only the producer would be able to sabotage the equipment, send three people to the hospital, one to the morgue, and still insist the station go on with the show."

"You're a lot sharper than most of the chefs upstairs. They're blinded by ambition, grasping for fame, stepping on each other to get ahead. You pay attention to what's going on around you and follow your instincts. I knew if anyone figured it out, it would be you." Horatio reached a shaky hand and touched the plaque under his picture. "Horace R. Snaarg. Poisoned twenty-one classmates and one grad student with salmonella."

I nodded at his portrait. "Is this why you killed her?"

He twirled his mustache. "This is just the scar you see. There are many more beneath the surface."

"It can't be easy to stand here and be reminded about the horrible way she treated you."

"I don't have to be reminded, dear, I think about it every day."

I took a long look at the dapper older gentleman. What amount of pain would fracture the soul to where one would be willing to snuff out another's life? "I get that she was horrible, but why would she go to this extreme over a bout of salmonella? It happens in the best of restaurants."

"For one thing, Bess Jodice took pleasure in being cruel." Horatio gave me a sad smile. "But, also because one of my classmates nearly died. He had a weak immune system from another disease and couldn't fight off the bacteria. He was in the hospital for weeks. I was traumatized even without her vilifying me. It's why I've spent my career being vigilant for proper food preparation when I review a restaurant. I never want another chef to experience the horror that I went through."

"Do you know how it happened?"

"It was a momentary mistake that resulted in a lifetime of consequences. Bess ran the classroom like a drill sergeant. Always behind you, barking out orders. Nothing was ever good enough. You were always on edge, terrified to make a wrong move." Horatio shifted his feet to lean on his walking stick. "She loved these timed tests, not unlike your competition upstairs. She said that in a restaurant kitchen you would have to move quickly or the whole line would fall behind. The demand was impossible. Fillet a sea bass in under two minutes. Trim a tenderloin in under five. On that fateful day, we were being timed on chicken fricassee, and I was behind. I was always behind. I forgot to flip my cutting board and wash my knife between deboning my chicken and chopping my finishing herbs."

That is a surefire way to spread salmonella. I tried to keep the look of horror out of my eyes. I didn't need anything flipping his switch. He'd already killed one person this week.

"Back in those days we had peer reviews. Within an hour of eating my fricassee, half the class was in the emergency room. The rest of the story is hanging there on the Wall of Shame before you."

I looked at the portrait of a hopeful Horatio, not marred by the ugly title Bess had hung on him. "She called you Horace the day she died. I thought she was slurring her speech because she was drunk."

Horatio tapped his walking stick on the floor. "That was the effects of the botulism taking hold. She knew who I was from day one, kept making offhanded comments about recognizing old students and knowing everyone's abilities. I tried to play it off like I didn't know what she was talking about, but she plunged that knife in my heart right from the start and twisted it a little every day."

"I would have thought she'd be impressed by your standing in the restaurant community. Everyone else is awed by you."

Horatio chuckled under his breath. "She knew I didn't want to be a food critic. After I flunked out of school here, I tried to apply to other community colleges, but she sent them all letters of censure, blackballing me from admittance. She said I didn't have what it took. I was too slow, too timid, and would never make a good chef. My family was poor. We didn't have the money for a top-tier school. So, I changed my name and got a job as an apprentice under a head chef in New York for a couple of months." He shook his head. "It was no use. My nerves were raw. I was frozen with terror that I would make another mistake and hurt someone else. After I was let go, I returned to New Jersey and went to night school for a journalism course. I thought maybe I could write about food, a little column discussing my own dishes. Today they call it food narrative, and it's wildly popular."

"Isn't that basically what Bess did for *Food and Wine Digest*?

Horatio tapped his walking stick on the floor again. "Yes, ironic isn't it? There she was—a chef—and she stepped down to do my backup plan. I hate being a restaurant critic, but I couldn't get hired to write anything else. Editors pigeonholed me because of my culinary school background. I understood what I was eating—or was supposed to be eating. But I never wanted to be sitting at the table. I wanted to be in the kitchen."

"A lot of people would love to trade places with you."

"It's not all they assume it to be. You're always an outsider. Chefs hate you. Some belittle you, others send death threats. No one will cook for you because they think you'll critique them. Eating out is going to work, and I am so sick and tired of truffle oil and molecular gastronomy, and pretentious chefs like Adrian Baxter who make mediocre food. They rely on big-school credentials, exotic ingredients, and plate designs—but what comes out of the kitchen is dry, tasteless, over spiced and under salted, and sometimes just plain weird. What I wouldn't give for a really good grilled cheese."

I shifted my weight to look around Horatio at the door. *Why is no one coming?* His expression grew wary.

He knew I was thinking about running. I had to keep him talking until help arrived.

"All this happened so long ago. Why kill her now?"

"It was her editorial on recipe development that caught my eye. Bess used *Food and Wine Digest* as her personal self-promotion column. She was boasting about the release of her new cookbook and her process for developing unique recipes. The recipe she used in the article was for pineapple bread stuffing. I knew the recipe instantly, because I'd made it up. It was the only time I'd ever gotten a B in her class. That's when I decided to delay my retirement and started formulating a plan. I called the Chamber of Commerce and the television station and convinced them that my Restaurant Week event was a great idea. Who do you think bankrolled most of the basket items?"

"I thought they were donated by local vendors."

Horatio gave me a patronizing look. "What local vendor in South Jersey would have Buddha's hand fruit or monk's beard?"

"Honestly, I was wondering that myself. Do the Chamber of Commerce and television station know that R. Snaarg is really Horatio Duplessis?"

"No, my dear. No one has called me by my given name for ages. It took me months to work out the details. Killing Bess by food poisoning would be poetic justice. I had confiscated a bulging jar of tainted peaches from a restaurant I'd reviewed. The 'chef,' a kid who'd turned himself into a human pin cushion and had a beard down to his belt, was so proud of the 'craft beer' that he'd distilled in a bathtub in his basement, that he offered me a tour of his 'culinary workshop.' He was so busy bragging about making sausage out of roadkill, that he failed to see the ticking peach time bomb in his artisanal pickle pantry. I was so irritated, I wanted to make him eat the peaches. But instead, I took them home with me to save his unfortunate patrons."

"So, you clearly had the murder weapon, your peach jar full of botulism, but what I can't understand is how you pulled it off. Bess was poisoned with your own spoon."

Horatio tapped his walking stick on the floor again. "I was originally going to do it at the inn. Maybe slip some peach botulism into her orange juice. But then I met you, and I recognized a kindred spirit. A woman of your age, starting over. I said to myself, now here's someone who understands regret and disappointment. I didn't want you connected to this in any way."

My stomach took a sudden drop. The murder almost took place right under my own roof.

"Then I went on the kitchen tour with the other judges and saw that some intern had set the place settings backwards. That's when I knew how to get away with it. No one paid any attention to my activities during the tour. They were far too concerned about their lighting and what camera angles would be the most flattering. I stole my own spoon away in my pocket and brought it back to the B&B to marinate it overnight in the poison. I did it three nights in a row. I had no idea it would take her so long to die."

"But how did you get her to use your spoon instead of her own?"

"Bess was frivolously petty, fussy to the point of tedium. She would only use the proper silverware in the right setting. All I had to do was poison my own spoon, put it back in the spot that should have been hers, and let her pick it up. Instant alibi."

"I've watched the video footage. I saw you swap the

name cards when no one was looking, to be sure she was next to you. But I never saw you put the spoon out. How'd you do it?"

"I was very clever about it. I carried the spoon behind my pocket square, and then when I mopped my brow I slid it down my sleeve before the other judges arrived."

"Then why'd you have to edit the file? I know something was removed from the finished clip. I saw the video jump."

Horatio's eyes narrowed. "I paid that kid to make sure the video was a clean cut. The camera caught me moving my spoon closer to Bess's plate. I wanted to be sure she thought it was hers. First, he botched the appliance sabotage—no one was supposed to get hurt. Then he was almost caught by Chef Vidrine sneaking around trying to peek in the baskets. That would have been a shame—she has a lot of promise as a chef, even if she is a cheater." He sighed. "And now the video footage. These kids today do everything so slap-dash."

"By that kid, do you mean Roger?"

Horatio waved his hand. "Oh heck, no. That one's a straight arrow. Thinks he's going to be the next Steven Spielberg of all things. No, I paid some tattooed kid I found hanging around the media booth."

"Is that who you got to rig my oven? You know I could have died from that explosion."

Horatio tossed his walking stick back and forth between his hands. "Actually, I did that myself. I thought for sure you heard me leave the bed and breakfast the night before. I waited for the distraction of Tess and Norman arguing to slip out. I did warn you to stay out of it. I told you that you'd force the killer to have to come after you. I didn't want to see you hurt, but a few days in the hospital would have done you some good. You really should have stayed there."

That sick twisted little man. An evil gleam was forming in his eyes. He was reminding me less and less of my Uncle Teddy and more like a deranged Monopoly Man about to go on a killing spree.

Horatio pushed a button on the handle of his walking stick and a switchblade shot out the bottom. "I like you Poppy. I really do. But I can't just let you walk out of here and turn me in. I've already suffered enough, and there's no way I'm going to spend my golden years rotting in prison."

Horatio lunged to stab me with his blade. His face twisted with bitterness, his mustache standing straight out across his lip.

I dodged the first swipe, but the second swipe sliced my upper arm. Searing pain shot down to my fingertips and my chest spread with wet heat. I instinctively grabbed the wound with my other hand. It came away warm and sticky. He was really trying to kill me. I looked for somewhere to run.

Horatio lunged back to strike again.

I tried to run, but I was backed against Bess's Wall of Shame. My foot caught on the edge of the table Bess had used to display some of her trophies of humiliation, and I stumbled, banging my knee on the cold concrete floor.

Horatio caught my shoulder this time. He'd narrowly missed my neck. I had to find a way to fight back before he overpowered me. I threw my wounded arm behind me and grabbed a rusty cast iron frying pan from the display and conked him on the side of the head. He cried in agony and crumpled to the floor. The weight of the cast iron was too much for my injured arm and the pan slipped from my grasp and clanged loudly on the floor.

I watched Horatio writhe in pain and then all movement stopped. He lay still, but his chest was rising and falling. He was alive. I kicked his cane out of reach and pulled my cell phone from my pocket. I dialed the cell number for a certain blonde police officer that I knew.

"Amber, I'm in the boiler room of the community college. You aren't going to believe this. Horatio Duplessis is Bess Jodice's killer. I have him disarmed. Can you send a cruiser and an ambulance?"

Amber replied, "Aww crap!"

Chapter Thirty-Nine

Officer Birkwell got to the basement almost before I hung up the phone. He cuffed Horatio and called an ambulance. Soon after, Amber arrived with half the police force, and everyone upstairs had made their way downstairs. Ivy had been in a panic that Horatio was missing. Aunt Ginny had been in a panic that I was missing. And Adrian had been in a panic that he was going to be blamed for my disappearance.

Philippe, Gia, and Tim were fighting their way to the boiler room. I could hear Tim arguing with Philippe all the way down the stairs. "Why would you tell her about this room? She has a nose for trouble. She'd better be alright. If she's hurt in any way, I'll kill you."

Gia was giving Philippe what for with the Italian version of Tim's rebuke.

The boiler room doors flew open and the three men burst in shoulder to shoulder. Their panic was quickly followed by relief and then anger when they saw my bloody arm.

Before any of them could take a step to help me, a loud "YAAAAAAH!" preceded a tiny red head in a glorified harem costume flying through the air, her little gold bells tinkling in the breeze she created. Aunt Ginny ran straight up to Horatio and kicked him in the side as hard as she could with her soft gold slipper.

"I appreciate the effort Princess Jasmine, but he's unconscious and handcuffed."

Aunt Ginny looked from me to Officer Birkwell to Horatio's still form curled on the hard floor. "It never hurts to be sure."

Gia pulled me into his arms. Then Tim shoved Gia and pulled me into his arms, with my face smashed against his chest. Gia pulled a fist back and was ready to start swinging.

I wriggled around and yelled, "Whoa! Okay, let's everybody just settle down."

Aunt Ginny nudged me in the side. "Wait a minute, let's see where this goes."

Amber saved me from finding out. "Everybody who is not connected to the events that took place down here, please return to the arena above us."

Nobody moved.

"If you don't return upstairs, I'll have to charge you with obstruction of justice."

Most everyone left after that. Aunt Ginny stayed, daring Amber with eyes of fire to make her leave. Tim and Gia stayed. Neither one was about to leave my side. Gigi stayed to keep her eyes on Tim. And Philippe stayed because he felt responsible for sending me here in the first place. "I would never have let Madame come by herself if I had known zis killer would be in zee room." Philippe gave me a raised eyebrow to see if I would out him for having his fake French accent back.

I gave Philippe a wink and a slight nod, and he grinned in return.

Paramedics bandaged my arm until I could go back

to the hospital to get stitches, while Amber took all of our statements, and by all, I mean mine. Philippe and Horatio, who was now conscious and handcuffed, gave brief answers as to their part in the matter, but Amber soon learned that no one else in the room had been involved.

Horatio was arrested and charged with the murder of Bess Jodice and the attempted murders of Marco Ubruzzi and myself. I felt a little sorry for him. Not a lot, because, you know—he tried to kill me. Twice. But a little, because he had been bullied and tortured by Bess. And I know what that feels like and how it can cripple a person to live a mediocre life of feeble effort.

We made our way back to the kitchen arena. Tim told me that the day was a bust. "When you and Horatio didn't return, Aunt Ginny refused to go on with the taping until you were found."

I smiled at Aunt Ginny and she waved me off.

"Then the old people in the stands started making bets about where you were and if you'd been attacked again."

"What odds did they give me?"

Aunt Ginny shrugged, making her bells tinkle. "I don't know, but they were in your favor."

The seniors cheered when we entered the room. Ivy rushed over and grabbed my hands. "I'm so glad you're okay. Who would ever have guessed that Horatio killed Bess? That's crazy, right?"

"You know what else is crazy? Horatio's real name is Horace R. Snaarg."

Ivy's mouth hung open and her arms dropped to her sides. "Oh. My. Gawd. Are you kidding?"

"It's true. He's your exec."

Ivy clicked on her headset. "Roger, have I got a

Snapchat update for you." Ivy ran off to let the rest of
Cape May County know what was going on.

I was being greeted by Mrs. Dodson and Mrs. Davis
when an unexpected visitor returned to the scene of
her Emmy-worthy performance.

Ashlee flashed a big smile to no one in particular
and waved to the room. "It's true everyone, I'm back.
I know you've all missed me, and everyone has probably been so worried . . ."

Tess folded her arms and shook her head. "Wait
for it."

Miss New Jersey tapped Ashlee on the shoulder.
"Uh, yeah. The police were just here. They have evidence that you fed yourself the peanut butter."

Tess said, "And there it is."

The audience gasped. Mr. Sheinberg yelled, "Dun
dun duuun!"

I watched the biddies check their lead sheets. "Well,
who bet that Ashlee poisoned herself? I know one of
you must have."

Mrs. Dodson tapped her cane. "That's mine. Pay up
those Marie Callender coupons, Thelma."

Ashlee tried to act innocent. "I don't know what
you're all talking about. I didn't—"

"I found the evidence under your bed, or rather,
Figaro found it. You had to use rubber gloves, so you
didn't dose yourself prematurely."

Ashlee nervously looked around the room. "I didn't
put that there."

"I'll bet you put the gloves on after you carried the
peanut butter and knife up to your room. That means
the police can pull your fingerprints off the jar."

Ashlee knew she'd been had. She laughed it off.
"Oh well, at least it was good for ratings. *Wake Up! South
Jersey* gained a few points in the ratings because of my

hospital stay. They're talking about sending me and Tess to cohost a dating show for Valentine's Day."

Norman threw a hissy fit. "What? She's going to stay on the show? This blows! I was promised her job! What gives, Tess?"

Tess yawned and fluffed her hair out. "Whachu want from me, *chico*? Those are the breaks."

Norman was enraged. "I provided certain services to you in exchange for the cohost position on your show."

Ashlee giggled and told Tess. "He performed the same services for me to get rid of you, too."

Tess snickered. "How was he?"

Ashlee cocked her shoulder. "Eh."

"Yeah, me too. Besides, he's too old to host a millennial morning show."

"Maybe he could be our weatherman. You can do that like, forever."

Norman was freaking out with primal cries of displeasure. He was finally able to form words. "This is sexual harassment! I'll sue!"

Tess shrugged him off. "It was your idea, dummy."

Ashlee rubbed her stomach and looked around the room. "What have you all got to eat in here? I'm starved."

Chapter Forty

I woke up stiff and bloated with Figaro rumbling on my shoulder. My arm throbbed where I'd gotten stitches last night in the emergency room. Both Tim and Gia had insisted on going with me. Keeping things light and casual with the two men was starting to seem more like smoke and mirrors on their part. I hadn't dated in twenty-five years, so I had no idea how to go about it. It seemed like there were a lot more games and innuendos than I remembered. Whatever happened to him standing on the lawn under her window with a giant boom box over his head playing "In Your Eyes."

I rolled to the side enough to tip Figaro onto the mattress. He was annoyed for two seconds then fell back to sleep. I let gravity spin me around to sit up. Why did everything hurt so bad? My hands and feet wouldn't bend. My face itched. I shuffled to the bathroom scratching my cheek and looked in the mirror. *Oh, this is not good.* The dark circles had taken over my face. I was breaking out like prom night all over again.

I stripped down, took off my rings, and stepped on the scale. I squinted because the number staring back at me had to be a trick of nearsightedness. I took off my earrings and tried again. The scale mocked me. Where was this thing made? Nazi Germany? I had to face the truth. I'd gained seven pounds in one week. Impossible, you say? I wish I could agree, but reality had a sharp stinger. I texted Dr. Melinda, asking if I could see her ASAP. I could tell something had gone very wrong, and I needed her advice.

I tried to plan my day while I took a shower. Today was a Restaurant Week bonus round, although, it was less of a bonus and more of a make-up day because yesterday was incomplete. I think everyone involved was dragging themselves through it at this point. With Horatio in jail, and his accomplice in custody, there shouldn't be any more sabotage or poisoning. One would hope, anyway. I was having trouble getting the shampoo and conditioner out of my hair. My wounded arm weighed a ton. That's where the extra seven pounds is. It's in the stitches and swelling. Hmm. Okay, probably not.

I made a valiant effort to get it together. Some days you had to grade on the curve. I went down the stairs to the first landing. This is ridiculous. Bess's door was wrapped in crime scene tape. Horatio's door was wrapped in crime scene tape. Now Ashlee's door was wrapped in crime scene tape. She'd learned the hard way that filing a fraudulent police report was against the law. You could read all about her arrest and up-coming community service on her blog.

I put a breakfast casserole in the oven and made a pot of coffee. Aunt Ginny and I sat together in silence and let the caffeine force our eyes open.

Aunt Ginny blew on her coffee. "That was some showdown last night."

"I think I pulled a muscle swinging that frying pan at Horatio's head."

"I'm not talking about Horatio. I'm talking about those two boys fighting over you."

"I'm not sure what to think about that yet."

"That Gia means business."

I smiled. "Yeah."

"What about Tim?"

I took a deep breath and stretched my shoulder. "I don't know about him. I'm afraid he might only be interested because he doesn't like to lose. Plus there's the Gigi factor."

Aunt Ginny nodded. "You'll figure it out."

Dr. Melinda texted me back that she could see me this morning before I had to be at the community college.

Aunt Ginny and I served our remaining three guests an eggs Benedict casserole and strawberry sweet rolls. Norman refused to sit in the dining room with Tess, but she was happy to have the table to just her and Miss New Jersey. I carried in a couple of mimosas to celebrate the Restaurant Week finale.

Miss New Jersey was waving a piece of casserole under the table. "Here kitty kitty. Come get an eggie."

Figaro looked at her hand, then turned his back to her and washed his face.

"I don't know what's wrong with him today," she said. "Why won't he come to me."

I put the mimosas on the table in front of them. "Because you want him to. When did you notice he started leaving you alone?"

"As soon as I got my antihistamine and could breathe again. I've been trying to hold him, but he won't let me pick him up."

Figaro turned his head to look over his shoulder at me. He winked.

You little devil. I smiled at Miss New Jersey. "I'm sure it's not you. Cats are funny."

"I think I'll get a cat when I start law school in the spring."

Say what now? "I didn't know you were going to law school." *I might have guessed beauty school.*

"Uh, yeah. That's why I do the pageants. Tuition money."

"My late husband was a lawyer. Law school was really hard. The course load is very demanding." I waited to see how that hit her. She hadn't struck me as someone who'd—let's just say—venture down the path of higher academia.

"I'm ready for it. My LSAT score was 171 and I have a 3.9 GPA in my undergrad studies at Princeton."

I was staring, and I knew it. I just couldn't stop. "Well. That. Sounds. Fabulous." I smiled at her. "Good luck with everything."

I asked Tess if she needed anything else. She gave me a knowing look like she'd seen right through me. "Oh no, I'm fine. Thank you."

"Okay then. Aunt Ginny will check you out when you are ready to call your Ubers to head out to the college. I have an appointment, but I'll see you up there."

The girls said good-bye, and I made a hasty retreat past Figaro who was napping in a sunbeam, now that his evil plan was complete.

I thumbed through an issue of *Paleo Magazine* in Dr. Melinda's cheerful waiting room. The sun was playing off the yellow walls and white bookshelves, setting the room aglow with morning light.

The receptionist, George, a kind man with a gentle spirit, offered me a drink. "You want to try that green tea again?"

"Nope."

George had a twinkle in his eye. "Come on, you know it's an acquired taste."

"So is bourbon. You got any of that?"

"Poppy?" The slim brunette in a red plaid skirt and tall black motorcycle boots was my holistic doctor. If you asked Aunt Ginny, alternative medicine was voodoo and magic potions, but Dr. Melinda was the first doctor to diagnose me with an autoimmune disease and set me on a path to health with natural supplements, yoga, and the Paleo Diet. "Come on back."

I made myself comfortable in her patient room, which looked more like a lounge in a trendy coffee bar, except for the exam table. She asked me what was going on. "You have me listed as your primary care physician, so I got an email from the hospital that you were admitted. What happened?"

"Someone tried to kill me."

"Again?"

"Do you believe in curses?"

"I didn't before I met you. I may have to start."

That made me laugh, and I relaxed. I filled her in on the last couple weeks of my life. It had begun with so much promise—I was on top of the world. But after a week of crazy sprinkled with sugar, gluten, and dairy, timed competitions, exploding ovens, and protesters throwing tomatoes, the stress had taken its toll.

Dr. Melinda listened and nodded along. Finally, she sat back and put two fingers on her lips to think. "How have you been keeping up with your yoga?"

"I haven't had time. I had to be at the college every morning right after the breakfast service."

She nodded. "And how about your nutrition? How have you eaten outside the competition?"

"Uhhhh." The *panzarotti* was the first thing to come to mind. It was followed by plenty of other bad choices.

"Okay. I think what you're feeling right now is a bad-week hangover. You've had unhealthy food, too much stress, and a very chaotic week. That's caused some flare-up of your symptoms and inflammation. Sometimes life just gets in the way. You don't have to be perfect, but I want you to be committed."

"I think I am committed."

"You're doing fabulous, and these are big changes. But I don't want you to put your healthy lifestyle on the back burner when life gets hard. I want you to be healthy committed—not just healthy convenient."

I wanted to balk, but I realized she was right. In the four months I'd been on the Paleo Diet, I'd gone off it every time I was under pressure. I was a stress eater, a celebration eater, an entertainment eater, and an emotional eater. My ancestors were probably just survival eaters. I bet even Adam and Eve would have been fat and sick in the twenty-first century. I followed the Paleo Diet when it was convenient for me.

Dr. Melinda took out a prescription pad and scrawled something on it. "I don't want you beating yourself up about this. That's only going to add stress to an already stressed system. You have an autoimmune disease we need to manage and heal. There's a place in every healthy lifestyle for birthday cake and Christmas cookies and that special night out. But for the rest of the time, I want you to make your health a priority. You need to take care of your body, or you'll have more auto-immune flare-ups like the one you're having now."

We talked some more, and she made some good suggestions for how to manage different situations I tended to find myself in. Then she handed me the folded prescription and said to call her in a couple weeks.

"I will, thanks."

She pulled me into a hug.

Once I was outside her office I opened my prescription. It said, "You can do this. You're stronger than you think you are." I teared up a little. This was not time for condemnation. Today was a fresh start.

Chapter Forty-One

The kitchen arena was purring again. It was just like the first day, before the sabotage and accusations ruined the vibe of camaraderie. The storm had broken, and it was time to celebrate. Louie and Vidrine were huddled together, chatting it up. He had his arm draped around her shoulders holding her close. She saw me and gave me a big smile, blushing before she turned adoring eyes back to Louie.

Using hand signals and universal grunting sounds, Momma was showing Philippe how to make fresh pasta. They were both covered in flour. Philippe looked like he was having the time of his life.

Even Tim and Adrian were deep in amicable discussion. They had finally buried the hatchet. Sawyer was right. Once Tim apologized, Adrian got over it.

Ivy grabbed my elbow before I made it to my kitchen. "I have some exciting news."

Her smile was infectious, and I felt the excitement bubbling inside me, right along with her.

"Because of the way things were handled this week, the TV station has promoted me to assistant producer. They're giving me the Annual Restaurant Week

Competition to develop as my own, and I have you to thank for it."

"Oh, I'm so excited for you. Congratulations."

The lights dimmed and came back up, signaling the two-minute warning. I put on my black chef apron and we all took our places. Me next to Gigi next to Tim. Gigi in the middle. Always in the middle. I looked over to Momma's kitchen. Gia was leaning against the counter, his arms crossed, watching me. He gave me a sexy smile. I felt the heat rise to my cheeks. I tried to look poised, but I smiled back in spite of myself.

Ivy took her place in front of the camera and opened the day, even though the judges' table was still empty.

"Okay everyone. Welcome to the final, final day of our Restaurant Week competition. The inaugural event that those of us who lived through, will always refer to as Hell Week."

The chefs roared with applause. We'd been through the trenches, and it had formed a bond between us that none of us would ever forget.

"Things have not gone smoothly for anyone this week. I know it's not what you signed up for, so I've worked out a couple of ideas for damage control. First of all, while only one of you will take home the ten-thousand-dollar prize, all six head chefs will have their pictures on the cover of *South Jersey Dining Guide*."

The room erupted.

"We're calling it the "Real Chefs of South Jersey." NBC has picked up our footage to turn it into a two-week miniseries. They said you can't make up stories like this. Now, down to the business for today. You're all aware that we lost another judge, and"—Ivy continued through the boos—"we've had to make some more substitutions. So, let's dim the lights and start the music as we bring in our celebrity panel for today."

Oh boy.

The club music started, and Tim came around Gigi to stand next to me. "This is new."

"Yeah, and I think I know whose idea it was."

"Stormin' Norman Sprinkler from News Channel Eight." Norman entered the room dancing, while recording himself with his cell phone. He took a lap around the room and pulled some fancy club moves before making his way to his seat.

"Miss New Jersey, Brandy Sparks." Miss New Jersey danced in the room and did a few runway twirls—an impressive feat in her gold stilettos.

"Ginny Frankowski from CrimeSceneHouse.com."

I sucked in my breath and gripped the counter. "She's gonna be what kills me. This is why I think I need an eclair—this, right here."

Aunt Ginny danced her way around the room wearing pink-leather hot pants and white go-go boots. She'd topped it with a pink-and-yellow geometric blouse that tied at the waist. I had a picture of her in that very outfit at my sixth-grade graduation. The whoops and hollers in the room weren't coming just from the seniors. The chefs and culinary students had grown to love Aunt Ginny's antics throughout the week. She gave me a twinkling finger wave as she passed my station.

"And last but not least, one of *L'École des Chefs* very own pastry students, Joanne Junk."

"No. It can't be."

But it was. One of the meanest girls from high school entered the room wearing camouflage cargo pants and a black T-shirt that had BEEF written across the front. Joanne hadn't changed at all in twenty-five years. Same bad haircut, same surly attitude, same inexplicable hatred of me. From the moment I'd returned to Cape May, she'd been calling me names and making my life miserable. She stomped around the arc on a frown and fell into her seat. The music was timed for her entrance, so it kept playing. Aunt Ginny filled the time by taking a second lap around the room. She gave me another twinkling finger wave as she passed again.

The music ended, and Ivy addressed the chefs. "Okay, based on the point system, there is a three-way tie between Chef Philippe, Chef Adrian, and Chef Tim. Today will determine the winner of the Restaurant Week Competition and the ten thousand dollars. Yesterday, we polled the audience as to what theme today's baskets should be. The overwhelming response was gluten free."

My heart did a flip. Excitement coursed through my veins. After the past four months of baking for the coffee shop, this was my wheelhouse. My mystery basket ingredients were Marcona almonds, rose petals, and canned lychees. A smile broke across my face. *I got this.*

"The results aren't just surprising, they're a mathematical miracle as one hundred and eighty votes came in from one hundred and six audience members."

I zeroed in on Aunt Ginny who was engrossed in her charm bracelet.

"As an added bonus, we're giving you an hour and a half to make your dishes. Begin!"

I rushed to the pantry for white chocolate, heavy cream, sugar, and eggs. Baby, I was making macarons. I'd spent hours practicing. Even though every third batch of shells still had something wrong with them, I was confident that I'd improved enough for today.

Gia met me in the pantry and slipped me a kiss.

"Your car is ready, Bella. Why don't you come over tonight and pick it up?"

I giggled. "Okay. I'm sorry Momma isn't in the lead."

"Bah. I told you, Momma was only here to let me know if things were serious between you and Tim. Then Marco said not to worry, because Tim was already married to his restaurant and didn't have room for you or Blondie over there."

Oh my God. Is that true?

"Good luck out there, Bella. You own this one."

Gia had me thinking, and that thinking was slowing me down. I had to shake these fears out and reexamine them later.

Gigi grabbed my arm, and I almost dropped my eggs. "Quick, where is the Dijon mustard?"

"Girl, you've been in here for a week. How do you not know where things are by now?"

Gigi looked over to where Tim was collecting chanterelle mushrooms. "I start out okay, but then I get flustered and can't remember what I'm doing when he's around."

I had a decision to make. Gigi was my competition for Tim, and she took every opportunity to make me look bad. Do I help her now, or let her fail? "The Dijon mustard is behind the olives."

I'm sure I'm going to regret that. I ran out to my station and started melting sugar for a caramel in one saucepan, and steeping rose petals in heavy cream for rose-infused white chocolate in another. Then I pulverized my almonds in the food processor.

As I put together my macaron batter, I looked around the room. I had grown fond of these chefs, and I enjoyed working with them. I loved creating desserts and fancy pastries. I'd felt for so long that my life had taken a bad turn and gotten off track when I didn't get to go to culinary school to become a professional pastry chef. But this past week, I'd seen firsthand that a chef's life is hard. They're on their feet all day. They work nights, weekends, and holidays. Gia was right, chefs are married to their careers. It's a profession full of drama and risk. I love baking and creating, but after one week of making desserts for Tim, I was sick all over again. If my dream had come true to become a full-time pastry chef, with my autoimmune disease and food allergies, I'd be sick and miserable all the time. Not to mention double my size.

I colored half my macaron batter gold, and the other half light rose. Then I piped my shells onto parchment and set them aside to dry. I turned to my fillings. I would make two flavors, white chocolate-rose lychee and rose-kissed caramel. The sugar was a nice golden amber, so I added butter. When it was finished splattering, I added some of the rose-infused cream and whisked it smooth. I poured the finished caramel into a large casserole dish and popped it in the blast chiller. Then I turned my attention to the white chocolate filling. I poured the rest of the rose-petal cream through a sieve over my chopped white chocolate to melt it and whisked it over an ice bath until it thickened and cooled.

I looked at Gia trying to flip something in a frying pan. Uh . . . it's on the floor. Now Momma is swatting him with a towel. Yeah, he's starting over again. He looked at me and made a face. I am so blessed to work for *La Dolce Vita*. I get to bake and create and make people happy, but without poisoning myself with ingredients I'm allergic to. Plus, he pays in coffee and kisses, so that's a huge bonus. I realized that baking gluten free for Gia is right where I'm supposed to be. And you know, after all the flack Gigi gave me this week, I am a professional pastry chef. I'm paid to make desserts. So, Gigi can bite me. Isn't it funny, life has a way of turning out just the way it should, despite what you had planned?

Ivy called the chefs to attention. "I'm going to send Tess around to give each one of you a chance to talk about yourselves and your restaurants for some added publicity. Try to keep it under two minutes so Roger doesn't have to cut it down too much. His chief editor was arrested for helping Horatio conspire."

I had just put my macaron shells in the oven when Tess made her way to our kitchen. "Chef Tim, can you tell us what your inspiration was for becoming a chef?

The camera followed Tim, who came to stand next to me. "This lady here is the reason I became a chef. She was my first love." Tim looked at me and smiled. "Poppy and I were high school sweethearts. We were even engaged to be married."

The audience awed, and there was a flurry of activity by Aunt Ginny. *I see some last-minute bets are being placed.*

"Cooking with Poppy this week has given me back a piece of myself that's been missing for a long time. No matter what happens in the competition, this has been worth every minute just to be with her again."

I smiled up at Tim. I felt the same way. I knew I would always love him. I looked past Tim, and my eyes met Gia's. He was watching me intently.

Tess said, "That is so sweet, Chef Tim. Can you tell our audience about your restaurant?"

"Maxine's isn't just a part of my life, she is my life . . ."

I didn't hear what else he said. I was lost in the

swamp of my emotions. I stood numb for a moment until I heard Aunt Ginny yell. "Focus!"

I took my macaron shells out of the oven to cool and filled my piping bags. I could feel the pull of Gia watching me, and Tim working on the other side, but I wouldn't look at either one. I had one job right now, and I was giving it my full attention. I piped mounds of white chocolate-rose filling into my pink macaron shells. I placed a lychee in the middle, and then matched the shells up top to bottom. Next, I filled the gold-colored shells with my rose-kissed caramel. I dusted the caramel macarons with a touch of flaked gold leaf and got my plates together. I had a few minutes before Ivy counted down the last ten seconds. When she did, the arena erupted in applause and the audience stood to their feet. I felt like an idiot for crying. I tried to play it off like I had powdered sugar on my cheek, and I was wiping it away.

The judging round was the best we'd had. It was amazing what lovely things the judges can say about you when they aren't afraid of being poisoned.

Philippe presented his entrée and for the first time, he owned it. "Judges, today I have made for you Julia Child's Lobster Thermidor, with my own special twist."

Vidrine and I looked at each other across the kitchen. Vidrine mouthed "Wow." I just gave her a big smile in return.

My macarons were highly praised, even by Joanne who could only find one little fault.

"They're not bad, but they could use more food coloring to make them pop."

When the end of the day arrived, it was time for the winner to be announced. Ivy and Roger brought in a giant cardboard rectangle that I assumed was "the check" for the winning chef. We all craned our necks to get a glimpse of the name, but Ivy had cleverly wrapped it in tissue paper.

My hands were shaking like a chocolate junkie in a Godiva outlet. *What if we lose? Tim worked so hard for this. What if he blames me and doesn't want to see me anymore?*

"Okay everyone. You've all done so well in the face of what can only be described as a pant-load of chaos. With all the disasters and interruptions this week, we were not able to factor every day into the final score."

Tim reached over and gave my hand a squeeze. I held on to him like it was the last time we would ever touch.

"So, please keep in mind that your best days may not have counted in the final ranking. Also keep in mind that the cameras are rolling, and I'm just the messenger."

Gigi let out a shaky breath and grabbed the counter. "Just get on with it."

Ivy and Roger began tearing off the tissue paper. "Tying for second place we have Chef Philippe Julian and Chef Tim Maxwell."

Oh no. My heart was sick.

"And in first place by a very, very slim margin, the winner of the first Annual Cape May County Restaurant Week Competition . . ." They spun the check around. "Chef Adrian Baxter."

Tim squeezed my hand so tight you would think he was having contractions. Adrian was so overcome that he dropped to his knees and wept that his mother would finally be proud of him. His show of humility was so different from the Adrian we had known all week. It didn't last long before he cued up "We Are the Champions" on his iPad and ran around the room reminding everyone that he was the best chef in the room, and he'd said he would win in the end.

Tim stood shaking his head with his arms crossed tight across his chest.

"Tim, I'm so sorry that we didn't win the ten thousand dollars."

Tim shrugged. "I didn't even know about the money when we started. I was just competing for the publicity, and we got a ton of that."

I let out a breath that I hadn't realized I was holding. "You're really not upset?"

Tim shook his head. "I'll get over it. I'm just glad you were here with me."

We smiled at each other, and Gigi gave an irritated huff.

Gia came over to praise my macarons. "I love this one. You need to make it for the shop. I think it'll be a big hit for Valentine's Day."

Louie and Vidrine joined him. "They're beautiful, *chér*. You did such a nice job. You think I could hire you to make these for Slap Yo Mamma! sometime?"

"I'd love to." I looked at Gia for confirmation.

He nodded. "Call *La Dolce Vita* and we'll set it up."

Louie took a rose caramel from my tray of extras. "Dude, these are amazing. You got some talent, girl."

I could feel rainbows shooting out of my eyes I was so proud.

"Vidrine." Louie nudged her. "Tell them our news."

Vidrine grinned. "We're merging."

"What?"

"That's right, dude. We're opening a restaurant together. We'll each still have our own places, but together we're starting a donut shop."

"Oh, I did not need to know that."

Gia laughed at me.

Tim joined us and opened his arms to hug me.

"Thank you for being here this week, Mack. It means the world to me."

"I'm sorry we didn't win. I know you really needed the money."

"Some things are more important than money." Tim looked into my face. He started to say something when Gigi grabbed his arm and spun him in her direction.

"Hey partner, we did it. We made a great team, don't you think?"

"Yeah, Geeg. You were fabulous. Wasn't she, Poppy?"

"Fabulous." My fabulous didn't have the same level of enthusiasm that Tim's did.

Gigi reached down and took one of my macarons and shoved it in her mouth. "Oh my God, these are so good." She stopped chewing and her eyes got real big.

"You've been stealing my extra desserts all week, haven't you Gigi?"

Gigi answered through a mouthful of caramel. "No, I haven't."

Tim cut in. "Yes, you have. I've seen you sneaking them out under your chef coat."

Gigi blushed to the roots of her blond hair. "Well, I was just making sure Poppy wasn't ruining our chances with the judges."

"Are you kidding me?" Tim laughed. "She's the only reason we tied for second. Her desserts were the highlight of our team four out of seven days."

Gigi rolled her eyes. "Whatever. I was wondering if you wanted to come to dinner with me tonight." She ran her hands over Tim's chest and leaned in until her chest touched his stomach. "Just you and me. I'll send the rest of the staff home, make a little chateaubriand, light some candles. We can finally celebrate. What do you say, Chef?"

Gia put his hand on my back to support me.

Tim had the faintest hint of pink rising up his neck. He took Gigi's hands in his and removed them from his body. "Um, Geeg. I'm sorry if I gave you the wrong idea." Tim cleared his throat. "I tried to tell you the other day when you brought her up. I'm only interested in Poppy."

I wasn't breathing. *Isn't breathing supposed to be automatic? Why aren't I doing it?*

"She was the love of my life, and that's hard to get over. I asked her to help us with the competition to get closer to her, and to get her away from spending so much time with Gia. Even though that part backfired some." Tim glared in Gia's direction.

Gia stiffened and tightened his posture to stand taller.

I sucked in a loud lungful of air and almost choked.

Gigi shriveled in front of me. Her eyes filled with tears and her bottom lip trembled. "Well, you'll be throwing your heart away. Poppy doesn't understand you like I do. She doesn't know the chef code. She won't be by your side on those long nights and holidays when you're in the weeds."

Tim looked into my eyes. "Maybe she will and maybe she won't, but I have to try. We have too much history to give up now."

Gigi had storm clouds brewing in her eyes. "That's a mistake. She's going to break your heart and leave you for this guy. It's written all over her face when she looks at him."

My mind had gone blank. I wasn't capable of conscious thought. I was only aware of the tension rolling off of Gia, and Tim's eyes locked with mine.

Gigi's anger sucked the light from the room like black descends before the hurricane. She slammed her fist on the stainless-steel counter that had been my workstation for the past week. "You'll regret this one day. Both of you. I'll make sure of it." The tiny tornado spun from the room, leaving a stunned silence behind.

Tim cupped my cheek with his hand. "What do you say, babe? You know I've always loved you. Want to give it a go with me?"

RECIPES

PALEO BLACK FOREST FRENCH TOAST

Ingredients

3 Tablespoons butter, softened (You can always use coconut oil if you are sensitive to dairy. Refined coconut oil will not have a coconut flavor.)

1 Paleo Chocolate Chunk Loaf, cut into cubes (let them dry out a little)

3 cups dark cherries, no sugar added (fresh, canned, or frozen). If you use frozen, let them thaw and drain first.

¾ cup chocolate chunks (or the rest of the bag that you didn't eat when you made the loaf)

6 eggs

1 cup coconut cream (both the solid coconut at the top and the liquid at the bottom)

¼ cup Godiva or other chocolate liquor (optional)

coconut whipped cream

Directions

Preheat the oven to 350 degrees and grease your ceramic or Pyrex baking dish with the 3 Tablespoons butter. **I use an 8" x 10", 2.3-quart casserole. If you use a bigger one, like a 9" x 13", the casserole will be thinner and will require less baking time**.

Layer half the chocolate bread cubes, dark cherries, and chocolate chunks in baking dish. Repeat with a second layer.

Beat the eggs, coconut cream, and chocolate liquor until combined. **I use a blender.**

Pour the liquid mixture over the layered bread cubes, cherries, and chocolate, and let sit 15 minutes.

Bake at 350 degrees for 45 to 55 minutes.

Serve with coconut whipped cream

PALEO CHOCOLATE CHUNK LOAF

I made this to use in the Paleo Black Forest French Toast, but it was delicious just out of the oven as a chocolate chunk loaf cake. This is best eaten a little warm while the chocolate chunks are gooey.

Ingredients

- 1¾ cups Paleo flour blend
- ½ cup unsweetened cocoa
- ½ teaspoon baking powder
- ½ teaspoon baking soda
- ¼ teaspoon xanthan gum
- ½ teaspoon salt
- 1 cup coconut sugar
- ½ cup butter, softened (You can always use coconut oil if you are sensitive to dairy. Refined coconut oil will not have a coconut flavor.)
- 2 eggs
- 1 cup canned coconut milk (use a fair amount of the cream at the top, top off with the liquid)
- 1 cup chocolate chunks

Directions

Preheat oven to 350 degrees.

Grease bottom only of a 9" x 5" loaf pan.

Combine flour, cocoa, baking powder, baking soda, xanthan gum, and salt in a small bowl. Mix together.

In a large bowl, beat together coconut sugar and butter (or coconut oil).

Add eggs; blend well.

Stir in coconut milk.

Add the dry ingredients and stir until the batter comes together.

Fold in chocolate chunks.

Pour into the greased loaf pan.

Bake at 350 degrees for 55 to 65 minutes or until toothpick inserted in center comes out clean.

Cool 15 minutes; remove from pan.

After the loaf has cooled, wrap tightly and store in refrigerator, or cut into 1-inch slices and lay out to dry out a bit for French toast.

LEMON CRÈME BRÛLÉE

Crème brûlée requires the aid of a blowtorch. Don't waste your money on the sad little kitchen store blowtorches. Do yourself a favor and go to the hardware store and buy a real one. They work so much better and they're cheaper.

Ingredients

6 large egg yolks
¾ cup sugar
½ cup fresh lemon juice
peel from 1 lemon, grated
2½ cups whipping cream
sugar for the top crust

Directions

Prehcat oven to 300 degrees.

Beat egg yolks, sugar, and lemon juice in a mixing bowl until thick and creamy. Add lemon peel.

Pour whipping cream into a saucepan and stir over low heat until it almost comes to boil. Remove from heat immediately. Temper the cream into the egg yolks and beat until combined.

Pour cream mixture into the top pot of a double boiler. Stir over simmering water until mixture lightly coats the back of a spoon, about 3 minutes. Remove mixture from heat immediately and pour into ramekins.

Bake at 300 degrees for 20 minutes or until the custard is set.

Remove from oven and cool to room temperature. Refrigerate for at least 1 hour or overnight.

Before serving, sprinkle the top of the custard with sugar. Using a blowtorch, caramelize the sugar until it bubbles and turns golden brown.

If you have gotten to this point in the recipe and neglected to buy a blowtorch like I suggested, you can always put the crème brûlées under the broiler and let the oven caramelize the sugar. I'm not putting a time here for how long it will take because you'll have to watch them constantly, so they don't burn or catch on fire. Next time, get the blowtorch.

GLUTEN-FREE LAVENDER SHORTBREAD
Ingredients

1 cup good, softened *butter or solid coconut oil
  *Butter is the big flavor here. Substituting with coconut oil or anything else will not make shortbread. The better the butter, the better the shortbread. However, with the flavor addition of lavender, someone who is dairy free could give the coconut shortbread a shot.

1 cup sugar

2 teaspoons dried culinary lavender (buds only)
  *or 1 teaspoon lavender extract

¾ cup cassava flour

¾ cup 1-to-1 gluten-free flour blend

¾ cup almond flour (this really gives the shortbread a crumbly texture)

¼ teaspoon sea salt
  *If you're using dried lavender buds and you know in advance that you're making the shortbread, add the lavender to the sugar and let the flavor infuse for a few days before making the cookies. That

*lavender will be creamed in with the butter and
sugar, but that's okay. You'll have a much stronger
lavender flavor.*

Directions

Preheat an oven to 350 degrees.

Combine the butter and sugar in a mixer and mix
until light and fluffy. Add lavender buds or extract. (If
you infused the sugar, the lavender will already be in
the butter at this point.) Mix well.

Add the flours (cassava, gluten-free, and almond)
and salt and beat until a dough has formed. Press between two sheets of parchment and roll out to ¼-inch
thickness. Chill until the dough is firm—two hours if
you have the time.

Peel the top layer of parchment off the dough. Cut
dough into desired shapes using cookie cutters, a
glass, a lid from a jar—whatever you want.

Sprinkle tops of cookies with decorative sugars, if
desired. Pat down slightly so the sugar doesn't roll off
when you pick up the finished cookie.

Bake for 10–12 minutes or just until the cookies
start to turn slightly brown on the edges. Remove from
oven and let sit on the pan for a few minutes to finish
baking before transferring to a wire rack to cool.

These go really well served with Lemon Crème Brûlée,
or with a scoop of ice cream or sorbet sandwiched between two of them.

NO-BAKE PASSION FRUIT
CHILI CHEESECAKE

I wouldn't normally make a no-bake cheesecake, but I
wanted to provide the recipe Poppy used during the
competition. This no-bake version uses gelatin instead

of eggs. Mini springform pans enable the cheesecake to set up quickly, or you could make one big 8- or 9-inch cheesecake if you'd rather. You would just need to let it chill for several hours to be firm enough to cut.

Ingredients

Cheesecake Filling

1–2 chili peppers*

1 envelope Knox plain gelatin

3 Tablespoons cold water

¾ cup frozen passion fruit pulp, thawed (You could also use fresh passion fruit, pulped, and strained.)

16 oz. cream cheese, softened

1 can *dulce de leche* (or sweetened condensed milk, about 1 ¼ cups)

almond meal—a few Tablespoons to dust the bottom of the spring form pans. (You could also make yourself a crust if you want, but Poppy just made the cheesecake without a cookie bottom.)

I used red serrano chilis for a gentle heat. If you want more of a bite you can use habaneros. Use rubber or latex kitchen gloves when cutting chili peppers. Be sure to remove gloves when you're finished and don't touch anything the gloves have touched.

Passion Fruit Jelly topping

1 envelope Knox plain gelatin

3 Tablespoons cold water

¼ cup sugar

4 ounces frozen passion fruit juice, thawed

Directions

Cheesecake Filling

Wearing rubber gloves, seed and chop your chilis. Don't touch anything else. Don't rub your eye or scratch your face. When your chilis are chopped very small, add them to your passion fruit pulp. Clean up the area and equipment you used and throw away your gloves.

Mix the gelatin with the water and let it bloom. Then, microwave the gelatin for 20 to 30 seconds until it melts. Add it to the passion fruit/pepper mixture.

In a mixing bowl, whip your softened cream cheese until it's smooth. Doing this now will help the finished batter not be lumpy. When the cheese is fluffy and smooth, add the dulce de leche (or sweetened condensed milk). At the lowest speed, beat for 1 to 1 ½ minutes until the mixture is well blended. Add the passion fruit/pepper mixture and fold or beat at the lowest speed until the mixture is incorporated.

Sprinkle the bottom of your springform pan(s) with almond meal. Use enough to cover the bottom to make releasing the cheesecake easier.

Pour the cream cheese mixture into the pan(s). Smooth out the surface because what it looks like now is what it's going to look like later. It isn't going to move. Refrigerate until set—30 minutes for minis or several hours for a large cheesecake.

Passion Fruit Jelly Topping

Mix the gelatin with the water and let it bloom. Then, microwave the gelatin for 20 to 30 seconds until it melts. Add in ¼ cup of sugar and microwave another 40 to 60 seconds, until melted. Keep your eye on it so it doesn't boil over. Using oven mitts or a towel, remove bowl from microwave. Add 4 ounces thawed passion fruit juice.

When this mixture is nice and cool—**it doesn't have to be cold, but it can't be warm**—and the cheesecake is cold, gently pour the passion fruit liquid on top of the cheesecake(s). Chill for another 2 to 4 hours.

When you're ready to serve, use a butter knife to gently go around the inside of the springform pan to help release the cheesecake from the liner. The cheesecake should come off the bottom easily because of the almond meal.

PALEO EARL GREY MADELEINES
Ingredients

5 Tablespoons unsalted butter, plus additional for molds, room temperature (**You can always use coconut oil if you are sensitive to dairy. Refined coconut oil will not have a coconut flavor.**)

4 Tablespoons loose Earl Grey tea or tea from 4 teabags

1/3 cup + 1 Tablespoon coconut flour

1/2 cup arrowroot starch

1/4 teaspoon baking soda

1/4 teaspoon baking powder

1/4 teaspoon salt

1/8 teaspoon xanthan gum

3 eggs

1/3 cup raw honey

1/4 cup butter, melted (**You can always use coconut oil if you are sensitive to dairy. Refined coconut oil will not have a coconut flavor.**)

1/4 cup coconut milk

zest of 1 lemon

Directions

Preheat the oven to 350 degrees.

Melt 5 Tablespoons butter in saucepan over low heat. Mix in the tea. Let steep 10 minutes.

Grease two madeleine pans with remaining butter.

In a small bowl, whisk together the coconut flour, arrowroot starch, baking soda, baking powder, salt, and xanthan gum. Set aside.

Whip the eggs until thick and lemon colored.

Strain butter/tea mixture well—you want as much of the butter as possible. Throw away the tea.

Add the honey, melted butter, coconut milk, lemon zest, and strained butter/tea mixture into the beaten eggs, while mixing on low.

Slowly add in the dry ingredients into the wet and mix until incorporated, scraping the sides of the bowl often.

Use a cookie scoop to evenly divide the batter among the greased madeleine molds in the pans. You should fill the madeleine molds just about entirely. Do not bang the pan or pat down the batter.

Bake for 12 to 15 minutes or until a toothpick comes out clean. Mine were done in 12 minutes.

Let cool in pans for 5 minutes before turning onto a wire rack to completely cool.

Optional: sprinkle with powdered sugar (not a Paleo option).

DARK CHOCOLATE POTS DE CRÈME
Naturally gluten free and grain free (not Paleo)

Ingredients

1½ cups heavy cream

½ cup whole milk

4 ounces dark chocolate, finely chopped

4 egg yolks

3 Tablespoons sugar

⅓ teaspoon sea salt

Directions

Preheat oven to 300 degrees. In a heavy saucepan, bring cream and milk to a boil. Remove from heat; whisk in chopped chocolate until smooth.

In a large bowl, whisk together the yolks, sugar and salt. Temper the yolks with a little of the hot chocolate. Then, whisking constantly, slowly pour the rest of the hot chocolate into yolks. Strain through a very fine mesh sieve into a large measuring cup, a pitcher, or your blender so it's easy to pour.

Divide mixture into 2- to 4-ounce espresso cups or small ramekins. I used ramekins and it made 6.

Put a large roasting pan on the pulled-out rack in the center of the preheated oven. Set filled cups in the roasting pan while it's in the oven. Add very hot tap water to pan, halfway up the sides of cups. Cover pan with foil; use a fork to prick holes in foil. Very gently push the rack into the oven, taking care not to splash water into your chocolate pots.

Bake until edges are lightly set (lifting foil to check) but the center—about the size of a quarter or less—is still jiggly. It will set as it cools—30 to 35 minutes. If the chocolate is still very runny in an area bigger than a quarter, you will need to bake it longer.

Transfer cups to a wire rack to cool completely. Refrigerate at least 3 hours before serving with whipped cream and an Earl Grey Madeleine.

PALEO BISCUITS
Ingredients

½ cup coconut cream—use the thick cream at the top of the can

1 teaspoon lemon juice

1 cup almond flour

1 cup tapioca flour

½ cup coconut flour

2 teaspoons baking powder
1 teaspoon baking soda
¼ teaspoon sea salt
5 Tablespoons butter, cold
2 eggs

Directions

Preheat oven to 400 degrees.

Whisk together the coconut cream and the lemon juice; let it set for a few minutes.

Line a baking sheet with parchment paper.

Combine the almond flour, tapioca flour, coconut flour, baking powder, baking soda, and salt in a mixing bowl.

Add the cold butter to the dry ingredients and cut in using your fingers, until it resembles a coarse meal.

Add the eggs until well combined.

Pour the liquid ingredients into a well formed in the dry ingredients and stir together until a wet dough is formed.

Let the dough rest for 5 to 10 minutes.

Using an ice cream scoop, drop the dough onto baking sheet. Flatten the tops and sides into a well-formed biscuit shape.

Place biscuits 2 inches apart.

TIP: I had to chill mine for a couple of hours on the cookie sheet because I had to go to a meeting before I could bake them. They were very firm when I took them out of the refrigerator. You don't have to do this, but if you have trouble with them keeping their shape, try it.

Bake for 12 to 14 minutes, or until the tops have turned lightly golden brown. I baked mine for 15 minutes because they started out cold. They came out perfect.

Cool on a wire rack.

Serve warm with butter and Aunt Ginny's Fig Jam.

AUNT GINNY'S FIG JAM

Aunt Ginny uses dried figs when she needs an excuse to use a bottle of port and fresh figs aren't in season. I serve this with Paleo biscuits, but it's yummy as a sauce over meat or ice cream too.

Ingredients

14 ounces dried mission figs, stemmed and
    chopped
1 cup water
¼ cup fresh lemon juice
1 cup honey
1 cup ruby port
pinch nutmeg

Directions

In a large, nonreactive saucepan, toss the fig pieces with the water, lemon juice, and honey.

Bring to a boil, stirring with wooden spoon. Add the port. Simmer jam over moderate heat with the lid on, stirring occasionally, until the figs are soft and the syrup is thick—about 30 minutes. Add the pinch of nutmeg.

Using an immersion blender (you can also transfer mixture to a stand blender), blend until smoother, *but not pureed*. You want to cut up the fig pieces without losing them altogether. Blend until you have the consistency you want.

Spoon the jam into a clean, sterilized mason jar. The jam keeps for several months in the refrigerator like this, or you can seal the jam either with paraffin or by using a canning method in a water bath. Then it keeps for a couple of years on the shelf.

Connect with

Us

Visit us online at
KensingtonBooks.com
to read more from your favorite authors, see books
by series, view reading group guides, and more.

Join us on social media

for sneak peeks, chances to win books and prize packs,
and to share your thoughts with other readers.

facebook.com/kensingtonpublishing
twitter.com/kensingtonbooks

Tell us what you think!

To share your thoughts, submit a review,
or sign up for our eNewsletters, please visit:
KensingtonBooks.com/TellUs.